PRAISE
FOR
**A SENSE OF HONOR**
AND
JAMES WEBB

"The narrative literally crackles with authority. James Webb has written a book of questions, has created earthy and humanly flawed characters to grapple imperfectly with the questions, to muddle through. There is love and adultery and the failure of poetry to cope with the latter. There is suspense. . . . As in war, no one truly triumphs. But the struggles are mighty and the victories impressive."

*Los Angeles Times*

"Webb is as much a moral philosopher of the military as a novelist. In a time when fiction seems to find it harder and harder to address moral issues, that makes him a valuable man at the typewriter. A SENSE OF HONOR is provocative and passionate."

*Washington Star*

"The question Webb asks is one that has been slighted for more than a decade: Is there a greater common good to be advanced and protected which justifies some degree of physical hardship for men who must bear it in their future lives? . . . It is a remarkable moral statement, one that might sooner have been expected from an older, more experienced man. But Webb learned many crucial lessons under the gun, and his call rings true."

*Boston Globe*

# PRAISE
# FOR
# A SENSE OF HONOR
# AND
# JAMES WEBB

"James Webb writes as only an insider could of that peculiarly costly education. His uncanny ear for the raunchy vocabulary of military life (he *must* have taken notes) is matched by his evocation of its spit-and-polish claustrophobia and its inherent contradictions: loneliness in the midst of camaraderie, brutality mixed with decency, pain with pride, honor with death and destruction."

*The New York Times*

"The book is a novel of ideas which probes the nature of the efficient military mind and the kind of leader who breeds heroes, even when he may destroy a certain element of humanity. It is also a complex dissertation on the nature of authority and the value of rules and regulations."

*Nashville Tennessean*

"In this powerful novel, Webb pulls the reader right into the cauldron of Annapolis, for a vivid picture of heroes and martinets living according to their various interpretations of 'honor'; and he illuminates the mystique that makes men voluntarily stay in such a meat grinder."

*Publisher's Weekly*

In Vietnam, their friends were dying.
At home, their country was torn by strife.
And at Annapolis, they battled to preserve

**A SENSE OF HONOR**

Bantam Books by James Webb

FIELDS OF FIRE
A SENSE OF HONOR

## ABOUT THE AUTHOR

JAMES WEBB graduated from the U.S. Naval Academy in 1968. A
varsity boxer and a member of the Brigade Honor Committee for
four years, he received a special citation for Outstanding Leadership
Contributions upon graduation. Commissioned in the Marine Corps,
he stood first in his class in Marine Infantry Officer Training and
went on to become one of the most highly decorated marines of
the Vietnam era. He has written on numerous topics and is the
author of the best selling, critically acclaimed novel of the Vietnam
war, *Fields of Fire*. An attorney, he currently serves as counsel to
the Veterans Affairs Committee in the House of Representatives.

# A SENSE OF HONOR

## JAMES WEBB

BANTAM BOOKS
TORONTO • NEW YORK • LONDON • SYDNEY • AUCKLAND

*This low-priced Bantam Book
has been completely reset in a type face
designed for easy reading, and was printed
from new plates. It contains the complete
text of the original hard-cover edition.*
NOT ONE WORD HAS BEEN OMITTED.

A SENSE OF HONOR

*A Bantam Book / published by arrangement with
Prentice-Hall, Inc.*

*PRINTING HISTORY*
Prentice-Hall edition published March 1981
Bantam edition / April 1982

If you ever
       Sat on the Green Bench, or
       Slept through Steam, or
       Dragged your grease girl in the Yard—
I dedicate this book to you. There'll be a P-work when you finish.

---

Thanks to Barb, who endured the living of it, JoAnn, who endured the writing of it, and Amy, who is a product of it and much else. Also to Jack Wheeler for his insights, even if he was a Woop, and to John Kirk and Oscar Collier for their editorial patience.

"It is by no means enough that an officer of the Navy be a capable mariner. He must be that, of course, but also a great deal more. He must be a gentleman of refined manners, liberal education, punctilious courtesy, and the nicest sense of personal honor."

*John Paul Jones*

# Contents

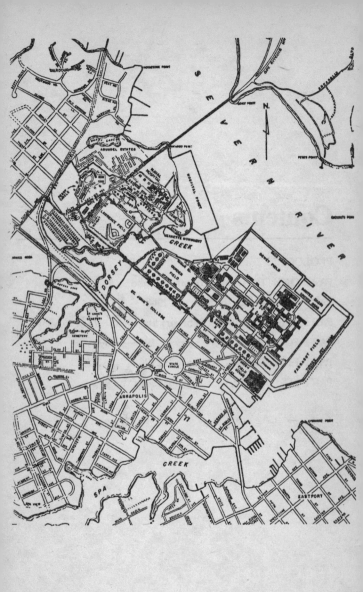

# PROLOGUE:

---

# TUESDAY,
# JUNE 4,
# 1968

*The drums begin. You can hear them, like a million heartbeats from the deepest corner of your own insides. A half-mile away, in front of Bancroft Hall, the snare drums peck and the bass drums boom: the Brigade is coming. The drumbeats are foreboding, speaking of power and exactness; military drums.*

*Bugles and brass join the drums, playing "Diablo," a tantalizing march written by a midshipman in the class of 1966. It cuts into you with a sense of longing, a yearning for action, and you stand on your seat, peering over a thousand other searching heads from the grandstands to the street that borders ancient Isherwood Hall. The sun-filled sky is a blue umbrella. Sailboats dance on the Severn River and its tributary behind the field. Hundreds, no, thousands of the most enticing women in America, who have traveled from all its distant corners, grace the stands with a color and beauty that is almost incomprehensible. June Week is a military Mardi Gras, five days of parades and ceremonies and festivities, a sensuous feast that celebrates a year of spiritual fasting. The men who are marching toward you on the crisp edge of the drums have given fifty days of drudgery for every one you will watch them play.*

*The music and the drums grow, filling the air like clouds until they surround your excitement with a tangible presence. Finally, along the narrow road by Isherwood, the Brigade Staff glides along, left feet with the drumbeat, its triangle of seven starched men swinging their swords and doing clever staff turns until they are on the grass field itself. Behind them comes the Brigade, company flags marking off the units, a mass of black uniform coats and white trousers, thousands of bayoneted rifles flashing as the bright sun welcomes them.*

*The field before you fills with their presence. They march across it, turning with precision, not a man out of step, and line up two companies deep, eighteen companies across, thousands of slim, erect, athletic men taking up the whole field. You find yourself applauding, feeling embodied in it, wishing secretly that you were a part of it. Power, precision, pride—they emanate from a parade like sweet smoke. Is there anyone on earth who does not thrill to it?*

*The drums stop. The Brigade is motionless and the crowd is mute.*

"Good afternoon, ladies and gentlemen. Welcome to the United States Naval Academy, and to this afternoon's dress parade. Standing before you on historic Worden Field is the Brigade of Midshipmen, four thousand young men from every state in the Union and several foreign countries, representing the cream of American youth. You will note by the formations on the field that there are two regiments in the Brigade, with three battalions in each regiment and six companies in every battalion. The Brigade's thirty-six companies are identifiable by the yellow guide-on flags at the head of each company.

"Today marks the final dress parade for the midshipmen of the class of nineteen sixty-eight. During the past four years the members of this class have undergone extensive indoctrination and training, both here at the Academy and with the operating forces of the Naval Service, developing the fundamentals of professional knowledge and personal character which have earned them the right—and the privilege—of undertaking the responsibilities of leadership in defense of our nation. Tomorrow, eight-hundred and forty-one of the original thirteen hundred members of this class will be commissioned as Ensigns in the United States Navy, or Second Lieutenants in the United States Marine Corps. Soon thereafter they will join the operating forces, following the thousands who have marched before them on this field. We are proud of them. We wish them success and Godspeed.

"Reviewing today's dress parade is Rear Admiral Donald Kraft, the Superintendent of the Naval Academy. This is Admiral Kraft's final dress parade as Superintendent, as he will be retiring from the navy following thirty years of distinguished service.

"Ladies and gentlemen, the Brigade of Midshipmen."

Applause. No, not merely applause: the robust, proud beating together of hands from a crowd that had spilled over from the packed bleacher seats and now surrounded the field. It was not quite real, this audience filled with nubile beauties in their bright summer dresses, the sailboats moving up and down the river as if someone had painted them onto a backdrop, the lush trees and green grass and flowers, even the brilliant azure sky. And on the field, of course, an ocean of black coats and white trousers in perfect alignment, at exact attentions.

Inside the Brigade formation looking out, all John Dean could see clearly was the back of someone else's head. He stood buried in the middle of his company formation, sweltering inside the thick wool of his full-dress blue jacket, holding his bayoneted rifle at order arms beside him. The man to his left, a second classman, swayed gently in the windless heat, and then abruptly burped. The second classman had been drunk when the parade formation began in Tecumseh Court a half-hour before, having barely made it to formation from the June Week cottage his girl friend was sharing with six others. The heat had already cooked the good parts of the alcohol out of him, leaving him ill. The second classman reached up very slowly as he swayed, the motion of his white-gloved hand imperceptible from the stands, and undid the high collar of his jacket. He was breathing deeply. He burped again. Dean wondered if he was going to throw up.

"Reeee-*port!*! The Brigade Adjutant, standing in front of the canopy at the center of Worden Field, put the parade in motion.

The first regimental commander responded with a slow sword salute. "Nineteen men absent, sir!"

"Very well." The adjutant returned the salute and looked toward the second regimental commander.

"Sixty...*nine* men absent, sir." The second regimental commander's report was the first official gesture to the next year's graduating class. It was a symbolic moment, emotional in its simplicity. The crowd recognized the symbolism and applauded again.

The adjutant reported the parade formed to the Brigade Commander, and marched back into his position in the Brigade Staff formation.

"Present ar-r-r-rms!" The Brigade Commander bellowed it and the two regimental commanders did an immediate about-face.

"Fir-r-r-rst regiment, present...*arms!*" Two thousand rifles moved into the air together, the sun again dancing on their bayonets, and one resounding whack echoed off of the old brick homes that surrounded Worden Field as two thousand hands met the rifles when they reached the proper place in front of their bearers.

"Secon-n-n-nd regiment, present...*arms!*" Two thousand more, in unison. The crowd rippled with comment, applauding once again.

The Chief's Band struck up the National Anthem. Dean struggled to keep his rifle perfectly still, perpendicular to the ground and one fist's distance from his body. The second classman next to him had hooked the M-1 rifle onto his bayonet belt buckle to take the weight off of his arms. Next year, thought Dean, watching the second classman out of the corner of his eye, I can do that too. But it was more than being a plebe that kept him from doing it.

The second classman had burped several times. Now he had taken to mild groaning. Several of the upperclassmen near him were chiding him.

"Order arms!"

The parade proceeded just as a thousand others before it had, a ritual handed down along with the uniform they wore. New commands and immediate responses awed the crowd, and yet were done with such a mindless, yawning precision inside the formations that the paradox was almost heresy. Parades were basically a pain in the ass, and during June Week they interrupted the parties. Parade rest. Sound off. Attention. Right shoulder arms. Port arms. Left shoulder arms. Order arms. Officers center march. Officers post march. Present arms again, the cannon firing a thirteen-gun salute for the departing Admiral, the second classman next to Dean finally going down on one knee and vomiting into the sweet spring grass. The upperclassmen near him taunted the second classman with that cruel acerbic humor that makes a man give more than a body tells him he rightly should, and he struggled back up on the eleventh or twelfth discharge of the cannon as smoke settled over the parade like low white fog, holding his rifle at a correct present arms.

*"Pass...in...review!"*

Half of the men in the company immediately responded in low mumbles that the crowd could not hear, *"Piss...in... your shoe!"* No one knew why they said it, it just came out, as it had for decades on Worden Field.

Music bounded off of homes and trees and people and they marched again, a company at a time, down the length of the field and then along its whole front, passing the entire stands where proud hands beat together yet again, interminably. At the center of the field, in front of the bright blue canopy where special guests sat out of the sun, the Admiral stood at a rather ungainly old man's attention, reviewing the Brigade.

"Company! Eyes! Right!" Dean jerked his head to the right along with the others, leaning back and digging his heels in, finally getting a quick look at the Admiral and the stands filled with proud excited faces. They were beautiful, really, all the girls in their pastel summer colors, their June Week tans giving off a sharp contrast to their dresses. A thousand faces filtered past his eyes but then suddenly he found one set of eyes staring back at him, locked inside his gaze with a startled, uncomfortable certainty. Dean's eyes went wide and his mouth opened, as if he had caught hold of an electric current, and he could not let go of the eyes; they held him like two fists on his ears. He wanted to scream, to go after them, but he could not break formation or even watch them anymore because—

"Company! Ready! Front!"

He snapped his head back to the front, again seeing only the back of someone else's head, feeling as if he had just been allowed one small peek into a door that was now closed forever. The crowd was still beating its hands and the company marched off the field, heading down another narrow alleyway toward Gate Three. Dean and the other plebes immediately started a Navy song, another ritual passed down with the uniform. He sang mindlessly with the others, tempted to simply break formation and try to explain it later, to take the gamble. But they would kill him if he did.

*I saw him. It was him.*

The first classmen were breaking formation, though, leaving their rifles with plebes and sprinting ahead, down the alleyway. Firsties from companies behind them began pouring by, screaming at each other, charged with emotion and release. The company marched past Gate Three and stopped in front of the Chapel. The second classman who had been left in charge dismissed them with three seconds of perfunctory commands that would have caused him to be written up for a conduct offense on any other parade day of the year.

"Company halt inspection arms dismissed!"

They all broke into a run then, Dean among them, knowing he could not go back to the parade field in his dress blues and thus giving it up. They sprinted through a small tunnel and around the eighth wing, finally ending up at the reflection pool outside the Library-Assembly area. The firsties were jumping into the reflection pool in full uniform, a final act of freedom from those choking full-dress blues and all they symbolized. It was ecstasy in the reflection pool, grown men wading around in waist-deep water fully dressed, splashing each other, daring to unbutton their uniforms in public, a moment of release almost as profound as the next morning, when they would throw their midshipman caps up into the air and walk away forever.

Dean grew tired of watching them. It was like viewing a private party, although perhaps a thousand people were standing around doing just that. You've got to be pretty far down, he mused, before standing waist-deep in a pool of dirty water makes you feel up. But I guess that's Navy in a nutshell.

He began walking slowly back toward Bancroft Hall, staring with hunger at some of the women who strode by, feeling the gazes from cars that drove along the roadway. It was like a zoo. You were always on display and so much of the world was out of reach. But you got used to that, too.

Then Dean saw him again. He was sure this time. There he stood, next to the Library-Assembly building, leaning casually against the wall, his arms folded as he secretly watched them frolic in the reflection pool.

Dean stood motionless for a second, washed with an aching that he could not define. Then he began walking toward him.

"Sir!" But he had seen Dean too, and was disappearing, moving along the sidewalk toward Gate One. Dean broke into a jog. "Sir!"

That did it. Dean knew he shouldn't have started to run. It was like a lynx powering away from him, blending for a moment into a crowd of tourists and then popping out on the other side. Dean stopped jogging and watched him fade into the distance, out Gate One, a part of himself evaporating forever.

And it had to be him. Nobody else could run like that.

# PART ONE:

---

# THURSDAY, FEBRUARY 8, 1968

# Chapter One: 0545

Bill Fogarty skimmed along the black road, his combat boots like pistons, pounding slush and pavement with the steady rhythm of a fine machine. The predawn world looked like an old newsreel, all black and white and gray. The road was black and looked like a river. The sky was black, washed with grainy speckles of stars. The Severn River beyond a low wall on his left was white, choked with ice and snow that gnawed and sighed in the lazy current. And the wide athletic fields were a murky, slushy gray, churned from the games his fellow midshipmen would not abandon, even in the cruel cold of February.

He passed a small snowman several of them had collaborated on the day before. The snowman wore a midshipman Dixie Cup hat, properly rolled and boxed, properly placed forward on its head, just above its nonexistent eyebrows. Its creators had awarded it the National Defense Medal, the red and yellow badge perfectly centered on the left side of the snowman's chest. Even snowmen were squared away at Navy.

Fogarty chased puffy clouds of his own breath in the icy dark, wrapped inside two sweatsuits and a parka, wool hat and scarf, wool gloves. His labored breathing had made a thin layer of frost on his scarf. The first gust of morning wind lifted a curtain of ice crystals from the Severn and flung it at him. It beat his face like cold sandblast, then melted and ran into his scarf. He winced, but did not so much as touch his numbed cheeks.

Dewey Field slowly disappeared behind him, giving way to Santee Basin, empty for the winter of its complement of sailboats. Far to his right, lights had begun to dot the darkness of Bancroft Hall, the largest dormitory in the world, as the plebes prepared for reveille. He crossed the short length of Farragut Field. His boots were soaked, heavy as lead. His legs were numb at the thighs. He had run three miles in the icy slop along the Academy grounds.

The seawall made a dark crisp line below the whiteness of the Chesapeake Bay, just across the road from Farragut Field. Fogarty ran it every morning, hundreds of large, flat stones piled on top of each other, each one four or five feet around, each one angled in a different way, so that anyone trying to run the wall would have to hop from rock to rock, rather than merely going in a straight line. Most of the rocks were covered with ice or moss.

Fogarty never ran the seawall until he was tired. He used it as a test, a game that pitted his fear against his courage. One wrong step, or one unlucky one, and he would fall, smashing his body onto wide, sharp rocks that could easily break his bones or crack his skull. But that was all a part of it.

He reached the wall. The icy confluence of river and sea surged along the lower rocks, ice scraping up at him with swells from the distant sea, sounding something like rats gnawing wood.

Fogarty broke into a sprint. His eyes came involuntarily wide and remained glued to the rocks in front of him. Without thinking long enough to make a decision, he jumped left, toward the sea, to avoid a dark, moss-covered rock, then back up to his right to avoid ice. Left and right, yet maintaining the momentum of his sprint, a ballet dancer, a hopscotch player, one hundred sixty raging pounds sometimes guided through his heavy wet boots with the simple flicking of a single toe.

Finally he finished the seawall, hopping back onto the road and resuming his normal jog. He completed his morning ritual, a lap around the Academy grounds, turning past the Halsey Field House on the other side of Thompson Field, then heading back toward Bancroft Hall, where in moments all four thousand men of the Brigade would begin a day of ceaseless motion.

Fogarty chanted as he jogged, in a mindless, repetitive whisper. "I can run all night ... I can run all day ... I can run all night..." His smooth face, red as if burned by an unrelenting sun, broke into a grin as he climbed the Sixth Wing steps. He banged on the door and the Mate of the Deck let him back into Bancroft Hall, that prison he had learned to hate after nearly four years with a passion that was almost love itself. Love, hate, fear, loneliness, a touch of anger tied up with a knot of pride: that was Navy. The whole universe, squeezed into a Hall.


No one ever got used to reveille, any more than one can learn to accept being whipped. At one moment most of the four thousand midshipmen who lived in Bancroft Hall were asleep, the Hall itself dark as a tomb, its corridors solemn and quiet as a church. In the next, when the clock ticked over to six-fifteen, hundreds of large school bells spaced every few yards along the corridors screamed in unison, a long thirty-second blast followed by thirteen one-second taunts, knives into even the dullest sleeper's dreams. By the time the bells ceased ringing every midshipman was required to be not only awake, but completely away from his bed and on his feet. Touching one's bed between reveille and morning meal was a serious offense, punishable with a weekend's restriction to one's room.

Bells controlled the midshipmen. Being one second behind the bell, letting it beat them by one hollow echo, meant trouble. Bells got them up. Bells told them when they were late for meal formations. Bells called them to class, and announced when they were late. Bells announced liberty. And when a midshipman returned from leave, it didn't matter if he had journeyed all the way from Hawaii, if he was one second late, he was down. Punctuality was the key to the naval service, officers reminded them regularly. What happens if you are one second late getting to your ship and it's just left Long Beach for the South China Sea? Bells bells bells. They learned to hate the bells.

But they also learned to split seconds, and to react like Pavlov's dogs. Like the time the spring before, when some dumb sleepy plebe on Main Office watch had accidentally tripped the reveille bell at two-thirty in the morning, and the entire Brigade had turned out and whirled into motion before anyone noticed the time. The clock had said two-thirty, but no one trusted the clock anymore. The bells were omnipotent, all-wise. In Fogarty's room, Swenson had completed his shower, McClinton had already shaved, and Fogarty himself had swept the dust from the room— all parts of their separate morning rituals. They hadn't even trusted McClinton's windup clock at first.

Fogarty climbed the final steps toward the first deck, his company area. The thirty-six companies in the Brigade were each imbued with the distinctness and the idiosyncrasies of an isolated clan of mountaineers. Fogarty had spent four years along this set of corridors with the same group of classmates, originally three dozen but winnowed down to two dozen, the seniors who were now in charge of the company itself. This collection of forty stark rooms was the womb of his adulthood, in many ways more of a home to him after four years than even the house in which he had grown up. In a few months Fogarty and the others would enter the operating forces, becoming pilots and marines and submariners and "black shoe" line officers. But until then they played games, suffered deprivations, studied the deeds of those who had gone before them, lived by bells.

Reveille sounded and the world transformed on command: black to white; night to day; Ghost Town, Wyoming, to New York City. The bells screamed out their first long maddening blast and immediately the Mate of the Deck began furtively clicking on the light switches for the hallway, proclaiming day. Screams and moans emanated from different rooms. Fogarty passed two plebes as he entered the company area, each under a school bell, standing on a chair, holding pillows over the bells as other plebes galloped from room to room, announcing reveille to slumbering upperclassmen.

Fogarty stopped in the center of the hallway, watching groggy midshipmen stumble from various rooms in their blue or gray bathrobes, rubbing their eyes, their shower shoes clopping along the hall like lazy horses. He smiled again, the same fierce, exultant grin he had worn when the Mate had let him back into the Hall.

"GOOD MORNING, EVERYBODY! YOU CAN GET UP NOW. AND IN A HUNDRED EIGHTEEN DAYS YOU CAN KISS MY ASS GOOD-BYE."

"Screw you, Fogarty." A half-dozen weak, uninterested rejoinders floated to him from various somnolent, yawning faces. It was a ritual. Fogarty laughed, walking down the hallway.

Rituals, rituals. A burly, disheveled man with the kind, morose face of a Saint Bernard dragged himself slowly from room to room, dressed in a gray West Point bathrobe he had won in a bet with a cadet on some Army-Navy sporting event, carrying a long cardboard sheet with the names of everyone in the company. Arnie Lesse was the muster-taker for that week, responsible for reporting every man turned out at reveille, locked in at evening study hour, and tucked in at taps.

Fogarty called to him, "You better make damned sure they're up, Arnie. The OD's going to be through here this morning, I can feel it in my bones."

Lesse stopped in the hallway, shrugging almost apologetically. "They'll be up. If I have to sign my name on this musterboard, you can bet your ass on it." He shrugged again, inspecting Fogarty. "That doesn't mean they won't go back to bed after I leave their room, but who the hell am I? Hey, Bill," Lesse shook his head at the soaked boots, the wet, mud-stained gray sweatpants, finally grinning in amazement at Fogarty's reddened cheeks and the dripping scarf below his mouth. "Plebe year was over three years ago. Didn't anybody tell you?"

Fogarty playfully slapped his classmate on an already softening stomach. "Yeah, well you're going to be sitting on your ass in the wardroom of some destroyer, sipping coffee and watching movies. I'm going to be in the mud, man. What's plebe year to Vietnam?"

"So what's that got to do with running around in the snow at five in the morning? You marines are crazy as hell. I never in my life seen a bunch of people work so hard to get their asses shot off."

"So, what do you want me to do? I hate ships. I hate wardrooms. I hate goddamn coffee, and Arnie, I'll tell you a secret: sailors suck."

"I can't believe it. You were right!" Lesse stared down the hallway toward the Fourth Wing doors, where a dark, narrow passageway connected the Fourth and Sixth wings of Bancroft Hall. His mouth was agape. It was as if an attacking army had unexpectedly appeared on the horizon. Lesse trundled away, leaving Fogarty with one finger in the air, in the middle of his lecture. Lesse madly waved the musterboard as he hurried from room to room.

Fogarty turned to where Lesse had stared and watched the Officer of the Day begin bursting into the first rooms of the wing, trying to catch midshipmen who had gone back to bed after Lesse's reveille inspection and were again asleep. Fogarty walked gingerly toward the Fourth Wing, his stocking cap now in his hand, fully accustomed to the marvel of a thirty-year-old man dressed in a service dress blue uniform, wearing a hat and sword as if at parade, running from room to room with a hapless plebe at his heels, trying to catch a grown man in the act of touching his very own bed. It was, as the midshipmen liked to lament, a Navy Kind Of Morning.

"GET THAT ONE, MATE!" The officer held a door open and pointed at one bed inside the room, then sprinted toward the next door. It was Lieutenant Von Yerks, a wiry, bespectacled little shrew who had graduated from the Academy a decade before, and was now living out his former frustrations while serving as a Company Officer.

"HERE'S ANOTHER ONE! ON THE RIGHT, MATE!"
The plebe who was following Von Yerks also wore his service dress blues, with the blue armband and a yellow *W* that marked him as a Mate on Main Office Watch. He seemed confused and exhausted. Later, he would be required to fill out a Form Two, the standard sheet for placing midshipmen on report, on each guilty midshipman. Von Yerks would then sign them and send them back to the midshipman's company officer. Sleeping after reveille: twenty demerits. Spend a weekend in your room.

"BOTH OF THESE! THAT MAN IS SITTING ON HIS RACK!"

Von Yerks sprinted toward Fogarty. As required, Fogarty stood at a rigid attention and formally greeted him. "Good morning, sir."

Von Yerks did not even acknowledge Fogarty. Doing so would break up his momentum, cause him to miss catching a culprit or two. He dashed into another room, then into another, the heavy wooden doors bouncing on their hinges as he pushed them open in his haste. Fogarty shook his head with faint amusement, his insides nonetheless vibrating slightly from the terror all midshipmen felt toward such officers.

Wait a minute. Swenson. Fogarty retraced his steps and entered the first room inside the Sixth Wing, where Von Yerks had begun his blitzkrieg. It was a standard Naval Academy two-man room, same in design and furnishings as a thousand others in Bancroft Hall. Just inside the doorway, a closet disappeared to Fogarty's right. Two M-1 rifles stood against a rifle rack in the closet, and two large white laundry bags hung from high clothes hooks, among overcoats, "reefer" class coats, and bathrobes. A sink and shower were on Fogarty's left. In the center of the room, a large square of Formica made a two-man desk, where the room's occupants sat face to face during study hour. Against each wall on the left and right were bunkbeds, the sheets turned back according to regulations governing post-reveille activities, with identical powder-blue bedspreads and navy blue blankets. Two high windows covered the far wall, their venetian blinds closed tight.

McClinton was in the shower, humming a bad rendition of a recent Beatles hit. Swenson sat naked at his desk, reading the morning paper. He shook his head winsomely as he noticed Fogarty, his thin, angular face cracking with a dry smile.

"You're dripping water on my deck."

"Did you get fried?"

"No. Get a sponge and wipe that up, will you?"

"When did you start caring about water on your deck?"

McClinton had heard Fogarty. He stuck his head out of the shower, his black hair framing a freckled face. He pointed a huge weightlifter's arm at Fogarty.

"Oh, it's the midnight miler. Meet any mermaids on the seawall this morning, Fogarty?"

"In this weather, I'd be more likely to run into a walrus."

"God spare us." McClinton was back inside the shower. "Then we'd have to listen to a goddamn sea story about how you beat the hell out of a walrus."

Swenson fretted at Fogarty like a grandmother, not even looking up from his newspaper. "Bill, either take your boots off or wipe up the puddles, will you? Captain Lenahan is really tight about clean decks. Don't ask me why. Goddamn marines. Crawl around in the mud and then complain about water spots on the deck. Tell me the sense in that. Anyway, wipe it up."

"You sound like my mother." Fogarty sat on top of the desk, scanning the headlines of Swenson's paper as Swenson read the inside. "See what happens when I move away? You assholes have to start cleaning up for yourselves. Get a plebe to do it, for God's sake."

"You can't do that anymore."

"Oh yeah? Don't you have a plebe coming around this morning?"

Swenson ran a thin hand wearily through the air, still staring into his newspaper. "Yeah, I have a plebe coming around. But we're discussing the war."

"*Discussing*?" Fogarty spun off of the desk. "Since when do you *discuss* things with a plebe during come-arounds, Swenson? You discuss things in class. What is this happy horseshit?"

"This happy horseshit is John Dean." McClinton had climbed out of the shower and was drying himself with a regulation white towel. "Dean has a brain that's even bigger than Swenson's."

"Careful, Mack." Swenson had still not looked up from his newspaper. "Comparisons are inherently invidious."

"So what the hell does that mean?" Fogarty's face was squinched up.

"It means it's fun to talk with him. Even if he is a scumbag."

Fogarty waved them both off. "So talk with him while he swabs your deck."


I am a failure, thought John Dean, making one last adjustment in the knot of his tie as he examined himself in his mirror. Every weary detail of his pale, round face presented itself to his sad inspection. His was a face that held all of its energy in the eyes. The thin, straight nose might have broken easily if its owner had ever submitted himself to contact sports. The small chin seemed weak and mousy. The skin itself was unblemished and unscarred, as a baby's. But the eyes were clear, ambitious in their own shrewd and cautious way, and plainly disapproving of what they were inspecting in the mirror.

I am a failure.

Dean checked his watch: six-twenty-three. In two minutes he would burst into Swenson's room, surrender his freedom for a half-hour of abuse, farm out his mind for Swenson and his friends to pick apart and malign. Come-around. Three times a day, six days a week, like voluntary flagellation.

I am here of my own free will. I hate this place and I hate them all, but I don't have the courage to walk away I am a *failure*.

Six-twenty-four. Dean took a deep breath and placed his cap carefully onto his head, measuring three fingers above his ears and adjusting the gold braid above the visor. He mashed his chin tightly against his throat and ran out of his door, squaring the corner in the middle of the hallway as he headed toward Swenson's room at an obligatory trot.

"Beat Army, sir!"

Five doors down, he again squared a corner and headed toward Swenson's doorway. "Beat Army, sir!" Outside Swenson's door, he stood at a stiff parade rest, his chin tight in its brace, watching the clock for the second it would tick over to six-twenty-five.

"So who the hell are you?"

A rough red face with a mashed nose and fierce blue eyes stared into his own, emanating an ambiguous fury. Dean came immediately to attention.

"Sir, midshipman Dean, fourth class, sir."

"Oh. So you're the guy."

Dean had no idea what the fierce man meant, but his responses were limited by regulation and custom to five: yes sir, no sir, aye, aye sir, no excuse sir, or I'll find out sir.

While the angry-looking red face dripped sweat into a steaming parka, cool eyes went over Dean's uniform, scrutinizing every detail from the top of his cap to the tips of his shoes. "You're not very squared away, did you know that?"

It was too much, this insult from a stranger after Dean had spent a half-hour shining and brushing and tucking, all the while chiding himself for doing it, because doing it was an act of failure, of not quitting.

"Sir, I request permission to make a statement, sir."

"Speak to me, turkey."

"Sir, Mister Swenson is my squad leader, and he seems quite pleased with the way I look, sir."

The fierce man stared at Dean for a long time, his square, muscular face jutting toward Dean's, only inches away. "Who the hell are you to say that to me, *huh*? You never talk to an upperclass that way, you slimy smack." Dean felt the man's boots slowly grind the polish off of one spitshined toe, then the other. "Your shoes look like shit."

Dean stood silent in his tight attention, the uncomfortable, denigrating "brace" reserved for plebes, hating the ass of a man who had just undone ten hours of spitshining in a callous moment of spite, hating himself for standing mute before such abuse, hating the U.S. Naval Academy for having created and perpetuated such stupidity in the name of discipline or degradation, or what did they call it, it was all the same.

"I said your shoes look like shit, dufus. Are you ignoring me?"

"No, sir."

"Then what have you got to say for yourself?"

"No excuse, sir."

"You bet your ass there's no excuse. Do you think Mister Swenson will be 'quite pleased' when he sees your shoes now?"

"Sir, no sir."

The man wiped his mashed nose with a thick hand and casually rubbed sweat and snot onto Dean's shined belt buckle. "Your brass is tarnished, too. Oh, you *are* a mess, Dean. A real mess."

Swenson appeared at the doorway, half-dressed, slowly buttoning his black drill shirt, part of the weekday uniform during the winter. "I see you've met Dean." The angry, scowling man had not stopped staring at Dean. "He's a little bit of a sea lawyer."

"I noticed."

From the corner of his eye as he stood in his brace, Dean caught the motion of Swenson slowly shaking his head from side to side, a gesture of disbelief. "Oh, Dean. Kiss your fat pink ass good-bye. You really did it, this time. Do you know who this is, Dean?"

"Sir, no sir."

"Who's the Brigade Administrative Officer?"

It was a "plebe rate," required knowledge, to know all the first classmen who held major positions in the Brigade striper organization. "Sir, the Brigade Administrative Officer is Midshipman Lieutenant Commander Fogarty, sir."

"Guess what, Dean."

"Sir, I have just met Midshipman Lieutenant Commander Fogarty, sir."

McClinton appeared behind Swenson, nodding toward Fogarty with an ironic grin on his face. "See? I told you he was smart."

"So what is smart, huh?" Fogarty grunted, still staring at Dean. "A computer is smart. Einstein was smart. Can you see him leading troops? Hell, he couldn't lead little old ladies across the street."

Swenson pulled his already-knotted tie over his head and began tightening it around his neck. "Ah, Bill. Somebody has to figure out nuclear subs. We're not all going to be marines."

"Is that what you want to do, Dean?"

"I beg your pardon, sir?"

"Why did you come here, troll?"

Dean's eyes stared into a vacuum, detached from the confrontation, his memory struggling to sort through the banal anguish of eight months of humiliation, to pan out all the fool's gold and come up with the one small pebble of reality, of precious pure reward that made it all worthwhile. "For the education, sir."

"Well, that's what I hate about you, you sorry prick." Fogarty's red face had exploded with his words. "You need an education about this place."

"Oh, Dean. Poor Dean. You really did it. You hit Mister Fogarty where it hurts." Swenson rested a hand on the frail plebe's shoulder. "You're supposed to say something about flying the jet, or driving a ship, or leading troops in combat. Really, Dean."

Swenson gestured at Fogarty, who still stood in front of Dean, his powerful arms folded and his face still dripping from sweat and steam. "Consider human nature. Look at this guy. He got up at five o'clock this morning and ran a lap around the Academy, the whole goddamned Academy, for *fun!* He wants to be a mud-sucking marine! Did you see the headlines this morning, Dean?"

"Yes, sir." It was another plebe "rate," a requirement of every first-year midshipman, to know the three most important stories out of the newspaper each morning. "The Special Forces camp at Langvei fell to the North Vietnamese yesterday, sir, and a key hill position at Khe Sanh is under heavy attack. The North Vietnamese still hold Hue City, although the marines are on the move, sir—"

"Alright, alright." Swenson smiled softly. "Consider all that. Am I getting through to you, Dean?"

"Not fully, sir. If I were to be honest, that is."

"Am I in your chain of command, Swede?" Fogarty had not taken his eyes off Dean.

"Are you in my chain of command? I suppose so. I answer to the Platoon Commander, he answers to the Company Commander, he answers to the Battalion Commander, he answers to the Regimental Commander, he answers to the Brigade Commander, and you work for the Brigade Commander."

"And Dean answers to you. Why don't you send him around to me for a few days? I'll see what I can do to help him understand fully."

"Oh, I'll bet he will." Swenson and Fogarty laughed, then Swenson nudged Dean. "Hey, Dean. Put your head between your legs."

"Aye, aye, sir." Dean obediently leaned over, holding onto his cap, and stuck his head as far between his legs as it would go.

Swenson laughed again.

"Now, kiss your ass good-bye."

"Goose Breeden's down." McClinton had dressed, and caught up with Fogarty as he strode the corridor toward the Fourth wing.

"Down where?"

"Up North. His wife called Ray Whitlow last night."

"Is he alive?"

"He was when he went down. A SAM hit him, but they saw a chute."

"He'll make it." Fogarty walked with measured paces, not looking at McClinton.

"I don't know. It was pretty rough country. They didn't give his wife much hope."

"He'll *make* it, goddamn it. All right? He's got a whole jungle to hide in."

"They'll get him. All they do is follow the chute. You know that, Bill."

"If he doesn't make it back I'll kiss your ass, McClinton."

"If I know you, you won't come back yourself in a big enough piece to kiss *anyone's* ass."

Fogarty's eyes rolled, his only sign of emotion. "Christ. So what do you want me to do?"

"Kiss my ass now."

"Mark the spot, McClinton. You're all ass."

He dominated the hallway as he strode toward his room, chiding other midshipmen, taunting plebes, possessed with a maddening certainty. Bancroft Hall, the Marine Corps, all things military, were Bill Fogarty's world. The clock ticked over to six-thirty-five and with the precision of a computer hundreds of plebes throughout Bancroft Hall began their "chow calls" at the same instant, standing at the end of every corridor and at the intersection of every joined passageway, figments, an army of windup dolls. Fogarty stood motionless, his face jutting to within six inches of one wide-eyed plebe near his room, daring the plebe to break his continuous, screaming chant. The plebe persisted, despite Fogarty's pressures.

"SIR YOU NOW HAVE TEN MINUTES UNTIL MORNING MEAL FORMATION, THE UNIFORM FOR MORNING MEAL IS WORKING UNIFORM BLUE ALPHA, FORMATION IS INSIDE. SIR THE MENU FOR MORNING MEAL IS CHILLED ORANGE JUICE SCRAMBLED EGGS FRIED CHICKEN LEGS ASSORTED DRY CEREALS TOAST BUTTER AND JAM COFFEE CREAM AND MILK. SIR THE OFFICERS OF THE WATCH ARE THE OFFICER OF THE

WATCH IS, LIEUTENANT VON YERKS, UNITED STATES NAVY, THE ASSISTANT OFFICER OF THE WATCH IS, LIEUTENANT CUCCIO, UNITED STATES NAVY, THE MIDSHIPMAN OFFICER OF THE WATCH IS, MIDSHIPMAN LIEUTENANT COMMANDER MORGAN, THE COMPANY MIDSHIPMAN OFFICER OF THE WATCH IS, MIDSHIPMAN LIEUTENANT PARKER. SIR THE MOVIES IN TOWN ARE, AT THE CAPITOL, *THE WILD FLIES*, STARRING ROGER MOORE AND CANDY LEFAVE, AT THE CIRCLE, *DAYS OF WONDER*, STARRING MALCOLM HENRETTY AND ISABEL SHINER, AT THE PLAYHOUSE, *IT NEVER HAPPENED HERE*, STARRING JULIA GONZALES AND BARRY SOUSER. SIR THE DAYS ARE, THERE ARE FIFTEEN DAYS UNTIL WE BEAT ARMY, FORTY-ONE DAYS UNTIL SPRING LEAVE, ONE HUNDRED FOURTEEN DAYS UNTIL THE SECOND CLASS RING DANCE, AND ONE HUNDRED EIGHTEEN DAYS UNTIL FIRST CLASS GRADUATION. *SIR!*"

Rituals, rituals. Every plebe on chow call said the same thing, the same way. It was as precise and exact as a rosary chant, and the whole recital took less than a minute. Fogarty grabbed the plebe's drill shirt just above the belt buckle, where a slight fold had gathered. "Go give yourself another tuck before the five-minute call, negat."

"Aye, aye, sir."

"And go around to your squad leader for standing in my passageway with your shirt hanging out."

"Aye, aye, sir."

"And don't look at me. I'm not your friend."


It took him four minutes to shower and dress. Such perfunctory mechanics were a vestige of his own plebe year, when it had been nothing, indeed a ritual, to shower, put on a uniform for inspection, and race to an upperclassman's room within the space of two minutes. Showering was quick. He had only a small tuft of hair to wash, and he used a bar of soap on it. His uniform was an extension of himself, so familiar that he could (and often did) put it on in the dark and have it fit perfectly, with an imposing exactness. "That rapier look," one woman had remarked as he strode the streets of San Diego while on liberty from his ship during his first summer at sea. He kept his hat inside a plastic bag, to keep it from picking up dust or lint. He kept his tie knotted perfectly, with a dimple in the exact center of the tie, underneath the knot, so that he could merely slip it around his neck and pull it tight. He could fit the wire "spiffy" collar stays underneath the knot and into the corners of his collar with his eyes shut. His brass belt buckle was jury-rigged, the belt tip extracted from the belt itself and fastened to the buckle so that it always appeared, with no effort whatsoever, that the brass of the belt tip was exactly joined to the brass of the buckle. After almost four years he could give himself a military tuck so tight that it appeared someone had painted his drill shirt onto his body.

Fogarty stood in front of the mirror and inspected himself before leaving the room. Four gold bars gleamed on each collar. Only four men in the entire Brigade of Midshipmen outranked him. His eyes were clear, his mouth was firm, unyielding, and his shoulders bulged out from his drill shirt. He was a recruiter's dream.

The chow callers were screaming that there was one minute left before morning meal formation. Fogarty waved briefly to his roommate, the Brigade Operations officer, and strode slowly down "striper alley," the hallway on the first deck of the fourth wing where the Brigade and Second Regimental staffs lived, on his way toward the Main Office, where he would perform his early-morning chores. Like an interloper in a temporarily-neutralized enemy zone, he passed through a double fire-door then marched slowly down an empty dark hallway where in an hour the Commandant of Midshipmen and his officer staff would arrive.

He opened another set of fire doors and entered the Rotunda, the high-ceilinged, dark, ornate shrine just inside Bancroft Hall's huge double-doored main entrance. He had walked through the Rotunda at least once a day for almost four years and still it always stirred him, much as it did when he drove around the monuments in Washington, D.C. Here was history, condensed and sanctified, his past and his future in the form of tributes to those who had served the naval profession and the Academy through the generations. And up on the open staircases that bracketed the Rotunda, scurrying to beat the formation bells, were the very embryos of such deeds, immersed in his present. The Rotunda was a pulsing heart that beat inside his own breast.

High on a wall to his left, above the large, heavy main

doors to the Hall, was a large mural depicting the U.S.S. *South Dakota* in a furious battle during World War II. Shells burst around it and the battleship fought back, churning through the high seas. The Japanese had reported sinking the *South Dakota* ten different times during the war, but she had always managed to limp back into port, to be mended and return to battle. The *South Dakota* had been nicknamed "Battleship X." And that was what it was all about, on the mural for them all to contemplate each day as they walked toward class.

Up a marble staircase to Fogarty's right, Memorial Hall haunted him like a Shinto shrine. Battle flags and souvenirs from all our country's wars lined the walls. In the center of the Hall, across a wide, solemn expanse of hardwood floor, under an always-burning light, a glass-encased series of pages with the typed names of those Academy graduates who had fallen in combat reminded all of them of the wages of their special calling.

Nearest Fogarty as he walked, at the bottom of those marble steps that ran up to Memorial Hall, were the deepest, most real reminders. On three large posters, eight feet high and six feet wide, lined up in rows as if at some final formation, were the photographs and short biographies of graduates who had died or were missing in action in Southeast Asia. The inscription on the center poster read: TO THOSE WHO WENT BEFORE US.

Fogarty knew several of the many faces on the posters. Everyone in his class did. They were men who had tortured him plebe year, who had stood near him in a thousand formations, who had marched with him to parades and football games. They were names he had seen on the blackboards in the Hall as Midshipman Officer of the Watch, or had cheered as they moved with strength and grace on the athletic field.

Fogarty stopped for a brief moment before the board. And now Goose Breeden will make the third board, he mused, studying the space at the bottom of it. Crazy bastard. Conduct case. God, how he hated the Academy!

There was no Brigade Staff formation at morning meal during the winter, when the Brigade itself formed up inside the Hall. Fogarty used the few minutes before breakfast to take care of the Main Office paperwork, which was one of his duties as the Brigade Administrative Officer. He entered the brightly lit outer room of the Main Office, nodding casually to the several midshipmen watchstanders who were manning phones and making various entries into several logbooks, then moved back to a secluded section in the rear of the office.

His In box was full. Fogarty felt his lips work into a grimace as he looked at the high stack of new regulations, amended regulations, deleted regulations, various types of mail and notifications: all the accoutrements of bureacracy. He hated paperwork. It got in the way.

Sighing, he sat down and sorted the mail into stacks, one pile for the regulations, which he would have to log in and file in one of a dozen blue cloth binders, one pile for materials to pass on to the Brigade Staff, and one pile for the Officer of the Watch.

He never read the new, amended, or deleted regulations. He simply logged them and filed them as quickly as he could. They were indexed by number and he reasoned that, if he ever needed to find them, he could index into them. He quickly filed them, feeling abstractly offended by the whole process, hating the thought of having to view himself as a paper shuffler, even the paramount paper shuffler among all midshipmen in the Brigade. Then he picked up the material for the Officer of the Day, and knocked three times, loudly, on the OD's door.

No answer. Fogarty knocked again, three times, loudly, as required. Still no answer. He felt relieved. He feared and disliked Von Yerks, and he didn't know Lieutenant Cuccio, and like most midshipmen he dreaded having to deal with officers other than those he wished to emulate. It was too easy to get into trouble. They had their world; he had his.

He entered the OD's room, marching past a large television set over the thickly-carpeted floor to the Officer of the Day's wooden desk, where he deposited the materials in the OD's In box. The Out box was empty. Fogarty was not surprised. Von Yerks liked to spend his time as Officer of the Day along the corridors of Bancroft Hall, collaring offenders. Von Yerks liked to fry.

There wasn't much mail left for the Brigade staff. Fogarty cupped it in his hand and strode quickly out of the Main Office. If he didn't hurry, he would be late for morning meal, and Von Yerks just might decide to fry him for arriving late to the staff table.

Fogarty jogged through the Rotunda, down the steps

through Smoke Hall, then down another flight of steps into the mess hall. The Brigade was still pouring into the mess hall from the four entranceways and again he could not contain his awe. Four thousand men descending into one collective area, filling the huge, T-shaped room in their same black uniforms, brought a noise and confusion, a collective energy and madness that had to be unique in the entire world. Meals were mandatory at Navy, and the mess hall was a circus.

Plebes "chopped" toward their assigned tables, a mimic sprint filled with motion but little forward movement, up-and-down, up-and-down, almost like running in place, their caps all held the same way, hands completely inside, visors pointing down, their chins against their throats and their faces blank, like innocence. Upperclass sauntered with deliberate slowness, as if disassociating themselves from the forced antics of the plebes. White-uniformed Filipino stewards raced about, still carrying large trays of juice and coffee to some of the tables.

Fogarty flipped through the Staff mail as he made his way among a sea of black uniforms toward the staff table. There were only a few items: two pieces of Yard mail for Banks, the Brigade Commander, a letter for the Brigade Supply Officer about mess hall menus, and three casualty reports for the Brigade First Lieutenant, who was in charge of the TO THOSE WHO WENT BEFORE US board.

Fogarty opened a casualty report, standing at the staff table.

"COPY/COPY/COPY DEAR MRS. LOUDENSLAGER I DEEPLY REGRET TO INFORM YOU THAT YOUR HUSBAND FIRST LIEUTENANT RONALD E. LOUDENSLAGER DIED..."

He staggered slightly, his face taking on an almost drunken look. Someone asked him if he was sick but he could not concentrate enough to answer yes or no. He wandered around the table as if lost, staring down the long high wings of the mess hall at chandeliers and tables and people, at nothing, merely walking and staring.

Banks was calling the Brigade to attention and the Chaplain was giving his morning prayer, something about making their lives more fruitful through work and study, and then the Brigade was seated, all without relevance, all without Fogarty. He walked slowly down the main aisle of the mess hall, his face now expressionless, the yellow paper in one thick muscled hand, his eyes peering vacantly above the many faces that stared up at him.

He reached the company tables, the small corner of the mess hall where he had passed through the rigors of plebe year and the million other special antics and miseries, his home. At the far end of one table McClinton and Swenson sat, presiding over their little fiefdom of a dozen men, the plebes furiously passing chow and serving the upperclass eggs and chicken and cereal and juice. This was normality, security, Fogarty's anchor, his sanctuary.

They watched him walk toward them, their smiles slowly fading. He stopped at their end of the table, his eyebrows slightly raised, the telegram by now wadded tight, squeezed into a ball.

Fogarty dropped the paper onto Swenson's plate. It landed with a settled plop on a mound of watery scrambled eggs. Fogarty put both hands on his hips and shrugged, almost with nonchalance.

"Ron Loudenslager's dead."

# Chapter Two: 0830

Ted Lenahan's face carried the perpetual look of having just lost a very close fight. He had defiant, disappointed blue eyes in weary sockets, the soft skin underneath them too dry and wrinkled for a man of twenty-nine. His craggy, rough-skinned Celtic face seemed in a perpetual squint, accented by thin lips that liked to smirk, and broken teeth behind them from having indeed lost a few too many fights in his youth. Ted Lenahan was for real. The marine captain with the jutting chin and furious, controlled presence was a landmark among the midshipmen he served as Company Officer.

He walked with flat, measured steps along the first deck of the Sixth Wing, inspecting rooms. Most of the midshipmen were in class, although some remained in their rooms, studying or asleep. Lenahan sought them out on his inspection tours, asked them questions about their classes, their girl friends, their aspirations. He was more than a Company Officer. He was a leader.

It was Lenahan's first year back at the Academy since he had graduated, and he had not yet fought his way past his memories into the present. Every time he walked the corridors, he again secretly marveled at himself for ever having been a part of the Brigade. Even after seven years, in his weakest moments Ted Lenahan would admit that, deep down inside, it was hard to believe he was actually a marine officer at all. A marine, yes. An infantryman, of course. But to have the status of a Naval Academy graduate and a commissioned officer still seemed like an alien, undeserved windfall.

He had grown up in South Boston, watching dozens of street corners take on the names of older Southies who had died in places like Anzio and Guadalcanal and Bastogne and Iwo Jima. By the time World War II was over and Ted Lenahan was six years old, it seemed as if most of the street corners had new names, and the possibility of having a street named after him was more real than anything called college.

Two of his brothers fought in the Korean war, one with the army, one with the marines. Neither of them claimed a street corner but the marine came back with the muscles of one calf cupped by shrapnel, and three puffed toes, immobile from frostbite. When small children would stare at his calf and then his toes, Lenahan's brother would wave his hands and wink and tell them that a Chinese man had scooped the flesh out of his calf and stuffed it into his toes. He was really pretty funny. Lenahan used to spend a lot of time helping him learn how to walk again.

His brother would go on about the Corps as if it were a combination of the Knights of the Round Table and the Jesse James gang, rough and ribald and yet steeped in the purest form of camaraderie. By the time Lenahan was a senior in high school, he had decided to enlist. The recruiter, who had no need to worry about making quota because South Boston flocked to the Corps with the eagerness that Scarsdale reserves for Harvard, took one look at Lenahan's test scores and advised him about the Naval Academy.

He almost didn't get in, and in fact had not expected to be accepted. Lenahan had a juvenile record for assault, one of those little moments that tends to follow an adult through life like a specially marked page in a very long book.

It wasn't really fair, but then it never is. When Lenahan was fifteen he was working as a delivery boy for a grocery store, making thirty-five cents an hour. Just outside of South Boston, in Boston proper, a cut-rate appliance store owner used to advertise progressive prices, depending on how long an item remained on the showroom floor. If the item had not been bought within ten days, it was marked down 10 percent. If it had not been sold within twenty days, it was marked down another 10 percent, and so on until it was bought. The store owner time-dated each item. He was very successful in moving merchandise.

Lenahan had been wanting a radio for years. The store owner put one on the showroom floor for twenty-six dollars. It was an ugly, old-fashioned, round-topped radio with bulging tubes, but it was made out of real wood. Lenahan fell in love with it.

He figured that, in thirty days, the radio would be on sale for eighteen dollars and ninety-five cents, plus tax, and that, in thirty days, he would be able to save up nineteen dollars and fifty cents. He visited the radio every day. He became very protective of it.

On the twenty-sixth day, he walked into the store in time to watch a middle-aged lady hover around his future possession like a vulture, staring at it from all angles, picking it up, even daring to plink the tubes. It was already marked down to twenty-one dollars and six cents. Lenahan had saved up eighteen dollars and seventy-five cents.

The lady started to walk toward the checkout counter with his radio. He hadn't any choice. He strode briskly up to her, craggy and tight-muscled, with the fierce, indignant scowl of the morally wronged, and hissed into her face,

"If you buy that radio, lady, I'll kill you."

So the lady had dropped the radio and screamed and the radio tubes had burst and the casing had split and the store owner had called the police. And in the end Lenahan had bought a broken radio for twenty-one dollars and six cents, just escaping a sentence to Juvenile Hall.

Lenahan's record had caused some debate when he applied for the Naval Academy. Finally, his high school counselors became convinced that he was thoroughly rehabilitated, mostly through their dedicated counseling, and was competent to be trained to kill enemies of the country rather than ladies who coveted his most prized belongings. The Academy, surprisingly, agreed.

So he had gone, uncultured and unwashed, and the whole four years had been like a dream. But he never escaped a slight feeling of unworthiness, as if all the pomp and ceremony, all the glitter and tinsel, were actually too much for him. He hated the marching regimens as much as everyone else, but every time Ted Lenahan stood at dress parade on Worden Field and listened to the announcer's voice careen across the magnificent old brick buildings, talking about the cream of American youth standing at attention before the stands, he would literally shudder with pride.

And he who had never been out of the state of Massachusetts in his life was suddenly spending summers cruising around the world, riding great gray fighting ships to Hawaii and Mallorca and Barcelona. He who had never dated anyone other than South Boston girls who were rapidly becoming secretaries and teenage housewives was now himself courting the brightest women from the best local Washington, D.C., colleges. He who had never driven a car in his life owned a Corvette by the time he graduated.

It was overwhelming. It transcended the miseries and deprivations of Academy existence. And when he graduated, Lenahan was left with more a sense of unsettled confusion than of joy or even accomplishment. He spent four full days of his precious commissioning leave merely sitting around the Academy grounds, for the first time studying monuments and buildings with a sort of removed, painful awe. He was not alone. On any of those days, he saw a dozen of his classmates sitting numb and incredulous on park benches or monuments, like distance runners who had just spent all their energies and could now only stare at an empty, dominating track.

He saw it in other alumni also, especially since he had been assigned back to the Academy as a Company Officer. Graduates would drive through the Yard in cars filled with wives and children, pointing at landmarks, faces quizzical, stares hollow with bewildering, painful memories and most of all with questions, as if all of life's problems had begun for them right there on those grounds and therefore the answers, too, should be lurking somewhere, underneath a monument or etched into a brick walkway.

When Lenahan first came back and watched a noon meal formation in Tecumseh Court, all the rows of impeccable, solemn, athletic men marching into Bancroft Hall, first to the tune of "Anchors Aweigh" and then to the "Marine's Hymn," he cried. It brought out too much of himself, too much of what his own four years spent marching to the same music on the same yellow bricks had done to him. And in the months he had spent back inside the Hall as a Company Officer, he had yet to transcend that emotion. When he stared at a midshipman he saw himself, and it never failed to bring on a tiny edge of confusion, of lament.

He was an outstanding officer, a good and dedicated marine. He had spent five months as an infantry company commander in Vietnam, in continuous combat, picking up two Silver Stars and a Bronze Star for heroism, and three Purple Hearts. The third time he was wounded, Lenahan's medevac flights hadn't stopped until he found himself in Tower Twelve of the Bethesda Naval Hospital, where he spent four months so immobile that he defecated through a hole in his bed. His brother wrote him a funny letter from South Boston about learning how to walk again, warning him to keep a baseball bat at bedside in case any horny queer navy-type squid corpsman tried to sneak up under his bed in the middle of the night and rape him through his craphole. Semper Fi, do or die. His brother knew what he needed to keep from feeling sorry for himself.

His marines in Vietnam had loved him. He was an irascible, aggressive leader, filled with wisecracks and the sort of black-humored courage that inspires the best out of men in combat. And his midshipmen loved him, too. Ted Lenahan carried combat in his scars and in the ribbons on his chest. He was what it was all about.

He entered an unoccupied room, the door left fully ajar as required by regulations when both inhabitants were gone. Lenahan inspected rooms in his company area every day, usually about a dozen rooms at a time, so that every room had a pass-through inspection at least once a week. Every month he conducted formal, white-glove walk-throughs on Saturday mornings, the classic, traditional sort of scrutiny that searched for dirt and dust in absolutely ludicrous places. No one liked such inspections, including Lenahan. But then that was the keynote to the military, anyway: doing things you didn't like.

For the midshipmen, he was ubiquitous. When they got back from class he had been in their room, leaving an inspection chit. When they formed up for noon meal, he was wandering amongst their ranks, a wiry, scowling demigod dressed immaculately in his greens, carrying an ever-present but never-worn pair of regulation black gloves rolled inside his left hand, his left chest covered with ribbons and shooting badges.

They did not comprehend his caution, but he was careful to leave them alone at night. He remembered Bancroft Hall in his midshipman days, the separate world that evolved after evening meal, company barbers and sandwich salesmen and souvenir salesmen crawling out of the dark walls like an army of roaches, all illegal, all part of the essence. And the "special instruction" sessions for problem plebes, again illegal, again essential. If he had reason to be in the company area after evening meal, Lenahan was always careful to mention it to his midshipman company commander, a subtle way of warning the men to abstain from their frolics for one evening. The mids never fully appreciated his subtlety. They always came away believing they had buffaloed him. But that was a part of it, too.

Lenahan tore an inspection chit from the small bulletin board just inside the doorway, and began marking it. Sink unsat. Shower dirty. Two pencils left out on the desk. Blanket improperly folded on left rack. Socks improperly stowed in left closet. Boondocker shoes placed on shoe rack with mud on them. It was a plebe room, and it was the worst room he had inspected that morning.

He checked the door to make sure. Yeah, Dean again. Lenahan tore the sheets off of Dean's bed and threw them onto the floor, tossing the blanket on top of them. He reached inside the "wall locker" closet and raked out a whole shelf onto the floor, then stood staring at its ruins, shaking his head in exasperation.

Poor Dean. In baseball they would have called him a "good field, no-hit" type. The plebe was brilliant in the classroom, and if he could only come to grips with the indoctrination, there would be a place for him in the navy someday, perhaps as a nuclear submariner, where his technical skills could be utilized. But he came apart whenever anyone yelled at him. Under the old rules, mused Lenahan, the upper-class would have made life so miserable for him that he would have either squared his act away or quit by now.

Lenahan left the room and walked to the end of the hallway, carrying the inspection chit. He entered the end room and Swenson came to attention from his desk, wearing his drill trousers and an undershirt, his drill shirt carefully folded inside-out on his bed, to prevent wrinkling and lint.

"Attention on deck, Midshipman Swenson, first class, sir."

"Carry on, Swenson."

"Aye, aye, sir." Swenson sat cautiously back down, his narrow, angular face intent on Lenahan. Lenahan handed him the inspection chit and he grimaced.

Lenahan grinned wryly. "Did somebody yell at poor Dean again?"

Swenson laughed softly. "Yes, sir. I think he misses his mother or something. He's not used to people being mad at him."

"I want him to have a full white-glove inspection Saturday morning. The whole works. Leave his roommate out of it. I can't see giving Peckarsky any more demerits because of Baby Blue."

"Aye, aye, sir."

Lenahan and Swenson had been through the whole routine before. Lenahan continued to grin wryly. "So what's the matter this time? I'm sure he'll be requesting mast to see me."

"Dean really pissed off Mister Fogarty this morning, sir. It was pretty funny. You know Fogarty, Captain. I thought he was going to tear Dean a new asshole. You should have seen Dean's face."

"Well, maybe Fogarty's just what Dean needs."

"That's exactly what we were thinking, sir. In fact, it looks like Mister Fogarty is going to be having Dean around for a while." Swenson examined Lenahan's face for any sign of disapproval. "It's all kosher, sir. Fogarty's in Dean's chain of command."

"Well, you're not going to get any argument out of me. Who knows? Fogarty just might square him away."

Swenson smiled brightly to Lenahan. "Well, sir, if anyone can square Dean away, Fogarty can. Fogarty's crazy as hell. I mean, he really *cares*."

"You don't have to be crazy to care, Swenson." Lenahan had not lost his knowing grin. "Sometimes it helps, though, I'll admit."

"Sir—" Swenson called to Lenahan as he turned to leave. "You ought to be aware of something else, sir. Fogarty's best friend was killed the other day. It was a guy out of the class of sixty-six. He just found out about it."

"Vietnam?"

"Yes, sir. He's acting pretty weird, if you ask me. I'm a little worried, to tell the truth."

"They were actually best friends?"

"Hell, yes, sir. This guy was as crazy as Fogarty. Fogarty sort of modeled himself after him. He was our plebe summer squad leader. They just really ended up good friends. They used to double-date together, run together, play marine together, you name it."

"He was a marine, then? What was his name?"

"Loudenslager, sir." Swenson shook his head, his pale eyes lost in the misery of some plebe summer triple-sweatgear come-around, dead Loudenslager screaming at the squad and laughing. "Ron Loudenslager. He was a crazy German out of Chicago. He was company commander during our youngster year, too. During parade season, he'd make the whole company march around the parade field one more time after it was all over, just to show we could do more than the other companies. It used to piss us off so bad we'd deliberately screw up during the parades, so he wouldn't be able to say our extra marching did us any good. He was a case, but the son of a bitch could lead, sir. He could really lead. He'd already been shot once. Mister Fogarty thought Loudenslager was still in the hospital on Guam. And here he is today, reading the casualty letters for that board in the Rotunda, and Loudenslager's name jumps out at him. Jesus, sir. He came walking down to our company tables during morning meal and dropped the telegram right into my plate and then just sort of shrugged, you know, and said 'Ron Loudenslager's dead,' like he might have said 'I forgot to put my laundry bag out in the hall this morning.' It was sad, sir. I'm a little scared for him."

"I'll talk to him."

Swenson smiled, somewhat relieved. "Thank you, sir. Not to get into your business, sir, but he really respects you, sir."

Lenahan rested a hand on Swenson's rail-thin shoulder. "Yeah, okay, Mister Swenson. And take care of Baby Blue, will you?"

They were great, the mids. Lenahan loved working with them. They responded to his offhand, nonregulation sort of leadership like eager children. Many Company Officers led by playing cops and robbers, placing as many midshipmen on report as possible without regard to making disciplinary situations instructive. Lenahan rarely wrote a midshipman up for a conduct offense. It was so much more effective to counsel a wrongdoer, to attempt to affect his future conduct rather than merely lock the man inside his room over a weekend where he could stew and fret about the System.

So many of the regulations were bullshit anyway, he recalled, walking down a stairway toward the battalion office. Silly restrictions carried down through the generations with no relevance to leadership development. Like not allowing a midshipman to have even an iron or a coffee pot in his room. Or PDA, Public Display of Affection. It was one thing to condone a mid's being seen in a passionate embrace with a woman. But it was really quite another to lock a grown man away for his only period of free time all week, simply because he had been seen holding hands with his girl friend. And yet, there were Company Officers who eagerly did just that.

The mids were great for other reasons, too. They were fresh, eager, and absolutely ingenious. They lived inside a sweatbox, with every moment of the day pressurized, so they learned to pick up even the slightest little crack, the tiniest dip in pressure, with a speed and certainty that was astounding. Woe be it to anyone in a position of authority, officer or professor or even another midshipman, who showed in the tiniest little way that he was afraid of them. Midshipmen developed a scent for weakness and attacked it with ferocity, because there was no room for weakness in their environment. Given every reason to resent authority, they gave genuine respect only to those who deserved it.

Thus, they learned to worship strength, to seek it out and emulate it. They reached toward men who were self-contained and strong, who had shown they could function under stress, who had guts and tenacity, who could fend off weaker men, and win. They looked for men like Ted Lenahan.

He pushed open the door of the battalion office and waved to several of his fellow Company Officers, already gathered inside. Yeah, the mids made it worthwhile. But Mad Pratt made it almost miserable enough for him to want to go back to Vietnam. The fat, crew-cutted battalion officer, Lenahan's immediate superior and thus the man who wrote his fitness reports and controlled his career, was a disaster. Pratt was walking testimony, mused Lenahan again as he entered the room, to what sort of military calamities befall the many when a few ignore their responsibilities to cull out the maladroits during plebe year. Somehow, Commander Pratt had made it through his own plebe year, had graduated from the Naval Academy in 1948, and had taken out the navy's mistake on various unfortunate subordinates for almost twenty years thereafter.

Pratt was the most dangerous man Lenahan had ever worked for. At his previous duty station a sailor had become so incensed by the Commander's rigid and unthinking disciplines that he had chased him halfway across the base during one workday, firing a .38-caliber pistol at him.

Unfortunately, mused Lenahan, pouring himself a cup of coffee from the small metal pot near the conference table, the sailor was a lousy shot. Pratt was dull and explosive, a devastating combination. He was impossible to predict. And he ran his six company officers, all men with more than a half-dozen years in the active military, as if they themselves were plebes. Pratt was fry-happy, and seemed to evaluate his company officers by the number of demerits they assigned. He had counseled Lenahan on several occasions to "put more discipline" into his company.

The mids themselves had named him Mad Pratt for his perpetual scowl and his madman's rages, which he obviously considered a part of his Academy duty. It was a vision of stark terror for any midshipman to look down a passageway and watch the waddling swagger, the round face with the wire-frame glasses that pinched the skin along the shaved head, the thin, pouting lips, and the cap tilted to one side, at the back of his head. Pratt went through a company area like a one-man Mongol horde, tearing up rooms, frying hapless mids who happened to cross his path, rousting out Company Officers and bringing them to the scene of his destruction to be counseled in front of the midshipmen themselves, the penultimate form of bad leadership: punishing in public.

Maybe *I'll* shoot the son of a bitch, mused Lenahan, joining the others at the conference table. If he's going to ruin my career with a series of bad fitness reports, I may as well make it worthwhile.

He nodded wryly to the others, the six of them gathered around the table for their morning meeting with all the eagerness and enthusiasm of a corral full of roped and hobbled calves. But I'm the worst, decided Lenahan, studying the faces of the other five, all navy officers. At least they have the ability to either laugh Pratt off or stay out of his way.

Or to emulate him. Lenahan elbowed Lieutenant Pruitt, a blond, baby-faced submarine officer who sat next to him. Pruitt did more than play Pratt's game. He actually seemed to believe in it all. Pruitt was Pratt's little brother.

"What's with your buddy Von Yerks, there, nukie-poo? I hear he tore my company a new asshole this morning."

Pruitt rubbed his crewcut and stared into his coffee cup, avoiding Lenahan's eyes. Lenahan was sure Pruitt had put Von Yerks, a fellow submariner, up to the assault, in order to gain an edge on Lenahan. Pratt became furious when companies in his battalion were caught sleeping past reveille, and would surely take it out on the decorated marine.

Pruitt looked out the window. "Yeah, Don can really be an asshole at times. I hear there's a whole stack of Form Twos on Pratt's desk. I guess he'll be pissed."

"Yeah." Lenahan continued to stare at Pruitt, enjoying the baby-faced blond's discomfort. "The Madman is definitely going to be pissed. But what's he going to do, cut off my hair and send me to Vietnam?"

The other officers chuckled comfortably. Lenahan grinned to them, lighting a cigarette. He envied their ability to take it all so comfortably, to let Pratt and Pruitt and Von Yerks, all of it, roll past them as if they were merely mids again, counting the days, waiting for it all to end so the real world could again begin.

It's like a come-around, he decided, watching them stoically prepare their notebooks for Pratt's daily harangue. You gear up for it, you endure it, and then you forget about it. See how well plebe year prepared us for life? He studied the movements each one was going through, the mental preparations, as if he were removed by a time or maybe emotional warp, merely studying an historical event. Wentzel, a small, hawk-nosed aviator, a wild man with a chest full of combat medals, Lenahan's closest friend in the battalion, sat at Lenahan's right, monotonously drumming a pencil. Pratt did not exist to Wentzel. Sometimes the Academy did not exist to Wentzel. His eyes would glaze and his thin hands would start drumming the pencil and Wentzel was over Haiphong again, or maybe setting his monster jet onto the angle deck of a carrier, zooming down onto a speck at hundreds of miles an hour. Wentzel was a brilliant man, an aeronautical engineer, but he described himself as a Hell's Angel with a jet instead of a cycle. *Just let me fly the jet.*

Foote sat across from Wentzel, meticulously diagramming in his notebook even before Pratt's first word. He was pure black-shoe navy, a destroyerman like Pratt himself, and had spent four of his first six years out of the Academy at sea. Foote lived, breathed, and drank the sea. Each year of his Company Officership he had begun with a lecture to his company about professional priorities. First, remarked Foote, came the navy. Then came God. Then came his country. And somewhere down the line, cobwebbed with afterthought, came his family. A hundred whores in ports around the world had felt Foote's dark, heavy body shudder over them, then quickly roll away as Foote's brooding mind thought once again of putting out to sea. The Academy was an interruption, necessary for his career, for command at sea. Whatever Pratt wanted out of Foote he got. But first he had to ask.

Then Karalewski, the clown. The barrel-faced Pennsylvania Pole was just off a tour as the weapons officer on a guided missile destroyer. Karalewski managed a happy balance, and indeed seemed to spend his entire energies doing so. His mids loved him and his wife loved him and his church loved him and even Pratt had a hard time getting mad at him. Karalewski knew when to be funny and when to be quiet, a trait Lenahan envied. Just then he was mimicking Pruitt's embarrassment, staring hollow-eyed at the boyish submariner's downturned face, Karalewski's own face squinched up, his tongue out and his head tilted. No, thought Lenahan. He's not really thirty. Nobody who's thirty can make a face like that.

And finally Parkhurst, another pilot, who next to Pruitt was the most disliked company officer in Pratt's battalion. Parkhurst had made a career of flying P-3 antisubmarine aircraft, a large, propellor-driven creature that the others teased him was akin to flying for the airlines. When he was a midshipman, Parkhurst had been an all-American halfback on the 150-pound football team. He was a bulldog, cocky and aggressive, and he liked to fry.

The clock ticked over to zero nine-hundred and Pratt immediately opened the door from his private office. It was almost comical, thought Lenahan, rising to attention with the others, that a man could put so much energy into such wasted routine, while being so absolutely empty of real leadership. Pratt's small blue eyes flashed at him as the Commander walked slowly to the head of the table. Lenahan briefly fantasized about the bulky battalion officer leaning against the door inside his office, hand on the knob, waiting for the clock to tick over. Punctuality, the thick brain would be pulsing, as he watched the clock. Punctuality is a key to good leadership. I will be punctual. I will have nothing important to say, but that's all right. I was exactly on time.

Pratt sank into his chair then nodded briefly, a silent order, his eyes on a manila folder he was opening. The six Company Officers sat cautiously back into their own seats, watching Pratt's hands with rapt attention, as if he would soon pull out a rabbit from the folder, or maybe a set of orders to Vietnam. Inside, captured in a tight scrawl, were two pages of notes Pratt had taken at his morning meeting with the Commandant of Midshipmen.

"We're winning in Vietnam." Mad Pratt spoke from his notes, as if reading a decree. Lenahan and Karalewski exchanged glances that went light in the eyes, just avoiding querulous howls. Now, just where the hell did he dig *that* out, wondered Lenahan. Who does he think he is, President Johnson?

Pratt studied his notes further, avoiding eye contact with his company officers, speaking to the notepad. "The enemy has lost more than fifteen thousand men since this Tet Offensive thing started. The word should go out to the companies. Tell the midshipmen."

All right, mused Lenahan, writing on his own notepad. *15,000. Winning. Tell mids.* Next item of business, before you ream me out for Von Yerks' little purge?

"Service selection is Monday night." Everyone knew service selection, the annual carnival where the soon-to-graduate first classmen chose their career fields and first duty assignments, was Monday night. Pratt's lazy, raspy voice had trailed off after "night," the only indication that more was to come. The commander glanced at Lenahan, then kept his eyes on his notes once again. "I don't want any heads shaved. The Commandant of Midshipmen doesn't want any heads shaved. There will be no heads shaved. Get the word out to your companies. No midshipman who signs up for the Marine Corps will have his head shaved, or I will personally write him up for a 'Class A' offense, direct disobedience of an order."

"Ah, sir..." Lenahan muttered his protest without real enthusiasm as he scrawled on his notepad, having been through the coming process so many times he could have written a script for how it would proceed.

Pratt sighed, still staring at his notes. "Yes, Captain Lenahan. You disagree. I had expected you to disagree."

"Just a small point, sir." Talking to Pratt was like trying to disarm a booby trap before it blew up in your face. "The mids who sign up for the Corps don't usually *ask* to get their heads shaved, sir. Their classmates do it to them. They don't have any control over it."

Pratt looked up from his notes, keeping a pudgy finger on the next item of business. His heavy jowls were pushed forward, toward Lenahan, as if he had been deeply insulted. "So..." His voice rasped and trailed off again, as if he were weary. "What are you telling me, Captain Lenahan?"

"Well, sir"—Lenahan stubbed out his cigarette— "a man can end up with a shaved head even if he's trying his damndest to obey your order, sir."

"Yes?" Another weary, irritated word.

"So a man who has his head shaved by someone else, against his wishes, isn't directly disobeying your orders, sir."

Pratt's finger remained comically fixed on his page of notes as he scowled at Lenahan, as if the paper would blow away if he took his eyes and his finger off of it. He spoke with a solemn profundity, as if he were opening up a very secret door for Lenahan and allowing him to peer in at universal truth. "Well, Captain. Someone is."

"Yes, sir." They watched each other as if across a chessboard on which the midshipmen were being bungled about as pawns. The other officers sat back in their chairs, Karalewski far enough away from Pratt's line of sight to make a face that emulated strangulation, his eyes bugged out and his cheeks filled with air. Lenahan barely restrained a laugh. This isn't really how policy is made, he thought. If the mids only could see this. "But it's not fair to the victim, sir."

"Life is unfair. I didn't say anything about being fair. I said we aren't going to have any shaved heads on service selection night. The order is, no shaved heads. Violators will be punished. Any further questions, Captain Lenahan?"

"No, sir." The air came out of Karalewski's face.

"And while we're talking about punishment..." Pratt pulled a stack of more than a dozen Form Twos from his folder, holding them in front of them, dangled in the air away from his body, as if their odor were so strong he could not stand to have them any closer to his face. "All these are from your company, Captain Lenahan. Thirteen men, almost ten percent of your company, went back to bed after reveille this morning. There really is no excuse for this. It embarrasses me, and it shows, it shows…" Pratt stared incredulously at Lenahan, as if Lenahan should be providing him the appropriate self-insult.

Pratt stared silently, looking old with his heavy, bespectacled face and closely cut gray hair, his glasses pinching at his temples. For a moment, Lenahan actually felt sorry for the tongue-tied Commander. Really, he thought. Get ahold of yourself, Mad. It's only sleeping in. Hell, two weeks from now you won't even remember it happened. Then he contemplated again that Pratt had the power to affect, and even ruin, his own career. He reached down inside his sock and pulled out his Marlboros, then casually lit one as he awaited Pratt's recovery.

"You aren't doing your job, Captain Lenahan." Karalewski's eyes rolled as Pratt spoke.

Lenahan put his cigarette pack back inside his sock, deliberately elbowing Lieutenant Pruitt, Von Yerks' friend, Pratt's little brother, as he leaned over. The boyish submariner inched away from him, not looking up from his notepad.

"For the next week, Captain, you will be in your company area at reveille."

Lenahan dragged on his cigarette, then flipped the ash into his empty coffee cup. That's the end of the rope, he decided, staring at the coffee cup as he tapped his cigarette again and again. I've commanded troops for seven goddamn years. I've stared at Castro's assholes in Cuba and I've stared at Ho Chi Minh's assholes in Vietnam and I've commanded every kind of platoon and company the Marine Corps can figure out, and I am a silly son of a bitch if I'll let this dumb ass destroyerman tell me how to lead troops.

"If you want them up, sir, I'll make sure they're up. In fact, I'll guarantee it. But it would be undignified for me and them both if I went racing around every morning at reveille for a week, checking beds. And besides"—Lenahan tapped another ash, then looked up at Pratt— "If they'll only do it because I'm around, they'll stop doing it as soon as I'm not around. I can straighten them out, sir."

"It's not them I want to straighten out, Captain. It's you." Pratt dropped the Form Twos on the conference table. His left index finger had never left the paper, where he would again pick up on his brief. "You don't do enough of this yourself. That's why Lieutenant Von Yerks had to do it for you."

Lenahan dropped his cigarette into the coffee cup. It went out with a hiss. "Aye, aye, sir." He stared into the pulpy features of Pratt's face, as if he were looking at an irrelevant irritant, a screaming child. "But I'll stand on my record, sir. I'll match it with anyone's."

"How long were you in the hospital, Captain Lenahan?"

"Five months, sir."

"I wonder if you haven't gone a little soft."

Lenahan fantasized briefly about putting his fist into Pratt's fat scowl, then sat back in his chair and smiled slightly. Karalewski had that strangled look again, leaning back in his chair so Pratt could not see his face. Karalewski gently shook his head from side to side, encouraging Lenahan to shut up.

Lenahan shrugged casually, his face marked with a bland smile. "Gone soft, sir? I haven't gone soft. I've always been soft. Except when I've had to be hard."

# Chapter Three: 1145

The instructor, a balding man in a frumpy brown suit, was telling them how to determine the water pressure on the side of a ship's hull at various depths. Fogarty sat slouched in the wooden chair, absently resting his head against one hand, the other hand tracing carved symbols that covered his V-shaped wooden desk.

He hated academics. He resented having an engineer's degree forced down his throat or, as they so often kidded, up his ass a nickle at a time, the price of a "free education." He would have absolutely no use for engineering once he graduated, and yet here he was sitting, as he had done for so many thousand wasted hours over the previous four years, bored and disaffected, staring at the carvings on his desk as professors went on about such irrelevancies as fluid dynamics (the subject now being droned) or electrical systems or oceanic navigation or differential equations. Not to mention the untold hours spent out in the Chesapeake Bay on the ninety-foot YP boats, going through antisubmarine tactics and wheels and corpens, being forced to learn the doings of a destroyer while yearning to be an infantry commander.

IHTFP. He allowed his pencil to carve through the letters once again. It was everywhere at Navy, like a secret code word that everyone nonetheless knew: I Hate This Fucking Place. Navy was a womb to all of their adulthoods. They even called Bancroft Hall "Mother B." But they fought it even as it nourished them, lived for the moment they would emerge flailing and innocent into the rest of their lives, snapped like a thousand twins off of the same umbilical cord. Such sameness, so many unrelenting demands that marked off every split second of every day with punishments and rewards, caused a depth of passion that was either love or hate. And only a masochist or a lunatic would acknowledge love inside a sweatbox.

The instructor pointed earnestly at a schematic of a ship's hull, the drawing filled with arrows that somehow conveyed the directions of various water pressures on that point. A $D$ in Fluids was inevitable; Fogarty could see it coming. Sometimes when the instructor was particularly entertaining, when he could make Fogarty forget what he was teaching, Fogarty could muster enough enthusiasm to wade through all the formulae and data. But otherwise it was a write-off. Science was a sadistic come-around.

Physics had been all right. The professor had been teaching at Navy for two decades, and held no illusions. He had explained refraction by reminding them about when they had looked into a bathtub and thought their penises were in one place, but had discovered, upon reaching for them, that they were somewhere else. That had made sense to Fogarty. He remembered refraction.

The bell rang and the entire class slammed their notebooks shut, cutting off the instructor in the middle of a sentence. The man could have been drawing up a formula for eternal life on the blackboard and he still would have been speaking to an empty classroom within thirty seconds after the bell rang. They ran from the bells. In twenty-five minutes another one would ring, and noon meal inspection held all the promise and the terror of an officer scrutinizing them for lint on their shoulders and tarnish on their brass. What was eternal life compared to the prospect of spending the weekend, their only precious free time, locked in their rooms?


Winter squatted on Annapolis like a dirty gray slush-breathing monster, ugly and cold and immobile. The sky was low and sunless above Fogarty as he walked back toward Bancroft Hall,

43

clouds gathered like great bunches of steel wool. The air was piercing and humid and cold, early February bringing weather that dumped snow and then partially melted it, until the athletic fields and the grounds were trashed with a slushy mess that was the same gray as the sky. A harsh wind whipped the walkway from the east, picking up ice from the frozen river and pelting the thousand blackcoated men who walked toward Mother B from their classrooms at Maury and Sampson and Isherwood halls. They walked past stone monuments under great old cobwebs of bare winter trees, the wind driving snow and ice into shaved faces and unprotected ears and closely cropped scalps. It was a sin, a reportable offense, to wear parkas or stocking caps or other protective devices as they walked to and from class.

The sky was gray and the grounds had become gray and the buildings were already gray, and the sullenness of the post-Christmas surroundings ate into their very minds until a whole gray mood permeated the Brigade, like a hostile nimbus. It was a time without color, without anticipation, and the mood was mean and uncomfortable, as if all four thousand men were collectively overwhelmed by cabin fever, an uneasiness with each other and with their harsh, isolated lives.

They had a name for it: Dark Ages. They wrote it on the blackboards along the corridors of the Hall and made plebes stand on their chairs and scream it in the mess hall, "Da-a-a-ark Ages," like some haggard medieval chant. Two years before, the officer staff, probably in its own fit of Dark Ages depression, had outlawed the term, ordered it abolished, making it a conduct offense to utter the words publicly. The midshipmen had retaliated by painting the words onto the statues and monuments in the Yard—the ultimate sacrilege, violating the symbols of the past—and by screaming the words out of anonymous windows during study hour. Finally, the officers had given up. The Dark Ages weren't going to go away because of somebody's edict. Only spring would destroy them. And until then, the mood was miserable. In their isolation, dumped into an icy pit of gloom, they often went entire weeks without seeing a single emissary from the outside world, not one warm bright smiling female body, not one old shriveled tourist.

Fogarty strode the cobbled walkway, the high collar of his reefer jacket up around his ears against the wind, every few seconds reaching up and screwing his cap back onto his head. Far to his right, down one brick walkway, the Academy chapel loomed, its dull green dome blending into like tones in the heavy leaden sky. Loudenslager had been married in the Chapel almost two years before, only a day after the class of 1966 had snapped the umbilical cords and tumbled into the real world. Fogarty had been an usher and had stood on the chapel steps after the ceremony, wielding a sword for the first time as Loudenslager and his new wife exited the chapel, a vision of white, of gaiety, a whole life finally to be lived after four years of deprivation.

Loudenslager had been in a hurry. Fogarty was in a hurry. The bells beat on you for four years, held you back, whacked at you like some mad Procrustes and it did not seem right that a man should be dead so soon after finally seizing back his human existence. They were all denied the normal implements of life for one full year: radios, stereos, the right to any privacy, the right to date women, the right to simply lay down and take a nap when tired, the right to drink coffee—the list was interminable. And they were denied other normal functions for years after that: the right to ride in a car, the right to drink a beer, the right to watch a television show, the right to take a study break and go for a walk in town. It was not fair that a man should be dead after he had finally regained the right to live. Not fair, thought Fogarty, but there you have it. Who the hell said life was fair?

Tecumseh Court teemed with midshipmen, a swarm of black-uniformed men in crisp white caps striding quickly toward the Hall in their haste to prepare for noon meal inspection. That was Navy: a walking pace that was almost a trot, everywhere outside of formations themselves. Even on liberty, the women they dated learned to step it out. Every journey was a race, and the clock laughed at their frenzy.

In the Rotunda dozens of faces smiled at him, black and white echoes forever frozen in their youth, three posters of identically posed, grinning midshipmen gathered on the boards like the formal sitting of a choir. Fogarty stared at the very bottom of the third poster and there he was, right next to Goose Breeden, the two of them side by side as if in formation, their yearbook pictures and biographies already Xeroxed and posted by Farrow, the Brigade First Lieutenant. See how efficient we are, mused Fogarty, his muscled frame taut and still before the posters.

Goose Breeden was a carefree goof, a perfect jet-jockey. His wild eyes danced merrily on his picture. Ron Loudenslager had a sober, confident set to his face, the eyes tough, blond hair like a halo in its brilliance. "The future Commandant of the Marine Corps," his biography proclaimed.

Loudenslager's hollow blue eyes challenged Fogarty, mocked him from some memory years before, the summer of 1964 as Fogarty hung from the top of Loudenslager's door like a monkey, his hands gripping the sharp wooden edges at the top of it, making his palms bleed as tears poured down his grimacing face. The summer of 1964, only days after the Gulf of Tonkin incident had signaled a real war in Vietnam, and Loudenslager pushing his squad of plebes with a delighted sense of mission that was wild and overwhelming. *Would you die for your country, Fogarty? How big are you? Are you bigger than yourself?*

*Yes, sir. Yes, sir. I would die for my country sir.*

To Fogarty, the men on the board were martyrs. No, they were saints.

To Midshipman Fourth Class John Dean they were victims, short and sweet. The boards terrified him as he walked through the Rotunda three minutes after Fogarty had paid his homage. It was all rather morbid, a celebration of the ghastly, a dark death dance on ash-filled sand. He couldn't even stand to look at the faces on the pictures. The notion struck him that it was bad luck, like speaking ill of the dead. If he looked at the pictures the ghosts could read his thoughts. It didn't make a lot of sense, but then, neither did their dying.

Like lemmings, he thought, now safely past the haunting pictures on his way to the Fourth Wing. Their friends come back in boxes and they romanticize it, build little monuments to it. But what the hell. I get out of here in 1971. It won't happen to me, it *can't* happen to me. The war will be long over by 1971.

He left the Rotunda, passing through a set of fire doors into the Hall itself, and immediately began running along the center of the corridor, following a long string of fellow plebes. It always reminded him of a trail of ants, all the black uniforms trotting along single-file, exactly in the center of the hallway, squaring corners on the metal plates that had been conveniently placed at every intersection of corridors.

"Beat Army, sir." Oh, yes. You always said it, every time you squared a corner or stood up or sat down or came out of one of the million little isometric torture positions the upperclass created for your own special misery, "Beat Army," as if the whole world revolved around a silly football game. "Beat Army." Who cared, really? The Woops up at the Point were taking it in the ass just as bad, poor bastards.

He chopped along the corridor into his own company area. Men filled the passageway, calling to each other, screaming jokes and taunts across the hall as they changed from class uniforms into clean inspection clothes. Dean felt his insides knot, as if someone were secretly tightening a corset around his courage as he ran.

"Hippety hop, plebe stop." Dean halted immediately, his chin pressed tight against his throat, staring straight down the corridor. "What were you looking at, Dean?"

I am a failure, thought John Dean. "Nothing, sir."

"You calling me nothing, weird one? Huh?"

I am a waste, a coward, without the courage to even end my own misery. "No, sir."

"Well, you keep your eyes in the boat, slime."

I hate this place I hate them all— "Aye, aye, sir."

"Get out of here."

"Aye, aye, sir." Dean began running again, hating the upperclassman but most of all hating himself for his very obedience. It didn't make sense. It wasn't what he wanted. It was cowardice, pure and simple, an act of running from himself.

"Beat Army, sir." Dean squared another corner and ran into his room. Peckarsky, his roommate, was hurriedly changing into his inspection uniform. He ignored Dean at first, then pointed toward Dean's bed, where the sheets had been left in a ball by Captain Lenahan.

"I told you your rack was unsat."

"The bastard!" Dean picked up the sheets and threw them against the wall.

"Swenson wants to see you, like ASAP."

"The *bastard!*" Dean threw the sheets against the wall again, for effect. Peckarsky sighed, his large pale transluscent moon of a face staring at Dean with the patience of a mother. Dean started to make his bed, then began to take his reefer overcoat off, then remembered that he had been summoned by

Swenson. Peckarsky chuckled, fitting his spiffy collar stay and shaking his head as he watched Dean flit around the room in his indecision, with the jerks of a water bug.

Dean mashed his cap onto his head, scowling at Peckarsky. "You probably think this is pretty funny."

"Hardly. John, you could fuck up a wet dream, did you know that?"

"Ease off, Peckarsky. I've got enough problems without you starting on me."

"Don't forget your gloves."

"What?" Dean halted just at the door's edge, on his way to leaving the room.

Peckarsky pointed to the desk, where Dean had tossed his gray leather gloves. "You'd better either take that reefer off, or put the gloves on. Somebody's going to fry you for being out of uniform." Dean threw both hands up into the air, addled, and quickly donned his gloves before sprinting into the hallway.

"Beat Army, sir."

*"Dean, you worthless piece of mung!"*

Dean halted in a stiff brace in the center of the passageway, not seeing his assailant or recognizing the voice. It didn't matter who it was. Anyone who rated yelling in the hall was God to a plebe. "Yes, sir."

"You didn't square that corner worth a damn, Dean. It makes me think you don't respect me. Give me twenty."

He didn't want to say it but it was his only way of preventing total self-hate. Such things just oozed out of John Dean's brain, unrehearsed, unprovoked. "Sir, I request permission to make a statement, sir."

"What?"

"Sir, the regulations provide that you can only ask me to do ten, sir."

"You asshole." Dean finally recognized the faceless voice. It was Potter, a second classman who lived two doors away. "You goddamned crybaby sea-lawyer. All right, Dean, hit it for ten."

"Aye, aye, sir." Dean dropped to the corridor and did ten pushups, plus one to beat Army, then came back to his tight attention.

Potter's voice was lazy, provocative. "All right, Dean, hit it for another ten."

"Aye, aye, sir." Dean slowly pumped out another ten pushups, feeling humiliated by his own hand. "Beat Army, sir."

"Now, get out of my sight, dufus."

"Aye, aye, sir." Every time he ventured into the hallway something happened. He was a proverbial "shit magnet." They would not leave him alone. They watched for him, delighted in his miseries. Sometimes it took him thirty minutes merely to make it to the bathroom. It never occurred to him that he visited all the taunts and anger on himself.

"Beat Army, sir." He raced into Swenson's room, removing his cap just before he entered the door, then taking the mandatory three large steps inside and pressing his back flush against Swenson's wall.

"Midshipman Dean, fourth class, reporting as ordered, sir."

"I don't know what to do with you, Dean." Swenson stood before the long wall mirror, brushing his shoulders and chest with a wet whisk broom. "You're a goddamn disaster." Swenson was not even looking at him. "Did you know you were a disaster, Dean?"

"Yes, sir."

Swenson strode slowly to Dean and playfully poked the whisk broom into his face. "Kiss Grandma." Dean flinched and kissed the stiff ends of the whisk broom. Swenson laughed softly. "So what does it take to get you to make your rack right, and clean off the top of your desk?"

"Sir, I just ran out of time this morning, sir."

Swenson whacked him on the top of his head with the whisk broom. "And that's another thing. I didn't ask for one of your excuses, Dean. I'm really tired of your sea lawyer bullshit. Really tired. Break out your 'sea lawyer' sign and wear it in the mess hall again, until I tell you to stop."

"Aye, aye, sir."

"Don't ever talk to me about time, Dean." Swenson handed him the whisk broom and Dean automatically brushed the lint off of Swenson's back. "You've got the same amount of time as every other plebe. I didn't even run you this morning. We just bullshitted the war around. You're on report. Bring around a Form Two."

"Aye, aye, sir."

Swenson sat down in his chair and began putting on his inspection shoes. "So tell me, Dean. What was so time-consuming about this morning that you couldn't make your rack right?"

"Sir, I had to repair the scars on my grease shoes. Mister Fogarty ground out both toes this morning."

"Poor Dean. Did it ever occur to you that Mister Fogarty

wouldn't have messed with your goddamn shoes if you hadn't played sea lawyer?"

"No, sir." It really hadn't. Sometimes talking back was his only revenge, even when he lost more than he gained.

"Go home, Dean. We don't want you around here."

"Aye, aye, sir."

"No, I'm serious. You don't want it bad enough. I don't know why the hell you came here in the first place."

Nor I, mused Dean, staring at one small spot on Swenson's far wall as he kept his tight brace. Nor I.

McClinton filled the doorway like a huge dark shadow and then walked right over the top of Dean, the bulky weightlifter knocking Dean three feet to one side as he deliberately brushed against him. "So, how am I supposed to change my clothes when you're blocking my locker, shit-for-brains?"

"Excuse me, sir." Dean relocated along another place on Swenson's wall.

"Get out of here, Dean." Swenson was tucking his shirt, tight as if form-fitted, for inspection.

"Aye, aye, sir."

"And Dean—"

Dean stopped abruptly in his race for the door. "Yes, sir?"

"Those shoes you repaired instead of making your rack right had better be perfect."

Dean grimaced, his face hidden from Swenson. "Aye, aye, sir."

When you're nineteen, time has no fluidity. It holds you in each moment like a cold vise, locking up your lonely present, fending off your dreams with all the passions of today. Plebe year was Forever After to John Dean, a miserable moment that would last through eternity.

Noon meal inspection ritual had been repeated with such regularity that it almost seemed to be normality. Dean changed quickly into his best, "grease" shoes, shined until they were black mirrors then rubbed with wet cotton balls to remove every speck of lint. He put on his grease cap, the white plastic cover scrubbed and Cloroxed, without a hint of dirt or smudge, the black band fitting the cover exactly, pressed to eliminate any small accidental wrinkle, the plastic visor rubbed every noon with Pledge furniture polish. He shined his brass belt buckle until it gleamed absolutely white. He took a wet whisk broom to a freshly pressed drill shirt and trousers, "brushing off" (a code word, a term of art, pure art). He put on a pressed tie, the Windsor knot so tight at the bottom that it came to a point, below which the tie flared out again, "dimpled" at the center. A tie without a dimple was a reportable offense. Behind the tie, he fit his wire "spiffy" collar stay so that the tie itself stood straight out at the knot, then curved gracefully back in where it disappeared inside his drill shirt, three buttons down. Finally, he and Peckarsky traded tucks, each pulling the other's shirt down and around as he buckled his trousers; no wrinkles whatsoever, no overhang in the back.

Normality at Navy. Dean raced down the corridor to beat the formation bell. At the end of the passageway a plebe was giving the one-minute call, in chorus with a hundred other plebes scattered across Bancroft Hall, all screaming it together in an undecipherable auctioneer's chant: *"Sir you now have one minute till noon meal formation sir time tide and formation wait for no man I am now shoving off sir!"*

Dozens of plebes sprinted toward the company formation area. Dean followed the stampede, then turned into his platoon formation area and stood in his squad ranks at a stiff parade rest, awaiting the formation bell. When it rang, he and the other plebes in the platoon, a dozen of them, snapped to attention together. Slowly, over the next three minutes, the ranks filled with upperclassmen, until by the time the late bell rang, every midshipman in the company was standing in formation, shined and brushed off and tucked, impeccable.

"Platoon, a-tenn, HUT. At close interval, dress right, DRESS. Ready, front." Dreiden, the Platoon Commander, a squatty, barrel-chested little South Carolinian with a face like a bulldog, one of those many Southerners who persisted in believing he was actually, secretly, serving in the Confederate Navy, barked out at the platoon. "The Captain's going to inspect us today. Stand by."

And here came Lenahan, the leather heels from his Marine Corps cordovans slowly clicking along the corridor, measured mayhem, controlled ferocity. Dreiden gave him a sharp, apprehensive salute. "Good afternoon, sir. Second Platoon, ready for inspection, sir."

Dean felt his fingers tremble, and made his hands into

fists, his thumbs perfectly along the seams of his trousers. He had never been able to control it, not in the seven months of regular inspections and procedures. Officers terrified him. Lenahan was the devil, dressed up in a green suit. Lenahan slowly made his way along the ranks, standing at attention before every man, scrutinizing uniforms and haircuts and shaves, closer, closer, like the dark funnel of a tornado growing larger as the moments passed.

Lenahan began the second rank, the Platoon Commander and Company Commander following him. Finally he reached Dean. Lenahan froze at attention and peered deep into Dean's soft face, questioning him without words. Dean unfocused his eyes and stared at Lenahan's throat. His hands still trembled. His palms were wet.

"You had the worst room in the company today, Dean. Plebes should have the best rooms. What's your problem?"

I have no problems, only those that others give me. "I had to work on my shoes, sir, and I lost track of the time."

Lenahan's eyes grew weary. His lips gave a tight grimace. "Everybody has to work on their shoes, Mister Dean. By the way. Your shoes are unsat. Place yourself on report."

"Aye, aye, sir." Swenson followed the Platoon and Company Commanders as Lenahan made his way further down the rank. He shook his head bemusedly when he stood in front of Dean.

"You never learn, do you, dummy?"

Company left face. Close, march. Forward, march. They filed down the stairway to the mess hall, unspeaking, still in formation, and Dean observed them in their rows. These were the Men of Annapolis he had watched on television as a child, immaculately groomed, fiercely disciplined even though they resisted every element of the discipline, a paradox, proud of the very things they hated.

Dean marched alongside them but did not feel he was one of them. He watched the snaking column of black-uniformed men disappear around the turn of one stairwell and envisioned the other end of the column coming out in Vietnam, seeking their friends who were in the combat units or being held as prisoners. He did not understand that aching in them. Or maybe they were diving to the bottom of the sea, swimming around like fish as they looked for the nuclear submarine that held other friends, who did not see any part of the world for a month at a time. Or perhaps they skittered along high sea waves, finding others who languished in small rooms on destroyers and cruisers, at sea for months at a time, away from home more often than they were there, wives becoming strangers and, for some, whores becoming temporary wives. He did not comprehend the longing and the pride that made those things worthwhile.

*The General's reward,* remembered Fogarty as he strode toward the company area in the crowded mess hall, plebes dancing past him with their silly chopping steps, *is not a bigger tent, but command.* Napoleon said it, Loudenslager made him learn it as he sat in a brace serving food to the thick-shouldered German, his knees rigged, pushing at the top of the table from underneath as he trembled and shuddered with exertion.

On this very table. Fogarty stowed his cap underneath a chair at the first-class end of the table and awaited the rest of the company's arrival. He stood, his arms folded, and absently watched the mess hall continue to fill with men, as if someone were pouring a black, viscid liquid into each entranceway. Each company broke formation as it reached the mess hall doors, the midshipmen taking off their caps in unison and the plebes then chopping all the way to their tables and standing in braces behind their chairs.

The plebes arrived, and after them the upperclassmen with their casual, practiced saunterings. Dean and three other plebes lined one side of the twelve-man table, their eyes straight ahead, "in the boat," chins mashed ridiculously hard against their throats, shoulders back and down and their hands in fists, thumbs along the outer seams of their trousers.

Swenson and McClinton walked languidly along first-class alley, the outer edge of the messhall where only seniors could roam. Fogarty nodded to them, a greeting.

"Mind if I eat with you? I can't hack the staff table today."

"Who said we can hack you?" McClinton pushed playfully at Fogarty, then pointed at one frozen blue image of a man. "Peckarsky. Go away." The plebe immediately grabbed his cap and dashed off into the mess hall's madness, looking for a table with an empty space.

Swenson stood erect, his arms folded in front of him, that classic upperclassman's pose, and stared at Dean. "I told you to wear your 'sea lawyer' sign, didn't I, Dean?"

"Sir, yes sir."

"So where is it?"

"Sir, it's in my cap, sir."

"So what's it doing in your cap, silly one?"

"I just haven't had a chance to put it on, sir."

"So what are you waiting for, Dean, a written invitation? Put the goddamn sign on."

"Sir, aye, aye, sir." Dean reached quickly into his cap and pulled out a handlettered sign affixed to three feet of laundry string. *SEA LAWYER*. He placed it around his neck and then returned to his brace.

Fogarty watched Dean, his face expressionless. "That's that guy."

Swenson chuckled, watching Fogarty's gaze slowly focus in on Dean. "Yeah, that's that guy. Hey, Dean, remember Mister Fogarty? I don't think he likes you very much."

Dean's blue watermelon eyes stared straight before him with all the innocence and anguish of the mortally wronged. "Sir, yes sir."

"So tell Mister Fogarty why you're wearing your sign."

Dean's lips puckered for a quick moment. He took a deep breath, fidgeting his thumbs against his fists. "Well, sir, I was trying to explain to Mister Swenson about why my room was unsat this morning when Captain Lenahan inspected it, sir, and—"

Fogarty cut Dean off. "Your room was unsat?"

"Yes, sir."

"Why?"

Dean's face went through several contortions as he pondered an answer. "Well, sir, after you ground out the toes of my shoes this morning, sir, I—"

"Oh, Dean, Oh, Jesus." Swenson shook his head bemusedly, a small smile creasing his thin face as if Dean were indeed a hopeless fool.

"So it's all my fault, huh, Dean?" Fogarty's muscular jaws were working, his cheeks rippling with their contractions. "You *are* a goddamn crybaby. Who decided to shine shoes instead of cleaning your room, Dean? Me?"

"Sir, no sir."

"Come here, mung." Dean trotted to the edge of the table. Fogarty grimaced. "Your shoes are still gross, anyway." He stepped on both toes again. "Start all over."

Dean's eyes rolled involuntarily. "Aye, aye, sir."

"Are you pissed at me, Dean?"

"No, sir."

"Well, that's good, because I'd hate to think you were going to get pissed *that* easy. Just wait, Dean. I think I'm going to give you a few things to get pissed about. What's your grade point, troll?"

"Three-point-eight, sir."

Fogarty whistled. "Almost straight *A*s, huh? What's your leadership standing?"

"Sir, I received a *D* in aptitude, sir."

"What's your ranking in the company?"

Swenson interjected, putting an arm on Dean's frail shoulder. "He's last. But there's a reason, right, Dean?"

"Yes, sir."

"It wasn't done fairly, was it, Dean?"

Dean's face twitched again, his thumbs still moving in tiny circles. "Well, sir, I don't think I've been treated—"

"You don't *think*, Dean. That's your whole goddamn problem." Swenson was losing his patience, his high voice a whip. "You don't stand there and tell me, after all I've put up with from you, that I haven't treated you fairly in your aptitude. Hell, Dean, if I'd treated you fairly, I'd have flunked you." Swenson grabbed Fogarty by the arm and moved him and Dean toward each other. "Dean, Fogarty. Fogarty, Dean. Run the hell out of him, will you?"

Fogarty's face was still expressionless. He stared at Dean without visible emotion. "You fucking *worm*."

"*Brigade, Atten - HUT.*" The loudspeaker sounded from the Anchor, at the center of the mess hall. The midshipmen ceased their frolics and their tortures and faced the Anchor as if it were the flag, standing at attention. Banks, the Brigade Commander, stood at the Anchor with the microphone in his hand. "Attention to announcements. There will be a bloodmobile in the Library-Assembly area this afternoon. All midshipmen are encouraged to donate. The blood will be going to the naval hospitals at Bethesda and Quantico, which are loaded with casualties from the Tet Offensive. Brigade, seats."

The upperclassmen sat leisurely down. Dean, the nearest plebe to the first-class end of the table, addressed Swenson. "Sir, I request permission to seat the fourth class, sir." Swenson nodded. "Fourth class, *seats*." The plebes scrambled into their chairs, sitting in a brace at the very edge of them.

Dean picked up a metal pitcher and held it out in front of him. "Sir, would you care for tea, sir?"

"Don't you know what I take, Dean?"

"Yes, sir, except I don't know what Mister Fogarty takes, sir, as he is not a regular member of the table, sir."

"Pour me some tea, Dean." Fogarty handed Dean his glass and leaned forward, examining Dean's soft unmarked face. "Get your chin in. So tell me, you little nord, Are you giving blood this afternoon?"

Dean immediately sat the pitcher and the glass back onto the table, as required, his hands again by his sides. "Sir, I hadn't planned on it."

"Why, not?"

"Sir, I hadn't considered it an obligation, sir. Needles really make me sick."

"Pour my tea, Dean. So needles make you sick. Do you thing anybody in this mess hall *likes* needles, Dean?"

"I doubt it, sir."

"Those hospitals are filled with guys who are *really* sick, Dean. They've lost arms and legs, pieces of their guts. They need your help. You're their comrade in arms. Doesn't that mean anything to you?"

"Sir, yes sir. Ah..."

"Dean thinks the college protesters are right." McClinton swirled the ice in his tea. "They're his comrades in arms. Right, Dean?"

"Well, sir, not exactly." Dean took a tray of cold cuts from the plebe next to him, and held it out for the first class to draw from. "That is, I think they're for the most part right. I just never considered them to be under arms."

"I'm not believing this." Fogarty and Swenson exchanged bemused smiles. "So what are they right about?"

"Don't get him on it, Bill." Swenson began making a sandwich. "I don't think you can handle it."

"Are you bigger than yourself, Dean?"

Dean considered it, holding a tray of tomatoes and lettuce and onions out for Fogarty and Swenson and McClinton. "No, sir. No one is, sir."

"Everyone is, if they make it a point to be. Give blood today, Dean."

Swenson muttered, almost under his breath. "You can't make him do it."

Fogarty reconsidered. "All right, Dean, let's put it this way. I can't order you to do it, but I'll kill you if you don't."

# Chapter Four: 1500

"I swear to God, you're the prettiest woman in the whole damn world."

She was dipping nonalcoholic punch from a large glass bowl, like the kind usually reserved for wedding receptions. She looked up, startled, then laughed with the soft, throaty giggle that had been her trademark for the entire ten years he had known her. "Ted! Look at this, you made me spill the punch."

"Ah, who cares? One of the Admiral's slaves will lick it up."

"You heretic! It's a wonder a lightning bolt didn't strike you just now."

"Hey, tell me. Do you do this every day? Why don't you just apply for a job in a restaurant? At least you'd be getting paid for it."

"Oh, but I am getting paid. Steve's going to get a super fitness report, and then someday he'll be an Admiral, and I'll have slaves to lick up punch when some dumb lieutenant's wife spills it."

Angie Wheeler gave him a goofy, faraway gaze that made him understand that she wasn't taking it seriously, either, that she had it all thought out and put in the right place. "Didn't you know that in the navy, the wife is marked on an officer's fitness report? Oh, yes, Captain Lenahan, you know that. Let's see: 'Force, excellent. Administrative ability, outstanding. Wife, above average.' How would that look? We wives have to score well, too."

Lenahan stood just a little too close to her, taking in the trim frame (would that be marked under "self-discipline," he wondered absently) and the heavy swells of breasts that made even her conservatively cut dress bulge invitingly. "Well, the Marine Corps takes a different perspective. As Chesty Puller said, 'If the Marine Corps had wanted you to have a wife, it would have issued you one.' Which, considering my situation, is a pretty good attitude, I guess."

"Lucky you." She poured another glass of punch, smiling to a naval officer and his wife. "Did you take Tommy to the doctor, Nettie? What did they say about his cough?"

The woman smiled back, carefully eyeing Lenahan. "He has to go to Bethesda in two weeks. They think it's allergies."

"Let me know when you're going. I'll take my three and we'll go shopping in Washington after Tommy's taken care of."

The officer, who had a company in another battalion, lifted his glass to Lenahan. "I hear Von Yerks purged your company this morning."

"Yeah, the asshole." Lenahan smiled quickly to the man's wife. "Excuse my French. Madman really came unglued about it, too. I think I'm on some kind of leadership probation."

"Leadership probation? What's that, Ted?" Angie Wheeler looked amused and curious, as if such a distinction could only fall on Lenahan.

"Well, Pratt's such a whiz at these things, he thinks I need to take lessons. So he's ordered me to hold reveille on my company for a week. I can think of better ways to spend my energies. And theirs."

"Well, while you're up, go take a look at my company area, will you?" The navy lieutenant lifted his glass to Lenahan again.

"If you were in my battalion, I might do that, just to get Pratt off my—" Lenahan caught the stare of the man's wife "—back. In fact, I just might go take a peek at Pruitt's boys, considering his Von Yerks connection."

"I smell a war coming on."

Lenahan reached into his sock and pulled out his cigarettes, ignoring the renewed staring of the officer's wife, and lit one. "Nah. I don't play those games. In a war like that, only the mids lose."

They were alone again. She looked at him with slightly narrowed eyes, as if she were working to contain some secret steam. "Steve's got the duty tomorrow night."

He watched her, just watched her, the high-ceilinged reception room with its ornate chandeliers and milling officers and wives blurring away as if it were all behind frosted glass windows, time and place losing itself in her steady blue embracing eyes. This was not the Admiral's house, the reception for the officers of the second regiment and their wives, and she was not forever entangled, the wife of his own best friend. For a moment that sliced into eternity, they stood alone on a barren spot of the coldest moon, their only warmth each other's need.

"All right. All right."

"Oh-oh. Here comes your friend. Be nice now. Really, he tries as hard as he can."

Pratt approached them, his plump, matronly wife at his elbow, reminding Lenahan of two stodgy ducks as they puttered along the floor. That woman's forty, going on sixty, he grimaced, watching them. Got her gray hair all done up in a granny bun, already picked out her granny glasses. Can't wait to get old. And look at her stare. She knows.

"Good afternoon, sir, Mrs. Pratt." Lenahan came to a semblance of attention, nodding to them. "You know Mrs. Wheeler, wife of Steve Wheeler, Admiral Kraft's aide?"

"Of course I do, Captain. You don't know how close we wives stay together. The Academy is like a small town." She was an illusion, a facade of makeup and frozen hair and bulky woollen clothes who wore her husband's rank like it was her own. And she doesn't like me, mused Lenahan. It's my fault I'm a divorced man. It's my fault my wife screwed me over while I was getting the shit shot out of me in Vietnam, my fault she wouldn't leave her goddamned engineer genius back-stabbing boyfriend, my fault the Marine Corps assigned me on the other side of the country from my son, so he'll forget what I even look like, much less am. Yeah, Mrs. Pratt, stare at me like that and talk about *we wives*. I had one once.

Angie had picked up the tension. "Punch, anyone?" She carefully poured two glasses, handing them to the Pratts. "Steve is thinking about volunteering for Vietnam, and Ted was telling me how I might disabuse him of the idea."

Oh, Christ, thought Lenahan. My only ace in the hole with Pratt and she's making it seem like I'm antiwar, or something. "That wasn't it, exactly, Angie." He shrugged to the Pratts. "I was just telling her he should look at all sides of it, that's all. That the experience is sort of a mixed bag."

"How do you mean that, Captain?" Mrs. Pratt stared with obvious envy at the ribbons on Lenahan's jacket. "I know you were seriously wounded and all that, but you seem to have recovered very well."

"Oh, yes, ma'am. I'm doing fine."

"Well, I just don't see how it's hurt you, overall. And I've always been led to believe that combat is, well, an invigorating experience."

Hurt me? Lenahan stifled a guffaw. Well, let's see, he

pondered. Shall we start with *we wives?* "The men were great, ma'am. I'll never get over that. It was more than I ever dreamed. They were magnificent. The media just doesn't capture how great they really are."

"And personally?" She had her beak into his brain and was shaking it furiously, as if he owed her a look into his insides merely because her husband wrote his fitness reports. "I see all this on TV, especially this week with this Tet thing, and I just can't see how you can walk away from it and be free of it. I mean, it seems so intense. Are you over it, Captain?"

I wonder if I should tell her, he thought. I wonder. "Well, you know Mrs. Pratt, I used to walk through the villages at night, on patrol or something, a company move, maybe, and it was the scariest thing I've every done. You couldn't tell where they were going to hit you from and you couldn't really tell exactly where your own men were. It was a mess, Mrs. Pratt, I mean it. I can't tell you what all that does to your insides. Anyway, all of those villes had waterbull pens, and there's nothing that smells as bad as a waterbull pen. I used to creep past all those hootches and smell the waterbull pens in the black night air and it reminded me of nervous diarrhea, that's what it smelled like. Now every morning since I've been back I crawl out of the rack and have nervous diarrhea and all I can say, Mrs. Pratt, is it reminds me of waterbull pens."

The three stared silently at Lenahan, motionless and all but expressionless. Angie's face seemed curious but confused. The Pratts held similar denials, chins forward like churchgoers confronting an atheist, or perhaps merely an agnostic. Finally, Angie motioned toward the punch bowl, smiling faintly.

"More, punch?"

"No, thank you, Mrs. Wheeler. Oh, look, dear. There's the Zellers." Mrs. Pratt took the dumbfounded Commander by the arm and they drifted off toward the other side of the room.

Angie shook her head sardonically, hopelessly, at Lenahan. "All right, what was that all about? Are you trying to ruin your career?"

"What the hell. She hates me anyway, because I'm divorced. Just thought I'd loosen up her brain a little, that's all."

"Ted Lenahan." Her blond hair piled in waves around her face. Her eyes did not conceal her attraction. "You've got balls."

Admiral Donald Kraft was of the battlewagon breed, old navy, a trade-school warrior who would talk of Coral Sea and Savo Island with the familiarity that comes from having watched the world through gaping metal holes, amid the screams of agony and courage. He had battled for his appointment to the Naval Academy in 1934, spending a year at sea as an enlisted man to convince his congressman of his sincerity. He had battled for his commission in 1938, overcoming poor grades and failing eyesight. He had cut his navy teeth on war, then suffered through the infighting that always comes with peace, fighting his way up through a morass of sycophantic desk officers to flag rank. During his two years as Superintendent of the Naval Academy he had battled in the same old way to preserve the institution as a seedbed for combat leaders, in the face of higher pressures to provide the operating fleet with a much-needed fill of technocrats.

The fleet was not simply changing, it was bifurcating. Vietnam called for combat leaders, people like Donald Kraft. But the nuclear navy needed brains. And the Academy was being pulled apart by the Department of Defense and Congress; they wanted both. In all, the nukes were winning, and Donald Kraft, together with his breed of fierce, unrelenting warriors, was being consigned to a role that resembled being a manacled cheerleader for the old, wise ways. He would not last another year as Superintendent. He would be replaced by a nuclear submariner, a disciple of Hyman Rickover.

Lenahan felt a rush creep around the edges of his pride as Kraft entered the room. Kraft was like a last, faint hope, a whiff of vindication. Lenahan joined the other officers and wives as they gathered in a half-circle around the admiral, who had finished greeting them in a reception line. Admiral Kraft placed his arm around his own wife's shoulder.

"Miriam and I would like to welcome you to our home. I hope to talk with each of you personally this afternoon. I'd like to emphasize to you again how important you are to the success of the mission here at the Academy. The academic section can teach our midshipmen how to be engineers, but only you can teach them what it means to be an officer in the naval service." The Admiral grinned warmly, an impish gleam in his weathered face. "So don't screw it up."

A titter went through the gathered men and women. Lenahan elbowed Wentzel, the fighter pilot who also had a company under Pratt. "When we went through this place it was filled with people like him. What happened to them all?"

Wentzel shrugged, his small face watching the admiral with admiration. "They're all mowing lawns down on their retirement homes in Florida."

"Well, next year I guess Kraft will be down there with them."

"Lucky him. And we'll be here with Rickover's little brother and Mad Pratt." Wentzel was flying the jet again, Lenahan could see it in his small eyes and empty stare. "Don't take it serious, Ted. It all counts on twenty."

"You've got a way out. I can see it in your goddamned eyes."

Kraft sought them out as he wound his way through the crowd. He grabbed Lenahan's arm and shook his hand warmly, even remembering his first name. "Ted, I know how you must feel being back here with your marines doing so much fighting this week. You have to take my word that this is just as important, at least for now."

Lenahan was drawn to the aging admiral. He felt a bond that transcended years and even services, a commonality that descended like blood. "Sometimes I wonder, Admiral. Sometimes I wonder why I'm back here at all."

"*You are the Academy.*" The admiral turned to Wentzel. "And you, too. How is it going, Joe?"

"Just fine, sir." Wentzel had just hooked into the cable again, and was back aboard the carrier after another searing mission. "But I think the good Captain here needs to drink a beer and get his mind off of ... things."

"Listen." Admiral Kraft peered at them from behind thick glasses, reminding Lenahan of a concerned father. "We're under a lot of heat, but we're not going to let them take this place away from us." He smiled at both of them, one hand on each of their shoulders. "If the man needs some liberty, get him the hell away from people like me and go buy him a beer. Go on! This reception will survive without you two. Get the hell out of here."

# Chapter Five: 1630

Speed bags rattled, heavy bags thumped again and again, crisp nasal snorts emanated each time a fighter threw a punch, even at the air. And down the length of the boxing area, as other fighters practiced footwork against canvas fighting shields, squash and handball courts popped and smacked with competition.

Ooomph. Fogarty danced around the heavy bag, jabbing, crossing, uppercutting, making the bag jump with every sharp combination. His sweatsuit was soaked as he emptied his energy and frustration into the bag. His mind coasted, though. The big bag was his mental resting place, his purest respite.

*Sports will be your mistress for the next four years.* A solemn, wiry lieutenant had told them that his second day at the Academy and Fogarty had never forgotten it. The lieutenant had been correct. He'd been a grad. He'd known all the emotions, all the ways of dealing with denial.

Every midshipman mandatorily carried a sport during all three seasons of academic year. Fogarty's sport, indeed his passion, was boxing. He had made love to a punching bag since 1964; not exclusively, but more regularly than to any other creature or object. He had spent uncountable hours dancing around the bag, perfecting his moves, throwing his greatest exertions at it, losing gallons of sweat to it. The bag helped Fogarty work out his most unsolvable frustrations, taking on the faces of his enemies and tormentors, allowing him to pound on them, have his revenge, exhaust his anger before it made trouble for him back in Bancroft Hall. It made him strong, gave him dignity. Fogarty loved his punching bag.

And this was his last day with it, the final full workout before the Brigade Boxing finals, which would be Fogarty's last fight as a midshipman. He beat on the bag with sweet melodic fury, like some madman's chorus of good-bye.

*That goddamned coward Dean. I'll bet he didn't even give blood.*

Fogarty had, hardly an hour before. The nurse in the Library-Assembly area had then told him he was excused from his commitments for the rest of the day, that he should drink tea with lots of sugar in it and eat sweets, to rejuvenate the pint of blood he had pumped into a plastic bag, his little gift to those who had so recently bled in battle.

But that was a bunch of bullshit. Fogarty had gone straight to MacDonough Hall and dressed for boxing practice, running four miles to warm up, doing thirty minutes of hard calisthenics, and then beginning the workout itself, round after round of shadow boxing and bag work and light ring work.

A man who loses a pint of blood in combat can't ask for the rest of the day off.

The bell rang and Fogarty left the heavy bag, walking across the large, high-ceilinged workout room toward one wall filled with high mirrors, where several men had been shadow boxing. He danced playfully in front of one of the boxers, a small Oriental man who immediately threw a dozen quick mock punches back at him, then he called abrasively at several others. MacDonough Hall was Fogarty's other home, the boxing team his closest group of friends outside of his company classmates. The Brigade Boxers were known for their camaraderie, and were famous for turning out combat leaders. The small boxing team, which produced only fourteen finalists every year, had already lost several members dead in Vietnam out of the classes of 1966 and 1967, and several others seriously wounded.

Fogarty chided the Oriental man. "Yahh, Mick the Prick. You better save those moves for Saturday night, Trajardo."

"You son of a bitch, I told you never to call me that." Mick Yamato was pure Hawaiian all-American, a mix of Polynesian and Filipino and Japanese. He jealously protected the identity of his middle name, Trajardo, and it was the easiest way for Fogarty to get under his skin.

"Hit him hard, Bill. Cut him bad so I won't have to do it Saturday." A lanky, baby-faced blond with a large eagle tattooed on one shoulder walked to them, his hands wrapped and gloved, sweat soaking into his sweatpants and sleeveless shirt. Little Stevie Wonder, child of the Washington, D.C. streets, looked white and talked black. He would face Yamato in the 127-pound finals. He was a year behind Fogarty and Yamato, and would follow them into the Marine Corps. Stevie and Yamato squared off, the closest of friends, faking moves at each other.

Fogarty watched them clown, laughing at their antics. He loved boxing. It was real. It was guts and pain, love and loss, all wrapped up inside a fat leather glove.

Fogarty had grown up fighting. He was from a family of fighters. One uncle had been a "packinghouse pro," a dedicated club fighter who had won some notoriety in the stockyards and packinghouses of Omaha. From the time Fogarty had turned fourteen he had lived down in the dank basements and small dark gyms of Omaha boxing clubs, fighting in smoke-filled, dusky air before hundreds of ravenous demanding buffs who reserved their cheers for only the most vicious displays of brawling. Boxing in Omaha had been like belonging to a cult.

It was also wildly individualistic, and a hell of a lot of fun. Fighters took on their own followings, and assigned themselves nicknames. Fogarty had become "Wild Bill" when he was fifteen. He had once fought "the Duke of Earl," a fiery-eyed mulatto who wore a blue beret into the ring and hung it on the ringpost, and whose friends would play the popular song "Duke of Earl" before each fight as he strode majestically down the packed, dingy aisles toward the ring. Fogarty's own coach, Whitey, had been the All-Navy champion a decade earlier, and had served in Alaska after that. Whitey would work Fogarty's corner wearing the traditional Eskimo shoes, mukluks, and would minister Fogarty's water between rounds out of a plastic ketchup squeezer, as if Fogarty weren't really bleeding at all, folks, but was merely being doused by Whitey in the corner.

And it had been like barrooms. Whitey taught him how to box, then spent hours teaching him how to do the other things. He learned how to lean on a fighter, how to hit on the break if he had to, how to throw an elbow, how to use the ropes to put more power in his punches. He couldn't use the other things at Navy.

Not that Navy boxing wasn't tough. It simply ceased to be some passionate display of the dark parts of a man's insides, and became a college sport, taking on overtones that were at first foreign to Fogarty, and confusing. He could not get used to ringside seats filled with officers and their wives peering with scrutinous faces, judging him not only as a fighter but as part of their military machine. His heart remained in musty gyms, hoping he'd find the chance to put an elbow into the Duke of Earl's face after having his eye butted closed in the first round.

Nor did he like fighting his friends. Intercollegiate boxing had been outlawed after several deaths, so Academy fighters had to fight each other. Working out with a man for six months deadened any desire to hurt him. The emotions of friendship became confused under the sun-hot ring lights.

"Hey, Jolly Chollie!" Fogarty called to a thickly-muscled black man who was jumping rope. Charlie Adair was a classmate, another future Marine. He would fight in the 135-pound finals on Saturday. "How's your weight, boy?"

"You see a boy, you knock him down." They laughed comfortably to each other. Adair skipped rope effortlessly, crossing it in front of him and doing a complex dance without losing the rope. "One-thirty-nine, on the dime."

"Go a couple rounds with me, then." Fogarty walked to the far side of the heavy bags and put on his headgear, then a pair of heavy sparring gloves. He climbed into one of the two full-sized canvas rings and Adair soon joined him. For several rounds they corner-boxed, close up at three-quarter speed, working on infighting.

And then it was over. The last bell rang, the boxers did their neck exercises and wind sprints, and headed for the showers. Fogarty felt a rush of melancholy as he unwrapped his hands and stripped off his sweatsuit. His last boxing practice was the first of many lasts as he left his youth behind.

"Hey, Fogarty." Yamato soaped himself under one shower head. "Did you hear Ron Loudenslager got killed?"

"Yeah." Fogarty stood motionless underneath a jet of hot water, letting it massage his neck.

"Casselli's in Bethesda." Little Stevie Wonder called from another shower. "He got shot in the spine. They say he can't hardly move a finger. What a bust, man. Hey, Fogarty, you fought him last year, didn't you?"

"Yeah." Fogarty still stood motionless, as if asleep on his feet. "I kicked his ass."

"Loudenslager was already hit, though, wasn't he?" Yamato stepped out of the shower and began drying himself. "Didn't you get a letter from him in the hospital, Bill? I thought he was in Yokosuka."

"Guam." Fogarty slowly rubbed his chest and stomach with a bar of soap. "You know who he saw in the hospital?" Fogarty warmed a bit, as if the letter were somehow proof that Loudenslager still lived. "Kentucky Cool, the Fighting Fool. He'd been torn up pretty bad by a booby trap."

"That's some ba-a-a-ad shit, man." Adair was sitting on bench, contemplating Fogarty, a towel draped over his middle. "You ever think about not going Corps, Bill?"

"No."

Dean was waiting outside his room, standing at a stiff parade rest, his chin pushed into his soft face and neck, making him appear even more cherubic, like some sort of Gerber Baby Food commercial.

"Did you give blood?"

Dean came to attention. "Sir, no sir."

"You dildo. You goddamn gutless wonder." Fogarty threw his parka at Dean. It fell from the plebe's face onto the floor. "Why the hell not?"

Dean's face moved around as he searched for his answer, as if his ruminating mind would churn his mouth. "Sir, the regulations don't extend far enough to make that a legal order, sir. And needles really nauseate me."

"The regulations, Dean? What do the regulations say about helping dying men?" Fogarty casually reached below Dean's throat and grabbed his tie at the knot, lifting him up onto his tiptoes. His voice was modulated, filled with a flat, unemotional threat. "What did I tell you about giving blood? What did I say would happen if you didn't?"

Dean's eyes stood out like large marbles. "You said you'd kill me, sir."

"Are you more afraid of a needle than you are of me, Dean?"

Dean contemplated it, his face so close that Fogarty could raise his mouth at any moment and bite off his nose. "I ... I really didn't think you were serious, sir. I just ... "

"Did it sound like I was telling you a goddamn joke?"

"Sir, no sir."

"Dean"—Fogarty bounced the fist that held Dean's tie off of the plebe's throat—"I'm serious. Got it?"

Dean spoke quickly, swallowing hard. "Sir, yes sir."

"And I don't want to hear another bullshit answer about the regulations. From now on, *I* am the regulations, Dean. Do you understand me?"

"Sir, yes sir."

"Good." Fogarty bounced Dean off of the wall, letting go of the tie. "Go get your sweatgear on and report to Mister Swenson's room. Two minutes."

"Midshipman Dean, fourth class, sir." He fit his back tightly against one of Swenson's walls, dressed in a sweatsuit, his unathletic frame appearing woefully out of place in such belongings.

"All right, Dean. Let's start with forty pushups."

He thought for a moment about mentioning the regulations, their limitation on pushups, then felt the heavy weight of Fogarty's words, like bludgeons. The regulations had definitely changed. Dean hit the deck and began doing pushups, counting them aloud. When he reached thirty he began to slow down, his stomach shuddering. At thirty-five, he stuck his ass up into the air, resting his chest muscles.

Fogarty stood over him, shaking his head with disgust. "I don't believe it. I goddamn don't believe it. Dean, did you know that the weakest member of my class could do sixty-eight pushups, any time day or night, by this time plebe year? You are an absolute abortion, Dean. Total scum." Fogarty nudged him with a foot. "Are you tired, Dean?"

"Yes, sir."

"Poor Dean. Would you like to take a rest, and think about it?"

"Yes, sir."

"All right, Negat. Think about it. Thinking position."

"Sir?" Dean undulated on the floor, trying to hold his pushup stance.

Fogarty looked at Swenson, who was studying, mindless to them both. "You mean he doesn't know what the thinking position is, Swede? What the hell have you been doing with this nord?"

Swenson shrugged, deep into a text on abstract mathematics. "That's the old stuff, Bill, you know that."

"So will Dean, in about a minute. Hey, Dean, didn't you say you came here for the education?"

Dean's whole body was shuddering. "Yes, sir."

"Well, what's an education if a man hasn't learned to think? Not much, eh?"

"No, sir."

"So, *think*. Stretch out flat, Dean, and only let your toes and elbows touch the deck. Put your hands underneath your chin. There, Dean." Fogarty smiled, pleased. "Now, think about things for a while."

Dean's body immediately began to tremble. Fogarty nudged him in the chest with a foot. "Get your knees off the deck, you pussy. Jesus, are you a disgrace. What's the menu for evening meal, Dean?"

Dean was grimacing uncontrollably. "Sir, the menu for evening meal is, ah—"

"Quit groaning, dummy. Your mommy isn't anywhere where she can hear you, and nobody else cares."

"Aye, aye, sir." Dean undulated in his pain.

"Evening meal."

"Aye, aye, sir. Sir, the menu for evening meal is, ah, Penthouse grilled steaks, mushroom gravy, ah, whipped, ah, potatoes, ah—"

"Oh, shut up. Come aboard, you drippy piece of mung. You make me want to throw up."

"Aye, aye, sir." Dean struggled up to attention again. "Beat Army, sir."

"Maybe we're taking the wrong approach." Fogarty paced in front of Dean, rubbing his chin in mock seriousness. "A friend of mine used to say, Dean, that leadership, in order to be effective, must be creative. Would you agree with that?"

"Yes, sir." Anything, thought Dean. I'll agree with anything.

"I thought you would. So, anyway, Dean, why don't I put some of Mister Swenson's records on and you can hang around and listen to some music and we'll talk about it. Would you like that?"

It seemed too easy, too out of character. But, then... "Yes, sir."

"I thought you would." Fogarty gave a small smile, his blue eyes mocking Dean. "All right, dufus. Up on the door. Come on. Up up up."

"Sir?" It made no sense. "On the door" was about as logical as "on the ceiling."

"On...the...door." Fogarty grabbed Dean by his shoulders and pushed him toward the doorway. "Up, Dean. How can you hang around unless you get up on the goddamn door?"

Reality flushed him like nausea itself. "Aye, aye, sir." Dean hesitantly grasped the sharp edges on top of the door, and lifted his feet off of the ground. He immediately grimaced, and let go of the door. "It cuts into my hands, sir."

"Well, that's the whole idea, dummy." Fogarty shook his head as if Dean were a hopeless idiot. "Get back up there, greasy. Hurry up."

Within two minutes Dean was sobbing, losing his grasp and then regaining it, the rough edges of the doorway causing his palms to bleed. Fogarty sat in a chair, calmly observing him. Finally he began to talk, in slow, measured tones. "What does it mean to hurt, huh, Dean? How much does that hurt? As much as a needle? Really, Dean, what is pain anyway? Just think. If you'd faced pain a couple hours ago and given blood to help somebody who just bled for you, you wouldn't be up there on the door. Does that make sense, Dean? Are you bigger than yourself? Oh, for Christ's sake. Quit crying. Come aboard, you goddamn girl."

"Aye, aye, sir." Dean dropped from the door, still sobbing.

"Quit crying, clown. You're not on the door anymore. What the hell are you crying about? Did I hurt your goddamned feelings? *Stop it.*"

"Aye, aye, sir." Dean still sniffled, humiliated. "Beat Army, sir."

"You're a real mess, Dean. It embarrasses me that you're wearing the same uniform I do. I don't want people to know we go to the same Academy. Now, you make up your mind about something right now, Dean. *Right now.*" Fogarty walked up to Dean and surveyed him with seriousness. "Either go home or square away. You can't have it both ways, Dean, because I won't let you. Now, what'll it be?"

*I want to leave. I want to go home and be a human and take out girls and drink beer and ride in a car and go to the movies and watch TV and go riding with my friends...* "I'll square away, sir."

"You're sure?"

*...take long walks in the afternoon and go to the beach on the weekend and have whole summers off to date and travel...* "Yes, sir."

"All right, Dean. Then we have to make you fit to wear that uniform. You are a disgrace, Dean. A mess. And that reminds me. Have you repaired your shoes?"

"Yes, sir."

"Go get them."

"Aye, aye, sir." Dean bolted out the door.

Swenson looked up from his book again. "Do you really think he means it, Bill?"

"I guess we'll find out."

Dean reappeared, carrying his shoes in one hand as he took three large steps into Swenson's room and went flat against the wall. "Midshipman Dean, fourth class, sir."

"Let me see them." Fogarty examined the shoes under the fluorescent lights. "Really shitty, Dean. Really shitty."

"Sir, I worked on them all afternoon."

"Did I ask you that?" Fogarty bristled. "Huh?"

"No, sir. I just thought—"

"Shut up."

Swenson shook his head, smiling hopelessly at the plebe. "Goddamn, Dean."

"You've got too many scrapes along the toes, Dean. You need to bring the wax all the way down." Fogarty walked over to the sink and ran the water until it was scalding hot. He stuck both shoes underneath the faucet, stripping all the polish, hours of work, off of each toe. The shoes went underneath the faucet like black mirrors, and came out like dull wool. "Like this."

He handed the shoes back to Dean. "Tomorrow morning, they'd better be perfect, or we'll start all over again. Do you understand?"

*... and play table tennis at the Student Union and join a fraternity and have long talks through calm evenings about nothing...* "Yes, sir."

"And I want you to start camping out."

"Sir?"

Fogarty looked over to Swenson again. "You mean you haven't let Dean camp out, Swede? What the hell's wrong with you? Tonight when you go to bed, Dean, strip your sheets off the rack."

"Aye, aye, sir."

"And your mattress."

"Aye, aye, sir."

"And sleep on the springs."

"Aye, aye, sir."

"In the nude."

Dean swallowed, blinking his eyes. "Aye, aye, sir."

"And tomorrow, Dean, you're going to start plebe year."

# Chapter Six: 1930

"We've got to get something to eat."

"I've got to get home, Lenahan. My bride's going to shoot me as it is."

"Well, hell. If she's going to shoot you, you may as well die on a full stomach. Come on, Wentzel. You got me drunk. You may as well break bread with me."

They sat at a table in the Officer's Club, four empty pitchers of beer between them. Lenahan leaned back in his chair, half lying down, his hands folded over his stomach. He belched loudly, then rolled to one side and farted. He felt a need to offend the other officers and wives in the room, to rub their faces in reality.

"No, really, Ted. I've got to get out of here. The wife is pretty jealous about my time since I got back from WesPac. I can't blame her. Hell, I've been out of the Academy for six years, and I've either been in training or at sea for four." Wentzel smiled mischievously. "I need to go take care of my obligations, if you know what I mean."

"Yeah, I know what you mean, Joe. If you don't take care of your obligations, somebody else sure as hell will. Sometimes even when you do take care of your obligations somebody finds a way to, uh—" he was thinking about too many things "—screw things up, shall we say?" Lenahan took a cigarette from the table and lit it. "See you tomorrow, turkey."

"Are you all right?" Wentzel peered steadily at Lenahan, veiling his concern with a smile.

"Well, my wife is living with another man, my son is in Oceanside, California, while I'm here on the other side of the goddamn country, I'm horny as hell, I'm drunk, my feet hurt, I've got gas on my stomach, I have to hold reveille on my company tomorrow morning, I'm so hungry I could eat the rag end off a skunk, and I'm thinking about volunteering to go back off to Vietnam." Lenahan dragged perfunctorily on his cigarette, grinning ironically. "Other than that, I'm fine."

"Sorry I asked." Wentzel rose, a bit unsteady, and waved. "Take care."

"Get the fuck out of here, you pussy-whipped squid."

He hated eating alone, especially in restaurants. Nothing accentuated his loneliness, his almost despairing sense of isolation, than sitting in a public dining place by himself, surrounded by people in their twos and fours. He always felt that they were secretly staring at him, commenting on his solitude. And he hated going home to the haunting empty cavern of his apartment, hearing only the echoes of his own self as he shuffled around from one room to another.

But being stationed at the Academy made it inevitable. Lenahan felt like an interloper. He couldn't socialize with the midshipmen; they were his military responsibility, his charges, and he was their example. And they were too young, anyway. Nor could he become comfortable with his officer peers. By the time an officer was assigned to the Academy, he had at least five years' commissioned experience, and they almost all were married, with families. Lenahan became the odd man out at most social gatherings.

The town of Annapolis wasn't much better. It had a small-town atmosphere that revolved around sailing and state government. The townspeople did precious little social mixing with the military. Once he left his company office or the Officers' Club bar, Lenahan was usually alone.

He buttoned up his long green Marine Corps overcoat and put on his garrison cap and began walking back toward the Sixth Wing parking lot, where he had left his car. Strolling the sidewalks and peering into black memories, Lenahan felt his chest go tight, his throat aching with an emotion that made him wish he were still young enough to cry.

He often had a vision, a fantasy, as he walked along the sidewalks of the Yard, staring at landmarks that had become a constant in his life. The sidewalk would narrow until only one person could pass. Another man, a well-built midshipman exactly his height and approximately his build, would walk toward him, stepping brisk and determined, filled with certainty. They would walk directly at each other, neither of them yielding the narrow walkway to the other. He would begin to stare at the midshipman's craggy face. Then he would realize he was walking into himself, seven years removed.

What I would give, he told himself again, passing the Chapel where he had married his wife, served as an usher in Angie and Steve's wedding, gone to mass each Sunday for four years, what I would give to be able to have a long conversation with what I used to be. I was stronger then, but I am fiercer now. I was so certain of life then, and of my place in it. I was so sure of my love, and of my future. I now have none of these certainties, but at least I can comprehend pain. I was so ready, so eager to fight and now I pay, I richly pay, for having fought.

I was so quick to judge, and now I judge myself.

He reached a terrace just outside Bancroft Hall. Every few feet inside the Hall he saw glimpses of activity, midshipmen undergoing their penitentiary-style study hour with a frolicsome elan, having created their own unique little worlds in each company area as they were locked away.

Seven years, mused Lenahan, peering through the windows he passed as if he were looking through a time machine, a constant conduit, at himself. And what has it given me? He tried to concentrate on that thought in his mildly drunken state, the cold air numbing his earlobes. Well, let's see. Hemorrhoids.

No, that's not fair. He stopped under the light that emanated from one room and took off his Academy ring and held it up in front of him. The oversize, ornate symbol of the Trade School glimmered before his eyes. He thought of the night he had finally earned the right to wear it, June Week of his third year, standing inside a huge replica of the ring as Mary, his future wife, took it from around her neck and dipped it into a cask filled with water from each of the seven seas and then pushed it along the third finger of his left hand. The whole world, life itself, had opened up to him at that moment, even if parts of it had slowly closed over the years that followed.

A ring. Lenahan put it back on his finger and inspected himself in the dim light, trying to place his memory back inside the Hall, looking out. What did I yearn for? This uniform, these precious silver bars. Command. Silliness, to a doctor or a lawyer or a banker. But a creed worth dying for, to me.

He reached his battered Volkswagen and then drove slowly through the Academy grounds toward the gate. The Yard became a ghost town after dark, almost completely shutting down following evening meal, except for Bancroft Hall itself. Lenahan drove through Gate One, waving to the elderly Jimmylegs policeman at the gate, then followed cobbled roads through Old Town Annapolis itself. It was indeed like riding on a memory, every day. Old Town was unchanged since long before Lenahan had journeyed from South Boston to become a mid.

How many pairs of shoes I have worn down on those sidewalks, he mused, side by side with she who now no longer loves me, in front of or behind Steve and Angie. So what is love, and what are memories? That's what she asked me when she met me in Hawaii for R and R, after I'd spent four months sleeping with the rain in my face and squatting in the weeds to shit. Four months, long enough to go through a hundred casualties in a company that fielded a hundred people, but hardly long enough to create a deep memory of love with someone else, much less destroy that memory in me.

He turned into his apartment building's driveway, parked, and entered his small dark home. Inside, he stood next to the light switch, not wanting to turn it on and face the stark emptiness. "Alone, alone, all, all, alone. Alone on a wide, wide sea. Samuel Taylor Coleridge, 'The Rime of the Ancient Mariner.'" He flipped on the light switch. An army of roaches scattered for their favorite cracks along the kitchen wall. Lenahan threw his overcoat and cap and military blouse onto a kitchen chair, then grabbed a frying pan out of the sink and began scrubbing it. "Ah, welladay, what evil looks had I from old and young. Instead of the Cross, the Albatross, about my neck was hung. Samuel Taylor Coleridge, 'The Rime of the Ancient Mariner.' I already said that."

Scrambled eggs were easy. He mixed four in a bowl and dumped them into the skillet, adding a slice of presliced ham and another slice of presliced cheese, then dumped them onto a plate and stuck the frying pan back into the sink, its permanent resting place. He was stone-cold sober, and was not quite comfortable with that, so he reached into an almost empty refrigerator and brought out a beer and drank it with his dinner. It didn't do any good.

He needed to hear her voice, just to hear her say a few words. He didn't love her anymore. He could never love her after having seen a part of her that would live with him in such completeness and then abandon him so completely, all within the space of a hundred casualties or four months, depending on how one was measuring time. But you get used to some things, he mused, pulling out his cigarettes from their perch in his sock. It's hard to break old habits, at least until a new one takes its place.

He checked his watch. It would be five-thirty in California. He walked into his small bedroom and sat on an unmade bed whose blanket was a Marine Corps camouflage poncho liner, and picked up the phone, dialing the numbers without looking them up. The phone rang several times. He was so tense his eardrums hummed from the increased blood pressure.

"Hello?"

"Hello, Mary."

"Hello." All the inflection left her voice. It was flat and rejecting.

"How are things?" It was too vague. "How do you like real estate?"

"I like it. Are you drunk?"

"No. What do you think, I run around drunk twenty-four hours a day?"

"No, only when you call. You've got to stop bothering us, Ted."

"I didn't think I was. And I wanted to talk to Jack, too. So, you like real estate. That's good. You always needed a career. It's hard in the military, with all the moves. It's a good choice, Mary. You'll be rich." He laughed softly. "Maybe you can pay me alimony."

"I don't need to be insulted from three thousand miles away."

"Sorry. It's my nature, remember?" He finally lit the cigarette, sighing. "Is my little man around?" My little man, he thought, the words cutting his insides like a dull icepick, stirring his emotions around until he felt his guts had hemorrhaged. My little man is a stranger, a voice that grows new words each time it speaks to me.

"Hello, Dad."

"Hello, Son. How are you?"

"Fine." The voice paused as if seeking something to talk about. "We haven't planted the corn yet. But Ralph said he would help me. Maybe we can plant it next week. Then how long is it?"

The day before Lenahan left for Vietnam his son had powdered him with questions, lost in his four-year-old mind about how long thirteen months would be, the time it would take to see his father again. Lenahan had told him three hundred ninety-six days, but the boy hadn't understood. He had then shown the boy an envelope, and told him he would write him every day, and when the boy had three hundred ninety-six of them he would come walking through the doorway. But the boy had no comprehension.

Finally, Lenahan had taken him into the backyard, where Mary kept a small garden, and stood next to a row of corn. "In a month," Lenahan had told him, "you're going to help your mom pick the corn. Then you're going to eat it. Then it's going to be Christmas, and Santa Claus is going to come. Then the Easter Bunny's going to come. Then, after that, you're going to help your mom plant some more corn. Then it's going to grow, from those little green things like grass, like these used to be. Remember? And *then*, when that corn grows up and you help your mom pick it, I'll be home."

Only the next spring, after the Easter Bunny had come, Mary hadn't planted a garden, and Lenahan was already back from the war, lying in a hospital. And his boy knew more about some engineer named Ralph than he did about Ted Lenahan. But he still seemed to believe, with his child's logic, that once the corn was planted and grew and was picked, Lenahan would return.

"How long, Dad?"

Lenahan began to choke as he tried to form words to answer his son. "I don't know, Son."

"Are you all right where they shot you?" He sounded so grown, even at six, so filled with adult perceptions even if his logic was a child's.

"Yeah, I'm fine."

"Will you show me your scars again?"

"Sure."

"I told my teacher at school that my dad was shot three times and she said it wasn't nice to talk about war, that war was bad. Ralph didn't go to the war. Is that all right, Dad?"

"I don't know, Son. You'll have to ask Ralph."

"I did, and he said the war was bad and nobody should go. Is it all right that he said that? Are you mad?"

The combination of innocence and perceptiveness and confusion was overwhelming, like a microscope that peered into his pain. "No, Jackie, I'm not mad. Listen, little man, I have to go."

"When will I see you? Do we have to wait for corn?"

"This summer. I'll come out this summer and we'll go to Disneyland."

"Oh, goodie. I went with Mommy and Ralph. I like Goofy. Can we see Goofy?"

"Sure, Son. We'll see them all. Now you take care of your mommy, you hear?"

"OK. Daddy—"

"Yeah?"

"I love you."

"I love you too. 'Bye."

I wish I had died, sobbed Lenahan, wrapped in his camouflage poncho liner blanket, still dressed in his uniform, his Marine Corps cordovans making black lines on his sheets. I wish I had died I wish I had died I wish I had died.

# Chapter Seven: 2300

"Lights out, Peckarsky."

"Aye, aye, sir." Peckarsky rose from his desk and hit the overhead lights, then climbed into bed. Dean remained at his own desk, still furiously rubbing a rag over the toe of one shoe. Finally he slammed the shoe onto the desktop and bounced from his chair, pacing the room in the dark.

"The bastard! I've got a Chemistry test tomorrow and I haven't even been able to crack a book. And look at these shoes. For God's sake, he ruined the leather. He'll fry me tomorrow morning, I *know* he will." Dean stared at Peckarsky, who lay unresponding on his bed. "I'll bet you think it's pretty funny."

"Better you than me, but it's hardly funny. You don't hear me laughing, do you?"

"You'd like to."

"Ah, come on, John. What do you want me to do, shine your shoes for you? I didn't piss Fogarty off. Now, come on, will you? I need to get some sleep."

"I just don't know what to do!" Dean sat back down, staring at shadows that were his shoes. "I need to study. I need to shine my shoes. He's going to fry me, the bastard."

"I'll tell you what I'd do." Peckarsky was almost a big brother to Dean. He had a way of tolerating and guiding Dean at the same time most of their classmates shunned the cerebral plebe. "You're smart as a whip, John. You can always catch up on academics. If you don't get Fogarty off your ass, he'll run you right out of here."

"He can't do that."

"You don't think so?" Peckarsky's soft laugh floated across the dark room. "He gave you a hell of a hint at evening meal come-around. If Fogarty told me to sleep standing on my head in the shower, with the water running, I'd have the water on before he finished giving the order. Shine your shoes, John. To hell with Chem."

"God *damn*, that reminds me." Dean was literally verging on tears. "He told me to camp out."

"What's that?" Peckarsky came up on an elbow, staring at Dean's silhouette.

The overhead lights went suddenly on and Fogarty strode into the room, his piercing eyes cold and in control, his West Point bathrobe flowing open at the front, revealing muscular legs that rippled in their sinews as he walked. Dean came to an immediate brace and Peckarsky jumped out of his bed.

"Attention on deck Midshipman Dean, fourth class, sir!"

Fogarty's presence was overwhelming, like a gun pointed straight at Dean's heart. Dean had become terrified of Fogarty, cold-shivering frightened of him in the space of one day.

Fogarty stood a foot away, looking at Dean with a mix of anger and disgust. "You're up after lights out. You're on report."

"Aye, aye, sir."

"Didn't I fry you at evening meal for your shoes?"

"Yes, sir."

"Why didn't you bring around a Form Two?"

"I forgot, sir."

"You're on report for forgetting."

"Aye, aye, sir."

"That's three Form Twos you owe me, Dean. Have them all filled out and ready for me at morning come-around."

"Aye, aye, sir."

Fogarty examined Dean's bed. "Forget something?"

Dean stood for a long moment, on the verge of shivering with unease. Finally he reached over and pulled his mattress off the bed, dumping it on end next to the bed.

"You can have the pillow. And a blanket."

"Thank you, sir."

"But take your clothes off."

… *and sleep in my own bed as the rain pelts windows outside, just roll over and hit the alarm clock…* "Aye, aye, sir."

Fogarty sauntered out of the room, hitting the lights as he closed the door. "Sweet dreams, turkeys."

Peckarsky jumped into bed, his eyes hollow with fear and amazement. "Good night, sir."

The door bounced as it fully closed. Peckarsky breathed slowly out, a sigh of relief. "Jesus, is he scary. I get the feeling he could kill you and laugh about it, John. You must have really pissed him off."

"The world pisses him off."

"Don't kid yourself. You *especially* piss him off." Peckarsky came up on an elbow again, and stared at Dean across the darkened room. "So that's camping out."

Dean attempted to become comfortable as he lay on the cold springs, shivering into his blanket. He rolled and metal scratched his legs and buttocks. "*Damn* it!" He usually slept on his stomach but he feared he might castrate himself on the springs if he even tried. "He doesn't rate doing this to me. They don't even let wardens do this to convicts in jail. I don't care what they did to him and his classmates plebe year. That's why the regulations changed."

"John," Peckarsky sounded weary. "You hate this place. You've done nothing but bitch about how bad it sucks since plebe summer. You hate the upperclass and you hate the military and sometimes I think you even hate me."

Dean sounded wounded. "No, I don't hate you. But I guess you're right about the rest of it." A spring scratched the middle of his back. "God *damn* Fogarty!"

"So why don't you quit?"

Dean pondered it, shivering on the springs. "I don't know."

# PART TWO:

---

# FRIDAY,
# FEBRUARY 9,
# 1968

# Chapter One: 0615

"Hear the loud alarum bells—brazen bells! What a tale of terror, now, their turbulency tells." Lenahan smiled softly, muttering to himself as the reveille bells shrieked, jangling even the dullest dreams. "Poe, you West Point asshole, come on back and finish your poem."

The Mate of the Deck clicked on the fluorescent overhead hallway lights one by one from the switchbox and in seconds night was day, slumber was motion, the empty passageway was filled with midshipmen. Lenahan strode the center of the hall with slow, measured steps, dressed in his greens, cap and all, carrying his gloves rolled in his left hand. He dug his heels in, their loud clicks a reminder to the midshipmen of his presence and authority.

The Mate saw Lenahan and sprinted to meet him, saluting as he ran. "Good morning, sir, Midshipman Hughes, fourth class, reports—"

Lenahan returned the salute, then waved the Mate away. "Carry on, Mate."

"Aye, aye, sir." The Mate sprinted away, back in the direction he had come from.

The word was out, it was obvious. The company area was a humdrum of forced activity. Arnie Lesse, the reveille inspector, moved from room to room with a briskness that he did not usually possess even on the athletic field, where he was a moderately enthusiastic, though somewhat lethargic, center on the company football team. Midshipmen coming out of the side passageways automatically looked for him as they turned the corner into the main hallway.

Ain't this a bitch, mused Lenahan. Mad Pratt gives Captain Theodore Lenahan an hour of Extra Duty.

"GOOD MORNING, YOU LAZY SONS OF BITCHES! A HUNDRED SEVENTEEN DAYS AND YOU CAN KISS MY ASS GOOD-BYE."

"Go away, Fogarty, for Christ's sake."

It came from the other end of the hallway, by the stairs, a taunt and a chorus of retorts. Lenahan continued his march and Fogarty looked up from thirty feet away, slightly startled, then grinned sheepishly, coming to attention.

"Ah, good morning, sir."

"Good morning, Mister Fogarty." Lenahan shook his head whimsically, inspecting Fogarty's soaked sweatclothes, the bottoms drenched and muddy from slush, his parka and the sweatshirt underneath it steaming with his sweat. Fogarty's face was blush-red from the cold, his gray scarf frosted from his own breath. "A little cold out there, isn't it?"

"Not bad, sir. Not bad. I'd say just below freezing."

"You did the seawall, I assume?"

"Absolutely, sir." Fogarty still grinned, somewhat docile in front of this demigod who had done all the things he wished to do: led men in combat and sacrificed and suffered. "It wakes you right up, sir."

"I'll bet it does." Lenahan remembered and walked closer to Fogarty, speaking softly. "Mister Swenson told me yesterday that one of your close friends was killed recently. I'm really sorry to hear it. I know what it feels like."

"We just have to learn to deal with those things, don't we, sir?" Lenahan might have simply mentioned that Fogarty had to go on watch, or shine his shoes again. "I couldn't believe it when I saw the telegram. He'd been in the hospital. I got a letter from him, maybe ten days ago. He was shot in the chest last fall. It was a funny letter." Fogarty smiled slightly, remembering. "He was really a funny guy." Fogarty shrugged, looking back to Lenahan. "I don't even remember what it was in the letter that was funny. It was funny, though."

"Where is his funeral going to be, have you heard?"

"No, sir. I imagine it will be Arlington, though. He used to joke about it. He used to say that if he ever bought the farm he wanted to be buried on a hillside at Arlington, so the gutless wonders in Washington will have to look at his grave every day when they drive to work. And that he wanted Johnny Cash to come and sing 'The Green, Green Grass of Home' when they planted him. The dumb ass. He was from Chicago. What did he ever know about the green, green grass of home? He liked Johnny Cash." Fogarty shook his head. "Jesus, he was funny."

"If you want to go to the funeral, let me know. I'll make sure you get a chit."

"Aye, aye, sir. Thank you, sir." Fogarty still stood at attention, now in the middle of a puddle of water his boots and clothes had created. He raised his eyebrows, smiling again. "You're at work a little early this morning, Captain."

"Yeah. Well, it seems like the troops need help hearing reveille. Although you seem to be contributing to that."

Fogarty grinned sheepishly again. "Well, yes, sir. It's a little game I've been playing for a while. It turns a few people off, but it's kind of fun. They like to tell me to kiss off, and they don't get much of a chance since I live out-of-company this year."

"Wonderful. How's your weight?"

"Right at one-fifty-nine, sir. No sweat. I weigh in this afternoon."

"Are you going to win?"

Loudenslager had asked him that, oh so long ago, plebe summer as he braced in a chair right next to his hulking squad leader, having eaten a pat of butter and washed it down with Worcestershire sauce for spilling Loudenslager's milk as he poured it. *If you don't win I'll kill you.* And he had said it with such a ferocity that Fogarty had almost believed him. *You don't build leaders by building losers.*

"I'll die trying, sir. You can count on that."

"Well, good luck. I'll be there."

"Thank you, sir. You won't be disappointed, sir."

"Carry on, Mister Fogarty. You've made a lake in my passageway."

Fogarty looked down and laughed. "Aye, aye, sir. Good morning, sir."

Lenahan walked away, his heels clicking like a metronome. Fogarty walked briskly to Swenson's room, where Dean awaited him, standing in a rigid parade rest outside the door.

"Dean, you maggot! How'd you sleep last night?"

Dean's eyes were dark with fatigue. He came to attention, dull and churlish in his response. "Not well at all, sir. I've got a lot of small cuts on my back and legs from the springs."

"Ah, well, Dean, after you've camped out for a while, you'll develop calluses. Besides, just think how lucky you are. A hell of a lot of men didn't sleep at all last night. They were in Vietnam, getting shot at. And a hell of a lot of others won't ever be waking up again. They got killed."

It came out, just came out, he didn't mean to say it. "Nobody in Vietnam has a chemistry exam this morning, sir."

Fogarty's face exploded in anger. His eyes flashed and his lips went tight, the blood drained from them, and his color went to a bright red. He checked down the hallway for Lenahan, and not seeing him, grabbed Dean by the throat and slammed him up against the wall, holding him flush against it. Dean's throat wheezed as he sought to breathe through a mashed windpipe.

"Don't you ever say anything like that again. *Ever.* You little pissant crybaby, I could kill you, did you know that? I could goddamn *kill* you. When are you going to start realizing that you aren't the center of the universe? There's a hell of a lot in this world that's more important than your silly little chemistry test, tool." He let Dean go. The plebe's soft neck was banded with finger marks. "The Princess and the Pea. Did those bad springs cut your little body, Dean? Tisk, tisk. Sweatgear, asshole. One minute."

"Aye, aye, sir." Dean bolted toward his room.

"Did you hear that?" Fogarty walked into Swenson and McClinton's room. "Did you hear what that idiot just said to me?"

Swenson sat naked at his desk, reading the paper, his aberrant morning ritual. McClinton sang in the shower, his own morning routine. They were like old men, fixed in their ways at twenty-two by bells that blocked out repetitive segments of time, identical through each day.

Swenson did not even look up from his paper. "Yeah. What a squirrel."

Dean burst through the door, dressed in his sweatgear. "Midshipman Dean, fourth class, sir."

"Give me forty, Dean." Dean immediately hit the floor and began pumping out pushups. He slowed at thirty-five, but strained until he completed forty, plus one to beat Army. Fogarty stood over him, arms folded. "On your back. Leg lifts, six inches off the deck. Up. Spread 'em. Together. Down. Up. Get them up, smack. Hold them right there. That's it, Dean. Let's see you grow some balls."

Dean's stomach shuddered. His face was beet red. He gasped and groaned. Fogarty leaned over and spoke very softly, just next to Dean's ear. "You'd better not let your feet touch the deck, pussy." Down they went, though, slowly, despite Dean's efforts. "Get them *up* Dean, I'm not kidding. Up up up." Slowly they rose. Slowly they sank again. Fogarty kicked Dean's legs. Quickly they rose. "Come aboard."

"Aye, aye, sir. Beat Army, sir."

Fogarty held out both Swenson's and McClinton's M-1 rifles, twenty pounds of irregular weight. "Rig these, Dean. And you'd better hold them straight."

Dean held them at arm's length, straight out in front of him. Soon the weapons began to fall, his shoulder muscles constricting, cutting off the flow of blood, temporarily killing the muscles.

"You goddamn girl, get them back up in front of you." Fogarty terrified Dean. Up the weapons went.

But not for long. Down they fell again, despite Dean's greatest efforts to keep them in front of him. They hit his knees. He grimaced in his pain and frustration, trying to raise them back up, to pre-empt the fountain of abuse he knew would soon erupt from Fogarty.

"Poor little Dean." Swenson looked up from the newspaper. "I think his arms hurt, Wild Bill. You should be ashamed of yourself."

"All right, Dean. You're not man enough to rig two. Give me one of them." Fogarty snatched one of the rifles from Dean's grasp. "Now, get the other one back up there."

For teh seconds it was easy. His arms almost went back up of their own accord. Then the single rifle began to fall. Down it went, and there was nothing he could do to stop it. He grunted and whimpered, swore under his breath at the falling weapon, ending up making a sound like a growl, low and animalistic, his eyes bulging in their failed determination.

"You baby." Fogarty leaned against a wall, shaking his head. "Are you afraid of pain, is that it, Dean?"

Dean's voice held its new animal growl as he replied. "I'm trying, sir. RRRRrrrrggggghhh." The rifle bounced on his knees, and then went back in front of him as he stared with angry fish eyes. Slowly it dropped again.

"I didn't ask you to try, Dean. I told you to do it. Now keep it up there."

Leather heels clicked in the doorway and Lenahan stood there, filling it with Marine Corps green and ribbons and shooting badges and himself. Fogarty noticed him and called them all to attention. "Attention on deck." Swenson and McClinton both came to attention, standing nude, McClinton dripping from his shower. Dean continued to gasp and moan, the rifle bouncing off his knees.

Fogarty glanced over to him. "Come aboard, Dean."

"Aye, aye, sir." Dean brought the weapon to order arms. "Beat Army, sir."

Lenahan surveyed them from the doorway, Fogarty all sweat and mud and something else, Dean red-faced and frightened, a victim's righteous grimace on the edges of his mouth, Swenson and McClinton plainly embarrassed at their nudity.

Lenahan nodded, working to hold back a smile. "And what . . . are . . . you doing, Mister Fogarty?"

"Sir, I am helping Mister Dean develop his shoulder muscles, in accordance with regulations that permit exercises to aid a plebe in certain weak areas of strength. Previous to that, sir, I was helping Mister Dean develop his stomach muscles."

"Are you getting any stronger, Dean?"

*. . . and I could play a game of tennis, maybe, leisurely, and call it a workout. Or do nothing, it would be my prerogative to get soft and old, what's so wrong with getting soft and old my mind would still be strong . . .* "Yes, sir."

"Wonderful." Lenahan nodded to Fogarty. "I hope you'll be able to report to me very soon that Mister Dean is the strongest plebe in the company, Mister Fogarty. I'd like you to work toward that end."

"Aye, aye, sir." Fogarty and Lenahan communicated with their eyes and with their knowing smiles, language that the regulations in their stark protectiveness would not let them utter.

"Carry on, Mister Fogarty. Good morning, gentlemen."

"Aye, aye, sir. Good morning, sir."

Lenahan's clicking heels faded down the hallway, a slow, measured dirge that marked the death of Dean's hopes for outside intervention. Fogarty was indeed the regulations. Fogarty folded his arms again, a menacing smile flitting across his still-flushed cheeks.

"So. Let's work on your arm strength, Dean. Pushups. Slo-o-wly. At my command. Halfway down. All the way down. Halfway up. All the way up. Halfway down. Hold it. Keep it there, Dean, that's it. Stop shuddering, too!"

Fogarty's voice sounded very close. Dean looked up as he undulated in his pain, his whole body shivering with isometric tension, and saw that Fogarty was doing them with him. Only Fogarty was doing them one-handed.

# Chapter Two: 0845

Lenahan walked into the battalion conference room and went immediately to the coffeepot, poured himself a cup, then faced Wentzel and Karalewski and Pruitt, who were already gathered at the conference table. He sat down, smiling ironically to Wentzel. "You look like hell, Wentzel. What's the matter, did the little lady beat you up for staying out too late last night?"

"No, on the contrary. You might say she went to sleep very happy." Wentzel smiled widely, rising to get another cup of coffee.

"See what a few beers will do for you? You ought to come out with me more often."

"I told her the Admiral ordered me to get you drunk. She was very understanding."

"I knew you couldn't just face her square." Lenahan leaned back in his chair, drawing a cigarette from the pack he always kept inside his sock. "Not that I'm exactly the best person to take advice from on family relations."

"Hey, that was facing her square." Karalewski grinned to both of them. "I heard the Admiral. You didn't see me with my hand in the air, 'Me, too, sir! I need to help Lenahan too'? Jesus, I got stuck talking with Mrs. Pratt for a goddamned hour, man. An *hour*, while you two were getting blitzed. I know more about potting African violets than any human deserves to be told."

Foote walked in, solemn and contained, heading for the coffee also. He nodded to them and then spoke to Lenahan as he poured his cup. "I take it all your mids made reveille this morning?"

"Yeah, all *mine* did." Lenahan dragged on his cigarette, dropping a piece of paper on the table top with ceremonial elan. "But I found eight of Pruitt's hogs nice and zonked out, ten minutes after reveille."

The boyish submariner looked up as if someone had told him his mother was dead. Lenahan grinned, taunting him. "Yeah, it's too bad your buddy Von Yerks didn't decide to go through your company yesterday, Pruitt." Lenahan could not contain his amusement at Pruitt's unease. Really, he thought. Let's spend all our creative energies trying to figure out how to screw each other.

"I didn't fry them." Lenahan slid the paper across the

table. Pruitt reached out and grabbed it, as if Pratt would immediately enter the room and ask for the incriminating evidence. "You might want to...counsel them. Or whatever. Just keep your goddamn friends out of my company area, Pruitt. All right? I'm tired of these silly games, and I'm tired of pretending they didn't happen. Stop acting like a little kid. Why don't you go hang out at the Charcoal Grill this weekend, Pruitt, and see how many mids you can catch holding hands with their girlfriends? Pratt would love it."

"Don't say that too loud." Wentzel's hawk face glared at Pruitt like he was a mouse waiting to be swooped down upon. "Somebody might think it's a good idea."

Parkhurst came in, a thick gorilla in his blues. "Hey, Ted, it sure looks like your marines are taking shit in Hue City. They still haven't taken it back."

Lenahan shrugged. "What can I say? I'd a hell of a lot rather be doing that than playing this penny-ante bullshit."

Karalewski made a patented clown's face and nodded goofily to the others. "That's why he's a marine. Thank God this place turns out enough lunatics each year that they don't have to draft the rest of us."

Tick. Zero-nine-hundred. The clock's minute hand touched the right place and Pratt tumbled through the door, wonderfully precise, his face dark with determination. Lenahan reached mechanically for another cigarette, on the verge of doing something patently offensive like giving the Commander a standing ovation. Instead he came to attention with the other officers, then sat back down with them, in unison, after Pratt took his seat.

Pratt adjusted his glasses, studying a page of notes. The glasses were so tight against the side of his head that he appeared to have grown into them. He cleared his throat, studying the notes.

"The Commandant has noticed a number of midshipmen exercising in sweatshirts that do not have *NAVY* on them." Pratt cleared his throat again. "This is against regulations. Individuals who do this lack pride in the Academy. Midshipmen should be proud to wear their *NAVY* sweatshirts." Pratt glanced quickly at Lenahan. "There will be no warnings. Midshipmen wearing nonregulation athletic gear will be placed on report."

Do I dare, mused Lenahan. It's such a small point. "Ah, sir."

"Captain Lenahan. As usual you don't agree."

"Just a word of caution, sir, if I may?" Lenahan dragged deeply on his cigarette, then put it out. "A lot of those sweatshirts were won by varsity athletes, the same way we win *ARMY* sweatshirts and bathrobes: by betting on games and meets. These guys see them as trophies, sir. They're really proud of them. It's a symbol of their pride, rather than any sort of … rebuke to this place."

Pratt stared impatiently at Lenahan. "And?"

*He doesn't like me.* "A mid running Farragut Field with a *DUKE* sweatshirt on is celebrating, sir. He's bragging about this place. He's wearing it like an Indian used to carry a scalp on his belt. He's saying, 'Look, we kicked the hell out of Duke.' It's pretty healthy, in my judgment, sir."

"Do you believe in the chain of command, Captain Lenahan?"

"Absolutely, sir."

"I said the Commandant is upset, Captain. The Commandant."

"I just thought maybe he had the reasons backwards, or something."

"Did you take ears in Vietnam?"

Lenahan squinched his face, somewhat startled. "Sir?"

"Ears. Did you cut off ears in Vietnam?"

"No, sir. That was really blown all out of proportion, sir. It didn't really happen very much. It didn't happen in my unit at all."

"It was an embarrassment to the service." Pratt's head was cocked. He stared into the distance. "Ears. We don't do things like that. We don't wear *DUKE* sweatshirts, either. We wear uniforms. There will be no warnings."

"Aye, aye, sir." Lenahan audibly sighed, writing on his own notepad. NO EARS OR SWEATSHIRTS.

"And speaking of judgment, Captain Lenahan." Pratt stared over at Wentzel also. The jet jockey's face was raised, his notepad still blank. His eyes were over Vinh, his whole senses rolling the jet hard to pull away from a Russian surface-to-air missile. "And Lieutenant Wentzel. Are you with us this morning, Lieutenant?"

"Yes, sir." Wentzel's gaze came slowly down from the ceiling, resting on Pratt's face. He smiled blandly. "Right here, sir."

"I noticed both of you leaving early from the reception yesterday. My battalion was the only one where officers left early. Lieutenant, you didn't even bring your wife." It was an accusation.

"She couldn't get a baby-sitter, sir."

Pratt was unfazed. "You were the only ones who left. We only get to visit the Superintendent in his home twice a year. You thoroughly embarrassed me."

"He told us to, Commander."

"You should have checked out with me first, Lieutenant. I am in your chain of command. Why did he tell you to leave?"

Wentzel and Lenahan exchanged glances. Such a small admission would be damaging. Pratt could never comprehend disaffection, the notion that duty at the Academy was not a greater delight than duty with the operating forces. Admiral Kraft had, in one small moment of conversation. But then, Admiral Kraft...

"He just said we looked like we needed a little liberty, sir." Lenahan stared at Wentzel, his face blank, knowing the comment would enrage Pratt.

"That could mean a million things. A million. You will both write a letter of apology to the Superintendent."

"Aye, aye, sir."

"Were your men awake this morning, Captain?"

Lenahan watched Pruitt go tight as a banjo string across from him. He smiled blandly at Pruitt for several seconds, enjoying the submariner's discomfort. Suffer, you little prick, he thought. "Yes, sir. My company did fine this morning, sir. I also toured the other areas in the battalion, and found it to be... *generally* satisfactory. I already reported to the others about their company areas."

"Good. Continue to do that, Captain."

"Sir?"

"Continue to inspect the entire battalion area for the rest of the week."

The son of a bitch, thought Lenahan. What does he think I am, a goddamn plebe? I've had it with this bullshit. "Sir, if I may say so, I think this is getting a little ridiculous. In any company in this battalion on any given morning, several midshipmen are going to go back to bed. It doesn't reflect on the Company Officers so much as it does on human nature." Pruitt looked like he was going to throw up. "I have a hard time seeing why you want me to tour my own company area, and I'm damned if I can understand why you want me to do the entire battalion."

"Some men can't handle combat decorations." Pratt uttered the comment as if it had spurted out of him unwillingly, escaped like an unavoidable hiccup. Wentzel's face came down from the ceiling again and he smirked to Lenahan. Wentzel would be next. "We don't owe you special treatment, Captain."

The old jealousy trick, mused Lenahan, reinforced by command. He sighed, lighting another cigarette. It would be a two-pack day. "Aye, aye, sir The entire battalion area, sir."

# Chapter Three: 1145

"All right, gentlemen. Stop all work. Put your pencils on your desks."

Dean slammed the pencil down, breaking the lead tip, on the verge of tears. I flunked it. I *flunked* it.

His whole head felt like soft wood, unalive and porous. He had been unable to study and he had not been able to concentrate on the questions. Fogarty is *killing* me, he mused, standing in line to hand in the test paper and the IBM answer card. The asshole. He'll be ecstatic. But at least my shoes were shined.

He placed his exam on one pile, the answer card on another, and dropped the IBM pencil into its box. Professor Thad stood behind the desk, an expectant smile lighting his chubby face, waiting for Dean's assessment. Dean was always the first to rehash each test with Professor Thad, to ask intricate questions and debate the nuances of hydrocarbons and precipitates.

"So what do you think, Mister Dean?"

"I don't know, Professor. I guess I failed it." Dean was too embarrassed to even look Professor Thad in the eyes. He began to walk out of the classroom.

"You've got to be kidding." Professor Thad had come to the Academy in 1967. He was as new as Dean, and was fond of remarking to his students that teaching at the Academy made him draft-exempt. "Mister Dean."

"Yes, sir." Dean halted near the doorway, his eyes dark from lack of sleep, still avoiding Thad's own.

"You're not serious, are you?"

"Unfortunately, I guess I am, sir. I didn't have much time to study last night."

"Are you ill, Mister Dean?" Professor Thad walked toward him. He was a rather tubby, soft-faced man of twenty-five, a product of M.I.T., one of the most brilliant acquisitions the Naval Academy faculty had managed in years. Dean was among his best students.

"Not exactly, sir. Just tired." Dean made his way toward the door again. "Sir, I have to get to noon come-around, or I'll get in trouble."

"Well, you let me worry about that." Thad watched Dean closely. "Are you being hazed?"

Dean laughed abruptly. The exact terminology had not even occurred to him. "You might call it that."

"What are they doing to you?"

Dean looked curiously at Thad. "They're running my ass." Then he walked away.

He grabbed his cap and donned his reefer class coat, then bolted back down Stribling Walk at a jog, trying to make up the time he had lost to Professor Thad. He jogged all the way to the Fifth Wing basement, on the other side of Bancroft Hall from his company area, making his way to the Press Shop. It was chill and blustery, a typical Dark Ages day, but Dean sweated profusely underneath his black drill shirt and heavy wool reefer. The odor of his own sweat mixed with the dry-cleaned smell from his drill shirt and almost nauseated him as he walked down the ramp to the Press Shop. Nothing in the world smells like a drill shirt from the Academy laundry, he thought again, surrounded by it. Somebody probably kept the same fluid in the damn machines since Nimitz was a mid, in the name of tradition.

Steam gushed near a far wall as fat, patient women sat at their large pressing machines putting military creases into uniforms, a never-ending stream of black wool moving along high racks toward them, inch by inch, uniform after uniform. A whole career, thought Dean, watching them, of reaching up from one rack and grasping the same uniform they just put onto another rack and putting the same crease in the same place, whoosh, then putting that one onto the one rack and grabbing another same uniform from the other same rack. I wonder what they do when they go home at night? Probably cook the same meal and put on the same old worn record and go to bed at exactly ten-twenty-two.

Thousands of black uniforms hung on long poles in the huge vacuous room, two rows of them along every aisle, one high and the other below it. They were organized by "alpha number," a four-digit number designed to correlate with a midshipman's alphabetical sequence. Dean searched through a long row of canvas tags, hooked along the sleeves of cleaned uniforms, for his number.

Finally he found it, and pulled down several articles of clothing: three fresh drill shirts, two pairs of trousers, two clean service dress blue uniforms. He hefted them over one shoulder and then sought out Fogarty's alpha number, just down from his own. I wonder what would happen if I got caught, he pondered, grabbing several other drill shirts and two more service dress blues, their sleeves ringed with concentric circles that denoted Fogarty's rank.

He fantasized about it, walking toward the Sixth Wing, past Smoke Park and the Library-Assembly area. Some faceless stern officer stopping him and asking about his carrying a first-classman's uniforms, his the victim's puzzled face, requesting permission not to answer the officer's questions, the officer persisting, demanding Fogarty's name. Fogarty "Class A"ed, maybe even thrown out for plebe servitude. Ah, sweet revenge.

But of course it wouldn't happen, nor would such revenge be sweet. He would be blamed by the other upperclass. And then it would truly never end.

Dean entered the Sixth Wing doors and began chopping, squaring corners as he raced up the stairway under his burden of uniforms. He dashed through his company area to his room, hung the uniforms inside his closet, then quickly changed into his inspection clothes and shoes and cap. Peckarsky wasn't even back from class yet. The lucky bastard didn't even have a noon come-around that day. Wouldn't life be sweet, mused Dean, grabbing Fogarty's uniforms from the closet, without come-arounds?

"Midshipman Dean, fourth class, reporting as ordered, sir."

"Dean, you fighting fool. Put those in my closet." Fogarty was at his desk, leaning back in his chair, reading *Leatherneck* magazine. "So, how did your test go?"

Dean came out of the closet and made himself a part of Fogarty's wall. "I'm certain I blew it, sir."

"Good, Dean. Good. How does it make you feel?"

"Pretty shitty, sir."

"So, why doesn't it make you feel pretty shitty to know you've blown plebe year?"

"It does, sir. One's just been...easier to control than the other."

"What was in the newspaper today?"

Somewhere in the cobwebs of his memory, in a dark room well before reveille as he furiously shined his shoes, before Fogarty, before a failed test, he had read the paper. "Sir, the loss of the Green Beret outpost at Langvei gives the enemy a key route toward the marine base at Khe Sanh, sir. And the marines are still fighting house to house in their attempt to recapture Hue City, sir. And Robert Kennedy is calling for an end to the 'illusion' on Vietnam, saying that the Johnson Administration is making us try to believe that the events of the past few weeks represent some sort of victory, sir."

"Do you believe that?"

"Sir?"

"Kennedy. Do you believe that bullshit?"

"I believe he has a point, sir. I'm not saying I agree with him."

"That's what I hate you, you sorry little mouse." Fogarty was shaking his head as if Dean were hopeless. "You don't believe anything. Everything is qualified. You don't even have the guts to give me an opinion. What the hell's so hard about forming an opinion?"

"Life isn't clear-cut, sir. There are very few absolutes."

"So what are you going to do, sit under a tree and think about it? When you're on the bridge of a ship and the captain says, 'Do we steer into the storm or away from it?' and you say, 'Sir, I see merits in both ways,' you don't exactly help solve the problem, do you get what I mean?"

"Yes, sir." Dean felt manhandled. He wanted to go back to his room and crawl into bed.

"What's going on these days, Dean?" It occurred to Dean that Fogarty sounded like an old man. The muscular first-classman paced slowly about the room, scratching an almost-shaved head. "You know, people keep talking about how the military makes you a robot, conditions your mind and all, but I've never seen the kind of conditioning that some of my friends who

95

went to college have come away with. You sit around a classroom like some Beta out of *Brave New World* and listen to the professor drone on and on, 'Pain is wrong,' 'People are oppressed,' 'You have the right to dissent, dissent, dissent,' but none of them are talking about duty, not one is being conditioned about duty, except maybe here, I don't know. We're pretty screwed up in this country right now, Dean. Hey. Do you believe in duty, Dean?"

"Oh, yes, sir." Or terror, or cowardice, or whatever else you want.

"Then come on over here. I want to look at your shoes." Fogarty shook his head as he inspected the two mirrors that gleamed back at him. "Unsat. Absolutely gross. Bring around another Form Two."


"Brigade, Atten-HUT."

The entire mess hall became silent, four thousand men facing the Anchor, where the Brigade Commander stood with a microphone in one hand.

"The Brigade is *honored*"—there was a tradition in the way a Brigade Commander said the word that conveyed an emotional reality; the word was always emphasized, and a pause always followed it—"to have as its guests in the mess hall this noon two of the most highly-decorated alumni of the Vietnam war. Lieutenant Joseph Purdy, United States Navy, class of sixty-three, holds the Navy Cross, the Distinguished Flying Cross with two gold stars in lieu of subsequent awards, and twenty-seven air medals earned from flights over North Vietnam; and Captain Frederick Packer, United States Marine Corps, class of sixty-four, holder of the Navy Cross, the Silver Star with a gold star in lieu of a second award, the Bronze Star, and the Purple Heart for wounds received in action."

The mess hall echoed with applause, reverberated, pulsed with it.

"Brigade, seats."

A dozen plebes sprinted toward the Anchor from one company area and lifted the two officers onto their shoulders, carrying them past every table in the mess hall, a ritual normally reserved for athletic heroes after important contests. The mess hall became pandemonium, each section of midshipmen standing at their tables as the alumni were hoisted by, cheering and applauding such links to their past and future.

The mess hall calmed down, resuming its normal circus. One table away, two plebes sat at a perfect brace, taking turns whacking each other smartly on the back of the head. A first-classman watched amusedly. His taunts drifted over to Fogarty and Swenson.

"Are you going to let Clayton get away with that, Del Vecchio?"

"No, sir." Whack.

"Are you going to let Del Vecchio get away with that, Clayton?"

"No, sir." Whack.

"Are you going to let Clayton..."

Noon meal was served, the Filipino stewards running from the kitchen areas with wide metal trays balanced on their shoulders, plebes at each table quickly unloading the trays and holding hot metal dishes for the upperclass.

Salisbury steaks. Swenson grimaced, drawing an oblong piece of spiced hamburger from one dish and covering it with spicy red gravy. "Elephant turds."

McClinton took one, nodding. "Sleeping pills, you mean."

In the mess hall's center area a plebe staggered, clutching his stomach, his face peering toward the ceiling. Finally he threw both hands up into the air and bellowed in a voice that carried through the entire wing.

"DON'T EAT THE MEAT! DON'T EAT THE MEAT! AAAAAAAGH!"

The plebe fell hard to the floor, clutching his stomach, feigning death. He remained still for several seconds and then rose, to the applause of the surrounding tables.

Then from the corner of one company area, the Pink Panther began his prowl, heading for the Brigade Staff table on orders from upperclassmen in his company, to perform for the honored visitors. A tall, gangly plebe with the legs of a man six inches taller than he, the Pink Panther stalked along the rows of tables, hands just under his chin like idle paws, his knees reaching all the way to his hands each time he pranced. Every few steps he stopped, looking left and right while in his absurd crouch.

The upperclass on the tables howled. The Pink Panther was right out of a Peter Sellers movie. Somebody screamed from a nearby table. "Do the fly! Hey, do the fly!"

The plebe immediately fell into a tight-kneed crouch, his

head jerking unpredictably in various directions, his hands like the front arms of a fly, busily rubbing his face and ears and the back of his head, one leg rubbing the other. He then hopped along the mess hall floor, facing this way and that, like a fly flitting from one piece of dung to another.

Finally he took off, making his way toward the staff table, responding to the screams and applause of midshipmen all the way through the mess hall.

"Christ, is the bastard funny." Fogarty watched the Pink Panther retreat.

"Speaking of funny, did you hear what happened with the stewards this morning?" Swenson swirled a glass of ice-milk, then grinned at Fogarty, who was sipping iced tea. "One of the stewards got chewed out real bad by a Petty Officer, and kind of took it to heart. The next thing you know they found him pissing in one of the tea vats." Swenson laughed hilariously as Fogarty stopped drinking his tea in the middle of a swallow. "No kidding. He was standing right there, pissing into a seventy-five-gallon tea vat."

"It's got to be the Dark Ages." Everything had a larger reason to McClinton, something that transcended the individual.

"I don't care what it is. Pour me some water, Dean." Fogarty held out his glass. He had drained the tea back into its container.

"The stewards don't have it that bad." McClinton was analyzing again. "Hell, they don't have to go to sea, they've got plenty of liberty, and all they've got to do is put up with us three times a day."

Fogarty took a swig of water. "Lucky them. You know who's really got it made? Yamato. Hell, whenever he wants to go over the wall, he just puts on his clothes and walks out with the stewards. Nobody believes he could be a mid, being part Filipino and all."

"Crazy Yamato." Swenson laughed, remembering. "Remember Pearl Harbor Day our plebe year, when the upperclass made him dress up like a kamikaze pilot and the plebes carried him around the mess hall in a cardboard Jap Zero? I never saw so many squares of bread tossed at anybody in my whole life."

"Excuse yourself, Dean."

"Sir?"

Fogarty leaned over toward Dean. "You haven't touched a

thing on your plate for two minutes, mung. I hate malingerers. Excuse yourself."

Dean appeared startled, confused. "Sir, I request permission to—"

"Shut up. I'm tired of your statements. All you're going to say is something about why you haven't eaten, right?"

Dean swallowed hard, his eyes wounded. "Yes, sir."

"All right. Take half of that meat on your plate."

"Aye, aye, sir." Dean grabbed the elephant turd and broke it in half.

"Put it on a piece of bread."

"Aye, aye, sir." He wrapped a piece of bread around it.

"Now, whammo it."

"Aye, aye, sir." Dean stuffed the whole thing in his mouth at once, and began chewing furiously, knowing what would come next.

"And Dean..." Fogarty had him. He now had only three chews to finish it. It filled his mouth, large hunks of mystery meat and gobs of bread. He opened his mouth for three slow chews, then squinched his eyes and swallowed. The mess slid slowly down his throat, a dry glob, as if he had just swallowed a baseball.

"Yes, sir?"

"I don't want you writing your mommy and telling her we don't let you have enough food. Did you get enough to eat, Dean?"

Dean swallowed again, straining his neck, trying to clear his mouth and throat. "Yes, sir."

"Good. You're excused, Dean."

"Aye, aye, sir." Dean rose quickly from his chair, grabbed his cap from the small shelf underneath the seat, and stood facing away from the table, his cap held properly in his right hand, such a simple act a chore of exactitude. His hand had to be all the way inside the cap, fingers spread wide so that the hat would not fall out, the visor pointed mandatorily toward the floor. His whole arm was close enough to his body to approximate the position of attention, but far enough away that the white cover did not touch his drill trousers.

Dean's mind was dull from tension and lack of sleep. The mystery meat sandwich was a lump, halfway down his esophagus.

Oh, I am a mess, he thought, feeling the stares as he stood behind his chair.

Two letters lay on Fogarty's desk when he returned to his room from lunch, left there by the Mate of the Deck. He picked them up, looking at one and then the other, one in each hand, as if they would disappear if he did not watch both of them continually. Finally he put one down on the desktop and sat in his chair, cradling the other one with meaty hands. He stared at the writing on the envelope for a long time, scrutinized it, turned it at various angles, trying to imagine the mood of the writer as he scrawled a letter to a friend from some muddy, rat-infested hole.

The letter that a dead hand wrote. Fogarty slowly opened the envelope, careful not to rip it as he would normally do, then unfolded the letter. The First Marine Division seal marked the letterhead. It was a brief note, obviously written in a hurry. "Back in Country—Got a company this time. Something big just blew. We move out in a half hour on trucks, God knows where. Keep your hands up and your chin down and your butt off the deck. Ron."

That was it. Fogarty stared for a minute longer, as if more would appear, then set it down, reaching for the other envelope. It was addressed in a controlled, loopy feminine style. The return address was Chicago. He knew who had written it. He didn't want to open it.

> Dear Bill,
>
> I don't know if you've heard but Ron was killed on Monday. I can't really get used to the idea, it's like it isn't really something that's happened. The marine officer who came to the house said he was shot in the chest again, and bled to death. We've arranged for a funeral in Arlington, Saturday at two o'clock. I hope you can come, and I hope you'll have some time afterward...

Fogarty held the letter on his lap and stared up at the ceiling. Bled to death. How the hell can a man bleed to death in Vietnam, with helicopter medevacs? Saturday, two o'clock. Arlington. Bled to death. Jesus Christ.

For the first time in his life, Bill Fogarty felt afraid of war.

# Chapter Four: 1400

"Hello, Angie?" Lenahan sat back in his chair, his feet up on his desk, and dragged on a cigarette.

"*Ted.*" She paused. "Hold on a minute." He heard her call to one of her children, her voice muffled as her hand covered the telephone receiver. "I'm back. You left early yesterday."

"Kraft ordered me out. The whole thing was getting to me."

"Well, dear old Commander Pratt and his goose of a wife watched you walk out. You and that little pilot. I think you really made him mad."

"Don't *I* know. Pratt ordered both of us to write the Admiral letters of apology."

"The Admiral will think it's funny. He's really a *dear* old man." Angie giggled. "Really. Pratt was so out of joint that he slobbered on his tie. You should have seen Mrs. Pratt chewing him out while she was trying to dab it off with her hanky. Poor Commander Pratt. His wife runs him like he was a plebe."

Angie had always been able to keep the Academy in perspective, even when she and Steve had dated, years before. She had kept Lenahan's former roommate in continual fear while he was a midshipman, doing things like embracing him openly in Tecumseh Court, pressing her body against him in flagrant displays that could have caused him to be put on report, and wearing sweaters that showed her voluptuous breasts much too well, driving whole companies of lonely midshipmen into a frenzy.

"Anyway, who gives a shit." Lenahan put out his cigarette.

"How have you survived, with an attitude like that?"

"Not very well. But like I said, who gives a shit." He took a deep breath, feeling he was about to commit an unpreventable, unpardonable sin. "Are you going to be able to see me tonight?"

"Well, just a minute. Let me check my schedule." She was chiding him. "Can you come between seven-thirty and eight? I have an opening. Either that, or how about after ten? I'll be taking a coffee break."

"You're really ridiculous, did you know that?"

"I suppose. But you try chasing after three kids all day. It doesn't do much to make you sane. But anyway, yes, I'll be able to see you tonight, if you feel stealthy and you don't mind parking your car a few blocks away and you don't mind sneaking into my back door. Isn't this romantic?"

"Why are we doing this?"

"Now, that's heavy. That's just—a million pounds. I feel like the heroine of some gothic novel when you say that. Quite frankly, Captain Lenahan, I crave your body." She giggled again.

"You're not like that."

"Then don't ask. Just let it happen, Ted. You go through life believing everything has to be reasoned out, charted, formulized. I'd like to see you tonight. Would you like to see me?"

"What are we, reciting school lessons? I already said so."

"Then come on over. Any time after ten."

"I'll think about it." He found himself smiling. "Okay, I thought about it. I'll be there." Someone knocked on his office door. "I've got to go."

"Duty calls."

"You're really a wise-ass. See you tonight." Lenahan came forward in his chair and picked up a pen, returning to a stack of evaluation reports he had been reading before he called Angie. "Come in."

Fogarty strode into the office, centering himself on Lenahan's desk as he stood at a practiced attention. "Midshipman Fogarty, first class, sir. May I have a word with you, sir?"

"Stand at ease, Mister Fogarty. What can I do for you?"

Fogarty seemed somehow perplexed. "Sir, I just got a letter from my friend's wife. You know, the one we talked about this morning? He's going to be buried in Arlington tomorrow, and I'd like to be there."

"That won't be any problem." Lenahan scrutinized Fogarty, searching for the rest of his puzzlement. "We'll get a chit in this afternoon. It won't interfere with your fight tomorrow night?"

"Oh, that." Fogarty dismissed it, almost absently. "No, sir. It's at fourteen hundred, and the fight isn't until the night. I got a letter from him, too."

"From him?"

"Yes, sir. Did you ever get a letter from a dead man?" Fogarty shook his head, searching Lenahan's face, smiling with a mix of irony and confusion. "It didn't say much. It wasn't even funny. She says he bled to death. How can a man bleed to death in Vietnam, sir? How can a man—she said he was shot in the chest again—how can a man bleed to death when they have helicopters? I just don't understand."

"Well, if you sever an artery." Lenahan lit a cigarette, his mind back in a vise, his stomach churning with cold ooze as he screamed into the radio, directing air strikes while he was so faint from loss of blood that he could not even hear himself shout. "Or, he could have had a sucking chest, and drowned in his own blood. Hell…" Lenahan dragged on the cigarette, and noticed Fogarty's almost nauseated unease. The powerful first-classman was in no mood for clinical comment; his question had been rhetorical. "It doesn't happen often, Bill. If the helicopter can make it into the zone, and if the man can be saved, he will be. It's not that frequent a man bleeds to death. I'm sorry it had to be your friend."

"There nowhere to unload. You know what I mean, sir? How did you take it in combat, when it happened all the time?"

"You don't deal with this part of it in combat. You medevac the casualties and you keep going. You don't even see them long enough, most of the time, for it to be real when they die. Once we couldn't get our dead out for almost a day. We had to stack them in this old pagoda, because the helicopters wouldn't come into our zone for dead marines. Dead marines are 'routine' medevacs. You don't come into a hot zone for a routine. Well, by the time we finally got them out of there, my whole goddamn company was crying, carrying friends who were stiff as boards and all blown to bits. But most of the time you don't see that. You won't dwell on it like you're doing now. And, hell, you've lost a very close friend. That eats at you more." Lenahan played with his cigarette as he talked, then dragged on it. "Are you worried, Mister Fogarty?"

"Yes, sir. I guess so." Fogarty looked directly at Lenahan, his perplexed face a mirror to his insides. "I never thought I'd react like this."

"What do you think you're supposed to do, laugh it off? I wouldn't want any man commanding troops who doesn't take it personally when someone gets hurt. A man who can't feel that is a danger. And like as not, he's a butcher, too."

"Yes, sir." Fogarty now seemed uneasy, as if he had shown too much of himself.

"You've got to suffer if you want to sing the blues, Mister Fogarty."

"Sir?"

"Nothing. It's from a song. Do you like poetry?"

"Not really, sir. I've never really read much of it, anyway."

"Too bad. Poetry will sustain your emotions. It's the lightning rod of the soul." Lenahan smiled easily. "Don't be afraid to be sensitive, just because you're a hard-ass. The way you feel about this friend of yours shows you're sensitive, Mister Fogarty. Poetry reaches that part of you. Have you ever heard of Dylan Thomas?"

"Well, yes, sir. I've heard of him."

Lenahan recited, staring straight into Fogarty's face, his words like a large hammer hitting a deeply clanging anvil. "The dream that kicks the buried from their sack/And lets their trash be honored as the quick./This is the world. Have faith." He smiled. "Dylan Thomas, 'Our Eunuch Dreams.'"

Fogarty seemed more puzzled than ever. "Yes, sir." He came back to attention. "Thank you, sir. I request permission to shove off, sir."

"Good day, Mister Fogarty. I'll see that your chit gets through Commander Pratt this afternoon."

"Thank you, sir. Good afternoon, sir."

Lenahan laughed softly, watching Fogarty's retreating frame. He probably thinks I'm goony, mused Lenahan. Eight years ago, I would have too.

He puttered about his office for fifteen more minutes, reading through leadership evaluation forms written on various midshipmen, checking room-inspection chits from a recent tour by the midshipman Battalion Officer of the Watch, talking to a few professors about midshipmen who were either deficient in grades or having trouble staying awake in class. That day's Mate of the Deck, a huge plebe who had played tackle on the plebe football team, entered and left, dropping the afternoon packet of Yard Mail in Lenahan's In box. Finally the phone rang again, and Lenahan set aside the paperwork, answering it.

"Good afternoon, Captain Lenahan speaking, sir."

"Captain Lenahan." The voice was soft, modulated, the voice of a thinker rather than a doer, of a man who had the leisure and the solitude to formulate loose, musical syllables. "This is Professor Thad, of the Chemistry Department. How are you this afternoon, sir?"

*Get to the point,* thought Lenahan immediately. So many professors made him itchy with their formalities. Professor Thad didn't give the slightest damn how Ted Lenahan was that afternoon, and Lenahan knew it. "What can I do for you, Professor?"

"I have a matter that concerns me greatly, Captain, and I want to bring it to your attention. It involves at least one midshipman in your company, conceivably more, and it could be a serious matter. Then again, I could be exaggerating it in my own mind. I'm rather new around here, so I hope you'll forgive me if I seem to be blowing things out of proportion."

*What?* mused Lenahan, almost ready to scream. For God's sake, is this twenty questions? Are you writing me an essay on the confused state of your insides, or are you bringing me a problem? "*What*, Professor Thad?"

"It involves Midshipman Dean." Lenahan leaned back in his chair, lighting what seemed like his thirtieth cigarette of the afternoon. The old eighty-twenty rule, he mused, waiting for the Professor's comments. Eighty percent of your time is spent on twenty percent of your people. "Midshipman Dean has been one of my best students thus far. I believe he has about a ninety-seven average. He is actually on the verge of being brilliant in this field." Thad reconsidered. "Well, that may be something of an exaggeration. But he is really very good."

"That's nice to hear, Professor. But it hardly sounds like a problem. Is there a problem that I can help you with? As long as it's not chemistry, I might be able to help." Lenahan chuckled at his little joke.

"Well, Midshipman Dean, who as I told you has been quite good in my class..." The Professor seemed to hesitate. "I really feel uncomfortable getting into this, Captain, but I do feel very strongly about the way so many plebes are treated. I think much of your plebe system is absolutely mindless and barbaric."

"Professor, if you don't spit it out, I'm going to hang up."

"I think Midshipman Dean is being hazed."

Lenahan almost laughed right into the mouthpiece. "*Hazed*, Professor?" It was a word out of history, like maybe *flogged*, or *keelhauled*. "Why, did he mention something to you?"

"No. No, I don't want Midshipman Dean to be implicated at all by my phone call. He said nothing at all to me. He was quite loyal to your *system*." Professor Thad almost spat the word over the phone. The receiver hissed in Lenahan's ear with the *s* sound. "But a man with a ninety-seven average doesn't just fail an important exam by accident. And it has to be more than merely losing the chance to study. Midshipman Dean is intelligent enough in my course to pass any exam of this sort without studying, Captain. There had to be more. He looked absolutely ill when I spoke to him. He was very vague about what was happening, also."

"He failed your exam?"

"That is correct." Professor Thad sounded somehow wronged, angry at Lenahan himself. "He has a ninety-seven average. Well, actually he has a ninety-six-point-seven average. And he failed the exam."

"All right, Professor. Thanks for your call. I'll talk with Mister Dean."

"I hope you will, Captain. I'm deeply concerned with all of this. Mister Dean impresses me as a very sensitive man."

"You are aware that a lot more goes on around here than academics, Professor? I mean, we're trying to make this guy into an officer, not a chemistry professor. No offense."

"I'm fully aware of that, Captain. I told you when I called that I am uncomfortable even talking to you about this. But I am also aware that there are certain mandatory...*limitations*."

"I'll talk to Dean and find out why he blew your test. Good day, Professor."


The door knocked hesitantly, as if the owner of the fist on the other side of the door was fearful of breaking his knuckles on the wood.

"Come in."

Dean took three steps inside the office and stood in a brace. "Sir, Midshipman Dean, fourth class, reporting to the Company Officer as ordered, sir."

"You don't need to brace up for me, Dean. Just stand at attention. There you go, that's it." Lenahan studied Dean's face, then inspected every detail of his uniform with a quick, consuming glance. Dean's face was washed-out, bagged from lack of sleep. Well, thought Lenahan, Fogarty certainly has his ways. His uniform was impeccable, though, as good as Lenahan had seen it all year.

"I just spoke with your chemistry professor. He says you failed a test."

Dean blinked slowly, and swallowed, registering no surprise. "Yes, sir."

"What happened?"

"Sir, I didn't have any time to study for it, sir."

"Why not?"

Dean blinked again, obviously struggling with himself. "Sir, I had other commitments that were more important, sir."

"Is there anything you need to tell me, Dean?" The question was carefully phrased. A direct interrogation would force Dean to spell out every minute violation of the indoctrination system that Fogarty had perpetrated, on penalty of committing an honor offense. Dismissing Dean without giving him the opportunity to come forward with his own recriminations would be a breach of duty by Lenahan. If he wants to unload on Fogarty, mused Lenahan, watching the frail plebe carefully, he'll have to do it on his own initiative.

Dean stood perfectly motionless for several seconds. Finally, he swallowed again. "No, sir."

# Chapter Five: 1600

"Boom boom boom." Little Stevie Wonder feinted and threw three mock jabs at Mick Yamato, standing in front of the large weigh-in scales dressed only in his jock strap. The eagle on his arm undulated every time he threw a punch. "Trajardo, I'm gonna have to kick your ass. C'mon, you! C'mon c'mon c'mon!"

Yamato studiously ignored Little Stevie Wonder, looking at Fogarty as he pointed a thumb in Stevie's direction. "Check this. You asshole, Fogarty. Why the hell did you ever tell him my middle name?"

Charle Adair walked up and leaned forward from the hips, his waist absolutely straight, staring up into Yamato's face. "Tra - HAR - do?" He kept his position and turned toward Fogarty, his angular black face lit with humor and excitement. "Hey, Fogarty, Did you say his middle name's Tra - HAR - do?" Adair laughed, long, high-pitched guffaws. "Oh, man! *We* take shit for having funny names, but I never in my *life* met nobody called Tra - HAR - do!"

Yamato stared calmly at Adair. "So, what's your middle name?"

Adair stood straight up, slightly self-conscious. "Langston."

"Langston, huh?" Yamato's face squinched up as he spat

the words out. "Well, *fuck you,* Langston!" He turned around and pointed at Little Stevie Wonder, who now was holding his stomach as he laughed at Adair. "And I'll deal with *you* in the ring tomorrow night."

Stevie Wonder threw three mock jabs. "Boom boom boom!"

"Ah, boom boom boom my ass." Yamato punched Fogarty on the shoulder, causing him to stutter-step. "Hey, man. Wake up. What the hell you dreaming about?"

"He thinks Chervanek's going to kick his ass. Can't get it off his mind."

Fogarty grimaced. "Screw you, Chollie."

"The man says he is going to knock ... your ... ass ... *out.*" Adair pronounced each word with crisp promise.

Fogarty laughed sardonically. "So what? He says that every fight."

"He's *got* a right hand." Adair threw a mock punch, whistling. "Whoooeee. Pow."

"Have you ever seen me on my ass?"

Fogarty stepped onto the scales and the manager recorded his weight, a perfect one-fifty-nine. He put his sweatgear back on and grabbed his boxing clothes, the shoes and gloves and head-gear and uniform that he would wear in the ring Saturday night, and began walking back toward Bancroft Hall, along the rows of handball courts and speedbags that lined the workout areas of MacDonough Hall's boxing area.

"Hey, Bill!" Yamato called after him. "We're going to the Steerage for a milkshake. Come on. Put some of that weight back on."

"Thanks, Mick, but I think I'm going to go get some rack time."

"Oh, yeah?" Adair's laughing voice chased him as he walked away. "Gonna dream up a way to stop Chervanek's right hand, huh?"


In the shadows of his darkened room, wrapped in his blankets like a warm cocoon, he mired himself in sameness as he dreamt of different things. Same blanket that had covered him each cold night since he had turned eighteen, same black clothes folded perfectly over a chair identical to every chair he had sat in for four years, same cardboard ceiling as he stared up at memories provoked by the unrelenting sameness.

*Ron Loudenslager died for something, call it Country or simply say that somewhere in eternity there was a little wave with a great big man on it, and now that tiny portion of the universe is as glassy as a Sargasso Sea. And Ron Loudenslager was me.*

He tried, just for a moment as he nodded off to sleep, to remember a time when he did not view the world as a chimera to be attacked, a progression of moments capable of violent destruction, a painful jungle designed to test his tenacity. He could not think that far back. He could get past first-class year and second-class year and youngster year. He could remember the incredible, unnerving scars of plebe year, as if his memory itself were falling into its own small sea and treading water there, trying to keep from drowning. He could identify each terror-filled event of plebe summer, those weeks that ripped his old self from him like someone reaching inside a plucked chicken and tearing out the guts, then packing in fear where they used to be.

But he could not remember how he had functioned before then, what had motivated him and what if anything had brutalized his psyche. His mind stopped at plebe year: the sweat, the misery, the exhaustion. Three sweatsuits in the boiling heat, fifteen-second showers, the long hours marching in the August sun as it burned morning mist out of the air, then dew off the ground, then the sweat right off his neck and fingers. Classmates dropping like flies during come-arounds and on the drill field. A year without so much as touching a woman's hand, a year where any upperclassman could walk inside his room and into the middle of his mind at any time, day or night. Fists on his chest, bats on his ass, humiliation.

Was there really ever a time when the deck was a floor, the bulkheads were walls, the overhead was a ceiling? Did he ever go to the bathroom instead of the head, climb a stairway instead of a ladder, find something easy instead of fruit? Was there ever such a thing as an empty afternoon, a weeknight spent drinking beer and shooting pool, a world where the dread of battle was not his most certain future?

If there was, it belonged to a child who merely had his name. And if it was, it was irrelevant.

He could not get inside.

Everywhere there was a wall and he drove over the river, looking downstream through a light haze at gray buildings and wide athletic fields, the meter on the taxi slowly clicking again and again, all his hard-won dollars disappearing with each click that had begun forty miles up the road at Washington National Airport. Click. Click. The old taxi driver sat settled in his cab like a bored Black Buddha, staring at the road as if he had been molded into the seat, plump and immobile.

Back across the river. Children played along a stretch of park just at the bridge's edge, fishing and chasing each other in the morning dew. The taxi passed a gate but it was the wrong one. Gate 8 it said and he was not allowed to enter through Gate 8, only Gate 1 or Gate 3. It was very clear on the instructions and he was not about to start his military career by disobeying his very first order. Click.

They wound through Old Town again, cobbled streets and bushy trees, large frame houses like in his grandmother's scrapbook. Experimentally the taxi driver made a left turn, driving with that sedate nonchalance that made him appear to be a fixture in his own cab, servant to it, only his hands and lower arms moving as he turned the steering wheel, even his cheeks and jaw perfectly still as he mumbled something about giving a side street a try.

And there it was. Gate 3, dead ahead, Old Town and all things civilian ending with abruptness, the high brick wall opening along cobbled roads just wide enough for a driving gate, flanked by two small walking gates. The taxi stopped at the gate and he asked the old, bored-looking gate guard about the Library-Assembly area and the guard responded with a terse sentence, obviously giving it for at least the hundredth time that morning, pointing, his washed-out, scarred face as immobile as the taxi driver's. The world was a slow collage of old, uninterested men moving him along toward deliverance. Click.

But it was beautiful, unimaginable in its colors and its odors, everything he had dreamed on cold Nebraska nights. Lush trees and magnificent stone buildings and monuments. Brick walkways curving through grass so green it was almost blue.

Athletic fields everywhere, flat and wide, many dredged up from the river. And the river, joining the Chesapeake Bay right at the Yard's edge, both of them a wide, clean, briny brown, dotted with puffy sailboats that rode the gentle morning wind.

Click. The taxi halted next to a reflection pool, its fountains spewing. Hundreds more like Fogarty converged on a set of double doors, dressed in their only suits or sportcoats, carrying bags filled with hope. The taxi driver said twenty-seven dollars. He gave the old Buddha forty, a nice round figure for good-bye. He didn't mind. Money had no relevance or even use inside those high stone walls.

It was like before and after, or maybe hot and cold. In the space of perhaps fifteen minutes, as he traveled a distance of a hundred feet, passing check-in stations and signing forms, his new world closed around him like a vise that would never, never release him. He walked out the back door of the large room in the Library-Assembly area and a scowling man dressed in crisp whites seized him and threw him into a line with several others, all the while screaming, punching.

Shortly they began running, this man in the crisp white uniform jogging at their sides, barking, prodding, punching. And the running would not stop for a year. Running, sweating in the humid scorching heat, his only suit soon ruined by sweat, the new pair of shoes he had bought from his savings to celebrate his new status in life becoming scuffed beyond repair. Running up steps and across streets and along metal gratings, a dozen of them lugging suitcases and guitars and tennis rackets, dropping those off in rooms that had already been assigned to them and running again. By afternoon they had all the gear they would need for the entire summer, beds in their rooms piled high with uniforms and bedding and navy-issue underwear and books and blotters and shoes and towels, soap and razor blades, even vellum stationery. They had burr haircuts and bookbags and the all-important sweatgear, three sets of gray sweatsuits that Loudenslager gloried over, guaranteeing them that the sweatgear would not dry out all summer. And raingear, the ankle-length black raincoat and waist-high accompanying cape. It was very important, insisted Loudenslager, that the raingear be inspected. So he dressed them in it and ran them in the heat for a half-hour, the world becoming a dizzying pool of sweat, a personalized steambath underneath the black plastic.

Later that afternoon he double-timed, eyes rolling with exhaustion, with more than a thousand others as they were herded like cattle into the low confines of Dahlgren Hall. The class of 1968. It seemed so distant, 1968, and then he would only be four-ninths of the way through it. He stood in the dark hall, suffocated by the heat and by the nearness of the others, and took the oath of office as a midshipman. Several boys around him were whimpering. Above them, mothers waved handkerchiefs from a high terrace where hundreds of parents and tourists watched the ceremony. It had lost its beauty, its romance. It didn't even smell the same. It would never be the same.

That evening he wrapped up every civilian item he had brought to the Academy, for shipment home the next morning. His suit was streaked with white salt stains. He stuffed it mindlessly into his bag. His shoes were ruined, scarred. He jammed them in also. His civilian underwear was soaked and stained. In it went. He snapped the suitcase shut and wrapped twine around it, carrying out this madman Loudenslager's exacting orders, and then stood up.

In front of him, staring back with hollow, frightened eyes, was a scalped youth dressed up in a sailor suit. It took him several seconds to realize he was looking into a mirror at himself.

They even played taps. It was a recording of a bugle, played over a loudspeaker in the hallway. It sounded terrible, like a flutophone, giving the whole scene a note of artificiality, a weak parody of summer camp.

He lay in his bed, trying to go to sleep with the doorway open, the hallway lights bright and the continual noise making sleep impossible. The doorway was open because Loudenslager had commanded it, would not let them be alone, even in their sleep.

Slowly, almost hesitantly, he began to pray. He had not prayed seriously in years. It was a short, embarrassed apology to God for not having prayed when things were going smoothly, and after he finished, he cried. He pressed his face against his mattress, heaving, trying to conceal his sobs from his roommates, two other frightened visions named Swenson and McClinton whom he had not even spoken to yet.

In a quarter hour, he cried away his youth. No matter what else happened, it was gone. If he quit he would have scarred his innocence with the knowledge or suspicion that he couldn't take it. He knew he would never quit.

So he cried instead for his youth. He cried because, with one decision, and after a day that he despised above all others in his life, he had committed himself to at least nine years of orders and abstinence and repression and confinement, worst of all confinement, the inability to decide any large aspect of his life.

And after nine years, if any portion of his happy wildness were to survive, it would be old.

# Chapter Six: 1800

The door was closed. The room seemed dark. Dean slowly pushed the door open, his soft face peering around it, into the cavelike shadows of the room. He carried his rifle in one arm. His body was bulky with the three sweatsuits Fogarty had ordered him to wear, making him look like some sort of stuffed teddy bear.

"Get in here, Dean."

"Aye, aye, sir. Midshipman Dean, fourth class, sir, reporting as ordered, sir." Dean placed his back against the nearest wall. He could not see Fogarty under the dark wool blanket in the corner of the room.

"Hit the overhead."

"Sir?" Dean squinched his face up, standing uncertainly in the dark.

"I said, 'Hit...the...overhead.'"

Who am I, thought Dean. He set his rifle against the wall and jumped into the air, slamming his fist into the ceiling. All right, he wondered in the dark. What do I do now? He retreated to the wall. "Uh...Beat Army, sir."

Fogarty sat up in bed, studying Dean with laughing cat's eyes. "That had to be the dumbest thing I've seen a plebe do in a long, long time, Dean. Really. Now, let me rephrase that: Turn on the overhead *lights*, shit-for-brains."

Dean rolled his eyes in the dark room, feeling like a moron. "Aye, aye, sir." He reached over and hit the light switch.

"Marvelous. Hey, Dean, you must be some kind of mechanical genius." Fogarty sat on the edge of his bed, wrapped in his blanket like a caricature of a disheveled Indian. His nap had beaten on him, left him weary. He rubbed his eyes. "So what's for evening meal?"

"Sir, the menu for evening meal is: roast young tom turkey, giblet gravy, mashed potatoes, buttered carrots and peas, bread and butter, fresh apples, devil's food layer cake, coffee cream and milk, sir."

"Bill the Goat's balls, Dean. Four minutes."

"Aye, aye, sir!" Dean sprinted from Fogarty's room, carrying his rifle with both hands in front of his chest, at port arms. Fogarty called after him as the door began to close. "High port, smack!"

"Aye, aye, sir!" Dean's voice echoed down the hallway as he disappeared, his rifle now high over his head.

Fogarty rubbed his face, trying to wake up, then finally rose from the bed and jumped into his shower. Dean's sprint to Bill the Goat's balls would give him time to clean up.

Bill the Goat's balls were more than a tradition; they were an unspoken Freudian shrine. The large bronze statue of Navy's fighting symbol, which stood in front of MacDonough Hall, was explicit in every detail in its depiction of a raging male goat leaping in the attack. It was the duty of each plebe class, despite continual warnings from the officer staff, to keep the statue's gonads brightly brassoed, so that they shone like a gleaming gold mirror from between the dull brown legs. And during come-around periods, plebes from all over the Brigade could be seen sprinting to and from the statue, slapping the brassoed balls.

Fogarty climbed out of the shower and began wiping himself with his white regulation towel. Dean burst back into the room, his face red, his chest heaving.

"Midshipman Dean, fourth class, sir."

"Oh, Dean." Fogarty grimaced, hanging up his towel, his sinewy nakedness like a statue come alive before Dean's eyes. "Hand me my B-robe." Fogarty caught his gray bathrobe from Dean and wrapped it around himself, staring tiredly at the winded, red-faced plebe. "You really think I get a kick out of running you, don't you?"

Dean peered innocently straight ahead, actually daring to hope for a long conversation, any mechanism that would postpone his pain, catch up with the clock. Fogarty could run him but even Fogarty was servant to the clock. At eighteen-thirty it was over, pain or not. "I'll...I'll find out, sir."

"No, you really do. I see it in your face." Fogarty walked slowly to his chair and sat heavily down. "I've got a whole life to get on with, Dean. And I don't particularly want you in it." He watched Dean's labored breathing. "Did you like it in college, Dean?"

*And I could sit outside the library next to a large fountain and watch the girls in their Bermuda shorts and halter tops, coming in and out of the library, calling to each other and waving and maybe sometimes on the right dark night or sunlit day they would call to me...*"Yes, sir. I liked it a lot, sir."

"Then why did you come here, Dean?"

"I really...I..." He couldn't say he didn't know. A plebe was not allowed to say he didn't know. It was a punishable offense to not know. "I'll find out, sir."

"Do you like it here, Dean?"

"I..." Dean blinked, puffing his face and grimacing.

"Hey, Dean. No one's here but you and me. You're not on TV. Nobody gives a shit how many faces you make. Do you like it here, Dean?"

"No, sir." Inside, he cringed.

"Well, that's good. You have to be crazy to like it here, Dean. Nobody likes it here." Fogarty smiled slowly, watching Dean's surprised eyes. "What, did you think I liked it here? Hey, Dean. I may be an asshole, but I'm hardly crazy."

"Yes, sir."

"What do you mean, 'Yes, sir'? Huh?" Fogarty's voice went hard again.

"Sir, I..." Dean exhaled with force, his chest all but disappearing under the bulky sweatshirts. "Nothing at all, sir."

"So, anyway, Dean," Fogarty rose slowly from the chair and began to dress for evening meal. "Eat shit. That's the military. The question isn't whether you like it, the question is why you're doing it, and what you're going to do *about* it. Do you think Roger Bannister *liked* it when he was running the four-minute mile?"

"Sir, I'll find out, sir. I doubt it, sir."

"Well, that's what this is, Dean. A real long mile." Fogarty grinned, anticipating his own little joke. "A four-*year* mile."

Fogarty pulled on his trousers and sat back down in his chair, lacing his shoes. "Did you learn your sports questions?"

"Sir, yes sir."

"I swear I can't believe any American male can live to be nineteen and not know how many runs a home run scores. That wasn't even tricky, Dean." Fogarty pulled on a crisp white shirt and began to fit his black tie. "So, how many points is a home run, troll?"

"Sir, it depends on how many men are on base at the time, sir. If—"

"It does not, dufus!" Fogarty turned from the mirror and began walking toward Dean. "Any time you answer a question around here, Dean, you don't give any goddamn 'it depends' bullshit, do you understand me? We've been *over* and *over* this."

"Aye, aye, sir." Dean blinked, his smooth face flushed again. "Sir, a home run scores one run. If there are men on base, the home run also allows them to score, sir."

"Better." Fogarty finished fitting his tie, looking at Dean through the mirror. "How many points is a soccer goal?"

"One, sir."

"Are you sure?" Fogarty glanced quickly at Dean again. "If you guess, it's your ass. I mean it."

Dean pondered it, his thin lips pursed, his eyes marbles again, the rest of him perfectly frozen in his brace. He blinked. "Yes, sir."

"Lucky man. All right, Dean," Fogarty took his service dress blue jacket from his wall locker and began meticulously brushing it with a whisk broom, removing every speck of lint. "How many points do you get when you make a goal in basketball?"

"Two, sir."

Fogarty's eyes flashed quickly at Dean. "You're positive?"

Dean swallowed hard, blinking his eyes again. He sweated profusely, from his run or maybe from Fogarty. "Yes, sir."

"How about a free throw? How many points is a free throw?"

Dean stared straight ahead, squinching his eyes and working his mouth.

"Be still, tool. I'm not interested in how hard you're trying, I'm interested in hearing your answer. How many points, Dean?"

"A free throw is only one point, sir."

"You're sure."

"Sir, yes sir." Dean's face looked as if he were on the down side of a high roller coaster ride.

"Uh huh. All right." Fogarty took the coat from the hanger and put it on, examining its fit in the mirror. "Now. If I kick a field goal in football from thirty yards out, how many points does my team get?"

Dean considered it for a long moment. "Three, sir."

"You're absolutely positive." Fogarty fastened the gold buttons of his coat.

"Yes, sir."

"What about if I kick it from twenty yards away? How many points?"

Dean was a frozen, contemplative statue on the outside, but inside he was still sliding down that roller coaster, falling so fast that his stomach was emptying into his throat. "Two, sir."

"You're sure." Fogarty adjusted his tie, still looking into the mirror.

"Yes, sir."

"Then I suppose you'll bet your ass on it. Do you bet your ass, Dean?"

He had to, of course. It was another of those things, those illusory questions to which only one answer was allowed. You bet your ass at Navy when you first opened your mouth, not when someone finally asked. "Yes, sir."

"Your bare ass?"

"My bare ass, sir?"

"No, your mother's bare ass. Your bare ass, Dean. I want to hurt you. I can't hurt you through three pairs of sweatgear and a pair of gym shorts."

"Aye, aye, sir. My bare ass sir."

"Drop 'em, Dean." Fogarty picked up his Naval Academy atlas, which weighed nearly five pounds. It was traditional punishment for a plebe who guessed; only the bare ass was Fogarty's little invention. He lectured Dean as the plebe busily unlaced and dropped his bulky load of sweatsuits. "I hate a guesser more than anything in the goddamned world, Dean. It means you're a coward. Someday somebody's going to *die*, just because you don't have the guts to say you don't really know the answer. Wrong answer because of one man's gutless bullshit, hundreds of men die." Dean stood against his wall again, three pair of sweatsuits and one set of dark blue gym shorts gathered at his ankles as if he were standing in a pile of dirty laundry.

"Lean over and touch your toes." Dean obediently came to the middle of the room and leaned forward. "Now, Dean. I don't want any guessing. I'm going to send you the answer in code. You just count the number of times I whack your fat little ass, and you'll have the answer." Fogarty took a two-step running leap and hit Dean as if he were swinging a baseball bat. The atlas whacked resoundingly and Dean came to an immediate attention.

"Beat Army, sir!"

"Oh, but we're not done, are we?"

"No, sir." Dean's ass and face had already turned red. He leaned forward again.

Whack. "Beat Army, sir!"

"Well, that's obviously not the answer, right, Dean?"

"Right, sir."

Whack. "Beat Army, sir!"

"How about three?" Dean's ass was quivering, as were his lips. Fogarty noticed that, and laughed. "Your ass and your mouth are both shaking, Dean. That must mean something. Yes, sir. Somebody ruined a perfectly good asshole when they put teeth in that mouth. So how about it Dean? Three?"

"Yes, sir."

"You're certain?"

Dean blinked his eyes, hesitating. He spoke softly, as if defeated. "No, sir."

"That's better. I didn't think you were." Outside, the chow-caller sang the five-minute call to evening meal. "Bring around a Form Two for failure to know a professional question: the number of points a field-goal scores."

"Aye, aye, sir."

"You didn't think I was going to forget, did you Dean, just because I took your ass for guessing?"

"No, sir."

"It just would have been easier if you hadn't guessed."

"Yes, sir."

"You're camping out tonight?"

"Yes, sir."

"Good. And tomorrow morning you're going to go running with me. Zero-five-thirty. Be ready to roll when I come knocking on your door."

*... And I could sleep on Saturdays, all the way to Sunday if I'd been out drinking or maybe with a woman and it had gone all right, I'm not any Casanova but then a lot of women don't ask for that and there would be time to develop it, time to think about it, time time time...* "Aye, aye, sir."

"Do up your sweatgear." Outside the chow caller announced four minutes until formation. Dean hurriedly tied the drawstrings, one at a time, fumbling at his waist. "Make sure you take a shower, with soap, before you go to formation."

"Aye, aye, sir."

"All right, Dean. When I blink I want to be able to open my eyes and not see you in front of me. That's how fast I want you to disappear. Got it?"

"Yes, sir."

Fogarty smiled. The chow caller screamed three minutes. Fogarty whispered the word. "Blink."

Dean was a whir of motion, a rat scurrying for quick sanctuary as he dashed by Fogarty for the door. Fogarty screamed after him, "Get out get out get out, mung!"


Dean bolted into his room, dropping his rifle onto his bed and peeling off the three sets of sweatgear, cursing and tossing clothes, on the brink of rage. The chow caller screamed two minutes. Peckarsky was standing in front of the mirror, putting on his jacket.

"Give me a hand, huh, Ski? Start the water."

Peckarsky ran to the shower and turned the water on and Dean finished stripping, then danced underneath the nozzle like a child running through a sprinkler, making sure he touched a bar of soap in order to comply with regulations about taking a shower, with soap, after a come-around. Peckarsky tossed him a towel as he jumped back out.

"You asshole. You left the water on cold."

"Bitch bitch bitch." Peckarsky followed him over to his side of the room, where he had left his uniform and shoes and cap as if on an assembly line, shined and brushed, ready to be jumped into. Peckarsky gave him a quick tuck, then held his coat for him as he finished his tie. One minute. "He ran your ass, huh?"

"Could have been worse." Dean fitted his cap and quickly inspected himself in the mirror, then bolted for the door with his roommate. "He's an asshole, but at least he makes sense."

# Chapter Seven: 1930

Her father was a navy captain, class of 1941, who had won a Silver Star as a destroyerman in the battle of Savo Island, and a Bronze Star as a PT boat commander in the battle of the Surigao Straits. Of his twenty-seven years' active duty, almost fifteen had been spent at sea. Sixty-hour work weeks on the Joint Chiefs of Staff in the Pentagon were a luxury for the family. They saw more of Captain Bruce Garnett than they had in years.

Her brother was a lieutenant (junior grade), class of 1965, who had gone through flight school and was at that moment stationed on an aircraft carrier off of Yankee Station, in the South China Sea. Bruce Garnett, junior, had already piled up a stack of air medals and a Distinguished Flying Cross from the front seat of his F-4 Phantom, and had been down inside North Vietnam after losing one plane to anti-aircraft fire, being rescued by a courageous helicopter pilot from the ship as virtually the whole squadron scrambled, providing close air support to prevent his capture.

Her mother was merry, brave in her own adamant way, a sturdy Pennsylvania Dutchwoman who converted chaotic moves and painful separations into normalcy, who was content not only to wait, but who had, over the years, made waiting itself an essential pastime, a reason to exist, a form of nobility. This is the world, her mother taught her from her first suckling gasp. Have faith.

When her brother graduated in 1965, her family had journeyed from her father's duty station at Long Beach, California, for the June Week ceremonies, and Bill Fogarty had been her blind date. A year later, Captain Garnett was assigned to the Pentagon, and she had entered American University, in Washington, D.C. She had somehow worked up the temerity to drop Fogarty a short note inside a funny card, announcing her arrival to the Washington area, and he had immediately invited her to Annapolis for a football game. They had been inseparable ever since, and would marry upon Fogarty's graduation. A marriage made in Valhalla, Swenson often teased.

Linda Fogarty walked through the fire doors into the Rotunda and she stood waiting for him in front of the TO

THOSE WHO WENT BEFORE US posters, in her own way as much a part of the Naval Academy as he. In four months, she would fill her mother's conduit just as fully as her brother had filled her father's.

She was all eyes and legs as he walked toward her, her body bundled in a maroon coat, her large doe eyes watching his every step and he transfixed by the eyes and his favorite part, the legs. She touched him on the elbow as he reached her, a controlled, comforting gesture.

"I see they already have Ron's picture up."

There was sorrow in her voice but there was something else as well, a tone that had a lot in common with some Irish fisherman's wife who had just learned of the drowning of someone else's fisherman, and who knew full well that the sea could in one quick turn devour her own, but who knew more deeply than perhaps her man himself that all the drownings in Ireland could not wash the sea out of her own fisherman's soul. The sea is a devil around a fisherman's neck, a laughing seducer, and so is combat to the professional military man.

"It's been terrible over there the last two weeks." She spoke with an authority equal to his own as he opened the large main doors of Bancroft Hall for her. "I talked with Mom today and she said Dad has been working eighteen hours a day. The whole Pentagon is going crazy. She got a letter from Bruce yesterday and he said he's been flying around the clock."

"Yeah, and what the hell am I doing?" Fogarty shivered underneath his heavy long overcoat, turning up his collar to protect his ears from the wind. "Working out and running douchebag plebes, studying the water pressure on the side of a ship at twenty feet. Damn, I wish I was out of this place. I feel like a malingerer."

"Bill, could I ask you something?" She eyed him hesitantly as they walked across the echoing bricks of Tecumseh Court. "Promise you won't make fun of me, now."

"I can already tell this is going to be good." Fogarty grinned ironically.

"I keep hearing that word, and I don't like to let on I'm so naive, but I really don't know what it means."

"What word is that?"

Her face squinched in curiosity and embarrassment. "Douchebag."

Fogarty laughed hilariously, briefly putting his arm

121

around her as they strode along winding brick walkways toward Gate Three. "Ahhh, I don't believe it. No, really, I don't believe it. You're something, Linda. You're really something."

"You promised you wouldn't laugh." The dark eyes dominated her small, pretty face as she joined his laughter with her own defensive giggle.

"No, I don't believe you can be a woman and live to be twenty years old and not know what a douchebag is."

"So why do you think I asked, dummy?" She reached out and punched him on the shoulder. She liked to hit him. It was a way of affirming his strength.

"All right." They walked through Gate Three and started down the cobbled streets of Old Town, on Maryland Avenue. He felt protective of her. She was knowing and yet naive, so mature when it came to large things like accepting separations and even deaths, yet so childlike when it came to simple things for other women, such as the definition of a douche. "When a woman and a man...you know, have sex?"

"Yeah?" Her eyes grew bright and smiled encouragingly to him, like a child waiting for a story. "Oh, I really chose a good one, didn't I?"

"Well, anyway, a woman needs to wash her insides out, sometimes, and when she does, she does it with a douchebag."

"That's what I *thought* it was."

"Oh, bullshit. You didn't have the slightest idea." She punched Fogarty again. It was true; she hadn't. "So, anyway, when you call a guy that, you're just ridiculing him. Like he's not even a man, he's a tool for cleaning out the leavings of a real man. Something like that."

"That's nauseous."

They reached the Little Campus Inn and walked inside, searching for a table. "Life's nauseous, Linda. You should know that."

"It is not. It's simple if you're simple. And it's happy if you're happy. And it's screwed up if you're screwed up."

They found a table and ordered two Cokes. Fogarty checked his watch. "Swede and Mack might come out. If they're not here by eight, they won't make it." He grimaced with exasperation, shaking his head. "Swede's going to pop the question to Sally Sue this weekend. Tomorrow night, it looks like. Talk about life being screwed up. Wow."

"Let's hope she says no." Linda's eyes went round in her disbelief. "Oh, my God. Can you imagine those two married?"

"There's no way she'll say yes. I just hope he can handle it." Fogarty sipped his Coke, shaking his head after he released the straw. "Yeah, old Swede has a tiger by the tail, and I don't think he can see far enough past her crotch to know that."

"Don't be crude."

"Well, hell. It's no fun seeing your best friend get kicked in the face." Fogarty grimaced again. "Yeah, Sally Sue is a real good lay. Just ask half the men on Capitol Hill."

"Bill, you don't know that."

"The hell I don't." Fogarty drained his coke. "*Swede* even knows it. He's literally bumped into men coming out of her place as he was going in." Fogarty looked dubiously at Linda. "Love is blind, and all that. He thinks he can change her."

"The first time he deploys for eight months to WesPac or the Mediterranean he'll find out just how much she's changed, too. Oh, who are we to talk like this, Bill? It's cruel. She won't say yes, so we're just going to have to help console him, that's all. All the rest of this is just out of place."

"That's Swede, every time he goes into D.C. Out of place. That's his biggest problem. In Battle Lake, Minnesota, when she goes to bed with you it means she loves you. He can't get past that." Fogarty's eyebrows raised. "Sally Sue loves the whole world."

"Anyway, here they come, so stop it." Linda waved to them, smiling. "Over here!"

McClinton waved back, then he and Swenson made their way past other tables and booths toward the two. Fogarty watched them, feeling he had experienced his whole childhood with them, grown up from the first incubator days of plebe summer all the way to 1968, saying that year over and over until it had become the benchmark for deliverance. Now here it was 1968, and he and Swenson and McClinton, like three Siamese triplets joined at the umbilical cord, were about to experience life. Already a small nostalgia mixed with that elation.

Swenson was a combination of intelligence and innocence, and the Academy had furthered both parts of that dichotomy. The lanky product of one of western Minnesota's rural farm-and-fishing villages had blazed through the Academy's academic program with almost straight A's, and often spent more time tutoring classmates than he did studying himself. He was undeniably brilliant in those areas where midshipmen were required to study, particularly mathematics and the physical sciences. At the same time, having been thrown into the isolation of the Academy directly after graduating from high school in the isolation of small-town Minnesota, Swenson was often baffled by the world outside Bancroft Hall. Navy had developed his ability to think, to withstand pressure, to lead. But it had kept him in a state of suspended adolescence. Swede Swenson fell in love at the drop of a hat, and spent many nights in canary-yellow sorrow, contemplating his misery like Goethe's young Werther.

McClinton was a monster, given to brash hyperbole, who underneath a muscular facade was as gentle as a puppy. His father was an army colonel, product of West Point, and McClinton in his brash confrontive way had picked Navy as the surest device to announce his adulthood, his independence from his dad. Secretly, McClinton had a hard time for more than a year simply convincing himself to declare his loyalty to Navy after having been weaned on his duty to West Point, and even spending three years growing up inside the Military Academy grounds, where his father had been an instructor. And, not so secretly, McClinton wasn't much for the military in any form. He wanted to be a pilot, a "jet jock," up in the air where no one but God could tell him how to crash.

In the dim light McClinton could be seen scowling at one particularly long-haired student from St. John's College, the other school in Annapolis. McClinton was famous throughout the Brigade for having mauled one "Johnny" the previous autumn. As the Brigade was marching, company by company, along the streets of Annapolis toward the Navy-Marine Corps Stadium for a home football game, the "Johnnies" had gathered in their usual way in front of their campus and harassed them. The midshipmen, in military formation, were powerless to retaliate. One long-haired Johnny had come too close, though, actually standing in the street, screaming "Fascists" at the midshipmen. McClinton, on the right-hand side of the company formation, had been unable to control himself. He reached out with one massive arm and grabbed the Johnny by his pony tail, throwing him into the middle of the company. The midshipmen had continued to march, solemnly keeping step, singing one of the many Academy songs, as the entire length of the company punched and elbowed the Johnny before he dashed out of the back end of the formation, hysterical and bruised.

And now every time McClinton saw a long-haired, wiry St. John's student, he scrutinized him, hoping it would be the one who had called him a Fascist. He wanted to finish the job. The student at the table glanced curiously back at McClinton, and the huge weightlifter moved on toward Fogarty and Linda, satisfied that he had not yet found last fall's offender.

"He ain't the one." Fogarty grinned comfortably at his former roommate as he and Swenson sat down. "If he'd been the one, he'd have shit right in his chair when you started staring at him."

"*Bill.*" Linda touched his arm, shaking her head at Swenson and McClinton.

"Well, I'd like to find that son of a bitch, I really would." McClinton looked around the room.

"Come on, Mack." Swenson smiled resignedly, used to McClinton's puffery. "They all think that way. It doesn't do much good just to dwell on one of them."

"Maybe we ought to kick all their asses, then." McClinton turned back around, forgetting the Johnnies. "You're coming to the party tomorrow night, aren't you?" He smiled mischievously to Linda. "Guaranteed to gross you out."

"Yeah, we're coming." Fogarty glanced uneasily at Linda. "I forgot to tell you. Mack and the boys are throwing a little bash out at their place. It'll be fun."

"My parents are coming down for your fight ... "

"No-o-o-o-o, you can't bring them." Swenson held his forehead, laughing. "Captain Garnett would *not* understand."

Fogarty shrugged. "We'll have a cup of coffee with your parents, then go to the party. Okay?"

"Come on, Linda, you'll love it." Swenson leaned across the table toward her, speaking easily. "Sally Sue's coming. You'll have somebody to relate to."

She smiled, giving in. "All right, if you really want to, Bill. I just remember the last one of these we went to, when George what's-his-name walked up and started to grab my...breasts when we walked into the door."

"Oh, he was pretty drunk. George is my friend. He wouldn't do that normally." Fogarty shrugged it off. "Hell, his girl lives in Mississippi. He goes stark raving mad most of the time."

"Besides," Mack grinned across the table. "He wasn't just picking on you, Linda. George is like that to *all* the little girls."

"Normal people don't go around grabbing women by the

breasts when they walk into the door, just because they miss their girlfriend in Mississippi." She paused, considering it. "Unless I've been more sheltered than I thought."

"No, you're right, Linda. It won't happen again. I promise." Fogarty put an arm around her, gesturing toward the whole world with his other arm. "Hell, I'll personally break a chair over anybody's head who tries to do a thing like that again."

She shook her head, smiling whimsically, defeated. "You'd love it. Then you could get into a brawl."

"No one will ever touch your breasts again." Fogarty smiled quickly, shrugging as he stared apologetically at her, then at his friends. "Heh heh. Except me, of course. But I guarantee, Linda, I'll protect them with my very own honor."

Mack's hands came slowly across the table, a wild gleam lighting his face. Linda's eyes went slowly wide, following McClinton's huge hands. Fogarty immediately grabbed a fork and raised it in the air, staring tautly at Mack, grinning with determination. "You son of a bitch! One more inch, McClinton, and I'm going to fork the hell out of you!"

Mack ceased his probing, laughing as he settled back into his chair. "See, Linda? I was just showing you he meant it. Now, don't worry about this party. We'll *all* take care of you."

"Oh, knights in shining armor. You'll probably offer me up as a target, just so you can get into a fight." She rose and leaned forward, an act of medieval courtesy.

"Excuse me, my lords, but I have to go to the bathroom."

Swenson watched her as she walked away. "She on the rag?"

"Goddamn it, Swede, stay out of my private affairs, will you?"

"Hell, I didn't mean anything. Most of the time when they get up real fast like that, with their purse in their hand, they're on the rag, that's all."

"Listen to Mister Smooth." McClinton shook his head, staring sardonically at Swenson. "Hey, Fogarty, talk this dildo out of proposing to Sally Sue, will you?"

Fogarty sipped from a second Coke, which Swenson had bought for them. The Johnnies were drinking beer. It always rankled him that midshipmen were prevented by state law and by regulations from drinking alcohol, while every other man or woman his age who visited Annapolis could do so at will. He felt like a high school boy sipping Coke after Coke in public places as

126

people younger than he enjoyed a brew. "I can't talk him out of anything. He's smarter than I am. But you'd better watch it, Swede, no kidding. You're moving too damn fast again."

"This is real."

"Oh, Swede. You never know what you're getting with a woman. You can sit over a cup of coffee or a Coke like this for five hours a day, every weekend of the year, or you can lay in bed with her for five hours, talking about everything under the sun. You can think you know the inside of her mind like it was your own. Then some silly thing happens and you see a whole new side of her, something that didn't come out when things were so hunky-dory and the waitress was pouring the coffee or you and she were all wrapped up in each other's bodies."

Swenson fiddled with his own Coke, staring at it. "I think I know people, Bill."

"So do I. But you've just got to be careful, you know? This Sally Sue, man, she's... Hell. Look, Swede. Women aren't like men, you know? With men you can look inside each other and read each other to your bones. You can talk with a man for five minutes and have a damn good idea whether or not he'll push back, how far he'll take it before you're going to end up on the floor with your hands at each other's throats. Men are easy to read. They don't have this...subtlety. Women don't have to fight head on to get what they want. They're more indirect. They have to throw up smokescreens, be pleasant. Hell, Swede. Only another woman can really comprehend what's really going on."

"Do you ever think this way about Linda?" It was a deliberate intrusion, an attempt to hurt Fogarty back.

"I guess I did, at first. But I've been around Linda for two years. I know her pretty well. And I'm the only man she's ever been with."

Swenson's normally placid eyes flashed. "You've got no right to bring that up. You can't hold a person's past over their head. It's irrelevant. Why the hell shouldn't a woman experiment? Men do it all the time."

"I'm sorry, Swede. It's none of my business." Fogarty finished his second Coke. "It's just that the three of us have been through an awful lot together, and I hate to see you get hurt. It brings out the mother in me."

"Some things you just have to do on your own." Swede's own face seemed puzzled, mystified at his predicament.

Fogarty studied him. Swenson was so proper, so painfully

shy around women, so much a product of Battle Lake, Minnesota, which still so gloriously celebrated his admission to the Academy. And he had somehow, perhaps through his ponderous, intellectual ways that often passed for worldliness, hooked into a tornado. Sally Sue Crown was playing, it was clear to everyone who watched them together. Men were her talent. She could attract a man, make him feel like heaven itself had descended on him, then once the challenge wore off she would cut him loose with unemotional abruptness. It was a game, a form of self-gratification, and Swenson had become powerless to interrupt the cycle as it worked its way through him.

"If she screws you over, Swede, we'll do a job on her." Mack leaned over toward Swenson, smiling devilishly.

"Yeah, we'll roll a frag under her door." Fogarty laughed.

"Shoot her in the kneecaps." Mack's eyes were bright again.

"That's what you know about women." Swenson, the sudden expert, the suffering cuckold, waved them both off.

"Yeah, he's right." Mack settled back into his chair. "We can't even grab her by the tits. The bitch would love it."

"Goddamn it, *stop* it!" Swenson's narrow, sharp-featured face was miserable.

"I see we're having a wonderful time." Linda walked toward them, smiling with irony.

"Well, we've got to make like an atom and split." Fogarty glanced at Swenson, the physics genius. "I thought Swede would *react* to that. Ah, well." He rose wearily, grabbing Linda's coat from her chair and helping her into it.

Mack nodded to Linda. "Don't keep lover boy out too late. He's got a fight tomorrow night, you know. Early to bed breaks the other man's head. Something like that. Quick to sleep kills the creep."

"Speaking of creeps," Fogarty slowly buttoned his overcoat. "I'm taking our man Dean out running tomorrow morning—the Academy tour. Hope you don't mind, Swede."

"Tie a weight around him and drop him into the river. I'll never tell."

"Ah, he's doing all right." Fogarty grabbed his cap. "He just never learned when to use his brains and when to use his balls, that's all." Fogarty gave his former roommates a short wave as he moved toward the door. "John Dean, the Plebe Machine. We'll make him a tiger!"

# Chapter Eight: 2100

"Hello?" The voice on the other end of the telephone was soft and modulated, too comfortable, actually, to be having anything to do with Navy's mad regimens. Classical music filtered into Dean's ear from somewhere behind the soft voice.

"Good evening, sir. This is Midshipman Dean, fourth class, returning a phone call to Professor Thad, sir." Dean held the yellow piece of paper in one hand as he spoke, examining the message the Mate of the Deck had left in his room. He sat inside a telephone booth in a room filled with them, a dozen telephone booths, all occupied by midshipmen calling home or girlfriends. He was in his full uniform, as was required whenever a plebe left his room for any reason. Sitting still in the booth after a day of Fogarty, he felt as if he would fall asleep at any moment.

"Mister Dean. Thanks for returning my call. I was beginning to wonder if you got my message, actually." Professor Thad was a rambler. Dean checked his watch as the professor droned on. "I called the Main Office to leave the message and I talked with the nicest young man, who fully explained the process to me. Midshipman Caligari, as I recall. He said something about the fourteenth company. A plebe. Well, anyway, he did explain to me that it took some time to get the messages actually to the rooms, that they had to be relayed to the battalion office, and then up to the Mate of the ... something. I've forgotten all of the gory details. But you did get it. Wonderful. How are you holding up?"

"Sir?" Professor Thad's question had an edge of camaraderie in it, as if he and Dean were undergoing some mutual ordeal.

"Are you making out all right? I want you to know that I've been asking some questions since our conversation today. I would feel, well, less than courageous if I simply let all of this slide by. It's so obvious that you have been maltreated, and I believe what they do over there is absolutely *enraging*, anyway. What does it really prove, except that some men have the capacity for unlimited cruelty? It confirms so much I've always believed about the military *system*—"

"Professor, wait a minute." Dean's instincts were ordering up nausea. "Sir, I don't recall saying I was being maltreated, sir. I—"

"You told me you were being hazed. Mister Dean, I asked you if you were being hazed and you distinctly said, as I recall, 'You might call it that.' Did you or did you not say that, Mister Dean?"

"I don't remember, Professor." Dean was wide awake now, sinking in quicksand. For some reason Professor Thad seemed intense, almost furious. "Really, I don't. I remember you asking me about the exam. That's all. I was in a hurry to get back to the Hall."

"I want to remind you of a few things, Mister Dean." The record in the background stopped. Shortly a new one began. "First of all, I am on your side. Second of all, you are bound by the honor system to answer my questions fully and completely."

Well, what do you know, thought Dean, the itchings of mistrust and even dislike overriding his gratitude at Professor Thad's interest. He bad-mouths the system and then invokes the system. "Sir, I appreciate it. I just don't remember telling you I'd been hazed."

"Are you being hazed, Mister Dean?" In the vacuum of Dean's hesitance, a piano played Chopin with all the delicacy of falling rose petals.

"They're running my ass, Professor. But that's all a part of it. It won't last long." Dean felt a panic crawl up his back, like the light hand of a laughing devil. "Professor, *please*—"

"I understand. I do understand, Mister Dean. I'm not trying to get you into any trouble. Are they breaking regulations?"

Fogarty's voice broke like an echo in his memory. *I don't want to hear another bullshit answer about the regulations. From now on, I am the regulations.* And yet he could not lie, above all else he could not lie, not even the smallest, tiniest small fib. Under the honor concept, he could be dismissed for even thinking an untruth. "Yes, sir. But it isn't material. What you don't understand, Professor, is that I'm doing alright. I'll make it out of this. You could hurt me more than you could help."

"I'm not going to get you into any trouble, Mister Dean. I want to help. When one of my brightest students fails a test that he could pass without studying, something wrong is going on. I have a *duty.*"

"If you want to help me, Professor, leave me alone for now. Please? If it gets worse, I promise I'll let you know."

"You're a man of courage, Mister Dean. I admire that. What are they doing to you that is against regulations?"

Thad was beginning to strike Dean as an unrelenting voyeur, someone who by virtue of his faint authority was peering inside of Dean's own mind. "Professor, you're going to get me into trouble. Can't you understand that? I won't fail any more tests. I've been trying all year to get these people off my back and now I have a chance to do it. Please, sir. Thanks and all that. But I don't need this."

"Did you speak to Captain Lenahan about this today?"

"Yes, sir."

"What did he say?"

"He asked me if there was anything I needed to tell him. I said there wasn't. That was it. Captain Lenahan knows how things work."

"He strikes me as something of a maniac."

"Professor, I've got to go. I've got a lot to do before taps, and I have to get up early tomorrow."

"I understand, Mister Dean." Again a sort of vicarious camaraderie crept into Thad's soft voice. "Well, I'll let you go. But you know I'm concerned for you."

"Thanks a lot, Professor. And if you really want to help me, I hope you'll let me work this out myself."

"Well, you hang in there."

"All right, sir. Good-bye."

What a gutless man, thought Dean, chopping back to his room, the hall lights a stream of fluorescent white above his head. What a goddamn loser.

# Chapter Nine: 2230

"You have scars."

"So do you."

"Yeah, but I'm supposed to."

"That's where you're wrong, Ted. That's where men are always wrong. I'm supposed to. You're not." She ran a long, delicate finger down the blue line where once her belly had been split open by a surgeon's knife, beginning just underneath her navel and then stopping when her finger touched her pubic hair. "That scar made a baby. It gave life. Women do it all the time." She reached across the sheets and ran the same long, neatly manicured finger along the side of his stomach. It dropped abruptly into the rough gouge where a bullet had dug and she massaged it gently, teasing him with a coyness in her voice. "And what did your scar make?"

Lenahan watched her, feeling an enormous warmth overcome his sensibilities once again, trying to tell himself that it was not a sense of absolute peace she gave him, but rather a numbness that was a parody of peace, that he had no right to make love to another man's wife. Not merely another man, but a friend. Not merely a friend, but a classmate who had spent four long years inside the same room with him, dreaming of this gentle messenger of tranquility who had borne him three children and who now stroked Ted Lenahan's belly with a fondness that had to come from somewhere other than animal attraction, from some sort of deep emotion, whatever he dared call it. So what is love and what are memories? That was what his own wife had asked him after four months or a hundred casualties, depending on how one was measuring the time.

"It doesn't seem that long ago, you know?" He stroked her hand as it massaged his scars. "You still have great tits, Angie." He leaned over and kissed them.

"I breast-fed, too. I can't explain it." She giggled softly. "I suppose if I'd worried about them, they'd be drooping to my belly by now. Was it bad, Ted?" Her fingers still explored several jagged holes in his midsection.

"They took my spleen out. And some guts." Lenahan laughed ironically. "What the hell is a spleen for, anyway? Nobody could tell me. But it made me go soft, that's what Pratt says. Ah." He touched her belly. "You probably hurt a lot worse when you had your kids. I remember Mary—" Her hand withdrew in an involuntary jerk. Lenahan came up on an elbow. "I'm sorry. We weren't going to, were we? Anyway, Mary told me after she had the boy that it felt like she'd shit a watermelon. God, can you imagine Mary coming up with something like that?"

"No." Angie reached over to the night table and took one of his cigarettes, then lit it. "I guess we can't just not talk about them, can we? I mean, we can't cut them out of our conversations like they weren't a part of our lives." She dragged deeply, not looking at Lenahan. "Steve's going over. He's been begging for orders, and the Admiral is going to get them for him." She gave her soft giggle again, shaking her head incredulously. "He actually envies you, can you believe it? Ted Lenahan has been in *combat*. Ted Lenahan has been *wounded*. And all Steve Wheeler has done is fry people who don't wake up when the reveille bell goes off."

"It doesn't take a whole hell of a lot of anything to get wounded. That's why they call it the Idiot Award."

"Yeah, but he doesn't know that. Yet."

"Well, I guess everybody has to find out for himself." Lenahan also lit a cigarette. "Like me. I couldn't wait. And look at all it did for me. I got hookworm, ringworm, gooksores, got shot, and my wife left me. Then, for my reward, they let me come back to my alma mater and fry people who don't wake up when the reveille bell goes off."

"Oh, Ted." She laughed warmly and kissed his stomach. "It really doesn't seem like seven years, does it? All the things we used to do together, you and Mary and Steve and me. The June Week cottages, everybody so careful to protest their purity, then being even more careful to rotate through, so no one would have to catch anyone else screwing in the cottage." She laughed again, deep in her throat. "You were doing it with Mary youngster year, weren't you?"

"Of course I was." He stubbed out the cigarette and examined her chiseled face. Her eyes showed just the first signs of wrinkling aging, like a green and flourishing tree that suddenly goes red and yellow at its outermost branches. "But I watched you, even then I wanted you, but I was so put on with honor and loyalty that I couldn't admit it, even to myself. I guess that's what the world does to you. It makes you realize that honor and loyalty are traps with no reward."

"Do you really believe that?" She reached over him, her heavy breasts resting on his chest, and put out her own cigarette. He grabbed her when she touched him, kissing her neck and then her face, laughing at her surprise. Then she pushed him away, staring deeply into his eyes, exuding a mellow warmth that calmed him, assured him of the sensibility of this deception that was almost as close as incest, the taking of a brother's wife. "I just can't tell you how I felt when I heard that you'd been wounded, and then that Mary had left. It was almost as if Steve had been wounded, it hurt so much. Then when I heard about you and Mary I felt...oh, I don't know." She flipped her hair out of her face, then regarded him with a steady open stare. "I just really worried about you. I couldn't stop thinking about you. Is that love?"

Lenahan lay flat on his back, staring at the ceiling. "So what is love, and what are memories?"

"Is that from one of your poems?"

He chuckled. "No, that's what Mary said to me when she told me she was splitting. Can you believe it, she came all the way to Hawaii to tell me she was leaving me. She didn't want to put it in a letter, she said. Jesus Christ. If she'd written me, at least I'd have been able to go on R and R in Bangkok or something." He lay very still, his eyes lost in the stars that would have been above him if he were able to see beyond the ceiling. "I know that's not much of an answer to your question. It's just kind of hard to think in those terms anymore. Is that love? Hell, who knows? 'Nay, whatever comes/One hour was sunlit and the most high gods/May not make boast of any better thing/Than to have watched that hour as it passed.' There's a poem for you. Ezra Pound."

She lay comfortably against him. "You're really good. That was beautiful. Somehow, I don't think people expect poetry out of you, Ted."

"Poetry is the haven of the homeless, the unanointed, the lost."

"Who said that?"

"Me."

"Really? You made that up?" She rubbed his chest and then his stomach, her fingers playing scars like coarse strings from a crooked banjo.

The phone rang. She startled in the dim light of her bedroom, her fingers involuntarily digging into Lenahan's stomach. It rang again, and then again. Lenahan nodded toward where it sat on a night table. "Go ahead, answer it."

"Hello?" Her voice sounded suddenly soggy with sleep. "Oh, hi." She raised her eyebrows to Lenahan. "No, I didn't see the news. What are you doing watching the news? I thought you were supposed to be out frying people." She rolled her eyes. "It was a joke, honey, okay?" Another pause. "Well, Robert Kennedy's an asshole. He just wants to be President."

She touched Lenahan's leg as she sat on the edge of the bed, an absent gesture that nonetheless seemed foreign to him as he lay there watching her speak to her husband, continuing a conversation that had no doubt begun years before, Robert Kennedy merely manifesting the latest particle in a stream that had run between them since they were both teenagers. And who am I, thought Lenahan, watching her hand run along his thigh. "Yeah, Stevie's fine. Okay. See you tomorrow."

She turned back to him, leaning over him, her breasts against his stomach once again. "I'm sorry. You're not upset, are you?"

"Mommy. Mommy." A small, hollow voice echoed from the other side of the door. "Why is your door locked, Mommy?"

"Because I wanted to be alone, sweetheart."

"Oh. Who was on the phone?"

"It was your daddy. He called to say he missed you. Now, go back to bed."

"Would you tuck me back in?"

Angie seemed beside herself with embarrassment. Lenahan touched her shoulder, whispering to her. "Don't worry. Go ahead. I'm all right."

She kissed him on the cheek, confusing him with her sentiment in the midst of all the normal sentiments of her life, the emotions he was endangering, that he had no right to share. Then she kissed his chest, his stomach, his raised thigh, and finally rose from the bed, grabbing her robe and walking to the bedroom door.

"Come on, sweetheart."

"Why's the light on?"

"How can I find my robe in the dark?"

It was almost evil, the tangle of deceptions that spun off such a pure thing as desire. Is this what happened to me, wondered Lenahan, lying naked on his former roommate's sheets, their whiteness already stained from the leavings of his union with his former roommate's wife. How many California nights, far before Vietnam, did I lie in bivouac, wrapped alone in a dirty sleeping bag on the side of a dusty hill, while someone stained my sheets after violating the very essence of my marriage? And what is love if it never existed, and what are memories if they are false? Is that what she meant? Or is this all women, all men, caught up in a greater vise than God?

*Thou hast committed—fornication; but that was in another country, and besides, the wench is dead.* Who wrote that, mused Lenahan. Marlowe, I think. He reached for another cigarette, then thought better of it. Her kids would smell the smoke, and then what?

She walked back into the room, closing the door without a sound and locking it again, then walked toward him, smiling. Her full breasts made the fabric of her long robe move, their swaying dance a magic that transfixed his eyes, arousing him again. All his doubts, all his resolve fell in a soundless crash with her robe as it gathered in a heap on the floor beside the bed, dropping from her shoulders with a suddenness that made him lose his breath as he stared at her rich flesh, her gently smiling face.

He sat on the edge of the bed and watched the scar below her navel, then her heavy breasts, finally burying his face between them, his arms around her. She held his head and they swayed as she rocked with a pivoting motion, again and again, holding his head to her breasts.

"I want you." She said it over and over, in time with her rocking motion. "I want you. I want you. I want you."

"I can't take it." He stood up, holding her firmly by the shoulders and staring into her shocked and curious face. "I've got to go, Angie. I feel like I ought to be shot."

# Chapter Ten: 2300

"Good night, John. Sweet dreams."

"Funny man, Peckarsky." Dean pulled his blanket over him as he lay naked on the springs. You could get used to it, he decided. Secretly he tucked a portion of the blanket underneath him, between his bare ass and the springs. He wondered absently if it was an honor offense to sleep on part of his blanket instead of the springs, and then decided that it was merely disobeying an order. It would be an honor offense if Fogarty asked him and he told a lie. But who would catch him? He grinned ironically in the dark. Fogarty would. He'd find a tuft of lint on one spring and that would be enough.

Oh, the hell with it. He pulled the blanket back from underneath him. It wasn't worth the trouble.

# PART THREE:

---

# SATURDAY, FEBRUARY 10, 1968

# Chapter One: 0515

The alarm clock cut through his sodden sleep with a laughing scream and Dean reached out, scratching a bare hip on a spring, and silenced it with a leaden arm. He sat on the edge of his bed, wrapped inside his blanket like a refugee, his mind so dull it was numb, his limbs heavy and weak. The room and the sky outside were pitch black but for a small light far out on the bay, like someone else's freedom. It was so still that when he rose the spring that squeaked behind him echoed off the wall.

He plodded toward the sink. It required thought, serious effort, to place one foot in front of the other. I wonder, thought Dean, turning on the small sink light and running water to shave, if this is what it feels like to be old. I can't even care enough in my own mind to be angry.

He lathered his face and shaved with a mechanical lethargy. There would not be another moment in the entire day to do so. He dried his face and slowly climbed into an athletic supporter and three separate pairs of sweatsuits, feeling vaguely like he imagined a mummy might, all tightly wrapped. He put a parka on over that, and his navy blue stocking cap, then sat down and laced his boondocker marching shoes, as ordered by Fogarty.

There, he thought, surveying himself in the mirror. Now I know what a teddy bear feels like from the inside out, or maybe a stuffed shrimp. Hey, that's pretty good. That's me. Stuffed shrimp. If I weren't so tired I'd laugh. He glanced at the alarm clock: five twenty-five. Five minutes to spare. Oh, Dean, you are a *fast* son of a bitch. And besides, maybe Fogarty would forget.

He only meant to sit on his bed, just to take the load off of his feet. Before he knew it he was lying down, the springs hooking into parts of his parka. If Fogarty forgot, I could sleep till reveille. Oh, sweet reveille. So nice…

"Dean, you asshole!" He woke suddenly, Fogarty shaking him furiously. "Did you go to bed in your sweatgear, you little candy ass?"

"No sir!" Dean bounced out of the bed and stood in a brace in front of it, suddenly wide-awake, his eyes wide and afraid. "I just finished getting ready, sir, and I lay back while I was waiting for you!"

"All right. I didn't think you'd do something like that. Well, let's get going, Dean. It's a brand-new day."

He could not contain his awe as he followed Fogarty through hallways and finally down a flight of steps. He moves like a lynx, thought Dean, watching the fluid, muscular motion of Fogarty's jog, his effortless, two-steps-at-a-time descent of the stairway. He looks like he could turn and disappear into a woods or run straight up the side of a mountain. He has honed himself, his body and his senses, until he is just on the edge of being wild. He is my anti-matter, mused Dean, thinking of his Modern Physics classes. If you folded him and me together, our energies would cancel each other out and we would both disappear.

"This way, negat." Fogarty broke through the doors and ran through a parking lot in the black icy air, following the edge of Thompson Field and then cutting up toward Ward Hall, the weapons building. He adjusted his gray scarf so that it was just in front of his chin. His legs were like well-timed pistons, his body loose and powerful. It occurred to Dean as he hobbled next to Fogarty in his uncomfortable boondockers that it was easier for Fogarty to run, actually, than it was for him to walk. Running was his natural state.

"You're going to get it easy this morning, Dean." Fogarty spoke effortlessly. "I'm just loosening up for my fight tonight."

They ran through a haunting ghost town. Nothing moved in the Yard: no people, no cars, not even the wind. Their boots clomped on the pavement and they breathed, Fogarty as if he were walking, Dean as if he were about to die. Little clouds of frosty air puffed in front of them with every breath. Other than that, it was like staring at a slowly changing dark watercolor of the Yard.

They passed a row of officers' housing, the huge old brick duplexes somnolent as normal people slumbered, not even an early bathroom light disturbing their solitude, then passed the Superintendent's house. Admiral Kraft's cavernous mansion was likewise dark. Up the empty street they ran, past great cobwebs of chestnut trees, and then the Chapel in its dominating place that made it the central feature of the Yard. On their right was the Herndon Monument, a gray phallus which Dean and his classmates would climb come June Week, the monument all greased, oozing with slick jelly, plebe year not officially over until the men of the class of 1971 had overcome the ooze and built a human wall and placed a cap on top of the monument, an ordeal that normally required hours.

The road bent and they followed it past the Naval Academy museum, repository of the exploits of famous graduates, and ran next to Sampson Hall, heading out toward Hospital Point. Everywhere they were surrounded by monuments and cannons, tributes and memorabilia to the naval profession.

Fogarty casually lectured Dean as they jogged. When they passed the chapel, he pointed at the heavy bronze front doors. "Do you know what's on the front doors, Dean? What does it say?"

It was required learning for every plebe. Dean gasped, trying to keep up with Fogarty as he responded. "Yes, sir. *'Non sibi, sed patriae,'* sir. A gift of the class of...of 1869, sir."

"That's right. What does it mean?"

"Not self, but country, sir."

"Do you believe that?"

"Yes, sir. Absolutely, sir." *Anything you say, sir. Leave me alone, sir.*

Next to Leahy Hall, the Language building, a large, ugly, ornate old monument had been erected to sailors who had died in Tripoli in the early nineteenth century. Fogarty pointed at it as they jogged past. "See that?" He grimaced in the dark. "Ugly old thing. A couple swabs bite the dust in eighteen hundred and they build a two-ton goddamn monument. Thousands die in World War One and Two and Korea and Vietnam, and we write their names on pieces of paper, even here. Eat shit, Dean. That's the twentieth century in a nutshell. We get so used to people dying that we forget each death was a gift."

He said the word so matter-of-factly, leaving it hang on the edge of a puffy little cloud of frost, that it echoed through Dean's conscience with each step. A gift a gift a gift. A gift?

"You better keep up with me, sweetheart."

"Aye, aye, sir."

They followed another turn in the road and jogged over a narrow wooden footbridge to Hospital Point, a huge, flat athletic field that had been brought out of the river years before with landfill. The field and river looked as one in the darkness, a desert of slush and ice. Far to their front, like a glimmer from

Dean's own memory, real people in real cars drove over a low drawbridge, on their way to early morning jobs.

Dean did not trust his legs on the icy slush. He could no longer feel the front of his thighs. He hesitated as he and Fogarty left the footbridge, running an icy path next to the concrete wall that kept the river away. One slip, he thought fearfully, watching the icy swells below him on his right, and I'll drown.

"Move it, Dean. Get going. We haven't even gone a mile yet." Fogarty nudged his shoulder, putting him off balance. It was a warning.

"Aye, aye, sir!" His hands were like ice. He could no longer feel his fingertips. He stepped like a dainty schoolgirl along the shadowed path.

"Quit *bagging* it." Fogarty pushed him suddenly and hard and he tumbled, bouncing off of hard spines of ice. He started to moan and Fogarty grabbed him by the neck, pulling at him. "I told you to move it. Now *get up*." Dean scrambled to his feet, terrified, jogging faster now, more afraid of Fogarty than of the swollen, ice-choked river.

"That's better. Don't hair out on me now, Dean."

Far across the river, on the sane side where normal people dwelled, a light went on in an upstairs bedroom. Dean watched the house from the corner of one eye as he struggled along the icy path, trying to imagine living on the other side of the river. Another light went on downstairs. A leisurely cup of coffee, Dean mused, picking his way along the path as Fogarty chided him from behind. Next year they'll let me drink coffee...

"Don't forget to turn, dummy, or you'll run into the river."

They ran the last leg of Hospital Point, the old hospital itself high on a hill before them. Dean found himself wishing for injury, a serious one that would remove him from Fogarty's tentacles. An operation, he dreamed, imagining himself languishing in a hospital bed for several weeks.

"Up through the cemetery. Come on, Dean. You're slowing down."

Dean leaned into the hill, feeling he had just run into a wall. His legs would not work properly and he gasped, slowing to almost a walking pace. Fogarty grabbed him by the arm and pulled him up the hill. He shook his arm from Fogarty's grasp, an act of unparalleled defiance.

"I can do it, sir. I can do it myself."

"Well, what do you know?"

The cemetery was dark as its own tombs, a haunting resting place for thousands who had passed through the conduit inside the Yard, graduates who had come back to the womb of their adulthood for their final rest. Fogarty elbowed Dean, grinning in the dark.

"You know why they put the cemetery next to the hospital, don't you Dean? So when those butchers who try to call themselves navy doctors fuck it up, they won't have to carry the bodies as far." He was almost funny, Fogarty, in his brutal sort of way.

They trod out of the cemetery, still the only moving objects on the road, and crossed a small bridge that spanned Dorsey Creek. The crew team's boathouse adjoined the creek, iced in for the winter. Worden Field, the parade ground that had sucked dull hours out of both their lives, lay like a large ice arena to their right, surrounded by huge red brick houses where the most senior officers lived. It looked peaceful to Dean, like a New England winterscape. It did not belong.

They turned on the road and ran along the water, coming up behind the laundry. Its tall smokestack was ornamented with a hand-painted inscription, "68 SEZ BEAT ARMY." Dean glanced at the words as they rounded Dewey Field, coming to the juncture of Dorsey Creek and the Severn again. He knew Fogarty was going to chide him for them. It took more than courage to climb the smokestack in the dead of night to put the class numerals on top. One had to first go AWOL from Bancroft Hall, an offense that could cost the perpetrator long weekends of isolation in his room. But still the game continued, members of different classes losing valuable sleep and taking great risks just to paint a number on a smokestack. The whole thing was beyond Dean. There were enough risks and there was never enough sleep.

Fogarty pointed to the smokestack, obviously proud. "So when is 'seventy-one going to get the guts to put their numbers back up there, Dean? Christ, my plebe year our numbers were never off the damn thing for longer than a day. And look at it now. Hell, Dean. We're just a bunch of tired old firsties."

"I'll find out, sir." It didn't matter. It just didn't matter.

He was wasted, drained, running on stone pillars of legs that somehow responded to his exhortations even though they were no longer alive. He felt his system shift gears again and he began to fade, running slower and slower even though his mind was still screaming at his legs to keep up with Fogarty.

Fogarty still breathed easily. Pull the air in. Force it out. Pull the air in. Force it out. He looked over to Dean. "Come on, Dean! Hell's fire, you drippy piece of mung! We haven't even done the seawall yet!" Dean was now gasping. "All right, Dean. I'm going to chant. You chant with me." Fogarty seemed even more energized. "I can run all night."

"I can run all night." They fit it to the cadence of their boots.

"And I can run all day."

"I can run all day." Dean picked up the cadence. His mind was off his pain.

"I can run all night."

"I can run all night."

"'Cause that's the Marine Corps way."

"'Cause that's the Marine Corps way."

"Great, Dean, great. You got it, baby. Come on, now. Keep it up."

"Aye, aye, sir." Dean felt better. Such a simple thing as a chant, he thought, making his boondocker boots hit the pavement in time with Fogarty's Marine Corps boots. But it works.

"Come on, Dean. *Sen*-try."

"Sentry."

"On guard."

"On guard."

"Bayonet."

"Bayonet."

"In the belly."

"In the belly."

"Bloo-o-ood!"

"Blood."

"Gu-u-u-uts!"

"Guts."

"Blood and guts!"

And so on. Fogarty reveled in it and Dean had to admit, secretly to himself, that it was indeed fun.

Bancroft Hall came nearer as they ran next to Luce Hall, the Navigation and Seamanship building. A few lights had now come on in some scattered rooms. Dean looked at the small blinks of his classmates just then beginning to prepare for reveille, and felt an undeniable, perverse pride in what Fogarty was subjecting him to. He was doing a little bit more.

"Left here, dufus." They passed Santee Basin and ran

143

along the edge of Farragut Field, another wide athletic ground that had been conjured up from the river's bottom. At the far corner of the field, luminous in the first streak of deep blue dawn before them, was the foremast of the U.S.S. *Maine*, whose sinking in Havana Harbor had touched off the Spanish-American war in 1898. And just past the foremast was the seawall.

"Are you ready, Dean?" Fogarty was peering at him as they ran, his eyes lit with anticipation. "Let's see what you've got inside you."

"Sir—" Dean's whole body was numb and drained. He gasped, watching the jagged, icy rocks that spread before him like sharp black terror. "Sir, I can't do it, sir. Not this morning, sir. I know I'll fall!"

Fogarty grimaced, almost nonchalant. "You goddamn worm, of course you can do it. Now, sprint right along behind me."

It was too dark to tell black rocks from mossy rocks from icy rocks. They simply erupted all along the edge of the water, great jagged shards that promised to split his skull. "No, sir! I can't do it, sir!"

"Why, you little shit! Get out there!" Fogarty pushed him hard, onto the beginning of the seawall. "Now, *walk* it, you goddamn baby. Walk the whole thing. I'm going to run it, and I'm going to come back and get you. I don't care if you have to get down on your belly and crawl, Dean, you're going to do the seawall. So *move*."

"Aye, aye, sir." Dean began hesitantly walking from rock to rock, feeling his way along the wall in the almost-dark, the juncture of the Severn River and the Chesapeake Bay surging just to his left, inviting him to slip in and have a cold drowning. Fogarty shot along the rocks like a madman possessed, a perfect human machine that danced so lightly on many of the rocks that it appeared he almost flew.

Dean stopped in his half-crawl, half-walk for a moment and watched Fogarty disappear in the darkness. A lynx, he thought, shaking his head in amazement and grudging admiration. A goddamned lynx! It was actually beautiful to watch, like football and ballet all rolled together.

Dean stood erect. He tried his feet tentatively, then hopped to the next rock. It made him feel good. He hopped again. Soon he was half-walking, half-running on the wide, jutting stones. I can *do* it, he decided, surprised at his success. I can really *do* it I can run like Fogarty, be like Fogarty you son of a bitch I can do your seawall. By the time Fogarty jogged back along the road, looking for him, Dean was very nearly running from rock to rock, only hesitating slightly as he picked out the next place to jump.

"Well, what do you know." Fogarty jumped onto the seawall again, and followed Dean. "We're going to have you sprinting this here seawall, Dean. Just wait and see."

Oh, Christ, thought Dean, hopping from stone to stone. Don't tell me I'm going to have to do this again.

Reveille raped Bancroft Hall, penetrating to its nerve ends. Lenahan strode the hallway, fully dressed in his green uniform, ribbons and shooting badges and barracks cover, carrying his leather gloves all rolled up like an imitation swagger stick. Click click click, his heels announced his approach in the silent numb afterwash of the harsh bells.

He watched with mild amusement as bathrobed midshipmen scurried back toward various rooms, passing the word that he was once again in the company area. They must think I thrive on this, he thought, marching down the center of the hallway. Ah, yes. Like I told Angie: my reward.

He turned along a side corridor and strolled it, digging his heels in to signal his approach. A tousled, baggy-eyed upperclassman in an Army bathrobe stumbled out of one room and almost walked into him, then came to attention, squinting and confused.

"Good morning, sir."

"Ah, Mister Boggs. It's good to see you're awake this morning, after Lieutenant Von Yerks found you otherwise disposed the other day. Restricting this weekend?"

"Uh, yes, sir." Boggs was still half-asleep, disoriented in his walking slumber.

"Well, enjoy yourself."

"ARE YOU ASSHOLES AWAKE YET?" It came from the main passageway. Lenahan could not restrain his mirth.

"Fuck you, Fogarty." A half-dozen rejoinders, from the hallway and from inside a few nearby rooms.

"OH, I HOPE YOU ARE, BECAUSE I WANT YOU TO SEE WHAT FOLLOWED ME HOME!"

Lenahan walked slowly toward the main passageway. He could hear the jeers emanating from a dozen upperclassmen.

Fogarty was still screaming and laughing. "OH, YEAH! MY MAN DEAN GREW HIMSELF ABOUT HALF A BALL THIS MORNING. HUH, DEAN?"

Dean stood against the centerpost of two fire doors in a ragged, weary brace, his eyes drained but focused, his face deep-red from the winter air. He still breathed heavily. Snot was dripping from his nose onto his lips and down his chin, drip drip drip, blending with sweat and melted frost. His leather boon-docker boots looked like black dishrags, wet and limp, and his sweatsuit trousers were soaked, caked with mud.

"DEAN MADE IT ALL THE WAY. HE EVEN CRAWLED THE SEAWALL. OF COURSE, WE HAD TO HELP HIM ALONG HERE AND THERE. BUT HELL'S FIRE, DEAN, BY NEXT WEEK YOU'RE GOING TO BE KICKING MY ASS. RIGHT, DEAN?"

Dean trembled from exertion. He did not look convinced. "Sir, yes sir." But nonetheless, noted Lenahan, studying the frail plebe as he approached, he seems…something.

"All right, Dean." Fogarty checked the clock. "You've got six minutes until come-around. Take a shower, read the newspaper, and report to me in your blueworks."

"Aye, aye, sir."

"Good morning, gentlemen." Lenahan stopped just behind Fogarty and slapped his gloves in his right palm, again and again, as if awaiting some explanation.

"Oh, good morning, sir." Fogarty came to attention, as muddy and wet and sweaty as Dean himself, but alive in the eyes, reveling in his condition. "Mister Dean and I have just completed a morning run, sir. I'm proud to report that Mister Dean made it the whole way, sir."

"With a little help, here and there?" Lenahan smiled, just at the edges of his mouth. "The seawall, too?"

"Well, he was a little slow on the seawall, sir. But he'll learn in time."

"I'll bet he will." Lenahan turned to Dean, whose eyes had become large marbles again in his terror of officers. "Mister Dean, I certainly hope you appreciate the extra time Mister Fogarty has been dedicating to your officer development. Years from now, you will look back and thank him, even if you resist that notion now." Lenahan turned back to Fogarty. "Well, don't let me interrupt you, Mister Fogarty. Carry on."

"Aye, aye, sir. Good morning, sir. Shower, Dean. Five minutes."

Word had gotten around in that magical way, through the grapevine that ties every military unit to itself with quick, excited phrases, warnings against trouble. The whole battalion was awake and industrious. Lenahan was glad. It made it all so much easier, really. Frying people was a drag.

He climbed a stairway, heading toward yet another company area. Steve Wheeler walked toward him on the steps, dressed in his blues and his sword, wearing white gloves and the epaulet that marked him as the Superintendent's aid. Lenahan saluted his roommate from those many years ago, half playfully. Wheeler saluted him back, laughing.

"What's up, roommie?"

"Fidelity." It was a dagger in his own heart as Lenahan gave off the traditional response, a vestige of their midshipman days. *Fidelity* was on the up-side of the Academy bayonet belt buckle that they wore to parade.

"You're up awful early. Can't sleep?"

"My little come-around. You haven't heard?" Lenahan smiled ironically, stopping on the stairway. "Von Yerks tore my company a new asshole the other day, so this is the wages of my sin. How's the Duty?"

"It sucks, what did you think?" They fell into the easy banter of their midshipmen years, Wheeler leaning on a railing as if they were both still midshipmen, discussing the officers who were creating chaos. "You know this new guy, Bankester? Class of 'sixty. My God." Wheeler turned to his plebe Mate. "Mate, go get a drink of water. I'll meet you at the fountain below." The plebe trundled obediently down the stairway, out of earshot. Wheeler watched him as he disappeared, then shook his head.

"This asshole Bankester. You don't know him?"

"Never even heard of him. He's new?"

"You haven't seen him? Fat little turkey with a heavy beard?" Wheeler rolled his eyes. "You're lucky. He's my O.D. today. He's been running me ragged. What a jerk. Last night he fried about half of one company over in the First Wing, for God knows what. Little things like tiny holes in their undershirts, walking barefoot in the passageway. Stuff like that. Well, he gets back to

147

the Main Office and one of the mids up there leans out of a window and screams at the top of his lungs into Tecumseh Court, 'Fuck you, Bankester!' and you know what he did? He sent a Mate up the First Wing and had him ask every mid in the wing, door by door, if he was the one who screamed. The Mate had to take down the names of any mid who wasn't there to be asked. They'll be asked personally this morning. So far every mid has said he wasn't the one. If one of them admits to it, Bankester will hang about a hundred demerits on him for disrespect and conduct unbecoming of a midshipman, uttering foul language in public, and who knows what else. If no one owns up to it, Bankester is going to demand a full-scale honor investigation to find out who lied, so he can throw the bastard out. Can you believe it?"

"Yeah." Lenahan gave off the tiny smile that was his trademark. "That's another reason why, Steve." It was like a codeword to their long friendship, a phrase they had used since their own plebe year, when the reason was why "Navy sucks." Only now, irony of ironies, they were administering the ridicule rather than taking it.

"Why what?" Wheeler grinned back, a tease in his voice.

"Why you'd rather be in Vietnam. And, if I must admit, me too."

"You've already done your part, Ted. I feel like a cop-out." Lenahan watched Steve Wheeler stare at him with guilty wounded spaniel eyes and hated himself, feeling as if he had gelded his friend the night before, taken his manhood from him by violating his wife.

"I haven't done shit, Steve. They're dying like flies and here I stand, perfectly healthy—well, more or less—watching mids get out of bed."

Wheeler shook his head, smiling whimsically as he started down the stairs. "You dumb-ass, Lenahan. I doubt you'd be happy until you came back in a plastic bag."

Lenahan waved Wheeler off, heading up toward the last company to be inspected. "What the hell. You're volunteering, aren't you? You die your way, I'll die mine."

# Chapter Two: 1115

Dean stood at parade-rest in front of his window, the venetian blinds exactingly half-masted for formal room inspection, dressed in his service dress blue, alpha uniform, cap and all. He stole a glance at his bed as he awaited Swenson's arrival.

If I'd done that kind of job the other day, he mused, feeling a numb tiredness that had become his natural state, I wouldn't have wasted the last two hours doing it again.

The bed was done up with scientific precision. The hospital tucks at the corners were a perfect forty-five degrees. The spread was fitted so that the Academy emblem was dead center on the mattress, both lengthwise and widthwise. The top sheet was turned down twice in six-inch folds, so that the pillowcase went from the top of the bed to the bottom of the folded sheet, blending in. The pillow itself was perfectly packed in its case, looking custom-made, the pillow shaken into one corner of the case and then beaten flat, with the rest of the case tucked underneath at two sides so that nothing lay loose. The blanket was folded into a military "nine," exactly the width of the bed and showing only folded edges to the open side of the room. The spread and sheets were tucked so tight that a coin would bounce if tossed on them.

The rest of the room was similarly precise. Inside Dean's wall locker, each pair of socks had been folded so tightly that they resembled rolls of quarters on his shelf, wearing identical "smiles" where the top of the sock had been pulled over the rolled section. Underwear shorts and shirts were stacked in rows, each item folded to the exact same width, as were his whiteworks uniforms and his gym clothes. The sink and mirrors were spotless, having been scrubbed and Windexed. The hanging uniforms and coats and shirts were done by categories, all facing the same direction, each exposed sleeve folded in front of the shirt or coat, to present a smooth outside appearance. The venetian blinds had been dusted, scoured, and Windexed. The desk was scrubbed and Pledged, and only Dean's and Peckarsky's blotters lay on top of it. The floor had been washed and Glo-coated twice, and the shower had been scrubbed and Windexed.

Dean had done it all during two free periods, except for the floor, which he had done the night before, after taps. He had not studied since he had met Fogarty in Swenson's room two days before. Saturday noon meal inspection, the most important personnel inspection of the week, would follow the room inspection, and after the meal itself Dean would report for extra duty from having been placed on report, working off his demerits through several hours of physical punishment.

Maybe I will quit, mused Dean, allowing himself a moment of fantasy as he stood in his parade-rest, awaiting Swenson. And if I did, let's see, this is Saturday, *I could get some friends and there might be a party or maybe we would just drive along the Strip, there's always girls and we could wave and maybe even if they waved back we could take them back to the House and if all went right...*

"What are you smiling about?" Swenson had drifted into the room behind Dean's fantasy and was standing in front of him, arms folded, smiling also.

Dean's mind snapped and he came to a quick brace, his eyes all round again. "Attention on deck Midshipman Dean fourth class reports room sixty-one-twenty-seven prepared for inspection, sir!"

"I said, what the hell are you smiling about, maggot?"

"Sir..." Dean smiled softly again, remembering. "I'm smiling because I like it here, sir."

"Then you're insane." Swenson stood over him, thin and erect, dressed in his drill trousers and an undershirt. His sharply featured Nordic face was clearly entertained. "Only crazy people like it here, Dean. That's why all the caps go up into the air when a class graduates. Wipe it off, dildo."

"Aye, aye, sir." Dean wiped one hand over his mouth and threw his "smile" onto the floor, then stomped on it. It was a ritual passed down from the navy's sailboat days, it seemed. "Hell on the Hudson, Hell on the Hudson, class of three, sir."

"Why three?"

It was one small way a plebe could get back. "Because there's three letters in the word *cat,* sir, and that's the kind of house your mother lives in, sir."

"That's lame, Dean. Can't you do any better than that?"

Swenson shook his head whimsically. "I give you a chance to unload on me and you use something that's as old as my father. Wipe it off again, Dean."

"Aye, aye, sir. Hell on the Hudson Hell on the Hudson, class of seven, sir."

"Why seven?"

"Because there's seven letters in the word *blowjob*, sir, and that's the only kind of job your girl can hold, sir."

Swenson's eyes flashed in quick, questioning surprise, as if asking Dean whether he knew something he did not say. Then he smiled easily, patting Dean on the shoulder. "That's right, Dean. She holds it so yours can drink it down."

"Sir, I don't have a girlfriend, sir."

"Shut up, Dean."

"Aye, aye, sir." Dean swallowed, examining Swenson from his brace. "Sir, I'm sorry if I—"

"Just shut up, alright?" Swenson looked casually around the room, examining it as he prepared to inspect. "Where's your gloves?"

Dean felt his eyes roll in self-disgust. "Sir, I forgot to put them out, sir. They're in my wall locker, sir."

"That'll cost you, Dean. Room improperly prepared for inspection. Form Two."

A small sigh. "Aye, aye, sir."

"Gloves, Dean. Gloves!"

"Aye, aye, sir." Dean scurried to his wall locker and took out a pair of white cotton gloves, handing them to Swenson. Swenson put them on, and began marching around the room, wiping underneath desks and around faucets and on top of doorways. The gloves remained spotless. Then he picked up Dean's M-1 rifle and opened up the buttplate cap, sticking a finger inside the buttwell. It came out black. Swenson clicked his tongue, then wiped a hand along the shower wall. It came out dusty and yellow from dried soap. Swenson clicked his tongue again. Swenson marched to the perfectly made bed and tilted the mattress and springs onto their sides, then lifted a flat board underneath and reached inside, coming up with a large ball of lint, the size of his gloved hand.

"Oh, Dean. I thought you reported this room ready for inspection!" Swenson examined the floor, which shone like glass. "Would you say this deck is clean enough to eat off of, Dean?"

Dean considered it, already upset by Swenson's other findings. I've washed it, rinsed it, and put two coats of polish on it. What the hell does he want? "Yes, sir."

"You're positive?"

"*Yes*, sir."

"Then lick it."

"Sir?"

Swenson was smiling easily. "Then lick it, if you really think that."

"Well, sir, I—" Dean's eyes searched the floor hesitantly, his soft face confused.

"You didn't exactly mean that, did you Dean?"

"No, sir. Not exactly."

Swenson grabbed Dean firmly by the shoulders. "Then, Dean, don't say things to upperclass that you don't exactly mean. I despair of you, Dean. Why does it take so long for a smart guy like you to catch on?"

"I'll find out, sir."

"Do that." Swenson sat on his desk, arms folded, considering him. "Well, let's review the bidding. You owe me a Form Two for room improperly prepared, and you haven't passed your inspection." Swenson restrained a laugh. "And but for the grace of God, you would have had a Glo-coated tongue."

"Yes, sir."

"So, I'll need that Form Two before noon meal. And tomorrow night, we'll just have to inspect your room again."

"Aye, aye, sir."

And you'd better look good at noon meal. Have you brought your shoes back up?"

"I have another coat or two to put on them, sir."

Swenson walked toward the door. "Well, get with it."

"Aye, aye, sir." Swenson left, pulling the door shut behind him. Dean wilted out of his brace and stared at his bed, now in disarray. He rubbed his tongue tentatively against the roof of his mouth several times, staring at the shining floor. Finally he sat at his desk, holding a head that felt like sodden wood, all heavy and numb and useless.

He checked his watch: eleven forty-five. Gee whiz, thought Dean, moving toward his sink in search of his shoeshine cloth. A whole half-hour before inspection. I hardly know what to do with myself.

The skylike limpid eyes,/The circular infant's face,/The stiffness from spats to collar/Never relaxing into grace;...

        Ezra Pound.

And there was the object of such poetry, standing at attention before him, holding a magnificent, practiced salute. See here, mused Lenahan, returning the salute. See what we have created with our torture and our praise: a weapon. A think-bomb, a smart-machine, a shepherd learned in the way of driving flocks to slaughter. A noble creature, yes, and I am his father.

"Good afternoon, sir. The company is prepared for inspection."

"Good afternoon, Mister Crowley." Lenahan motioned to his midshipman company commander. "We'll look at all three platoons today."

Rank after rank, squad after squad, immaculate and erect, dressed in their "grease" uniforms, their finest regalia. Fresh haircuts, gleaming brass, every uniform right out of the Press Shop, the black wool coats and trousers then brushed until not even a speck of lint remained. Mirror shoes, ties pressed and perfectly knotted, white shirts clean and starched, white gloves over their hands like the bindings of innocence itself. A celebration, mused Lenahan, standing at a brief attention before each man. An orgy of exactness.

It went quickly. He knew they were anxious to go on liberty, and they had prepared well. There were a few bad haircuts, a few wrinkled uniforms, a few pairs of shoes that needed new heels or were poorly shined. But overall, they looked like Lenahan himself.

"Real fine, Mister Crowley. Real fine. Give the company my congratulations, and have the Form Twos of those placed on report in my office on Monday morning."

"Aye, aye, sir."

"Are you going to the fights tonight?"

Crowley smiled with anticipation. "Yes, sir. We've been waiting for Mister Fogarty to win this one for four years, sir."

"Well, I guess you won't have to wait much longer." Lenahan watched Crowley's face and felt a sad warmth, like a hot mist from his past. Classmates, he mused, remembering his own midshipman days. What a raw mix of love and rivalry, like two dozen brothers, admiring each other and yet competing for the graces of Mother B. They've been waiting for four years and after tonight, win or lose, that vigil will be a memory, forever lost to the future. When a way of life so excruciating and exact ends with an abruptness after only four years, he thought, walking away from the formation, his clicking heels a good-bye, it prepares a man to die young.

"Sally Sue!"

Oh, she mangled him, left him spent each Sunday from her chaos and her unpredictability. But what a way to reach exhaustion, what a journey through new sights and smells, like some Oriental bazaar. Even Swede knew, in his private moments, that Sally Sue Crown had been belittling him for months. It just didn't matter.

She stood in the Rotunda in front of the TO THOSE WHO WENT BEFORE US posters, such a stunning blonde that few among the dozens of midshipmen who walked past her could do so without keeping their eyes fixed on her in open lust. Tall, long-legged, blue-eyed, dressed in French designer clothes that scoffed at most of the eyes without requiring her to even acknowledge the stares, she emanated the protected arrogance of beauty and money mingled in one person.

"Well, hey, Swede!" One melting smile and for that moment he was king of the universe. She took his arm briefly and started chattering as soon as they walked out of the door, all grace and presence, an entertainer. "I still have a hard time believing I drive up here to pick you up like this on Saturdays, Swede, I mean it's a pretty drive and all but Jesus Christ here you are twenty-two years old, and here I am twenty-three if I have to admit it and it's like the way they used to come pick us up in boarding school when I was fifteen or something, I mean, when are they going to let you all grow *up*?"

Swenson shrugged easily, mindful of the many envious stares that followed him as he strolled with Sally Sue. "Let's not talk about that, all right? We've said it all before. Anyway, in four months I'll be out of this zoo."

"Oh, yeah, but then what happens? Let's not even talk about *that,* Swede, I mean really, it's like the frying pan into the fire, do you know what I'm saying? It's bad enough the way this place keeps you locked up, but at least you're locked up near Washington. When you leave it's on the boat in the middle of the ocean." She looked up, summoning the dull gray sky's agreement, looking horrified. "I mean, my God. Oh, let's drop it."

He eyed her hesitantly, walking toward the road where she had parked. "Did you get the flowers?"

"What flowers?"

"You didn't get the flowers?" Swenson shook his head, irritated. "Well, *damn* it. I'm calling that son of a bitching florist and getting my money back."

"Oh, *those* flowers." She looked straight ahead with a vacant stare. "Yes, I got those flowers."

"Well, why didn't you call me and let me know?"

"I didn't know you wanted me to call you, Swede. I just got the flowers and there was a note that said...well, it didn't say anything about calling, that's all."

Swenson scratched his head, holding his cap briefly as they walked, afraid she would disappear if he pushed her too hard, but irritated nonetheless. "Well, I surprised you with the flowers. I thought you'd want to call me and thank me. You know, without being asked."

"Oh, Swede. You can't put words into my mouth, or actions into the rest of me. I did like the flowers. I've just been busy. I was out with some friends, and I didn't have the time to call you yet. I'm here, aren't I? Don't demand a response."

"You're always out with friends."

"My friends are very important to me." Her voice softened, with defensive concern rather than tenderness. "I swear you are so goddamn jealous I just don't know what to do with you, Swede. I mean, do you want me to give up all my friends and stay at home and knit, waiting for you? Really."

"No." He breathed in and held it. "Just give up the ones you've been to bed with."

Her voice went cold, flat. "You're a son of a bitch. Who are you to tell me something like that?"

"Nobody. Nobody at all." His anger was gone immediately, like the air from a popped balloon. "I'm sorry, Sally Sue. I'm sorry." He knew even as he apologized that he had been right to say it, that he was being deceived, that his deception was willing and would continue. But somewhere in the back of his mind, like

155

a laughing little devil, was the notion that she would eventually fall so madly in love with him that she would become a different person. "I just don't know what's coming out of my mouth sometimes."

"Well, I'm not going to take too much more of it." Her full lips were tight, her face empty of emotion. "Shit. I need a beer. Where the hell can we get a beer, where they won't treat you like a ten-year-old just because you're a middy?"

"Let's drive into Washington. I can drink there."

"Oh, great! Drive all the way into Washington. I just came from Washington. A hundred miles just to drink a beer with your lunch."

"Wait a minute. Mack will probably be out at the house by now. We can go there. He'll have cases of beer."

She smiled again, her mercurial emotions now bright, almost childlike. "Oh, great! We'll pick up some submarine sandwiches and eat out there!"


He was not equipped to understand her, and in the haste of her weekend visits there was little time to try, anyway. Swede Swenson was dazzled, on a wide-eyed roller coaster ride, hooked on her like a drug, willing to throw away everything, even his pride, just to keep that roller coaster going.

He could not comprehend the needs and moods of a woman who was reared by a maid, a black woman with five children, and who had never stopped to wonder who was rearing the maid's children while the maid was raising her. He could not understand the natural deception of a woman who grew up watching her mother lie to her father; gentle lies, meant to protect her from her father's misunderstandings, his absolute Southern patriarchal autocracy. He could not appreciate the natural child-ishness that came from her father's overwhelming protectiveness, a childishness that allowed her to bounce checks with elan, to spend two week's pay on a set of clothes and then forget to pay the rent, to dine continually in the finest restaurants because it was too boring to cook.

Sally Sue had come to Washington to grow up. Her father had gotten her a job with one of his friends, a congressman from their native Alabama, and had remarked that, finally, Sally Sue was going to learn to live off the land. But Sally Sue knew how to deal with her father. When she bounced a check or forgot to pay the rent, she simply called him and sweetly, helplessly informed him. Daddy always came through. Back home, when he got too close, got too much of a sense of control, she would seek out the raunchiest, sexiest wrong-side-of-the-tracks gas station attendant and screw his brains out, never even admitting to having seen the boy, but dragging herself in at four in the morning, disheveled and faintly smiling, and Daddy would know. Even in Washington, when a stern note on fiscal responsibility arrived with the latest check that bailed her out of the rent that had become unpayable because of a new Yves St. Laurent dress, she would merely consent to one of the myriad of offers and spend a Saturday night in someone else's apartment, so that Daddy and Mother's Sunday morning phone call would go unanswered until late in the afternoon or maybe Monday, and again she would issue that array of vague denials, and he would know.

She had devoured Swenson, mauled his emotions the way a gorilla would have done his body. He had stopped in her congressman's office on Capitol Hill to ask for directions to his own congressman's room the previous summer, and had been stunned into suavity as he took in her deep blue pools of eyes, her wonderfully full mouth, her rich blonde hair that framed her face in natural waves, muting the occasional devil's look her eyes gave off. Shyly, in sentences that she herself took for a sort of urbaneness, he had asked her out for that night, his last night of leave before returning to the Academy.

She had naively thought that, since Swenson was of Swedish extraction, he was a purveyor of free love. Calvinist that he was, servant of the harsh Minnesota winters and then locked lonely inside Bancroft Hall for years, Swenson believed in true love at first sight, like divine providence. God had delivered him Sally Sue, and it was his duty to make it work. When she brought him back to her cluttered apartment after their first date and casually took him on her unmade bed, a slow smile on her classic face, one knee up in the air as if she were sunbathing on a beach, he finished by delivering a speech to her about the sanctity of their act, its spiritual significance. Swede Swenson was in love.

Sally Sue Crown was both confused and amused. But Swede was tender and emotional, except for his bursts of morality, and was not really a hindrance, being locked up most weeks from Sunday night to Saturday noon. She gutted and filleted him with her dances and her lies. And he followed her mermaid's song toward oblivion, uncaring, his senses swamped in her perfume as his whole life laughed at him.

# Chapter Three: 1400

Fort Myer looked like history, with wide parade fields, huge reaching trees, and old brick buildings. Fogarty half-expected George Patton himself to come galloping down a roadway at any moment on a white horse.

"Turn here, Bill." Linda pointed toward a side road. "That's the Officers' Club. Take a right, and the Chapel is at the end of the block."

The Chapel sat off of the road on his left, the final conduit for sending young men to their tombs. Fogarty stared uneasily at the simple brick building, parking his car and walking toward it. How many, he wondered, have passed through those double doors inside wooden boxes today?

He had not accepted it, despite all of the programming. The military man learns early to bury his friends, and to move on. Men have traditionally sought danger in the military, and have traditionally found it. Servicemen are always in motion, in the air at more than the speed of sound, underwater at depths whales could only dream of, or on the surface of the water cruising at thirty miles an hour through crashing seas with another ship almost touching theirs, hoses connecting them like weird sex, replenishing their oil supplies. Or they are on the ground, in the dirt, testing and training weapons that may someday kill others but today may deal them that same irony. The smallest margin of error separates a live man from a dead one, even in the boring vacuum of peace. And in war, of course, they are the first and usually the only ones to pay. The President and the Congress may suffer bad news stories and ulcers and hemorrhoids. The military man suffers the death of his friends, early and often.

So he learns young to accept the inevitability that some of his friends, those he deals with every day, will beat their parents to the grave. He never admits, even to himself, that he might beat his. But some of the men he drinks with and drives to work with and plays bridge with will be gone, perhaps next week, perhaps in a year or so, and it will not leave a military man's mind. It squats on his relationships like a wet toad, warning him not to touch the inside of a friend's soul too deeply or he will someday come away scarred, covered with warted ugliness from some quick unexpected death.

And then occasionally the barriers break down and there comes an unadmitted clinging, a friendship desperate and close as love, born of mutual fear, however unexpressed. And all the inevitabilities, all the programming and the lectures and the ceremonies that replace grief with pomp, will not help him hide his heart.

Ron Loudenslager's dead, man.

A hearse pulled up, sleek and somehow ominous, like an ugly black beetle that had been sucking off of strong people instead of crops. Fogarty stood in the parking lot and watched it, frozen by its presence. Linda grasped his hand and squeezed it tightly as four Marines in their full dress blues marched up to the rear doors of the hearse, shuffling in a stiff, artificially slow march. These were ceremonial marines who buried casualties for a living. Fogarty watched them as they extracted the casket from inside the hearse, the black wooden box wrapped in a flag. The flag seemed somehow incongruous, brightly colored amid the black of the casket and hearse, the dull leaden sky, Fogarty's own dark mood. Old Glory, he mused numbly, trying not to be melodramatic. The blanket for a dead man.

He could not fully comprehend that it was Loudenslager in the box. He had been through too many meaningless ceremonies in four years to place credence in a stiff march. No, he thought. No. I have seen him *is* but I have not seen him was or used to be. I have not seen him not exist. He isn't really in there I can't admit that but they say he is and until they find him starving but alive inside some Vietnamese cave and bring him home and find out who this joker imposter is who insists he is dead Loudenslager and give him his own marker, until they do that I'll go along with this charade. They said he bled to death, couldn't stop the bleeding but Loudenslager wouldn't ever do that he would goddamn *order* the blood to stop so it couldn't be him.

But don't open it up. *Please* God don't let them open that box up and make me stare at his used-to-be.

A small contingent from the marine band began to play a soft hymn and the body bearers did a slow march into the church, the casket perfectly still in their hands, as if it were gliding on glass all the way, the flag itself not even gaining a wrinkle. Fogarty and Linda walked behind. The others were already inside. In the church they sat on a hardwood pew and listened to a minister who had never known him toll his virtues like a lonely bell. Fogarty tuned out the tumid mourn, staring numbly at the casket, trying to remember the poem Lenahan had recited two days before. Somehow it made more sense than prayers, but he could not remember it. *This is the world. Have faith.*

The rear doors of the church creaked open and the body bearers once again moved with practiced skill, carrying the casket toward a caisson. The band struck up again, a melancholy version of "Abide With Me." Six muscled, impeccably groomed horses pawed restlessly in front of the caisson. The body bearers strapped the casket onto the caisson and very carefully tucked the flag in, as if it were indeed a blanket. On the other side of the caisson, a squad of marines stood at a perfect attention, their rifles at present arms as the casket was being loaded.

It was almost too much, like marching to chapel to "Onward, Christian Soldiers," a procedure Fogarty found not only unsettling but faintly vulgar. Ceremony is killing reality, he said to himself, watching the band march off, tapping a drum, the squad of marines just after them, marching sharply, then the chaplain himself, that pudgy holy agent of Loudenslager to God, alone and sanctimonious.

The horses took off, their clopping immune to drumbeats, pulling Loudenslager to his dirt hole, dropping disrespectful piles of horse manure along the road behind them, and Fogarty followed the procession with the handful of others who had shown up: Loudenslager's parents and his wife, heavy with their child, two classmates who were assigned in the area, one other marine who had served with him in Vietnam. Fogarty held Linda's hand again, grasping it tightly, and managed to put his other arm around Sharon, his dead friend's wife, as they walked. It was a parade, a spectacle where everyone was marching and no one was watching. Only a half-dozen tourists, come to view the spectacle of Arlington and happening on a Real Funeral, and the hundred thousand markers, silently welcoming this latest dot of insignificance.

There. The goddamn band did it. They broke into "On-ward, Christian Soldiers" just past the Lee mansion, as a tourist busily snapped a dozen pictures of the procession for later on some sterile basement wall. Fogarty glared at the tourist. It did no good.

The road bent into trees and hills, graves lost to terrain for a narrow moment, then opened up into an explosion of identical white markers. Fogarty stared at a whole hillside saturated with spent soldiers and shook his head hopelessly as the band broke into another verse of "Onward, Christian Soldiers."

Abruptly, the band and the squad of marines turned onto a little side road and halted. Three rows of crosses away, up a gentle slope, was a reddened patch of recent graves, five of them still markerless, and next to those a new hole, surrounded by artificial green carpeting that hid the mound of dirt that would soon smother Ron Loudenslager's earthly presence. The body bearers unstrapped the casket and carried it up the hill, the flag still wrinkle-free, and eased it onto a metal holder that had been placed inside the hole.

They followed the chaplain up the hill, Loudenslager's parents leaning into it, his father's blue eyes watery, looking like brilliant jewels on his gray face, his wife and mother weeping steadily now, wiping tears with almost identical white hand-kerchiefs. Standing stolidly before the casket, the small group became overwhelmed by ceremony: the body bearers now taking the flag and holding it absolutely tight above the casket, flat and taut as a board, the squad down the hill going through various motions with their weapons, present arms and order arms, precise actions that were more confusing than meaningful, and now a firing squad just up the hill, looming over the whole ceremony like vultures over a carcass.

The chaplain was saying a series of prayers. Fogarty had tuned him out, watching the faces of those who had come to bury a friend, contrasting them with those others who were performing a military duty. Down the hill and far away, parts of Washington, D.C., loomed through ugly gray ground fog. Fogarty smiled slightly, remembering Loudenslager's frequent jokes about wanting to be buried facing the Gutless Wonders in Washington, and wanting to have Johnny Cash sing "The Green, Green Grass of Home" at his funeral.

Fogarty began humming the tune, a soft, secret melody

161

that was easily drowned out by the chaplain's prayers. "Ashes to ashes," the chaplain was saying. Fogarty continued to hum, a small smile on the edges of his mouth. You dumb shit, he mused, staring at the casket. What the hell does anybody from Chicago know about green grass? "Lord have mercy."

The squad downhill came to present arms and the squad above them erupted with three volleys over the grave and finally a lone bugler from the band played "Taps." Loudenslager's mother sobbed loudly, like retches, when the bugle played. The body bearers folded the flag with an incredible, agonizing precision, passing it down to the body escort, a marine lieutenant whose chest gleamed with medals.

The lieutenant walked tall and erect to Loudenslager's wife and presented her the flag. She took it in her hands, all blonde and beautiful and pregnant with their first goddamn little Loudenslager oh Christ, thought Fogarty, fighting back tears, Christ could that bastard lead. And it passed before him, like his own life moving by, the summer of 1964, hot and sticky and filled with pain, hanging from Loudenslager's door, fighting back different tears, the huge muscled man whose classmates claimed would someday be the Commandant of the Marine Corps taunting him, challenging him, *Would you die for your country, Fogarty? Are you bigger than your goddamn self?*

The military procession faded down the road. Across from them, a knot of anxious workers stood, waiting for the small group to depart so they could move the fake green rug down to the next site and plant dead Loudenslager.

Loudenslager's wife was crying uncontrollably. Fogarty walked to her and held her tightly, squeezing her, feeling the only part of Loudenslager that still lived as it pressed from her stomach into his. She grasped him suddenly, on the shoulders, with a grip so strong that it popped one of the shoulderboards on his overcoat.

"What am I going to do, Bill, oh what am I going to do?"

It unnerved him. She wasn't supposed to be asking that. He'd never been to a funeral before and here was his best friend's wife losing control. You didn't lose control. You felt it but you didn't say it, that was the military. But Sharon Loudenslager wasn't exactly military. She had simply lived in proud awe of this boasting, jesting madman who would soon disappear inside a cold hole. He had been a man first, whose passion simply happened to be the military. She had never understood it all the way, and above all Loudenslager was not supposed to die. The heroes never died in the movies.

And wives didn't lose control. Fogarty couldn't even talk to her or pull her face from the front of his overcoat. She just stood there grasping him as if he might disappear if she let go of his shoulders. The others stood in a tight circle around them, saying nothing, offering no assistance, too frozen by their own emotions to interfere.

Finally Linda walked forward and placed her arms around Sharon, hugging her like a mother. They rocked back and forth, the three of them in a cold tangle of arms, Linda and Sharon mixing tears. Linda was saying something, it didn't make a lot of sense but her voice was a purr.

"Don't let him go, Linda." Sharon still would not look at Fogarty. "Don't let him."

"There, there. Come on. Let's go get some coffee, okay? Come on, now. We can talk about it where it's warm."

"I don't want to leave, I just don't want to leave him here. He'll disappear and then it will just be dirt. Oh, don't let him go, Linda."

Fogarty found himself secretly checking his watch as he and Linda ushered Loudenslager's widow back to the roadway. It was too much. He couldn't take it anymore.

# Chapter Four: 1600

Ted Lenahan turned off of Wisconsin Avenue and drove up the long horseshoe drive in front of Bethesda Naval Hospital, its towers reaching skyward above him too far to see the top as he parked in front. It's almost a homecoming, he thought, slamming his car door and jogging in the brisk, icy wind toward the front doors. Five months on the inside looking out, four of them shitting through a hole in my bed, two more months coming in every day for therapy. I know more people in Bethesda Naval Hospital than I do in Annapolis.

He checked the admissions office for Bard's room number, and sure enough, he was in Tower Twelve, Lenahan's own alma mater. Lenahan felt a curious excitement as he rode the large, ridiculously slow elevator to the twelfth floor. An emergency case lay strapped and comatose on a wheeled bed next to him as he ascended. It was a young sailor or marine, pale and mangled, his skin so ashy gray that he appeared to be a corpse. The I-V bottle dripped fluid into one arm from a post just above the man's head. Rather than repulse Lenahan, it imbued him with a familiarity, a sense of belonging. He had mastered the esoterics of surgery and recovery and intravenous feeding, of pain pills and boring hours spent floating on his back in a dark room, dreaming of nothing.

Tower Twelve. The elevator doors opened and Lenahan stepped out at the nurse's desk. He recognized both nurses standing in front of him, and they both, after a pair of startled smiles, recognized him. Nurse Goodbody, dark and voluptuous (Lenahan had forgotten her actual name, it was something long and Italian), was a bedtime friend to many of the doctors in Bethesda. She had hinted to Lenahan one dull afternoon as he dozed along on Percodan that she simply could not contain herself. Doctors tending to patients, she explained, aroused her. Morphine Mary (again Lenahan could not remember her exact name) was a thin, nervous drill sergeant type, a disciplinarian who did not allow her patients even to complain. Lenahan was convinced that Morphine Mary did not even sleep with her husband. She wasn't bad looking, he mused again, staring at her thin frame. If she'd just get laid every now and then she'd mellow out and stop being such a damn witch.

"Well, Captain Lenahan. How's your leg?" Goodbody embraced him with her eyes.

"Leg's fine. I'm running some. Stomach could be better but what the hell, you never promised me a rose garden, eh, Morphine?"

"Don't call me that!" Morphine Mary looked left and right for patients and enlisted corpsmen. "I've finally gotten everyone on this ward to stop saying it, and here you come, saying it again. What are you doing here, anyway?"

"They're probably all still saying it behind your back anyway, Morphine. Don't kid yourself. Patients know everything, right, Goodbody?" Lenahan smiled conspiratorially to the short, full-breasted nurse.

"God, I hope not." She giggled.

"So where's Lieutenant Bard? Neil Bard? He's probably the

one who had his hand down your blouse when you leaned over to take the thermometer out of his mouth."

Nurse Goodbody quickly lost her smile. She and Morphine Mary traded skeptical glances. Morphine Mary spoke, biting off her words, still irritated with Lenahan. "No, I'd say he isn't exactly the most active patient on the Tower. In fact, I'm not even sure I can let you see him."

"He's got a head wound." Nurse Goodbody's eyes were dark apologetic moons.

"I knew that."

"Well, he's lost... what did Doctor Cohen say?" Goodbody looked to Morphine Mary. "A cup?"

"About a cup and a half."

"Anyway, he's lost a lot of his brain. Not so much that he's a vegetable or anything. But his system is in incredible shock." Nurse Goodbody seemed to be taking responsibility for the whole world's suffering. "I'm really sorry. He's still completely paralyzed from the neck down, and he doesn't talk. The doctors say he'll come out of the paralysis, at least partially. But he might not even recognize you."

"So where is he? I drove all the way out here from Annapolis in a car without a heater just to see him."

"Why didn't you call?"

Lenahan scowled. "Listen, Morphine, if people called me when I was in there shitting through my mattress, I'd have told them not to come. I was too embarrassed. But I liked people to come. This guy is a good friend of mine. We went through the Academy together. We've been drunk together all over the world. He's a squid, but that's all right. And I don't give a shit if he can't talk to me, Morphine, I want to talk to *him*. Do you get what I mean?"

Nurse Goodbody took him by the arm. She looked like she wanted to make love to him. "Come on, Captain. I'll take you to his room."

The room was dark and gray, like Bard's own skin. Bard's eyes moved when Lenahan entered, just the eyeballs themselves, a fleeting glance that followed him for a couple steps and then lost the ability or the interest to keep up with him as he made his way into a chair.

Lenahan sat back easily in the chair, reaching inside his sock for his cigarettes. He casually lit one, staring at his paralyzed classmate. Neil Bard had been a basketball player, a good one.

Lenahan squinched up his mouth, then drew slowly on his cigarette, his eyes never leaving Bard. " 'Thou hast nor youth nor age, but as it were an after-dinner sleep, dreaming of both.' Shakespeare, Neil. Hah. A lot you care. Hey, Neil, your goddamn head looks like it was stolen off a mummy! Yeah." He flipped an ash, then dragged off the cigarette again. "Now, don't you worry about a thing. You don't have to try and answer me, Neil. When you get better, you're going to remember I came here to talk to you. That's right. I'm going to talk your silly *ass* off, you little Jew. Yeah."

An intravenous tube dripped slowly into Bard. Lenahan watched the tube fill up with fluid from the bottle, drip drip drip, slowly marking off the afternoon. How many hours I lay on my back and watched a bottle drip into me, he mused. Each drip is one less moment I will feel pain, that's what I used to say.

"Well, Neil, where do we begin? The last time I saw you, we were drunk on our asses at the 'O' Club in Pendleton. What was that, two years ago? Christ, time flies when you're having fun. Hah hah. Well, Angie's still out there, I guess you heard, she's got the boy with her, too. Did I say Angie? Oh, shit, good buddy, did I just let a big one out of the bag. Maybe it's a good thing you can't talk yet. How's your memory? What the hell part of your brain did the gooks shoot out? Let's hope it's the side where you keep all your math smarts. That side was empty anyway, huh, Neil? Hah hah. Yeah, well, let's see. I was on Tower Twelve myself, you know? Just down the hall there, for a few months, that is. Nothing serious, all things considered. I walk, I talk—" Lenahan rose from the chair and stood in front of Bard, wiggling his fingers and jumping up and down "—see? Not a goddamn thing wrong with me!"

"Captain?" Goodbody stood in the doorway, peering at him as if he were among the forever lost. That girl cries with her whole *body*, noted Lenahan, ceasing his insane dance.

"That's all right, Nurse Goodbody, don't you worry about a thing. I know Neil and he knows me, he recognizes me, I can see it in his eyes. He's going to remember when he starts talking again. He thinks it's funny, even if he doesn't realize it yet."

"Captain, you're going to have to go. Lieutenant Bard is in pretty weak condition, and Mary is mad at both of us. I'm sorry. Really."

"Goodbody, you're in the wrong business." Lenahan put an arm around her shoulders, pulling her breasts against his lower chest. "No fooling. You walk around feeling sorry for everything on this ward. Christ, woman, you're going to flip out before this fucking war is over, did you know that?"

Goodbody put an arm around his waist, a sad purr in her voice. "Yeah, I know, really, I know. I hate nursing. Sometimes I just go home and cry. Look at him. He was a whole man and now he can't even go to the bathroom. I'm not cut out for this." She squeezed him, a small but insistent pressure, her breasts now flat on his chest.

"Yeah, old Neil's going to pull through, though. Huh, Neil?" Lenahan's face lit up. "He winked! Goddamn it, he winked! Did you see it, Goodbody?"

"I wish I could say I did, I really do." She held him tighter. He squeezed her back, feeling himself become aroused.

"Well, no bullshit, I saw it. Neil old buddy, I'm coming back tomorrow and we're going to talk again. I'm going to finish the story. OK?" Lenahan was grinning fiercely. One hand dangled over Goodbody's breasts. He fondled her left breast as they watched Bard. She made no objection. "Hey, Goodbody, you ever been to the fights?"

"Boxing matches? No." She rubbed against his chest.

"Well, come with me tonight. All right?"

"Well, I have a date with a—"

"I know, a goddamn doctor."

"How'd you know?"

"You're famous, Goodbody, all right? Hell, you forget. I did a lot of laying around, listening to scuttlebutt. You even told me about how bedside manner turns you on, something like that."

Goodbody blushed. "Did I say that? Well, it *is* erotic."

"Jesus Christ, woman, you've been emptying too many bedpans. Forget this doctor, he's probably married anyway. Huh?" She said nothing. "Come to the fights. I need to be consoled. I'm shot up, my marriage is kaput, my good buddy Bard is laying here with a hole in his head. Hell, Goodbody, I need some attention."

Her nipple was hard underneath his hand. She squeezed him. "All right."

Walking out the doorway, Lenahan was sure he saw Bard wink again.

# Chapter Five: 1700

Heaven on a Saturday: Apple pie and coffee, in a booth next to the window where they could sit and stare at the women who walked by. It didn't matter whether the women were with a man or even if they were pretty, it was so nice just to see a female face. And of course the jukebox, pouring melodies into their souls after a week with no music of any sort, a whole year without food for the spirit.

"Play it again, Ski."

Peckarsky walked across the small room and put another nickel in, hitting the buttons on a record that had been played dozens of times each Saturday since Fogarty himself had been a plebe. Dean stared out the window onto the bleak sidewalks as the song began again, watching women stroll briskly by, their coats buttoned and their chins high in the air, forbidden luxuries.

> Lonely
> I'm mister Lonely

Dean tested his arms painfully, having run three hours of extra duty. "I'm so sore I can hardly move."

"Why don't you go home, John?"

> Letters
> Never a letter
> I get no letters in the mail

"Maybe I will." His eyes were lost out on the street again, watching normal people walk the sidewalks and cross the brick roads of Old Town. On the waterfront the boats were iced in for the winter. Like my soul, thought Dean. "I really hate all this bullshit."

> Yeah I'm a soldier
> A lonely soldier
> Away from home
> Through no wish of my own

Peckarsky grinned at him. "You'll never leave."

"Why do you think that?"

"You'd miss all the bullshit."

*I'm mister Lonely*
*I wish that I could go back home.*

"When we go on cruise this summer I'm going to get so raunchy. I'm going to get drunk and get laid and, and, goddamn…"

Peckarsky laughed softly. "So I guess you'll be around for a while."

They walked back through Gate One and strolled past the Field House, killing time before they had to return to the Hall. Dean found himself steering his roommate toward the seawall. They stopped at the edge of it and stared down its narrow length, watching the green flashes of the beacon at the end of the wall, a gift of the class of 1945. It was distant. The seawall stretched forever in the darkness of a winter afternoon.

"I ran this thing this morning." Dean said it with earnestness, even disbelief. "I didn't go very fast, but I made it. In the *dark*. I ran it, Ski."

"If Fogarty was on *my* ass, I think I could figure out a way to walk across the river."

"Don't make fun of me."

"Who's making fun of you? I was serious."

# Chapter Six: 1930

Fogarty took his boxing gear from his closet and wrapped it inside his gray Army bathrobe, then threw it over his shoulder as he walked almost empty hallways toward the exit that led to Mac-Donough Hall. Inside MacDonough Hall he made idle, nervous chatter with several other fighters as he examined the gymnastics area, which had been converted into a boxing arena. The ring sat low amid perhaps a thousand seats. The emptiness of arenas before a night of fights always charged Fogarty, conjured up a passionate devil within him and held it like feathers in his throat, causing him to breathe differently, to laugh more often, to want to start beating on something and not stop until it was over.

"Say, Wild Bill."

"Say, Trajardo. How you gonna act? That's what I mean."

"I'm gonna kick ass, man. I'm gonna kick some goddamn ass."

"Yeah, baby. Kick ass and take some fucking *names*. That's right." Fogarty put his hand on the squat Hawaiian's heavy shoulder as they walked. They were as close as blood.

Yamato's body could not keep still. He fidgeted as they walked, his shoulders going through the motions of various combinations even as the rest of him walked forward, down a stairway, heading for the locker room. He glanced at the ring again as he and Fogarty descended the stairs. "Oh, man, in an hour that place is going to be *loaded* with people, man, *loaded*. Hey, there's Adair. Hey, Chollie!"

Adair put a fist quickly into the air, bouncing toward the locker room with a soulful dance. "What's happening, Tra - HAR - do?" He waited for them, bobbing and weaving as he stood there. "Yeah, we better be doing it tonight. There ain't no next time when you're firsties. Next time is in the Fleet, with an M-sixteen, you hear what I'm saying, man?"

Little Stevie Wonder was already dressed, standing outside the locker room and shadowboxing in little bursts, his long, graceful legs carrying him through feints and slips and body punches. He saw Yamato and called to him from across the room. "Hey, Mick! Boom boom boom." He threw a quick, tight combination.

"Yeah, yeah. Save 'em, Stevie. You're gonna need 'em."

They dressed slowly, suddenly in their own worlds, then reported upstairs to Misery Hall, the taping room. Fogarty made idle chatter, now babbling nervously as the corpsman taped his hands. He watched the gauze go around and around, over the thumb, back around his thick wide hands, then the tape go between his fingers, then more gauze, until his hands themselves were smooth fists that would barely fit inside his gloves. But nobody could pack a hand like Whitey, he remembered, thinking of his high school coach and days inside the dark, smelly gyms of Omaha, Whitey packing in little pieces of tape, ridges along his knuckles, secret weapons.

He packed the gauze down by hitting the corpsman's outstretched hands, and then held his arms rigid in front of his stomach as the gloves were forced over the wraps and taped onto his arms at the wrists. It was a final act, an imprisonment. Fogarty was now denied the use of his hands except for violent acts. He was totally changed until someone cut the leather clubs off of him; he was Mr. Hyde.

He climbed inside the practice ring next to Misery Hall and sat dumbly, staring at his gloves. Chervanek, his opponent in the Brigade Finals, lay flat on his back across the ring, similarly manacled. Stay away from his right, Fogarty chanted to himself as he sat on the canvas, waiting.

Slowly they began to fill the arena. He could hear them from the practice ring, the stamping feet of swarms of people and the pulsing of male voices, like distant, rolling thunder. Then suddenly the coaches were yelling at the fighters to line up by weight classes, Gold corner in one line and Blue corner in the other. Fogarty stood nervously with the Gold corner team, jumping up and down, the devilish feathers now underneath his arms and in his crotch and up and down his back.

A band just inside the arena from them began playing the Gillette fight song. He actually laughed. He was so high and he could never get used to it. It was so innocent after dark dungeons in Omaha, entering the ring to lusty brawlers' screams for his own blood as the "Duke of Earl" marched ominously along the crowded aisle from the other side. They trotted into the brightly lit arena and the crowd of midshipmen and their dates and the officers with wives and children all stood up and screamed with some sort of demonic release and bloodthirst all rolled up together and Fogarty thought about it again. It was lust in those screams, pure and simple. Lust for someone else's blood on the end of one of his smoothened fists, lust for his blood on someone else's gloves. Lust that resembled passion, an outlet for the fury they were all trained to keep controlled, to stifle, to channel into productive energy. Fogarty was going to hit something back for them.

Loudenslager had scowled at him from the upperclass seats during plebe summer those long years or lives ago, *You'd better win, dipshit, we don't build leaders by building losers,* but Loudenslager wasn't there anymore or was he. Fogarty chewed absently on his mouthpiece, standing at attention as the whole arena faced the American flag during the playing of the National Anthem, then scanned nearby seats as he took his place on the fighters' bench. Linda was nearby, sitting with Swenson and Sally Sue and Mack, who had a small, cute, dark-haired date Fogarty had never seen before. Fogarty nodded to them, his mouthpiece sticking from his lips, his face all greased with Vaseline and already sweating, the gloves making his hands feel like animal paws. Linda looked worried, but what did women know. Two rows from ringside, Captain Lenahan sat with Nurse Goodbody, who looked like she was going to cry already. Not bad, mused Fogarty. Get some, Captain Lenahan.

The fights started, Little Stevie Wonder and Yamato, and Fogarty sat watching them, wanting to see Yamato and also Adair fight before he warmed up. It would be cutting his warmup close; he was the fourth fight. But they had been together for four years, and this was the last chance to win the big one. He wanted to see it.

Lusting roars surrounded him, engulfed him like the hollow inside of a breaking wave, coming at him from four sides in a jerky rhythm of delight. Stevie and Yamato were outdoing themselves, two class acts, bobbing and weaving and throwing tight, clean punches that were landing, landing, landing. Up came the crowd from their chairs, loud were the screams as Stevie Wonder popped Yamato's nose with a hard right cross, spattering blood like vomit on his shorts. Down they sat, with a murmur, as Yamato opened the distance, jabbed jabbed jabbed, taking control of the pace. Up they came again when Yamato slipped the next hard right and dropped Stevie with a crisp, booming hook that sent the lanky, tattooed fighter rolling like an egg, trying to find his feet. Balloop. Stevie rolled up on an elbow, then went over a shoulder onto his back.

The bell saved him, and the crowd applauded the two friends' ferocity. The second round was the same, fierce and exhausting. Yamato bled freely, his mouth and chin covered with it. The referee examined him, and almost stopped the fight, but Yamato's corner stuffed cotton up his nose. In the next round the cotton balls came out with one quick snort, two red blobs on the canvas, and Yamato's face shook with blood each time Stevie Wonder landed a punch.

The two friends embraced each other at the end of the fight, standing spent in the center of the ring as the spectators rose from their seats. Little Stevie Wonder won the decision. Yamato climbed from the ring and strode back to the bench, a towel over his head and another pressed against his nose. He was weeping. Fogarty moved to the end of the bench and put his arm on Yamato's shoulder.

"It's all right, Mick. It's all right, man. It was a good fight."

"It ain't all right." Yamato's voice was hollow from his mashed nose.

Jolly Chollie Adair's fight began, he and a muscular Philippines exchange midshipman trading bombs. A handler grasped Fogarty's shoulder. "Come on, Bill. Let's get you warm."

"I want to watch this one."

"If somebody gets knocked out, you won't be warm. Come on. Now."

Downstairs he loosened up, the crowd oscillating with its murmurs and its screams, Fogarty wondering about Chollie. He shadowboxed, got his mind and blood going. Feathers were everywhere, raising goose bumps on his legs and arms, making him almost laugh every time he merely breathed out, causing him to jump up and down, jump up and down, the bottoms of his feet springy with nerves.

A light-heavyweight came down to warm up and told him Adair had lost.

Finally it was his turn. They led him toward the ring, down a narrow aisle between two seats, and he was the one inside the bright lights, he the one waiting to be ravished by the screams, to provide delight and release, to attack and hurt a man for no other reason than pride (or did they call it sport). And to show Loudenslager win, to show him kill, or did that even make sense he didn't know anymore.

Commander Marion was working his corner. He smiled easily and rubbed Fogarty's neck as they announced his name. Marion had been a football player at the Academy, as well as a boxer. He was a hulk, a brawler. He patted Fogarty's back.

"Remember, Chervanek's a puncher. He goes for the big one. Stick and move, Bill. Take it from him and don't get caught."

Stick and move, stick and move. Somewhere in the cobwebs of his memory, like a dance in another person's dream, Whitey screamed at him, pounding on the canvas of a raised ring. It was his fate to be hard and lean, to have his meat in trunk and triceps, to stick and move, stick and move, not get caught in a corner. Whitey chanting in a dust-filled room that stank of other peoples' sweat and he moving, moving until his legs were numb at the thighs. And this was the last time he would ever do it.

The bell rang and his mind was nowhere, it was everywhere. It was in the ring while Whitey yelled, it was seeking Loudenslager in the face of a determined opponent, it was screaming at him to move or be demolished. He moved, jabbing, jabbing, circling as Chervanek made tight charges at him. He was a matador and Chervanek was the bull. His strength was in counterpunching, in avoiding Chervanek's attacks and picking careful shots.

Here he comes sidestep jab jab jab go get him jab cross hook cross uppercut, now push him up onto the ropes, rough him up, hook down and bring it back up cross hold on and wait for the ref. When he lands, land back. Hit him hard and hold on.

The bell rang and he walked back to the corner and sat down, listening to Marion or was it Whitey it didn't matter they all said the same things. He stared across the tiny square at Chervanek or whoever, it didn't matter after eight years of doing it, they all did the same things, hit hit hit, hurt hurt hurt, and he was hitting back. He felt good; he felt alive.

The crowd had been screaming so it must have been a good round. He could never tell, all he ever really tried to do was survive, hit the other man as many times as he was being hit. He could feel the ones that bent his face but it was always hard to tell how badly he hurt the other man. But they had screamed and he was not really hurting anywhere badly, so some of his must have hurt Chervanek or whoever. Marion was patting him on the back, confident, and Marion didn't lie.

"You're killing him. You're looking great. He can't even find you. Just don't trade with him."

The buzzer went and Marion popped his mouthpiece back in. He sucked it into place and bit it down, tasting Marion's hand. The stool disappeared from under him and for a quick moment Fogarty felt abandoned, staring at Chervanek's pink muscular bulk. He smiled at Chervanek: just you and me, baby, and all that light from the ring lamps.

The bell rang again and he didn't feel anything, his guts and instincts took over and he danced, circled by himself, beating on a wild chimera that threatened to expose him in front of a thousand lusting eyes. Chervanek charged and he stepped to the side again and jabbed jabbed jabbed then moved in with a hate that he did not own, that had seized him when those gloves had been taped inextricably over his hands, and Chervanek staggered, his lip popping with a red gush. Fogarty followed the red, himself the bull now, the red like a cape waved in front of his face, and the face he pounded was anyone's, it was the gook asshole soldier who

174

had killed his friend, it was all the maddening hassle of a life that beat on him with every tick of a clock, with every deprivation and restriction.

Chervanek lay on the ropes, one eye closed and his lip spurting blood, both hands together near his chest. He rolled and swayed, waiting for Fogarty to attack again, having slowed the pace of the fight with his retreat. Fogarty planted his feet, getting ready to put him away *Whitey screaming in a musty gym and Loudenslager in the cold dirt like a winter tulip bulb he bled to death my jaw feels fine but look I see blood bled to death bled to death*…

It was like being mugged in some back alleyway, a club to the side of his head that he did not see or really even feel, its impact so brutal that his nerves refused to register the pain. A baseball bat connected on the lower left side of his jaw and he felt his heels skid backward as his air left him like a quick burp and then he was on his ass, his gloves pressed into the canvas. The crowd screamed its ugly delight and he shook his head fiercely several times, clearing it, then stood back up.

"…six, seven, eight!" The referee looked quickly at him. "Okay, that's it." He raised Chervanek's hand.

Four years of running, pounding, hitting and being hit, one small second where his mind took off and that was it. Fogarty followed the referee across the ring, pleading loudly, his eyes unbelieving. "Hey, you can't stop it like that! *Hey, ref!*" The crowd had been cheering. Now it was silent, Fogarty's screams drowning them out. "You can't do this to me! You can't do this!" The referee would not look at him. He walked around the ring, his hands folded, as if being chased by Fogarty. Fogarty danced in front of him. "You son of a bitch, I'll never forgive you, I'll never forgive you! I'm *fine*, goddamn it, can't you see? I'm fine!"

The referee continued to ignore him, now holding Chervanek's hand in the air. Yamato climbed into the ring, throwing Fogarty's robe over him and pulling him back to the corner. "Come on, Bill. Come on, man. They made up their mind, all right?"

*"They can't do this!"* Fogarty stared at the referee with a look that brought a frightened response from many at ringside. The referee still would not look at him. The next fighters were in their respective corners. The crowd was still silent, faint murmurs traveling through it like breezes.

Yamato manhandled him out of the ring and made him sit

down on the fighters' bench. He held his head inside two hands, more ashamed than disappointed, unable to comprehend it. The corpsman cut off those manacles, his gloves, and he stared numbly at his wrapped hands, tears pouring down his face. There was no way ever to redeem it; his boxing days were over. The crowd was already screaming at the next pair of fighters, insatiable in its lust, and he decided he did not like them anymore.

Nurse Goodbody was crying, too, her dark moons of eyes reaching out toward Fogarty as if she wanted to consume him, to make love to him and squeeze out all his pain. Lenahan shook his head and lit a cigarette, ignoring the censuring stares from surrounding officers and wives.

"Christ. The kid got screwed without getting kissed."

Goodbody patted his leg. "The poor boy. He tried so hard. I'm sick. Lenahan, why do you keep your cigarettes in your sock?"

"I'm not Lenahan, you dumb-ass Wop. I'm Ted. Come on, you're not on the ward, all right? I keep my cigarettes in my sock because it's unmilitary for a marine officer to keep anything in his pockets."

"Hey, that's, I mean, *really* the military, isn't it?" Goodbody was falsely impressed, teasing him. "So why do they give you all those pockets?"

"It's to throw people off, you see? Really, Goodbody, why do they give us hats? They don't keep our heads warm."

Goodbody seemed enthralled. "I don't know. Why do they give you hats?"

"Well, how the hell do you salute without a hat on?" Lenahan grinned secretly to her, putting his cigarettes back into his sock. "It has its advantages, all this. I mean, when the Colonel's wife comes up to you at some party and asks for a cigarette and you pull a sweaty pack out of your sock and offer her a bent-up Marlboro, it sort of makes her want to throw up." Lenahan watched Fogarty sitting on the bench, his head still in a towel. "He'll be alright. He's got to learn this part of it. Sometimes you do everything right and it still doesn't work out."

McClinton swore, shaking his head and pounding his fists on his knees, looking like he was being forced to sit on hot coals. "He was all right! He was fine! For Christ's sake, he chased the referee halfway around the ring and back! The goddamn ref didn't check his eyes or ask him to talk or even tell him to put his hands up and move. What the hell is going on?"

Linda cried softly, watching Fogarty on the bench. "Well, there's nothing we can do about it now."

"Oh, Linda, is that all you can say?" Sally Sue was incredulous. "He was robbed! That silly old ref just jumped the gun, even I can tell that and I don't know from anything about boxing. Bill had that other boy bleeding like a stuck pig. It wasn't *fair*."

"Well, I don't think it was *fair*, either." Linda had stopped her sniffling and was now giving a small smile to Fogarty as he sneaked a stare at her from behind his draped towel. "But it's *over*, Sally Sue. We can't change it. And if it's the worst thing that ever happens to him, we can all count our blessings, can't we?" *This is the world*.

Swenson leaned forward in his chair, apart from the others, watching Fogarty's misery, feeling it as if it were his own. "What a week."


Further up the stands, Dean and Peckarsky sat with a dozen other plebes from the company who had come prepared to carry Fogarty around the arena on their shoulders after he won his fight. Dean seemed stunned. Peckarsky nudged him, speaking over the roar as the crowd cheered for more blood from the next two fighters.

"He's going to be in a great mood Monday morning, John. You're going to get your ass royally run."

Dean watched Fogarty rise from the boxer's bench, the towel still draped over his head, and walk slowly out of the arena toward the locker room. He felt protective of Fogarty's early-morning rages, like some brutalized beneficiary, the wielder of a perverse but nonetheless very real pride. He is my anti-matter, thought Dean again, watching Fogarty turn and walk down a stairway. Fold him into me and we would cancel each other out, implode, disappear. So what should I be doing now if this is him, walking lonely away from his greatest love, that brutal, lit arena? *Walk into it*.

"So what? I can take it."


Fogarty sat on a wooden bench inside the locker room, his still-taped hands between his knees as he leaned forward on his elbows, staring at the floor. A pair of muscular black legs crossed in front of him, followed by a pair of sinewy, golden-brown legs. He looked up. Adair and Yamato nodded, then sat on the bench next to him.

He pointed at a drainhole in the concrete floor. "I wish I could crawl right into that hole and never come out again. I goddamn *blew* it. Eight years of fighting and I end it all with my ass on the deck. God damn, right out my *ass*, standing there like a tourist watching the asshole bleed while he was winding up the big one."

"Weren't any of us too lucky tonight." Jolly Chollie stared at the drainhole.

Yamato honked through a swollen nose. "Boom boom boom."

"If I was a civilian I'd take off for somewhere and not come back for a week." Fogarty started pulling at the gauze on his hands, commenting idly to himself that it was indeed the last time he would ever perform such an esoteric chore.

"If I was a civilian I'd go with you."

Adair started undressing. "Well, I know a mama out on the other side of West Street who's got just what I need, and I don't need to be no motherfuckin *civilian* to get any of it, either."

Yamato laughed softly, watching Adair. "Boom boom boom."

Upstairs in the arena the crowd still pulsed with screams, waves of bloodwishes pouring down the stairway, haunting their own failures. Adair danced through a shower and dressed quickly. "If Coach be wanting to see me, you don't know where I am."

"Well, ain't you something, lover-boy."

"I need me some soulful rest, my man." Chollie pulled on his overcoat and grabbed his cap. His mouth was smiling but his eyes were not. "Later."

Fogarty and Yamato sat side by side for several minutes, silent, their heads still ringing from recent punches. Finally Yamato mumbled in his honk, "So what do we do now?"

"Eat shit." Fogarty spat toward the drainhole, his spittle mixed with blood. "Where I come from they say the woods are always empty if you're a lousy hunter. Know what I mean?"

"Terrific." Yamato grimaced, then smiled. "At Navy they say only losers turn into philosophers."

# Chapter Seven: 2200

The message sat on his immaculate Formica desk top like a little yellow sail on a calm and empty sea. He picked it up as he trotted into his room, read it quickly, then stared at the ceiling with exasperation. Peckarsky nudged him.

"Who's it for?"

"Me."

"What's the matter?"

"It's Professor Thad again." He jammed the note into his pocket and put his cap back on his head, running out of the room again. "I'll be back."

"Hello?" Same soft music, other voices in the background. A party, perhaps? Have I been the subject of his dinner conversation, a little local color to blend with local seafood?

"Good evening, Professor. This is Midshipman Dean, returning your call, sir."

"Mister Dean!" It was said too loud merely to answer him. Was the professor announcing him to the others, delivering the brilliant, wronged victim of the System to his cohorts as promised? Dean suspected it. "How are you holding up? I'm glad you were able to return my call. I was beginning to worry about, well, whether they might be controlling your ability to get in touch with me. It's been far more than an hour, although I do understand how these things work in Bancroft Hall. Going through the Main Office, having to have your messages filtered through the command structure—"

"I was at the fights, Professor."

"Oh. Well." Thad seemed taken aback. "I didn't really know they let you out of your rooms at night." He recovered. "Well. Anyway, I have a friend here, a man who was at M.I.T. with me. He's an attorney now, if you can imagine a chemistry major switching to law—you know, from cookbook chemistry to the amorphous ranges of the unanswered." It was obvious that Thad was cheerfully taunting his friend as he spoke to Dean. "We've been talking about your case."

Dean startled at the phrase. So now I'm a *case*, he pondered, his stomach beginning to go acid with anticipation. "Professor, I'm—"

"He's really a very good lawyer. Hammond and Kittrie, in D.C." The names were supposed to mean something. "I'd like for you to talk with him if you would. I think you might be able to benefit from each other's experiences."

"Professor, I already tried to explain to you that—"

"Hello, Mister Dean?" It was somebody else. "My name is Tom Stiles. This is a rather weird way to meet, but I thought I might be able to help. How are you?"

Scared, thought John Dean. Scared shitless. "I'm fine, sir."

"We've been talking about your case. Jonathan—that is, Professor Thad—is very concerned, and wants to do something about this. I can understand your reluctance, but I can pretty well guarantee you that no one will hurt you. It's you who've been hurt. You should understand that your rights are being violated. That's not only against the regulations as they have been clearly stated to everyone on duty over there—" Stiles said "over there" with a taste of foreignness and even contempt— "but is violative of the Constitution of the United States. You don't surrender your constitutional rights when you put on a uniform. We have fought these battles in many arenas, John, and I just want you to know that you are on firm ground. I'll be helping Jonathan whenever he needs it. This sort of brutality is simply a symptom of a much larger disease."

Dean felt like he was going to throw up. "Professor—Mister—listen. I'm doing okay, can't you believe it? This whole—"

"Hello, Mister Dean?" It was Thad again, the vicarious sufferer, warm and enthused. "I won't hold you any longer. I know the pressures you're under. But I hope you appreciate the quality of help we're getting, *pro bono*."

"Professor, *please*. I told you, I can work this out myself."

"You're a brave man, Mister Dean. A very brave man."

# Chapter Eight: 2300

"In four months you're going to graduate. And then we're going to be married, in the Chapel. And when you get back from Vietnam we're going to have five kids and you'll make general and the whole world will be our rubber ball."

"I don't even want to go in there."

"*Bill.*" Linda grabbed his arm and shook it, a teasing rebuke. "You're stronger than that. Besides, they're all probably so drunk by now that they don't even remember that there *were* any fights tonight."

"Entirely possible. But irrelevant." Fogarty climbed slowly out of the car and walked toward the house, viewing the lights and the motions beyond the uncurtained windows with a pained reluctance. All the lights upstairs were off. Another typical weekend at Mack's, he mused, as a gust of dark icy air crawled inside the bruises on his face.

Mack and five other classmates rented the house, which had been "passed down" to them by several members of the previous year's graduating class. A local real estate agent had rented the place to midshipmen for years. On the inside, it was a disaster. There were almost no furnishings, and only the sink and refrigerator worked in the kitchen. But it was a haven, a place to come and be normal. Or whatever.

Fogarty rang the doorbell, one arm protectively around Linda. Mack opened it, dressed in jeans and a T-shirt that accentuated his weightlifter's build. Someone screamed inaudibly behind him. Two midshipmen sprinted toward the kitchen from the living room, laughing and growling. In the living room, on the only piece of furniture downstairs, a stained, overstuffed sofa, two women talked animatedly to each other, sprawled out, obviously drunk.

"Hey, Bill! I thought it would be you." Something crashed in the kitchen. Mack looked quickly in that direction, then turned back around and shrugged. "Who the hell knows? Come on in."

"Bi-i-i-ill." Linda's eyes went wide. She had just begun removing her coat. Fogarty followed her gaze and immediately stepped in front of her, pointing at a classmate.

"If you so much as start to put a hand on her, George, I'll punch your lights out. I'm serious, man. I'm in no mood tonight."

"Ah, Bill." George put a hand on Fogarty's shoulder. "I heard about that. I'm really sorry, man. And you—" George smiled drunkenly at Linda, inspecting her body with hazy eyes. "You sure got nice tits." He looked quickly back to Fogarty. "No offense, of course."

"Of course." Fogarty gently prodded George across the room, whispering into his ear. "Go fuck yourself, George."

"Hell, I'm going to have to." George looked miserable for a

moment, like an Emmett Kelly clown. Then suddenly he brightened. "But come spring leave, ah, my sweet Mississippi Pearl..." His voice trailed off wistfully.

"I hope I get to meet her, George. The first thing I'm going to do is twist her goddamn tits off."

"She's an angel! A goddamned angel, Fogarty. You'd kill her."

"I'd sure as hell try to. Payback is a motherfucker, George."

In the kitchen someone had bent an ice tray in two, smashing it against the sink to free the ice. It lay useless on the floor. Fogarty grabbed two beers, and seeing a half-dozen empty cans on the counter, shook his head fitfully and collected them, giving the two cans to Linda. He opened the door to the garage and tossed the empty cans casually inside. They clinked, hitting other metal rather than the floor. Linda's eyebrows raised with curiosity.

"What kind of sound was that?"

"You haven't seen the garage?" Fogarty held the door opened, gesturing cavalierly inside, and turned the light on. The light reflected off of a mass of beer cans four feet deep that covered the entire garage floor. Linda put one hand over her mouth and laughed, her eyes bright.

Fogarty grinned through his swollen face, turning off the light. "Six years of parties. That's how long the mids have had this house."

Sally Sue was standing in the middle of the living room, word-slurring drunk, her shoes off and her hands on her hips. She looked striking, like an animal designed for the rawest forms of passion. Her eyes were stuporous, but at the same time were lit with electric irritation.

"So, who the hell ripped the toilet seat off? Huh? Where the hell is the toilet seat? I have to *pee!*" Several men laughed hilariously, taunting her. "Now, how the hell is a girl supposed to pee when you stole the goddamn toilet seat? Ha. You all think it's funny. You all can stand up to pee. Well, all right. I can stand up to pee, too." The taunts increased. Sally Sue grew a devil's face. "And you don't believe me. All right. You all never seen a woman stand up to pee? All *right!*" She walked briskly out of the room, the men close behind, losing her footing as she turned the corner in the hallway.

In a few minutes a loud chorus of male cheers emanated

from the bathroom. Swenson sat on the sofa, his head buried in his hands. Fogarty sat next to him as a new wave of cheers came from down the hall. Swenson looked over, and tried a smile.

"She's pretty drunk, that's all. She's just drunk, Bill. Hey, I'm so sorry about your fight."

Sally Sue returned, with five men in tow. She had a triumphant smile, a victor's walk. "So, the hell with your goddamn toilet seats! You all think you're so hot, just because you're men!"

George shook his head, his wild, hazy, drunken eyes in awe of Sally Sue. "You wouldn't have believed it, Swede. She just dropped her britches and lifted up her skirt and pissed like a man. Didn't lose a drop, either. Not a drop."

"Shut up, George." Fogarty looked at all of them, his lips tight.

Sally Sue walked across the room like a cat, angling this way and that, never approaching Swenson head on, a sly smile on her magnificent face. "Swede's mad at me, uh huh. Swede thinks I'm dis ... *gusting*. Well, Swede, if you're mad at me, why don't you just tell little Sally Sue to kiss off?"

"You're pretty drunk, Sally Sue." Swenson stood and took her by the arm, heading for the stairway. "Come on. Let's go upstairs. I think you need to lie down for a while."

"Oh, ho!" Sally Sue wagged a finger at the others in the room, following Swenson toward the stairs reluctantly, facing the others as he dragged her by the arm. "Are you really worried about me, Swede, huh? Well, good-bye, folks. Swede wants to ... talk."

Linda sat next to Fogarty on the couch and they watched Swenson's retreat and the others' laughter. Linda touched Fogarty on the arm, leaning against him.

"It's not right, Bill, It's just not right. Poor Swede."

"How anybody that smart can be that dumb." Fogarty shrugged. "Sally Sue comes free. It doesn't mean anything to her. Everybody but Swede sees that. Why the hell does he make himself pay? Come on, Linda. Let's start saying our good-byes."

Sally Sue knelt astride Swenson, her long fingers playing the muscles of his stomach like a piano, those lean shoulders high in delighted shrugs and the rest of her undulating around and around, then forward and back, her face searching the ceiling for that shuddering moment, her round high breasts pointing this way and that into the night. Swenson lay back on the mattress in the stark room, at first feeling free, mingled in space with her like a blend of music, his fingers into her thick pubic hair, watching whispering lips alive in every detail, even in the darkened room.

Then, subtly, he again understood that he was being used, and he watched the poetry above him and said over and over, I am a phallus, I am a phallus. I point straight up to God and she rides me like a hydrant, like the Washington Monument, like the Eiffel Tower. I am her machine.

She shuddered, a croak in her throat, holding his hand to her as her eyes still searched the ceiling and he held back his own climax, a gesture of triumph and despair. I made her need me more I won but then I lose because watch her stare into the dark I could have been a hydrant.

"Sally Sue," he said, pulling her from her distant perch and holding her, "I love you I love you I love you."

She patted him on the back, an almost formal gesture. "Thanks, Swede. I really needed that."


"Where's Mack?" Fogarty peered around the room, one last visual sweep before departing. "I wanted to say thanks."

"Mack's upstairs, too." Arnie Lesse, of company football and reveille musterboard fame, smiled at Fogarty through panda's eyes. "You're the only one from that room that's still down here, Bill. Why don't you make it unanimous?"

"Yeah, sure." Fogarty guffawed, his arm around Linda. "Mack's up there with that little brunette he just met? That's hard to believe. She just didn't seem the type to me."

"Well, you know Mack." Lesse grinned again, making gorilla gestures. "One look at him in a muscle shirt and they all flip."

"Oh, bullshit." Fogarty laughed, shaking his head knowingly. "He's probably up there holding hands, making up a story for us."


She stared up at him, childlike in her straight innocent gaze, so small that she would not have even made a shadow of him. "So what did you want to show me?"

184

"Just the room, I guess." He sat on the bed, his face now nearer her own. "I really like you. No, really I do."

She walked over to the window. Outside, Fogarty and Linda were climbing into his car. The door slammed. "Your friend Bill Fogarty is leaving. Don't you want to say good-bye?"

"Oh, I'll see him back in the Hall. You don't get too far away from each other when you all go back to be locked up in Mother B at night."

She gave a quick giggle, still staring out the window. "You know, I feel sorry for you guys. There aren't very many of you who seem normal."

"What do you mean?"

"You're all either super-straight or super-crazy. Oh, I can't explain it, exactly." She turned away from the window and leaned against the wall in the dark, watching him. "I guess that isn't fair when I've only seen this place for one day. I've just never seen anything so dominated by the clock before. It's *Pavlovian!* It must drive you crazy." Her voice was like a muted alto sax, all mellow and melodic and unawed. "You eat by the clock, you study by the clock, you even have to party by the clock." She gave a small smile, measuring him with an exactness that made him laugh involuntarily, with unspoken embarrassment. "I saw you check your watch as soon as you closed that door. Do you do this by the clock too, Mack?"

She had a clarity about her, an honesty that squeaked like well-washed bone china dinnerware and rang just as resonant. Mack found himself craving her. "Really, I didn't have anything … specific in mind at all. I just wanted to be alone with you, and the hardest thing about being at the Academy is trying to be alone with a girl. Can you imagine what that does to someone? I never even thought about it before. I mean, I spent my whole *life* around the Army, and West Point, and I never even thought about this part of it. When I was a kid I'd see the cadets dragging their dates on the weekends and I'd talk to them about all of it and they said it but I never really heard, I guess. But it's—it's *devastating.*"

She was watching him with that small, unconvinced smile. He leaned forward on the bed. "All right, I want to tell you something. I'm not trying to make myself into a loverboy, either. But last year I was dating a girl and she came down to see me. It was in the late spring. I really liked her, you know? On Sunday afternoon we tried to find a place to be alone. I'd thought about it all week. The only place I could come up with was the Jeanette Monument, over in the cemetery. It's a big cross with icicles hanging from it, in memory of a crew that froze to death on their ship up in the Arctic. Anyway, on one side of the monument there's a bunch of bushes, so you can't see the base of the monument from the road." He could see her amused smile, her angled head in the dark. "Okay, it was dumb. But here I am, twenty-one years old, hiding in the bushes in a cemetery just to be alone with my best girlfriend, in the middle of the day. There just wasn't any other place! So, you guessed it. There we were, lying in the grass about half-dressed, and an officer decides to show his kids the famous goddamned Jeanette Monument. They come bouncing around it and walk right on top of us. Oh, I mean right on top!"

Mack raised two heavy arms in a helpless shrug. "You should've read the Form Two. It broke up the whole Main Office watch squad." She was laughing, eyeing him with a humorous warmth. "And I picked up seventy-five demerits, seventy-five big ones. That's a month and a half of sitting inside my room all day every weekend, standing inspections every hour, not seeing anything or anybody outside of that goddamned Hall, just because I wanted to be alone with a woman for a while." Mack's eyes darkened. "And that officer called my girlfriend a whore. My best girl. She refused to ever see me again, or to even *talk* to me. So—" Mack shrugged, peering at her with an intensity that was so real that the space between them tingled with it. "So now I have this dump, me and some other guys. And it's nice to be able to be alone with a woman, even if the stopwatch never quits running."

"I had no idea it was that bad." She was slowly shaking her head, still against the wall, her arms folded in front of her.

Mack laughed softly. "Oh, yeah. You remember Fogarty? Mister super-straight, right? Well, before he started dating Linda, Fogarty was a wild man. He still holds the record for the quickest slam-bam-thank-you-ma'am in the Brigade. He had taken this girl to one of those rock concerts and was walking her to the bus stop over by Gate Four, and on the spur of the moment he asked her to go across the street behind some bushes, I mean like twenty feet off the road, on the edge of the St. John's campus. She reminded him about the bus. So they ran across the goddamned road and laid there in the bushes, bare ass and all, with the headlights bouncing on them." She was laughing. So was McClinton. "And talk about beating the clock, the chick still made her bus! Fogarty came in all grass-stained in his trop whites, cussing up a storm because he couldn't even remember the girl's name and she'd made him promise to marry her if she got pregnant."

"You poor guys. Why do you put up with all of this?"

"Duty, honor, country. Forty bucks a month. The chance to fly a jet. Hell, I don't know. I just take one day at a time. It's almost over, now." He watched her oval face in the dark. "Can I kiss you?"

"I'm not getting on that bed."

He lost himself in her too-young eyes, the child's eyes that kept staring back at him, trying to understand the need and anguish in his own. He kissed her as she stood against the wall, his mouth speaking the pain of an unrelenting loneliness with his searching tongue as it caressed the inside of her mouth, a little girl's lips whispering back that she didn't French-kiss unless she was in love. He held her rounded, neophytic breasts, one at a time, their soft silkiness giving him such pleasure that his eyes went moist and the inside of his chest burned.

He caressed her thigh and she grabbed his hand and said no, no, no, and placed it on her breasts again and in a moment it was back along her thighs and she said no no no it isn't nice but it was so nice, how could he tell her what it meant to him, how could she understand? He was lost inside her dark eyes and then his tongue measured all the caverns of her mouth again, his hands out of control, beyond denial, *why must this part of my life be so removed?*

She stood straight up, turning her face toward the window. It was over.

"You don't respect me," she said softly, her words making little clouds along the icy window.

"I'm sorry," McClinton groaned, she like a child next to his bulky frame. 'I'm sorry. Really. I'm sorry."

She walked toward the door, fastening her brassiere. He watched her with a sad clown's face. "Will you see me again?"

"Not up here I won't."

"I'm not usually like this. It just gets to me. You will see me again?"

She stopped by the door. Downstairs they were screaming about something, some latest mad drunken party excuse. "You're nice, Mack. I like you, too." Then she walked out of the door, leaving it open behind her.

# Chapter Nine: 2400

"Oh, Goodbody, I swear to God you are an *original*, did you know that?" Lenahan lay back on his bed, dragging on a cigarette as she came bouncing from his bathroom, totally nude, her long hair unfastened and around her shoulders, doing some weird dance that seemed to be a cross between a waltz and rock and roll. He laughed from the belly, something he had not done for months or maybe years. "You're about three kinds of crazy, woman!"

She stopped in front of his bed and did a curtsy, then spoke in a falsetto, grabbing one of his forearms. "Nurse Canigliaro at your service, sir. May I take your pulse? Was your bowel movement all right yesterday? Did you pee on your sheets when you tried to use your bedpan? You really should stop smoking, you know." Her comment about his smoking was serious, said slowly in her normal voice.

"Come on, Goodbody, I don't need a mother."

"You've never had to scrub on a lung cancer operation, you dumb asshole marine. Lungs are like a sponge, do you know what I mean? And smokers' lungs are like sponges soaked in ... in dirty motor oil! It's grotesque to look at. *Terrible*." She sat on the edge of his bed, her breasts so large that when she leaned over they almost rested on her thighs. "I'm not made for this racket, Lenahan. It literally turns my stomach to watch a doctor make an incision. Ack!" She made a face, shaking her head. "I hate it."

"Then why the hell did you become a nurse?"

"Oh, now he wants answers!" She held her forehead, staring at the ceiling. "Catholic girls are doomed to nursehood at birth, Lenahan. You should know that."

He found himself laughing again. "Melodrama leaves me weak."

"Oh!" She pushed him back onto his pillow. "Rest up, you poor sick man." She looked around his cluttered bedroom. "How long have you lived here, Lenahan?"

"Will you stop calling me Lenahan?"

"You call me Goodbody."

"Well ... all right. What the hell is your first name?"

"Maria." She smiled demurely. "But you can call me Goodbody."

"No, Maria, I like that. Goodbody is so goddamned perjorative." He raised his eyebrows. "Hey, you like that word? Huh? I ain't just a dumb-ass marine."

"I don't even know what it means."

"It means people talk about you, about the way you swing your ass around. Doesn't it bother you that they talk?"

Her eyes went wide for a quick moment as if stunned at his comment. Then she shrugged. "It doesn't mean anything, really."

"What do you mean, it doesn't mean anything? Of course it does."

"It doesn't matter, Lenahan, all right?" She folded her hands over her breasts. "You're just about ready to talk yourself out of a lay, did you know that?"

"Big deal. What's a piece of ass, anyway, huh? What do you do to yourself, just to dispense a piece of ass? Hey." He poked at her arms. She had gone completely silent. "Come on. I just worry about you, that's all. I don't like to see good people being used. And you're damn good people."

"You don't know that."

"The hell I don't." He grinned frivolously. "You forget, we go back a long way. You can tell a lot about somebody when you ask them to empty your bedpan. Goddamn Morphine Mary used to make me feel guilty every time I had to go. You never bitched once. You were terrific."

"So I'm easy." Goodbody shrugged, smiling with a sort of helplessness. "Don't make me anything I'm not, Lenahan. I'm not sure I can handle it."

"Oh, bullshit." He prodded her on the shoulder. "Do you like it, being talked about that way by everybody?"

"Why are you asking me all this, Lenahan?" She had taken his poncho liner and wrapped herself in it, and was staring at him with defensive moons of eyes.

"I guess it's because I like you." Lenahan shrugged, putting out his cigarette. "If I didn't like you, I'd just screw you and keep my mouth shut. But I like you. And I have to make sure you know I think it's wrong for somebody to use you, so you'll know I'm not using you."

"So what are you doing? Or planning on doing?"

"Hell, I don't know." Lenahan smiled, his craggy face lined in his cheeks and forehead with his amusement, his blue eyes searching hers. "Make love to you, I guess. Or with you."

"You're really very sensitive." Just her head stuck out of his green poncho liner, accentuating her deep searching eyes. "I'm not used to that."

"I'm pretty screwed up, actually." He continued to grin. His voice took on a formal tenor, bouncing resonantly off of his undecorated bedroom walls. " 'Would it have been worthwhile to have bitten off the matter with a smile, to have squeezed the universe into a ball, to roll it toward some overwhelming question, to say: I am Lazarus, come from the dead, come back to tell you all, I shall tell you all,—if one, settling a pillow by her head, should say: that is not what I meant at all; that is not it, at all.' " He shrugged nonchalantly. "T. S. Eliot."

"That's beautiful." Her eyebrows raised curiously. "What does it mean?"

"Anything you want it to. That's the great thing about poetry."

"Then why did you say it, Lenahan? What did it mean to you?"

"I guess I was trying to ask you what it would do to me if I made love to you, if I violated that most secret and special part of your insides, and opened my insides to you, then had you kiss me off in the same breath as a quick screw in the Duty Surgeon's room. And what does it say about you if you can throw your ass around like that, without a second thought?"

"Oh, that's deep." She actually shuddered underneath the poncho liner. "You're so deep it's scary, Lenahan. Maybe you'd better just take me home."

"I'd like for you to stay. Really. That's the hell of it."

"You don't keep a gun under your pillow, do you?"

"I keep one under my bed, but—"

"Oh, Christ. Let me out of here."

"Goodbody, knock off the bullshit, will you? You don't have to make love to me, but at least you can take what I said seriously."

She stared at him for a long time, her face solemn now. "All right, Lenahan, I'll stay. But don't make any moves on me. And you can take me back tomorrow morning?"

"After church I can." He squinched up his face. "I'm under orders to be in the Hall every morning for a week, including Sunday. But after that, I have to go see Neil Bard anyway. I can take you back then."

She shook her head sadly. "I don't know why you're going to see Lieutenant Bard. He's so sick and brain-damaged he doesn't even know you're there."

"Hah. That's what you think. You and your goddamn medical friends, thinking you know all the answers. He'll remember. Besides, don't try to talk yourself out of a ride back, Goodbody. It's a long and complicated bus trip to Bethesda, believe me."

"You're right." She lay under the covers in his bed, turning away from him. "Good night, Lenahan."

"Good night, Goodbody."

Then later in the night she came to him, kissing his chest and throat and face, awakening him and infusing him with a warmth and depth of emotion that overwhelmed him, even in his slumber. They loved for an hour, touching and exploring, and when it was over he felt her tears drip from her face where it lay on his shoulder.

"Thanks, Lenahan. You're a real human being."

He kissed her eyes, his lips becoming wet with tears. "You're an original, Goodbody. A goddamn original."

# PART FOUR:

---

# SUNDAY,
# FEBRUARY 11,
# 1968

# Chapter One: 0715

Sunday mornings in Annapolis were slow and historic, as if they had been drawn from a Currier and Ives print. The town had no industry, and in fact did not even boast a railroad station, making it the only state capital in the continental United States without one. Old Town Annapolis, which clung to the Academy walls like fine old ivy, had not changed for decades, maybe even a century. And its narrow cobbled streets with the high square buildings and the old trees whose roots pushed bricks right out of the sidewalks went silent as museums on Sunday mornings.

The almost vernal solitude of Annapolis was one of the main reasons Secretary of the Navy George Bancroft decided to establish his Naval School there in 1845. Having originally begun the school in Philadelphia, Secretary Bancroft was persuaded to remove to the "healthy and secluded" location at the mouth of the Chesapeake Bay in order to "avoid the temptations and distractions that necessarily connect with a large and populous city to the detriment of young officers," according to a journal of that time.

The army was only too glad to abandon its old Fort Severn in favor of Secretary Bancroft's plan. Annapolis in the nineteenth century was an antiquated, dying sea town. And the first man chosen to head the Academy's medical department refused his orders after inspecting Annapolis, calling it "the dullest and most horrible place in the United States—it is very old, and I do not suppose a house has been built there in 40 years—the place is finished and will not improve…confound the place I hate the thought of it."

Thus, for those assigned to the Academy, "IHTFP" became a slogan even before the institution formally existed.

Ted Lenahan thought none of those things as he drove past ancient buildings, his tires stuttering on the cobbles of old brick roads, and yet he felt the same mix of isolation and enchantment that had been passed down through the continuum, like the uniform itself. Church Circle, State Circle, the Governor's mansion, St. John's College, a hundred huge old houses that looked as if they belonged on the seacoast of New England: they had all been there when he was a midshipman. They all reminded him of the lonely years spent walking on weekends inside the infamous "seven mile limit," of different women, of football games, of a whole esoteric life lived and gone in four years. Even seven years later he resisted it, resented it, and yet, strangely, longed for its innocence and simplicity. Annapolis was not a town, especially on Sunday mornings. It was a memory.

The midshipmen were a dark-uniformed, churning reality. Sunday morning was the only time of the week when reveille did not go. The hall lights remained off. Morning meal was optional, although chapel was mandatory, Catholic formation going at seven-fifteen and Protestant formation following, at nine-fifteen. Those of other denominations were allowed to attend church in town, forming up and marching out the gates or being picked up by parishioners. It was a major offense to miss chapel on Sunday in one of its many forms. Even the most avowed heathen was required to sit through somebody's sermon.

Lenahan strode through Tecumseh Court in his long green overcoat, his cheeks ruddy with the raw air, scrutinizing every company's Catholic formation. The midshipmen seemed astonished at his presence, incredulous that he would be examining them so closely on an early Sunday morning. Sunday mornings were normally a free ride, without inspections.

They stood in their little rectangular groups, oblivious to an early-morning wind that rose raw from the river. A drum pecked in the distance and they marched company-by-company along Stribling Walk, with a solemnity that was punctuated only by an occasional yawn, and then turned up another walkway. They marched in perfect, mechanical step, two long rows that disappeared inside the Chapel doors.

What the hell, thought Lenahan, striding slowly behind the last company. I'm already here. I may as well go to mass.

He sat at the very back of the chapel, among the handful of dates and tourists who had awakened early enough to come to mass. The chapel was huge, awesome in its caverns, with room enough for several thousand people. Lenahan gazed down the aisle, along a blue carpet that reminded him of the sea, and in between him and the distant pulpit were so many memories that the pulpit blurred; or was it tears again? Goddamn, thought Lenahan. Here I go *again*. Twenty-eight or is it nine now, who the hell counts anymore, and I'm acting like I'm five. Plebe summer in those front pews praying fervently for some dark deliverance, every Sunday after that for four years talking to Whomever, lamenting, striving, and later even consecrating that which is inalterably violated right down that same blue sea *I do I do*

I need a poem, decided Lenahan, blinking self-pity off his face in two salty little streams. Something biting, maybe a little humorous *How long, O Lord? Wilt thou forget me forever? How long wilt Thou hide Thy face from me? How long must I bear pain in my soul, and have sorrow in my heart all the day?*

Well, what a creep I am. What a goddamn crybaby.

Steve and Angie were outside together after the service, the perfect couple, smiling and greeting other officers and their families. The Pepsi-Cola kids, mused Lenahan, walking slowly over to them, getting that same raw feeling in his guts that he used to get while making night patrols in Vietnam. It was as if the earth would explode underneath his feet with any step, or the sky itself would erupt with little pellets singing death. There was Angie, there was Steve. Angie and Steve. I can deal with Angie, thought Lenahan, I can deal with Steve. I can't deal with Angie and Steve.

Steve stood on the front steps of the chapel, laughing as Lenahan approached them. "Well, hell itself just froze over. This must be the first time you've been to mass since we graduated, Lenahan."

"Wrong. I got married, didn't I? And I came to your wedding. Hi, Angie."

"Hi, Ted." She made it sound so perfectly distant, warm and yet impersonal at the same time. Who the hell would ever know, mused Lenahan, trying not to search her eyes. She had her arm around Steve's waist.

"Well, once every three years, whether it does any good or not. Are you all right, Ted?" Steve was scrutinizing him through the stare of a long-time, intimate friend, with eyes that had watched him suffer and perform for more than ten years.

"Huh? Oh, yeah. I'm all right. I'm a little tired, that's all."

"Bachelor life's getting you down, huh? I hear you had a real piece of cake at the Brigade Finals last night."

Angie started, the pupils in her eyes expanding and then contracting again, like a cat's. Lenahan gave a small, irascible smile. "Word gets around, doesn't it? Ah, she's just a friend from the hospital. I was in seeing Neil Bard yesterday."

"How is he?"

"He's a *carrot*." Lenahan shot the word at his old roommate like a spear.

"What?"

"He's a potato."

"What are you talking about, Ted?" Steve's face was pinched, alarmed more at Lenahan's demeanor than his words.

"He's a stalk of corn, that's what I'm talking about. A piece of *squash*, because that's what happened to his goddamned brain; it got squashed. He's a vegetable, Steve."

"Oh, God." Angie held her forehead, looking down at the chapel steps.

"But I'm going to talk him out of it." Lenahan said it so evenly, with so much quiet conviction, that he himself began to believe it. "Stay out of Vietnam, Steve. Or if you go, get yourself a nice staff job briefing some fat ass in Saigon. I'm tired of going to that fucking hospital, I really am."

Both Steve and Angie seemed embarrassed at his display of emotion. He tried to remember a poem, a funny one, but again he couldn't. Finally he shrugged, finding an ironic grin instead.

"Well, anyway, I have to go watch the Protestants do their little chapel trick, so Pratt won't fry me for missing a formation or something. Hah hah. That's why I'm here, really. I'm still doing my little dog and pony show for my Leader."

"Yeah, well, you better get going, then." Steve put an arm around Angie's shoulder. "Drop by the house sometime."

Lenahan waved as he walked away, looking at Steve and then at Angie. Angie had smothered all her emotions underneath her navy-issue officers' wives patented smile.

"Thanks, Steve. Have me over for dinner sometime. It's a pain in the ass cooking for myself."

# Chapter Two: 0915

"All right, listen up." Dreiden drawled it, as if he didn't really care whether they did or not. His pointed nose was red from the cold and his puffy rooster's chest stuck out, even through his overcoat. "The Commandant's on the rag again. He noticed last Sunday that too many mids were marching to chapel with their collars undone, and that we weren't squaring the corner at the top of the chapel steps with enough military pre—*cision*."

The midshipmen in formation jeered at the chapel Company Commander. He shrugged his shoulders, responding in his uncaring drawl. "Come on, give me a break, I'm reading this. Laugh all you want, but the O.D. is going to be watching and taking names, so if you don't want a pap, wake the hell up and march right. If you haven't shaved, it's too late. Try to look young." Dreiden signed the musterboard, indicating who was present and who missing from formation, then looked around Tecumseh Court. "Besides, Lenahan's in the area again, so knock off the noise. I don't need to get fried."

At the edge of the court, over near a high wall, they suddenly heard the unmistakeable tight-throated tenor of Commander Pratt publicly abusing someone. Dreiden shivered, blowing onto his white gloves. "Oh, Christ. Mad Pratt's in the area, too. For God's sake, don't do anything dumb."

"He's chewing out Lenahan!" A midshipman from the far end of the ranks called to the others, keeping his head and face perfectly still. Dreiden called back.

"Shut up in the ranks."

They listened intently. Through the stillness of their military formation, as adjutants reported units prepared to march, Pratt's invectives echoed like rifle blasts.

"I didn't see you at Catholic formation, Captain."

"Sir, I was at the formation, sir. I walked through the entire Court, inspecting the companies."

"Did you find anything *wrong*, Captain Lenahan?"

"No, sir, I didn't."

"Then how do I know you were there?"

In the pause that followed, several quiet solutions floated in whispered invective from Lenahan's own company, none of which Pratt heard.

"I guess you'll have to take my word for it, sir."

"You've been doing this for three days, Captain, and I've yet to see one Form Two. Are you trying to tell me the Brigade no longer commits offenses?"

"No, sir."

"Are you telling me there is no value in reporting these offenses?"

"No, sir."

"Then maybe you're telling me you don't have the stomach for your job, Captain."

"I know how to command troops, sir, and I believe they've been responding."

"These aren't troops, Captain. These aren't troops. They're *midshipmen*. Do you know the difference?"

"No, sir. I guess I don't, sir."

"Midshipmen learn to lead troops. We—"

"All troops learn to lead troops, sir. That's what troops are for."

"We put them through, through...hell, Captain. That's discipline. We'll talk about this again, Captain Lenahan. I can guarantee you it won't go away."

"Yes, sir. Aye, aye, sir. Good morning, sir."


Quiet murmurs floated through the thousand midshipmen standing in the cold silence of Tecumseh Court. Dean stood in the back rank of the formation, trying to see Lenahan and Pratt without breaking attention. So we're not even troops, he thought, confused and wounded. What are we, dogs to be whipped? Great. Then in a few years we can all try to be like Pratt.

The drum started in the distance, near the chapel, and one by one the companies began to march up Stribling Walk. The band cut in, playing "Onward, Christian Soldiers." It played "Onward, Christian Soldiers" every Sunday, just as Lenahan's company split the distance between Tecumseh's statue and the turnoff from Stribling Walk toward the chapel. Dean, in his scientist's way, had it down to fifteen steps, plus or minus five. Clockwork, he mused, having reached seventeen when the band cut in. Even the church songs are programmed and synchronized.

Chapel wasn't so much for God as it was for tourists. They turned up the walkway that led to the chapel and in front of them, standing in the street and along the chapel steps, was the usual gathering of girlfriends and parents and tourists, collected in the cold to view them as if they were indeed marching off to war.

Up the chapel steps. Dean carefully paced himself so he would hit the first step with his right foot. Otherwise, the wrong foot would hit the top step and he would be unable to pivot properly and the Commandant of Midshipmen would grimace darkly and the Officer of the Day would send his plebe Mate chasing after the formation to get Dean's name and he would have another batch of demerits. Dean pivoted on the top, exactly as he was supposed to, and emitted a sigh of uncontrollable relief: Praise the Lord, who called me to this test. I made it.

A plebe Mate chased their column as it made its way along the side of the chapel, pencil alertly touching his notepad, calling to an upperclassman just over from Dean.

"Name, sir? Sir, can I have your name?"

"Whitlow." The upperclassman automatically gave his service number. "Sixty-nine, thirty-seven twenty-six."

"Thirty-seven twenty-six, sir?"

"Thirty-seven twenty-six. Hey, Mate."

"Yes, sir?" The plebe had been moving right along with the company's march as he recorded the necessary information to place the man on report.

"Fuck you."

Dean glanced quickly over to Whitlow, wondering why he had been fried. Whitlow's collar was unbuckled. The full dress blue collars were high and irritating, and Whitlow had a thick, bulging neck that strained against it. Dummy, thought Dean. What's ten minutes of pain compared to a weekend of restriction?

Inside the chapel they filed into rows of pews, the upperclass ordering the plebes into the center sections that offered greater scrutiny from officers and tourists, many upperclass then scrambling for a side alcove that had come to be known as "Sleepy Hollow," since it was unviewable from the officer and tourist sections of the chapel, and hence allowed the unrepentant to sleep during the services without punishment. A nod of the head was worth twenty Big Ones in chapel.

Dean dropped his overcoat underneath his pew, watching the upperclass scramble into Sleepy Hollow, envying their sanctuary. You can send a mid to chapel, he thought sardonically as he noticed many of them unbuckling their uniform collars and settling back into their hidden pews, but you can't make him pray.

The higher-ranking officers and their families filed down the long blue carpet toward the front-center pews, like royalty. Finally, the Brigade stripers marched in, two by two, Fogarty among them, and sat at the very front. Later the stripers would march to the rear of the chapel with the exactness of a parade, two by two, and pass collection plates among the nonmidshipman guests. There would be hymns, a scripture reading by one of the high stripers, and then a sermon.

Then we will pray for our country's navy, thought Dean

absently, wondering how the navy got along during the week. And sing a hymn for those in peril on the sea. It was archaic. It was obsolete. It was faintly vulgar. But it was, secretly, something he admitted only to himself, a hell of a show.

The routine began. Dean stood up when the Brigade stood up, sat down when they sat down, prayed when they prayed. Up and down, sing and pray, precise and somehow meaningless, military, like a parade. He watched Fogarty sitting just in front of the Admiral himself, erect and expectant, one side of his face still slightly swollen from his fight. I've got to tell him about Thad, thought Dean. I've got to figure out a way to let him know without having him kill me in the process.

Finally the goddamn thing was over. Fogarty had felt them stare at him all through the service, free looks as if he were on display, taking in each bruise on his face, every flicker of his eyes. Oh Christ, thought Fogarty, grabbing his overcoat, who the hell am I? I used to be Ron Loudenslager but Ron is now used to be or maybe never was so who the hell am I? Ron Loudenslager is dead and I am knocked out so what is left except courage?

He could feel the momentum of a dozen friends moving toward him to commiserate with him, to pity him, to bitch about the fight and cry about his friend. He ducked quickly out a side door, then moved around to the front of the chapel to find Linda.

"Well, fancy you, Bill Fogarty!" Sally Sue stood next to Swenson as they waited with Linda for him on the chapel steps. She looked stunning, like a movie star, as if she had been dropped into a crowd of ordinary people in order to film a commercial extolling wholesomeness. "Up there in front, passing out the plate, marching up and down the aisle like that. Oh, I am *impressed*."

"Yeah, Sally Sue, I just jangle when I walk, I'm so full of glitter and tinsel." Fogarty smiled ironically. "I'm sure God was pleased to see how well we marched to chapel today, even if the Commandant wasn't."

Swenson's grin matched Fogarty's as he dared to hold Sally Sue's hand. "So we got to him again."

"The Brigade looked ragged coming up the steps. That's what he told Banks."

"Well, I thought you all looked terrific."

"You're easy, Sally Sue." Swenson's eyes flashed as Fogarty said it. He immediately regretted his choice of words. "What I mean is, you're too kind. Hey," he put a hand on Linda's shoulder. "We're going over to the Pancake House after noon meal formation. Want to come?"

Swenson winked quickly, secretly to Fogarty. "No, thanks, Bill. Sally Sue and I have some talking to do. Maybe next Sunday, all right?"

Oh, I don't believe it, thought Fogarty. Even after last night. What does he want, a wife who stands up when she pees? He forced a smile. "You're sure, now? All right, then, the hell with you if you can't stand good company."


Down the walkway, next to the Superintendent's house, John Dean stood facing the gathering in front of the chapel. He felt isolated and alone. Snow flurries danced on bursts of icy air that made him shiver, looking into a leaden sky. They were meeting girlfriends, laughing, planning what they would do that afternoon and his mission was to go back and take his room apart and wipe it all so clean that a white glove would come away unmarked, even off the floor *this is the world.*

He saw them standing there, joking, Fogarty and Swenson and those two absolutely beautiful women *how long has it been since my hand touched one, simply touched one? Maybe if I see him now he'll let me shake her hand and smell of her perfume.*

He began gliding toward them, actually fearful of intruding into their weekend world but being pulled along, needing some contact. Right through the crowd he walked, pulled like a magnet by the thought of it, and suddenly he was standing just outside their tight gathering, having arrived with nothing prepared to say.

"Well, John Dean the war machine!" Fogarty's eyes went fierce and amused as he nodded to Dean, watching the plebe's almost childish hesitance. "You all ready for tomorrow morning, you fighting fool?"

"Sir?" He stood awkwardly, embarrassed at his own intrusion. "Oh, yes, sir. I'll be ready, sir."

Sally Sue was watching him with some sort of secret delight that obviously made Swenson nervous and irritated. His squad leader spoke roughly. "What do you want, Dean?"

"Sir, I—" Dean turned to Fogarty. "Sir, I watched your fight last night and I'm sorry, sir. I just wanted you to know that. And sir, I—"

"I don't want to talk about it, Dean." Now he had irritated and embarrassed Fogarty, whose shoulders actually bristled when he spoke.

"And sir, I...there's something else we need to talk about, sir."

"Can it wait?"

"Sir, yes sir. I suppose, sir."

"Then wait, Dean. I don't need to think about all that when I'm on liberty."

"Sir, I—" They were all staring at him, not unkindly, but he had intruded and he had no business in their Sunday lives. "Aye, aye, sir." *Can't you even introduce me?* "Well, have a nice day, sir."

They watched him walk slowly away. Only Linda seemed sorry for him, despite her life of having been around the Academy. "What do you think he really wanted?"

Swenson shrugged, watching Dean's slowly retreating frame. "Ah, Dean's just a geek, that's all. A weirdo."

# Chapter Three: 1245

Swenson changed quickly from his full dress blues into his service dress blue alphas, the uniform for town liberty. After four years he had it down to a two-minute science. As soon as Sunday noon meal formation was dismissed, he began running down the hallway, undoing the dozen buttons on his full dress coat as he ran, and by the time he reached his room he was almost completely out of his antique church-and-parade uniform, the coat in one hand and the trousers already unbuttoned and unzipped. In seconds his full dress blues were in a pile on his bed, to be picked up in the dull Sunday evening afterwash of weekend liberty. It was another minute at the most before Swenson peered quickly into the mirror, inspecting himself in his liberty uniform, adjusting the tie and smoothing out the fit of his coat.

He dashed out the door again, pulling on his overcoat and crossing the thin white scarf underneath it, then buttoning it up as he ran. Plebe year uniform races were more than mere harassment, he thought amusedly again, racing down the hallway to the Rotunda. They prepared a man for the exactness of free time measured by a jealous clock.

She was waiting where she always waited, right in front of the TO THOSE WHO WENT BEFORE US posters, basking coyly in the awed stares that always honored her presence. They'll like her in Minnesota, he assured himself again, she's so beautiful and friendly and she's really just a small-town Southern girl at heart. Washington has been hard for her; I can understand how so many temptations can affect even the most morally grounded people. It's almost a curse to be so beautiful, but I have what she needs, I can give her everything she needs, all the attention and understanding. And in Minnesota she will be Queen of the Universe.

"Well, hey, Swede! Where to?" Bright and friendly, eager like a child.

"Let's go somewhere nice." He opened the heavy main doors of the Hall for her. "Your choice. A really good restaurant."

"Oh, Swede, don't make me choose! You know I'm not any good at picking things. You surprise me."

"We'll think about it while we walk." They strode quickly in the brisk, knifing winter air, his nose soon numb and his ears burning. He flipped the collar of his overcoat up, protecting his neck from the gusts of wind. She walked beside him, her cheeks blushing from the cold, her deep blue eyes flitting merrily from person to person, object to object, consuming everything for her own use, taking in each aspect of the Yard and its inhabitants. Sally Sue was in a good mood.

They passed through Gate Two and walked along cobbled streets, Sunday in Annapolis giving off an antiquity that was invigorating. Swenson felt the sort of thrill that had only come during his childhood, on early summer mornings as he crept out of the house alone and took his small fishing boat out on a wide, calm lake that was erupting with the energy of bass ripping up the shallows as they fed. It was electric anticipation, a sense that the world was beautiful and right in spite of itself, and that there was at least one small corner of it that was perfect.

"Sally Sue," It was the first time he had spoken since they left Bancroft Hall. "I'd like to marry you."

They continued to walk and she made a point of watching every surrounding event with interest, communicating neither with him nor with the people and objects she passed, as if the whole world were her personal zoo. He began to wonder if she had heard him, or if perhaps in his nervousness he had said it too softly.

Finally she spoke, keeping it just as light and airy as if he had mentioned the weather or the make of a passing car. "Really, Swede. Don't ruin a perfectly good afternoon."

"I didn't think I was." His limbs began to tingle. "Did you hear what I was asking?"

"You want to marry me." She recited his deepest wish as if she were commenting that he wanted to walk on the other side of the street, or to stop and tie his shoe.

"That's right, Sally Sue. You've known that, I think. I love you and I love making love to you. You must know it's been on my mind."

"Oh, Jesus." She stopped on the sidewalk, not even looking at him, and drew a cigarette from her purse, then lit it. Smoke rose into the air as she exhaled and she watched it as if it would produce some truth-inducing genie. Finally she smiled, changing moods abruptly like a car switching gears. "Let's go to the Harbour House today. I feel like having a carafe of wine and some crab. A *whole* carafe! You won't mind if I drink in front of you, will you, Swede? Maybe I could sneak you a sip or two, if some asshole officer isn't eating in there with his grandmother."

"Ah, Sally Sue." Swenson studied his shoes defeatedly. They were scuffed. They looked like hell. "All right, we'll go to the Harbour House." He brushed small flakes of ashes from his overcoat, where they had drifted when the wind hit her cigarette. "I can tell you don't want to talk about it."

"Talk about it?" She began to walk again. "Dear sweet Swede, there is nothing to talk *about*. I am not getting married, I don't feel like being married, none of my friends are getting married, I don't even feel like *talking* about getting married. It upsets me. Besides, you hardly know me, really. You don't know me."

"Know you? Hell, Sally Sue." Swenson snuggled into the upturned collar of his overcoat as they walked. "Just hell. I've known you for seven months. And I'd say we've been pretty damn

…intimate." The word hung in the cold air, neither of them seizing it for meaning or examination, as if he had spoken it in English and she had chosen to listen only in French.

Finally she spoke. She was walking ahead of him with short, rapid steps, so that it might appear to passersby that she was trying to open a distance, to be rid of this persistent pest in his funny black uniform. "So what's that supposed to mean, huh, Swede?"

"I guess that's the real question, isn't it? What is it supposed to mean when you make love to someone almost every weekend for seven months?" He felt out of control, as if he were shouting at a fading image on a screen, something bright and beautiful that he suddenly realized was only acetate reflected once, a mirage, the bulb behind the acetate now burnt out and the reflection slowly disappearing, leaving only the white desert of an empty screen. "What is it supposed to mean?"

"I don't know what you're talking about."

"You probably don't." She was ignoring him. He searched the sidewalks for someone who might hear them arguing, and saw no one. "I'll tell you what I'm talking about. I'm talking about fucking. That's all it is to you, isn't it? Just bare-ass fucking, like two dogs in a barnyard. Got an itch between your legs? Knock off Swede this weekend. Oh, he's graduating? Well, maybe he can leave you a reference in the class of sixty-nine. Yeah, that's an appropriate number, isn't it? Don't take it serious, though. It might make a human being out of you, instead of a—a—"

She stopped on the sidewalk and faced him, speaking with a flat coolness that froze him motionless, his mouth partly agape and his head forward, looking down at her as if bent in prayer.

"Get the hell out of my life. I don't need you or what you're saying."

"Sally Sue, I—"

"If you don't leave me alone I'll call the police."

"Look, it can't happen like this, right here on the street after seven months!"

"It can't?" Her eyes were deep unforgiving ice. "Just watch. And as for this seven months bullshit, I'm sick of hearing about it. You can't say you've learned to know someone just because you've been able to see each other inside a goldfish bowl, on the weekends. You don't know me, Swede. You don't, or you'd never have mentioned marrying me. Do you think I could really be a damn navy wife? Oh, my God." She laughed, tossing her cigarette.

"Come on, *really*. If there's one thing I am it's spoiled, and I admit it. Coming up here has been…fun. Well, a little different, but alright, fun. But when you all leave Annapolis you enter the great world of drudge. That's right. And I'm damned if I'm going to sit on my ass up in Newport, Rhode Island, or in Long Beach while you play sailor on some boat for six or eight months at a time."

"So you're going to get yourself a rich congressman."

"One's already asked me." She smiled slightly, her eyes still keeping him distant. "But he's a toad. No, I'm not marrying anybody. I don't even like men, really. They're all so goddamned possessive. They do you a favor and expect to own you." She shrugged as he shook his head, mystified. "Sorry, Swede."

"Let's at least eat. The Harbour House?"

"Nope. I'm going back to D.C. I have a lot of things to do before…well, before tomorrow. 'Bye, Swede." She waved teasingly, walking away.

"Just like that?" He stood with his back to the wind, the high collar of his overcoat flapping against his neck and head, his hands deep inside his pockets, staring down at her picturebook face.

"Just like that." She turned her head over one shoulder as she walked, and smiled slightly. "Maybe I'll call you sometime."

"All right. Sally Sue—"

She turned again. "What?"

"I love you."

"Jesus H. Christ." She threw her hands into the air, walking quickly away.

# Chapter Four: 1400

"Now, listen up, Neil. This is important."

Lenahan sat back in his aluminum visitor's chair, his feet propped up on Bard's bed. Bard lay motionless, his arms limp and his head perfectly still inside heavy wrappings. "There'll be a test when I finish. Hah hah. Anyway, here you are out on this river in a silly-ass little boat, what the hell do they call them … a Swift boat, yeah. If Kennedy didn't get his own head shot off down there in Dallas they'd be calling them P.T. boats, that's right. Kennedy would be in his second term, just getting ready to pass the crown down to Bobby, and every swinging dick in Vietnam would be driving a P.T. boat. But then I'm Boston Irish, so I know how the whole scam works."

Lenahan pulled a cigarette out of the crumpled pack he had earlier removed from his sock, and lit it, his eyes never leaving Bard's face. "So here you are on this goddamn boat with a bunch of other squids, I don't care what we call it but we'll say Swift boat. And you're tooling down the river, just grooving on the countryside like you were on some weekend cruise out on the Chesapeake or something—" Lenahan mimicked his friend, coming out of his chair and pretending to be standing on the bridge of the patrol craft. "Hey, Chief, look over there! It's a Mandau monkey, did you see it flip us the bird? Jesus Christ, Chief, a goddamn VC monkey. I'll tell you, they got the whole country trained up against us, and that's no bullshit. Well, that does it, Chief. The next monkey who flips us the bird gets blown away, and I'm taking a kill for it, too."

Lenahan stopped quickly, hoping to see some attentiveness or curiosity in Bard's sleepy, heavy-lidded stare. Bard's eyes continued to gaze vapidly from behind dark blue, swollen skin. "Then that goddamn monkey opens up, *pow!* And you say, 'Hey, Chief, that ain't any goddamn monkey, that's a gook bastard.' And you try to turn the Swift boat around and get the hell out of there. You get it halfway around, all the engines swirling in the water, you know, and they open up from the bank and you say, 'What the hell are they trying to do, *kill* us?' and you start running up to the bridge and then you feel this gentle tap-tap-tapping on the back of where part of your head used to be. Got it so far, dummy? Or should I say, mummy? That was a joke, Neil, you don't have to get pissed off. Hell," Lenahan sat back down, wearily shaking his head. "On second thought, get pissed off, Neil."

Lenahan pulled on his cigarette, staring at the far wall. "Anyway, here you are, you lucky puke, having everything done for you like you're some kind of a king or something." The intravenous bottle dripped a metronomic patter that measured off slow moments of a hollow, quiet afternoon. "You should have been married, Neil. Then you could have experienced the ... meaning ... of being abandoned. 'Ah, tis better to be left than to have never been ... something.' That wasn't very good. I was making it up, anyway. Let me try another one. 'Being abandoned suddenly puts meaning into a life that otherwise would have seemed dull and unrewarding.' Does that make sense? Hell, a lot you know, you goddamned whoremonger. You've never even been found, much less left."

Bard had not so much as twitched. "The odd thing is, I miss it, Neil. Not Mary. Vietnam. Yeah, that's right. Out on the street they'd call me a fucking *war*monger, but you know better. You know what it is to give up all the aspects of a normal life and work your ass off to prepare for something like that, and then have it just long enough to know when it's gone. It's sort of like—" Lenahan leaned forward, his head close to Bard's, staring intensely at Bard's empty face — "like holding a small, warm bird. It pulses in the cup of your hand, fragile and foreign, and then it flies away. Whish! And you're left with just the warm emptiness in your hand that used to be the object you held. Is that too pretty a thing to say about combat? I guess it is. Well, let me change it around. It's like a small, warm pile of birdshit, right there in the cup of your hand—"

Nurse Goodbody knocked gently on the door, as if intruding on two people making love. "I'm sorry, Lenahan. There's somebody else to see Lieutenant Bard. They say they know you. I couldn't tell them to leave when you were already in here."

Across the hallway, from another room, someone yelled for her. "Hey, Goodbody! Get over here, will you?"

Lenahan shook his head, exasperated, as Goodbody yelled back, "Keep your britches on. I'll be right there." She shrugged casually to him, starting to leave the room. "So I'll send your friends in."

"Stop letting people call you Goodbody, do you understand?"

"It's just a joke." Her moon eyes were wounded. She gave off a silly smile, staring at the floor.

"Yeah, and you're the punch line." Lenahan leaned forward, speaking in a modulated, concerned tone, "You better wrap yourself up a little tighter, Maria, or you're going to go through life as a doormat."

"They're sick. It helps their morale to joke around."

"Good. Then why don't you come to work in a clown suit, or a G-string? What the hell do you owe this place out of your insides, Maria? Come on, now. Bang the doctors and be the butt of all the patients' jokes. Get all dry and used up before you're old."

"You're cruel." She seemed confused, on the edge of tears.

He had said too much. He avoided her face, staring instead at Bard's. "Nah. I'm sorry. I'm just a little screwed up, that's all."

"No, you're not. That's what's cruel. You're reading me, Lenahan. A lot of peole do, I guess. But you're doing it out loud."

It came from the other room again. "Hey, Goodbody! Hurry up, damn it!"

"So are a lot of other people." Lenahan stared evenly at her. "Go on in there and tell that asshole to shut up."

"I can't." She shrugged, her breasts jiggling through the white nurse's uniform. "He'd laugh at me. Look, you still call Morphine Mary that. I can't stop it. It's been going on too long."

"Well, goddamn it, I can." Lenahan strode from the room, then quickly came back to the doorway and spoke in a fierce whisper. "And the next doctor you go to bed with, I'm going to beat the living shit out of."

Lenahan walked briskly into the room where the patient had been yelling for Nurse Goodbody. It was a navy lieutenant commander, flat on his back from surgery, his head propped up on two pillows. Lenahan stopped abruptly, within two feet of the man's stunned face.

"Knock off calling her Goodbody. Her name is Nurse Canigliaro, or Ensign Canigliaro. Do you understand?"

"What the hell's the matter with you?" The man seemed astounded.

"Not a goddamn thing. But there's going to be a hell of a lot wrong with you if you call her Goodbody again, because I'm going to take that I-V needle out of your arm and break it off in the middle of your fucking forehead. Do you understand what I'm saying?"

"Hey, man, I don't know who you are, but you have to know the stories about her. Don't you? Come on, she's screwed—"

Lenahan clutched the man by the throat, squeezing until the man's eyes bulged in terror. "They're going to be telling some stories about you in a few minutes, too. Only you're not going to be here to listen to them. Now, you just shut the hell up. I'm not going to tell you again. Got it?" The man nodded, unable to speak. Lenahan gave off a tiny smile. "Good."

Nurse Goodbody was standing in the doorway, crying, shaking her head. Lenahan kissed her on the forehead and she sobbed even louder. Lenahan turned back to the lieutenant commander, one arm on Goodbody's shoulder. "And if you think I'm kidding, you just say one more word."

Steve and Angie were in the room with Bard when Lenahan re-entered it. They were hushed, shocked at Bard's comatose, unmoving condition, standing close together, arm in arm, staring at Bard as if he were on display in his coffin at some funeral home. Lenahan sat back down in his visitor's chair, and placed his feet deliberately on Bard's bed again.

"Neil's better off than he looks. He's going to remember you came to see him when he comes out of this. Don't stare at him like that, you'll hurt his feelings." Steve and Angie shifted their gazes to Lenahan, both of them upset and curious, like two same stares from twins. Steve I can deal with, thought Lenahan again, returning their stares. Angie I can deal with. Steve and Angie I can't deal with. "Really, I'm serious. Head injuries are funny things. He's still got most of his brain. He's got more of his brain than he can ever use. He's just in shock, that's all, and you should be nice to him. So how have you all been?"

"Are you all right, Ted?" Angie said it, her arm still around Steve and her face filled with something that he would have called pity had he not seen her need him with every fiber of her soul two days before.

"Am I all right? What the hell does that mean anymore? Are you all right, Angie? Huh?" They continued to stare at him as he lit another cigarette. "Hey, I'm sorry. I'm a little worked up, that's all. A lot of things seem to be happening all at once."

"What were you doing across the hall?" Steve spoke as if his words might further anger Lenahan.

"Across the hall? Oh, that. What the hell does it take to get someone to show women a little respect around here? I was just talking with the man about it."

"You had your hand on his throat."

"He's lucky I didn't break his neck for him."

"Why?"

"So who needs a reason?" Lenahan gave off a small laugh. "Ah, he was saying some really bullshit stuff about Maria and it got to me."

"You mean Nurse Goodbody?"

Lenahan looked quickly at Steve, going stiff in his chair just for a second. "How would you feel if people called Angie that?

She's got a nice body." Lenahan watched her discomfort. "At least what I can see of it, that is."

"Well, sure, Ted, but Angie's well…you know what I mean. Nurse Good—whatever her name is—"

"Maria."

"Okay. Maria has a certain reputation. And anyway, you were calling her Goodbody yourself."

"So I'm an asshole, too." Lenahan stared at Angie for a penetrating moment. "So we trample the weak, make objects out of well-intentioned women … "

"I'd say she's done a pretty good job of making an object out of herself, at least from what I hear."

"So you fall into a hole, Steve. A deep hole. Sometimes you need help climbing out, and all you get is rocks thrown in your face by people up there where you fell in. People who are faking it themselves, half the time, and don't like it because you've blown their cover. What's the girl supposed to do, go around with a big scarlet A around her neck for the rest of her life? Hey, man, if we're going to make everyone who's slipped do that, I'm going into the A-making business."

Angie studiously avoided Lenahan's face as he spoke, peering along the floor, then painfully at Bard's immobile frame. Steve slowly began to grin, then nodded toward Lenahan, an encouragement. "Well, I'll be damned, roomie. I'd say you're taken with the lady."

"Maybe I am." Lenahan dragged on his cigarette. "Neil likes her. Yesterday when I invited her to the fights he winked at me."

"Oh, really?" Steve feigned seriousness. "Is that right, Neil?"

"Did you see it?" Lenahan came quickly forward in his chair. "He winked again! I swear to God! Hey, Neil, baby, all right!" Lenahan grinned widely to them. "Did you see that, huh? Well, I'll be damned."

Steve and Angie looked quizzically at each other. Steve finally spoke. "No, I didn't see it, Ted."

"You goddamn nonbelievers." Lenahan leaned back in his chair again. "You've got to be quick. Neil's a real fast winker."

# Chapter Five: 1500

You don't talk about it, especially to a woman. Sometimes when another man is going through the same thing and he can look inside your ferocity anyway you say a few things, all surrounded by puffery and black humor, and the two of you can share a secret moment of honesty about it. Otherwise you don't even talk about it to other men because unless another man is feeling it at the same time he won't admit he ever really has. Not to you, anyway.

So you bury it. It interferes. It makes you small. It makes other men afraid to follow you and it makes women think you're like them when the most important thing in the world is to not be like them, to be a man. Some day you will learn that men cry too, that the distinction between men and women isn't whether life can hurt you or whether tragedy breeds doubt. The real difference, the one you follow viscerally and the one that women will later debate as if it were untrue, is that women show strength by talking about it, while men show strength by not talking about it. At least while it's going on.

"I just wanted to see it one more time, that's all."

"Well, of course you did, Bill. He was your best friend."

"That doesn't matter. I mean it does, but that's not why. Not all the way why, anyway."

"Well, it's got to be why. You need a way to be able to deal with it, and you need to come here and see it and think about it so you can get it straight in your mind. I miss him, too. If it happened—"

"Stop it, Linda, all right? I don't want to talk about it."

"Bill, you need to talk about it. For God's sake, if you can't communicate with me, we don't have much hope in a marriage."

"Well, we're not married yet. I'll talk to you then." She threw her hands into the air and walked along the cemetery row, past a half-dozen raw, markerless graves. He watched her depart, drinking coffee from a Styrofoam cup and feeling guilty for having driven her away.

Across the river, under a dull gray sky, were monuments that made him stand taller every time he saw them, that literally sent proud chills up his spine, even as he sat in Arlington National

Cemetery among a mass of graves. Did the monuments cause the graves, he wondered absently, or did the graves produce the monuments? Or is there a difference, and if there is does it even matter?

He shrugged, shaking his head, clutching the coffee cup for warmth. Linda was walking back toward him. Something was wrong, so she would want to talk. She didn't understand, not even she, that talking about it would be obscene, unproductive, even sensationalistic. In a few years he would be able to talk about it.

The sky was cold and his hands were cold and Loudenslager's bones were cold. But Linda's lips were warm as she pressed them firmly against his numb cheek, an act of forgiveness which he did not deserve or even desire. He still stared at the monuments. Was it the monuments or was it the graves?

He took her hand and walked back toward the car. It didn't matter. Ron Loudenslager died for whichever way it was, and he had never asked or known.

# Chapter Six: 1730

*She will dial the numbers and in one small moment I will be back in the womb, floating in a bath of kind words, connected to home through the wire umbilical of a telephone line...*

"Collect call for anyone from Midshipman John Dean in Annapolis. Will you pay for the charges?"

"Sure, operator, put him on."

"Hello, Dad."

"Johnny!" The voice turned away from the phone, calling to what Dean knew would be a kitchen filled with family. "Hey, it's Johnny." It came back to him, warm and intense, as if he were phoning from a foreign post or perhaps a war zone. "So how's my favorite mid?"

"About the same, I guess. I have a formal room inspection in thirty minutes. I just wanted to call and say 'hi.'" Dean cradled the telephone receiver with delicateness, as if it were his memories. "How is everybody?"

"Hey, Johnny!" It was his younger brother. "We just got back from Sugarloaf, maybe ten minutes ago. *Great* skiing, man. I mean it. Cissy was up there, with that guy Greg Spinner. You remember him?"

"Oh, yeah. He's a Sigma Phi over at State, isn't he?"

"Yeah, big man. They looked pretty cozy. Sorry to be passing you the word."

"What the hell." Dean shrugged absently, staring around the telephone room at booths filled with a dozen others, mostly plebes, many of them probably receiving the same inevitable obituaries on high school romances. "She doesn't owe me anything. It's not like we were married."

"Are you going to quit?" It was as if his brother had slapped him, publicly proclaiming a frustration that he was working so diligently in private to overcome.

"I don't think so. I think it's working out. But I need to talk to Dad. Can you put him back on?"

"Sure. Sorry about Cissy."

"Ah, to hell with Cissy. Next year I can date. There are a lot of girls in the D.C. area."

"Right, John. It's good to hear you say that. I was a little worried, but I had to tell you. Anyway, here's Dad."

"Is something wrong, Son?"

"God I hope not." Dean's eyes flitted around the telephone room, uneasily searching for someone who might hear him and take it wrong. "Dad, I need some advice. Things looked like maybe they were finally going to work out and now I may be in a mess. I don't know how to handle it."

"You're not having trouble in any of your courses, are you?"

"Good God, no." Dean startled involuntarily. He had forgotten about his grades. "I mean real trouble, Dad. I don't even know what's going on for sure, but it scares the death out of me. I was finally getting them off my back. This guy Fogarty's been running the hell out of me. He's done a lot of things, a *lot*, but it's been all right, I've been able to take it, I've finally figured it all out, but Professor Thad won't leave me alone."

"Who's Thad? Who's *Fogarty*?" His father was a father again, and he was a child. "Calm down, Johnny. Take it slow."

"Fogarty's a firstie. He's an asshole, but he's got it together. He makes sense, Dad. Anyway he's been running me, pretty bad. He's made me camp out and run before reveille and a lot of—"

"Camp *out*? In the winter?"

"No, no, not outside." It was all coming out involuntarily. It didn't make sense when he considered it, and there was no use trying to make it logical for his father. "On my springs. He makes me sleep on my springs, in the nude. And I get up before reveille and run—"

"Why, that's barbaric." It took his father three full seconds to say "barbaric."

"You get used to it." He felt, in a small way, beyond his own father. "I was being really wise. I'm not saying I *deserve* it, but I can take it, Dad. And Thad doesn't understand. He thinks he's helping me but he's going to blow the whole thing. The whole goddamn thing. I can't—"

"Who's Thad?"

"Thad. Professor Thad. He's my chemistry professor. He thinks he understands. He keeps talking something about the Constitution, violation of individual rights. Something like that. He's got a friend, *Jonathan*. Jonathan somebody. Who the hell knows? Jonathan says he's going to help me out. I asked them to leave me alone, but I don't think they will. They think they're some kind of goddamned crusaders, I guess. He keeps calling me in the Hall, you know, to let me know he's pulling for me. I swear to God I wish he'd just leave it alone. It'll go away if he just leaves it alone. But no, he's got to—"

"Johnny, Johnny. Calm down. So what's the matter with this guy Thad trying to help you?"

"Oh, Jesus, are you kidding?" He was indeed beyond his father. What the hell did a dermatologist know about plebe year? "This is for *real*, Dad. If he goes to somebody, Fogarty gets it. Bad. It goes on all the time, but when it's reported, the guy is down the tubes."

"It sounds like that's where he belongs, if you ask me."

"You don't understand. This isn't the goddamned University of Massachusetts, this is a *tribe*. Fogarty's everybody's idea of the perfect mid. Jesus, Dad, he even dreams about the military. If he goes down the tubes, they'll get me. They'll get me bad, unless I literally move in with the Company Officer. And come to think of it, he'd probably get me, himself. Fogarty is his prize mid. Besides"—Dean was surprised to hear himself so readily defending his antagonist—"Fogarty will be a hell of an officer. Really. I was acting like a space cadet, Dad. I was sick of the place and I blew it, that's all. So now Thad's going after him with a platoon of goddamn lawyers. I really don't know what the hell to do about it, either. What does Thad know, for Christ's sake? He went to M.I.T."

"This other man, Fo—the one who's bothering you."

"Fogarty."

"Fogarty. He's not allowed to do these things, is he? Obviously he isn't, or there wouldn't be any problem."

"Not by regulation. But it goes on, Dad, it's all a part of it and—"

He could actually feel his father's mind working. "So, actually, if you don't do anything about it, it will keep happening. You'll be condoning that sort of conduct."

"Dad, are you going crazy? I'm not in a position to condone *anything!* Do you understand what I'm going through?"

"Are you a man of courage, John? I always thought you were."

Dean swallowed hard. "I try to be. Sometimes I am."

"If you are a man of courage, you'll go along with Thad. You might not understand it, but he is reaching for the greater good."

"Oh, G-o-d, damn it." Tears welled in Dean's eyes. There was no way to make his father comprehend. He was on his own. "He isn't reaching for anything, Dad. He's just screwing the hell around, butting in. I didn't even ask him to help! I don't even know what you're talking about when you say the 'greater good.' All I know is I'm finally getting them off my back, I'm finally going to be a *part* of it, and Thad tells me I've been maltreated."

"Well, you have. Maybe I should call the Admiral."

"Oh, Christ. A hell of a lot of good that'll do. What are you going to tell the Admiral?"

"I don't know." His father for the first time sounded doubtful. "I'm sorry, Johnny. I guess I haven't been much help. I just hope I and your mom gave you enough in your first nineteen years that you can figure it out."

Dean swallowed again, wiping his tears on his sleeve. "I guess you're right, Dad. It's about time I grew up."

"Do you want to talk to your mom?"

"I can't. I've got to go stand inspection. Tell her I miss her."

In Battle Lake the Meisinger brothers owned a grocery store and on Saturdays all the farmers came to town and the Meisingers doubled their bagboys and Swenson would work from seven in the morning until ten-thirty at night, for fifty cents an hour. That was all there was, the Meisingers fired anyone who even hinted at the idea of receiving a tip from the farmers, and that was fair. He got two breaks and a lunch hour. The Meisingers didn't pay for the breaks or the lunch hour. But if any of the produce was damaged the bagboys could eat it for free.

So he and Dave Johnson would coax the little farmboys up piles of watermelons in the summer and the watermelons would come crashing down and then he and Dave would haul a watermelon apiece down the dirt roads toward the lake. He would take his shoes off and the dirt on the road would pour through his toes like talcum powder and the sun would burn his bare shoulders and he and Dave would sit on old logs and watch the small boats on the lake, eating watermelon until both of their thin bellies bulged like frogs inside a snake. The frogs themselves would splash and croak in the tall reeds and turtles would crawl clumsily off of other logs when they approached. It was heaven on an August Saturday, dust and watermelon and dreams of becoming a man.

*I'm going to Annapolis, Dave. I'm going to be an engineer and I'm going to marry an airline stewardess.*

Dave had been drafted in 1965. He was already back in Battle Lake, the ordeal done, working in the produce department in Meisinger's goddamn grocery store. He'd married a German girl and she hated Battle Lake.

And I, thought Swenson, bundled in his blanket in the darkness of his room, am an idiot. Last summer he said he envied me, said I was the only person he had ever met who actually had gotten what I had always wanted. She hates Battle Lake but she loves him. What the hell do I have? Evening meal formation in thirty minutes.

The door opened and a shaft of light from the hallway pierced inside, hurting his eyes. A head appeared, then a hesitant, creeping figure.

"Sir?" Dean whispered to him, an uncertain warble in the dark.

"What do you want?"

"Sir, it's eighteen-hundred, sir. You told me to report to you so you could inspect my room, sir. The room is prepared for inspection, sir."

Swenson stared numbly at Dean in the dark, still lying on his bed. "Go away, Dean. Get out of my goddamn life."

"Sir, I—" Dean stood in a brace by his bed. It seemed so stupid, actually, to see a grown man in such an absurdly stiff position, imitating a relic from some militaristic bygone era that would have applauded the rigidity. Swenson felt a sudden need to be done with it, all of it, and yet here Dean was, intruding, reminding him. "Sir, I've worked all afternoon on my room, sir. I've got it—"

"Go away." His voice was an octave lower than its normal tenor.

"Aye, aye, sir." Dean started immediately for the door, agent of his whimsical power. Now Swenson felt guilty. Here the bastard spends all Sunday wiping up specks of dirt and all I can do is ignore it.

"Oh, all right, Dean. Wait a minute. Go stand by in your room."

He could actually feel Dean brighten. "Aye, aye sir." Dean raced from his room.

Swenson stumbled into his bulky gray West Point bathrobe, wrapped up in it like another blanket, and strode slowly toward Dean's room, his eyes dull with sleep and something else. Dean came to attention as he entered, his own eyes bright with anticipation.

"Attention on deck, Midshipman Dean fourth class reports room sixty-one-twenty-seven prepared for inspection, sir!"

Dean had done it all, to perfection. All the laundry was refolded and the shelves themselves had been scrubbed. The shower had been scrubbed and Windexed, the sink shone like a mirror, the floor had been washed and waxed again. Every pair of shoes in the closet was spit-shined, including the soggy boondockers Dean had worn when running with Fogarty. Swenson poked around inside shelves and drawers, upending Dean's bed and scraping shower walls, methodically combing every nook and cranny of the room. The white gloves he wore came away unmarked, absolutely clean, even when he jammed a finger into several places in Dean's rifle. Finally, Swenson took the gloves off and tossed them back on Dean's desk, shaking his head in amazement.

"What did you do, Dean, hire a maid?"

"No, sir." Dean's soft face was clearly ecstatic. "I just took a super-strain, sir. I worked all day on it."

"There may be hope for you, after all." Swenson filled out the inspection chit, giving Dean a perfect 4.0 as a grade. "I want you to know that's the first four-oh I've ever given, Dean." He worked up a dull grin and put one hand on Dean's shoulder. "Too bad you didn't work this hard a couple months ago. You wouldn't be in the shit, Dean."

"Yes, sir. I can see that, sir."

"Carry on, Dean." Swenson strode slowly out of the room, both hands inside his bathrobe pockets.

"Aye, aye, sir." Behind him, as the door closed, Dean raced over to the inspection chit that lay on his desk and held it up in front of the light as if it were an award citation for a medal earned in combat. Then Dean danced alone in his impeccable room, around and around his desk, waving the chit to empty walls.

"I did it! I did it! I did it I did it I did it!"

# Chapter Seven: 1930

"WHO GETS THE BRICK? WHO GETS THE BRICK?"

Just after evening meal the slow chant echoed through the company area, deep as thunder with the low musical rolls of men's voices. The company's plebes lined up in a long column of twos with the front two plebes holding a brick between them. The column itself did a native dance, a slow stutter-step in time to the chant. They were indeed a tribe, and this was but one pagan ritual.

"WHO GETS THE BRICK (UH!) WHO GETS THE BRICK (UH!)"

They picked up a calypso beat, all dressed in underwear or whiteworks uniforms or gym gear, whatever they had on when the litany began, their energetic, smiling faces throwing in the grunts as they stared at gathering upperclassmen with anticipation. Dean ran from his room and joined them in the passageway, falling in at the end of the line, his senses charged with curious intensity.

"WHO GETS THE BRICK (UH!) WHO GETS THE BRICK? (UH!)"

The column snaked slowly down the hallway, passing every room in the company in one long turn, then retracing its passage, throwing dread into the heart of every upperclassman who had taken out even a marginal-looking woman that weekend. Someone had been stuck with a date who possessed neither looks nor redeeming grace, and would soon be the recipient of a brick... and a cold shower. There weren't five plebes in the entire column who knew who was getting bricked, but on they stutter-stepped, their eyes bright and their voices loud and ominous.

"WHO GET THE BRICK? (UH!) WHO GETS THE BRICK? (UH!)"

Many upperclassmen now followed the winding, snaking column, most of their faces not only curious but secretly uneasy, only those who had steady girlfriends (exempt) and those who had not dated that weekend feeling safe. Bricking was judgmental, discretionary, a seed planted by anonymous upperclassmen. The two plebes with the brick smiled devilishly, making several false starts toward upperclassmen who got too close, stepping quickly toward them and beginning the motions of tossing the brick underhanded at them. The first slight motion caused each upperclassman to bolt in unconcealed terror, as if the brick were a live hand grenade. Every man knew that, once the brick left the hands of the plebes, the entire column would follow it, like a school of piranha moving for a speck of blood.

"WHO GETS THE BRICK—"

Suddenly the brick flew into the open door of one upperclass room. The orderly, chanting column immediately disintegrated into a fierce, growling mob, inundated with a lyncher's mentality, fighting its way into the room as if the door itself were the only exit in a building consumed by flames. George, the brawny upperclassman who persisted in attacking the breasts of his classmates' dates at parties, looked up from his desk where he had been writing a lonely letter to his fianceé in Mississippi. His face went aghast and he rolled his chair toward the column, interrupting their flow for a moment as he literally leapt onto the top bunk on one side of the room. The plebes surrounded George, alternately growling with animal passion and laughing with delight, pulling at his thick, stumpy legs like a pack of dogs going after a polecat caught in a tree.

George almost casually knocked arms away, screaming at the plebes. "God damn it, get out of my room! Get out of here, you idiots, that's an order! Get the hell out of my goddamn room!"

Someone caught an ankle and clutched it to his breast. George was pounding him on the head. Another plebe caught George's hand as it beat on top of another man's head. Then a half-dozen plebes grabbed portions of George's leaning frame, and finally toppled him from the bunk.

Slowly, as if they were carrying a struggling, screeching gorilla, they brought him to the shower. The cold water was already on. A plebe backed off, holding his face from where George had pummeled his nose. Blood gushed down his front. Finally George went into the shower, carrying several growling plebes with him.

Immediately the entire array of participants and upperclass observers broke out into wild cheering, the plebes from victory and the upperclassmen from relief that it had not been them. George burst suddenly from the shower, cursing, kicking several plebes in the legs and ass as they raced from his water-splashed room. His books and desk papers were torn, and some stuck wetly to the floor. Both beds on that side of his room were disasters, sheets scattered and torn, the mattresses on the floor, soaked with water. George's underwear was ripped and wet.

He screamed after them as they fled back to their rooms. "You sons of bitches! You idiots! Who put you up to this, huh? I didn't even have a date this weekend!"

Fogarty, Lesse, and several others who had been victimized by George at various times leaned against a far wall on the other side of the hallway, laughing and slapping each other on the back. Lesse called to George.

"Hey, you keep it up, George. The next time you start grabbing boobs we'll have them throw you over the goddamn seawall!"

Sunday nights were the hardest. It would be a week before most of them so much as saw a woman's face, or took a walk out in town. They milled the passageways on Sunday nights, not wanting to return to their rooms, asking each other about those few hours of freedom from Saturday noon to Sunday evening meal. *How was your weekend?* It was so glorious, so different, that each time a classmate asked it he might be wondering if you had spent it in Rome.

Anything to keep from fitting back into the harness and

plowing through the books. Fogarty and Lesse sauntered down the hallway, merely cruising, half-dressed and lazy. It was like watching a confession to see a midshipman take off his dress blue coat and walk down the hallway in his shirt or undershirt. In formation, everything was exact; each anchor and ribbon and visor all the same, indistinguishable, *Academy types are robots,* and then the coats came off and a simple white dress shirt became a work of art. Sleeves cut off, gargoyles drawn on the backs, *screw you Navy, I am myself.* And as the layers came off, that same message repeated itself. A speck of lint, a pinhole on the outside was grounds for a Form Two, but peel it down to a man's undershirt and sometimes you saw holes as big as oranges. It wasn't a question of being able to afford a new undershirt; it was a matter of principle. *Polish up my outside like some gem you own, but peel off my wrapper, brother, and you get me.*

Bancroft Hall pulsed and throbbed, its heart beating inside Fogarty. In one room a poker game had just begun, and would continue well into the night. In another, two "youngster" second-yearmen were having a flamethrower fight, chasing each other with cans of Right Guard deodorant held behind cigarette lighters. And in the hallway they walked as though at an open-air market, dozens of them in half-uniforms and bathrobes, casual observers of their own existence.

A group had collected in front of two second-classmen who were screaming at each other in rapid, biting sentences filled with curses and insults. Fogarty and Lesse nudged each other and stopped for a moment, watching. A gross-out contest had begun down on the company tables an hour before, slow taunts burgeoning until both egos were consumed. Brustein, a former enlisted sailor, was considered unbeatably gross. Gibson, a high-toned member of the debate team, was better with words than anybody in the company.

Gibson was waving long arms in the air, appealing to the gathered crowd " ...that is, if you knew who your sister *was,* Brustein, and if she'd been born with anything between her legs except an asshole, I'd be happy to bring some class to your low-rent name by knocking the bitch up."

Lesse nudged Fogarty. "I'd say this has deteriorated beyond repair." The crowd had applauded, though, and was awaiting Brustein's answer.

Brustein rubbed his chin, staring at Gibson. "If you had

anything between your legs except a pussy, you might be able to give it a try!" More cheers.

Gibson strode indignantly into Brustein's room and returned with the former sailor's toothbrush. He then ceremoniously dropped his trousers and wiped his ass with the toothbrush. The crowd of midshipmen groaned and jeered, incredulous.

Brustein stared straight at Gibson, taking his toothbrush back, and unflinchingly brushed his teeth.

"Oh, sweet Jesus." Gibson threw his hands into the air again and retreated into his room. "You're a *maniac*, Bru, a goddamn wild man!"

Brustein was taking his bows in the center of the passageway, to the cheers of the onlookers. He called after the retreating Gibson. "Never serve on a submarine, Hoot. I'm the only one they'd let off the fucking boat."

Dreiden saw them strolling and came from his room, his massive chest and piano-stool legs making him look like a bantam rooster. The long-nosed South Carolinian with the barking drawl seemed even more sardonic than his usual self. "Hey, Bill, you hear about chapel this morning?"

"You mean Mad Pratt?"

"Yeah." Dreiden started walking with them, his shower shoes clopping as if he were a workhorse. "That asshole. Chews the Captain out, right in front of the mids like that. Said mids weren't even troopies. What do you think about that, Wild Bill?"

"What do I think about that?" Fogarty mulled it, daring to touch a swollen jaw as he rubbed his face pensively. "In four months I'm out of this shithole, that's what I think about that."

"Those are some lo-o-o-ong months though, brother." Lesse's mind was at work. "Four months over four years, factor out summer cruises and leaves, and I'd say that's roughly twelve percent of the time you've already spent in here in the first place."

"You goddamn engineers. Stop talking like Swenson, will you?"

"He ain't going to let you get your head shaved tomorrow night, either. Says if we shave your head after you sign up for the Corps, you all is gonna get yo' fat ass Class Aed, Fogarty."

"They always say that."

"Yeah, but Pratt means it."

"He can't stop it."

"Oh, he ain't gonna *stop* it." Dreiden cackled, reaching playfully for Fogarty's crew-cutted scalp. "He's just gonna make you pay."

"Let's fuck him over." Fogarty's pace had not changed. His hands were still stuffed inside his pockets. Only his face was different, the eyes laughing with anticipation, his lips pursed in an amused grin. "Let's fix his ass. Tonight."

# Chapter Eight: 2200

Arnie Lesse took taps dressed suspiciously in a gray sweatsuit, with his blue Academy parka zipped up and his gloves sticking out of both pockets. In half the rooms, the midshipmen who reported to him as present were similarly dressed. As soon as the muster was complete and the musterboard signed, the company's passageway filled with scurrying, intent figures, like hungry roaches pouring out of cracks after the lights went off.

They gathered, then broke up into small groups, heading down the stairway. Conversation flitted among them like bursts of electricity. In moments most of them had disappeared from the company area.

Fogarty stuck his head into Swenson and McClinton's room. Mack was putting on his parka and stocking cap. Swenson was curled into a ball on his bed. Fogarty nodded toward the sleeping Swenson, looking at Mack.

"What's with him?"

"He's in the hurt locker, man. That goddamn bitch cut him deep."

Fogarty walked over to Swenson's bed and shook him. "Come on, Swede."

Swenson rolled away from his hand, facing the wall. "I don't want to come. Leave me alone, all right?"

"Hell no, I won't leave you alone." Fogarty pushed his shoulder again, and drew another retreat. "Come on, Swede. It'll take your mind off of it."

"This goddamn place." Swenson would not turn toward

him. "Fun on Sunday night at Navy. Dress up in your sweatsuits and go play like you're ten years old, out in Tecumseh Court."

"All right, so you hate it. Big shit, Swenson. Who loves it? What—"

"You do." It hung in the air, like an accusation.

"I'm going to ignore that. What—"

"You do, Fogarty. You love this shit. I mean, it's *real* to you, isn't it?" Swenson rolled over onto his back, staring up at Fogarty's powerful frame, his still-swollen face, his energetic eyes. "From those first days in plebe summer when Loudenslager hung us on the goddamn door and you came off of it crying, so goddamn pissed I thought you wanted to kill him, but then it all of a sudden became *real*, man, I can't explain it, but you don't understand anymore." Swenson sounded like he felt sorry for Fogarty. "I'm not going to go push airplanes around tonight."

"Come on, Swede. Snap out of it, man."

"No, *you* snap out of it. Snap into life, Fogarty." Swenson sat up in his bed, not looking at Fogarty anymore.

"So what are you going to do, sit here and write her a long, sad letter? Come on, Swede. She'd love that. She's rubbed your face in shit for months, man. It's probably the best thing that's ever happened to your young ass."

"Fuck you. Do you hear me? Leave me alone."

"*So what are you going to do, Swede?*" It was the first time they had seriously argued in four years.

"I'm going to go see her. I need to sit down and talk with her. I said some things I didn't need to say, and I want to apologize."

"You're going over the wall."

"I have to." Swenson rose and went to his closet, taking down a sweater and a pair of slacks.

"You don't have to do anything, Swede, except make reveille tomorrow morning." Fogarty followed him to the closet, standing at the entrance as he watched Swenson dress. "Please, Swede. Take a couple days and think about it. She isn't worth ruining your career over."

"My career?" Swenson gave off a forced chortle, grabbing his heavy corduroy coat. "That's what I mean about you, Bill. What are they going to do, cut off my hair and lock me up inside a ship for six months in the middle of the goddamn ocean? They lock us up inside this shithole for four years, keep us in a suspended state of adolescence, and then for our reward they lock us up for five more years. Sally Sue was right about that. Don't talk to me about ruining any damn career. I've had it." Swenson measured his friend from the dim light of the closet, this seeming machine who had bought all the offerings of a life of denial, who had poured every last hot ounce of his own youth into the Academy's demanding, bottomless suck machine. "You tell me how all this relates to life."

"I can't tell you anything anymore. Just be careful, Swede." Fogarty walked away without looking back.

"Hey, Mate! Come here!" Arnie Lesse stood in front of the battalion office with his long, narrow musterboard, scratching his head. The Mate of the Deck trotted over to him, leaving the Mate's desk in front of Pratt's office. Lesse stood so that the Mate's back was to the desk and as they spoke DeVita, a third-classman who had grown up in the bowels of New York City and whose idea of a good time was running Central Park to see who might try to mug him, easily broke into Pratt's office with a piece of firm plastic, springing the latch.

"Yes, sir?" The Mate stood expectantly in front of Lesse, awaiting instructions. DeVita was inside the room, and had quietly closed the door behind him. Lesse smiled amiably, watching DeVita disappear over the Mate's shoulder.

"Take my musterboard into the Battalion office, will you? I'm a little late and I don't want anybody in my company to get into trouble. Especially me."

"Yes, sir. Aye, aye, sir." The plebe went into the office. DeVita didn't come back out the door, which meant that he had been successful in exiting through Pratt's office window, onto the ground-floor railing beyond.

Lesse jogged heavily to the double doors that opened onto the Sixth Wing terrace and peered outside. DeVita was standing outside on the terrace, blowing into his hands, jumping up and down. He grinned widely to Lesse as Lesse let him back inside, giving him the "thumbs up" gesture of naval aviator fame.

"All set, man. Let's get with it."

Outside, like a long column of ants bringing their burdens back to the anthill, dozens of midshipmen began carrying newspapers to the terrace, collected from rooms throughout Bancroft Hall. A handful of others, directed by Lesse, busily wadded the papers, page by page, and tossed them into the now-open window of Pratt's office. Within an hour the entire office, floor to ceiling, wall to wall, was stuffed solid with newspapers.

Along the roadway that ran from the Field House to Tecumseh Court, past the Admiral's house and under the very noses of the sleepy old Jimmy-legs police, an A-4 Skyhawk attack plane slowly rolled from its normal place on Thompson Field, heading for the Court. A dozen midshipmen pushed it, calling to each other in excited, hoarse whispers. Such levity and frolicking was potentially disastrous: if they were caught, each might receive a Class A offense for being out of the Hall after taps. In minutes the A-4 rested in Tecumseh Court, its blunt nose pointing toward the Rotunda doors. They hung a large sign on it, like a bomb: PRATT SUCKS.

DeVita had also jimmied the door to the Battalion conference room, where Pratt met every morning with his Company Officers. Fogarty and several others now hoisted a long torpedo along the terrace. The torpedo, which had been captured from the Japanese during World War II and returned to the Academy as a war relic, normally lay with other such souvenirs in a park near Dahlgren Hall. It was more than twenty feet long, and had been painted park-bench green, over scabs of rust that now peeled off onto their shoulders as they lugged it. A midshipman opened the window to the darkened conference room from the inside, and they gingerly fit the torpedo into it, laboring until it stretched from the center of the conference table, across the room, and again out the window. It filled the conference room, like a whale washed up onto a tiny cove.

Fogarty and Lesse surveyed their wreckage with pride. Small retaliations, but in the all-risk environment of the Academy, they were large statements of dissent. Lesse nodded with uncontained glee. "Pratt will go bonkers, man. Absolutely insane."

They just don't understand, mused Swenson as he slipped out of the Sixth Wing doors and jogged across the parking lot toward Dahlgren Hall. He felt like a fugitive making his break from prison. Take Fogarty, I love him like a brother, but everything in

228

his life is military. Even Linda is military. Military military military. It takes someone like Sally Sue to wake a man up. What a joke we all must be to her. Locked up in our bird cage, practically killing ourselves to learn a trade that's designed to kill us later, anyway.

He walked quickly along the edge of Dahlgren Hall, then next to the fenced tennis courts beyond, and finally dashed across the street to the Halsey Field House. Gate Zero was behind the Field House. A chain-link fence extended from the banks of the Chesapeake Bay out into the water, a continuation of the wall that kept midshipmen inside and civilians out, except for the periods when the Academy gates were open and visiting was authorized. Swenson had never heard of a civilian braving a dangle along the chain-link fence to get in, but it was little more than a routine experience among midshipmen wanting to get out.

He hung to the icy fence, half-expecting a spotlight to go on and a megaphone to order his surrender, all the while contemplating a drop into the ice-filled, seething bay below him. Neither fear materialized. He made a short hop to a concrete landing and was suddenly in Annapolis, at the harbor area. He began to jog, feeling like a refugee who had just made it into West Berlin.

The air was sweet and somehow not so cold. The downtown area was dark, except for a few diehards who were drinking beer and shooting pool up at Pete's on Main Street. Swenson ran harder, afraid of being seen by someone who would recognize him as a midshipman. His car was parked in a lot near the Stadium, another mile away. It would be almost an hour's drive to Sally Sue's once he reached the car. That would make it one o'clock by the time he got there. A quick reconciliation, he mused excitedly, maybe a little, well, making up, and I have to be back here by five, at the latest.

This goddamn place, he thought, his feet pounding out a rhythm on the sidewalk that surrounded Church Circle. You have to feel like a criminal just because you need to talk with your woman.

# Chapter Nine: 2400

"Want to talk to my boy?"

"Isn't it awful late?"

"Ah, hell, it's only nine o'clock in California." Lenahan and Goodbody lay naked in his small double bed, the sheets and blankets pulled up to their middle parts. Lenahan reached for the phone. "He's a good kid. If he asks you when the corn is going to grow, just tell him it's growing."

Goodbody squinched her nose. "What corn?"

Lenahan was dialing numbers. He turned back to her, his craggy face wearing a small, sad smile. "I told him when I left for Vietnam that when the corn grew back again, I'd come home. Only she didn't plant any and she didn't want me back. So he thinks when the corn grows, things will be like they were. It's too complicated to explain to him over the phone. Just tell him it's growing."

"I'm not sure I want to talk to him, after that. That's sort of spooky, Lenahan." She contemplated it. "If he asks me about corn, I'm going to give you the phone. I don't know anything about corn, anyway. I'm from Philadelphia."

Lenahan finished dialing. "Hey, you think we grow corn in South Boston? The only corn we ever got in Boston was from the politicians." He concentrated on the phone, holding one hand over an ear. "Hello? Oh, hi, *Ralph.*" He made his voice go high and nasal when he said the man's name. "What do you mean, 'who is this?' This is your predecessor, you asshole. Now, let me talk—" Lenahan slammed the phone down on the receiver. "The bastard hung up on me."

Goodbody laughed, her head back and one hand on his shoulder. "So, what do you expect, calling him an asshole?"

"Well, he is one!" Lenahan's brow was furled as if he could not understand why Ralph could have been upset. "Even if he wasn't screwing my wife. That nonhacking, underachieving miserable son of a bitch probably couldn't even do twenty pushups." Lenahan's arms waved in the air, his face suddenly electric. "He makes *bombs!* Ah, yes! He makes bombs like some Doctor Strangelove and then screws the wives of the guys who go drop them. Now, who would do that except an asshole?"

"So, let me dial him." Goodbody took the phone, giggling with excitement. "What's the number?" She dialed as Lenahan dictated the number, then waited for the answer. Her eyes went round with surprise and she mouthed the words to Lenahan: *Your wife!* "Uh, hello, this is Maria Canigliaro calling from Annapolis, Maryland, on behalf of Captain Ted Lenahan. Captain Lenahan just attempted to speak with his son and was cut off. I'm a nurse and I can tell you, he is deeply upset over this. Deeply upset. He may even be on the verge of a serious depression." Goodbody paused, winking at Lenahan. "Well, I don't know anything about that. He seems entirely sober to me, and sane as well." Lenahan started tickling her and she wriggled away, stifling her laughter. "He doesn't even want to speak to you, ma'am, he wants to speak to his son. Don't you think it would be humane and appropriate to allow him to say hello to his own son? Really." Goodbody held Lenahan's arm away from her, then placed his hand on her ample breast. "Well, thank you very much." She handed Lenahan the phone.

Lenahan put his hand over the receiver. "Who am I talking to?" She shrugged, making a clown's face, and he then ignored her. "Hello?"

"Hi, Dad. Are you all right?"

"Sure, I'm all right, son. I'm just as fine as I can be."

"Ralph says we can plant the corn in April."

"Ah, the heck with Ralph. I'm going to plant some corn right here, Jackie, and you can come out and help me pick it. Would you like that?"

"Will it grow in Annapolis?"

"You bet. Hey, I want you to meet somebody. She's a nurse. Her name is Maria. She helped them fix me up where I got shot."

"Was she in the war, Dad?"

"Not exactly. She stayed back here to help people who got shot."

"Ralph says the war is bad, that nobody should go."

Lenahan gripped the telephone receiver so tightly that his knuckles turned white. "I want you to go ask Ralph something, Jackie. Are you ready? I want you to go ask Ralph why he builds bombs if the war is bad."

"Mommy might get mad." Silly me, mused Lenahan. A six-year-old possessess more wisdom than I in dealing with his own self-preservation.

"Okay, you talk to Maria, and then I want to talk to Ralph. Alright?"

"Okay, Dad."

Lenahan gave Goodbody the phone. She appeared absolutely puzzled, as if she had no idea what was going on. She smiled, though, hearing the boy's voice. "Hello, Jackie. Is that your name? Yeah, mine's Maria. I'm short and I have brown eyes and dark hair. Yeah, your daddy has some big holes but they got all better. He's fine. He's all right. He's a funny man and I like him a lot. Just a minute." She looked quickly out of Lenahan's bedroom window at the yard in back. "Well, I guess we could grow some corn out there. Sure. Alright. Good night. Wait a minute, your daddy wants to say something."

Lenahan grabbed the phone again. "I love you, Son. Now, go get Ralph for me, will you?" Lenahan waited for several minutes. He cursed. "The son of a bitch is running up my bill. What is he doing, writing a speech?" Finally Mary came on the line.

"Hello." She was a polar bear, a penguin.

"I just wanted to ask Ralph a question, that's all."

"Leave Ralph alone, Ted."

"Poor Ralph. Listen, I'll just tell you, and you can tell Ralph. You tell him to stop poisoning my boy's mind about this war, do you hear? If the war's so goddamn bad he can leave his job and go design fireworks displays or something." Lenahan slammed the phone down. "She hung up too, goddamn it."

Goodbody grabbed him by the ear, pulling him to her as she smiled wistfully. "So what did you expect, Lenahan? A standing ovation?"

"Beware when you play with the mind of a child." Lenahan reached over and turned out the light. "The fury of the misled can bury kings."

"Who said that?"

"Me."

She seemed awed. "You're really good, Lenahan."

"I am a veritable fount of platitudes."

"Your boy sounds cute."

"He is sensitive and fierce, a poet and a warrior, as Irish as the day is long. He is, in fact, myself in a matchbox." Lenahan stroked her hair, falling to sleep. "And someday he will tear this Ralph apart, tarsal by tarsal."

# PART FIVE:

---

# MONDAY, FEBRUARY 12, 1968

# Chapter One: 0100

Swenson took the turn coming off the Beltway at seventy miles an hour, the wide tires of his "graduation-special" Corvette whining at the road, then screeching as he stopped for a red light at Connecticut Avenue. He raced and screeched as he drove south into the District of Columbia, gunning his car and braking for the inevitable red lights. The street was almost empty, apartment buildings and restaurants and liquor stores lining the plush northwest section of the city like a quiet white haven from the steeping black reality that surrounded it. Northwest Washington was a fortress where people who took taxis to the theater to avoid the hassle of parking a car, were surrounded by people who rode cabs home from the grocery store to avoid being robbed of their food.

He drove for several miles along Connecticut Avenue, past familiar landmarks, places he and Sally Sue had frequented on his weekend leaves when he had stayed at her apartment. The restaurants and bars he had enjoyed with her were melancholy in their darkness, dingy and ordinary with the lights turned off. Northwest Washington in the heart of a bleak winter night looked as dead and boring as Battle Lake, Minnesota. And there was something else as Swenson drove through it: a dishonesty, a lack of charm.

At Cathedral Avenue he pulled over and parked his car just off the corner along a street crowded with late model cars, and walked briskly to her apartment house, a twelve-story brick complex with its own little U-shaped driveway out front. Entrance to the apartments was protected by a security guard, but Swenson knew the man on the night shift, who was a student. The man sat behind the entranceway kiosk, reading for his next day's classes. Swenson waved to him, and was immediately allowed to come inside.

He stepped into the lobby. It was warm and the carpet clutched at his shoes, thick and comfortable, like a putting green.

"It's cold out there." The student spoke without even looking up from his book. Swenson was a regular. He had visited Sally Sue on so many weekends that he might have lived there.

"Yeah, but that's what Februarys are for, I guess." The student chuckled halfheartedly, indulging Swenson in the immediate rapport of night people. Swenson walked to the elevator, and pressed Sally Sue's floor.

His heart dropped to his stomach as the elevator rose, then shot up into his throat when it stopped. His hands were wet with nervous sweat. Goose bumps covered him. He was so intense, such a bundle of fears and desires, that he thought he might throw up before he reached her door.

But he didn't. He banged with the knocker, then leaned against the door itself, uncertain of what he was going to do once she answered. He waited for what seemed an eternity, then knocked again, more forcefully. She's got to be here, he thought, rubbing his face as he stared at his shoes.

The doorknob jangled, and she opened the door an inch, the chain latch still fastened. One deep blue magnificent eye stared at him through the crack, blinked in disbelief, and then moved from side to side as she shook her head.

"Swede, what in the *hell* are you doing here?"

"Let me in, Sally Sue. I need to talk with you."

"You're crazy, you really are! Do you think you can just barge into my place at two o'clock in the morning without calling me or anything? How'd you get up here, anyway?"

"I just walked up. Now, let me in, please?" He felt a flat despair staring at that one blue pool of eye, as if it were peering at him from the end of a long tunnel that led into yesterday.

"No, I won't." A low light in the room behind her shone around the edge of a bare thigh toward the bottom of the door. She was naked. "You're supposed to be back at the Academy! Aren't you going to get in trouble?"

"Maybe. I just decided to take the gamble. I need to talk with you, Sally Sue." Even as he said it he knew she no longer needed to speak with him.

A new movement blocked out the dim light and allowed it to penetrate again. Someone had walked in front of it. Someone was in the apartment with her. The prospect had never even faintly occurred to Swenson. He audibly gasped, his eyes unbelieving. Finally the man behind her spoke.

"Is there anything wrong, Sally Sue?"

He had gray hair. A red towel covered his midsection. His chest was hairy and atrophied, the chest of a man old enough to be Swenson's father. Swenson tried to look into his face but was unable to catch enough of it through the crack in the door. The man's voice was deep and modulated, as if used to authority. Swenson could not control his anguish.

"Who's in there with you, Sally Sue? What's going on?"

"Dear Swede." She said it with the same tones that she might have used for "dear sweet child," or "poor baby." "I told you not to bother me again. Now, please leave me alone or I will call the police. I'm serious." She slammed the door. He heard the dead bolt slide. She had closed him out of her life.

He didn't even remember calling the elevator. He rode it down to the lobby and paced quickly out of the front door, not even acknowledging the farewell of the student night-guard, the cruel February air pushing blades of ice down his throat every time he breathed. He slammed the door of his Corvette and screeched recklessly out onto Connecticut Avenue, unsure of exactly where he was heading but pointing the car back toward Maryland.

Race and screech, race and screech, stoplight to stoplight. The radio was playing so loud it felt like it was coming from inside of him. His mind was roaring in its pain, laughing at his foolishness. Chivalry, she had once laughed. Chivalry is something for grade-school fiction. So what replaces it, he had wondered in his Calvinistic pose that she had misread for worldliness. And besides, Sally Sue, your dad practices chivalry every month when he pays your rent and covers your bounced checks. You asshole, she had spat at him with clipped words that enunciated his own truth. *You asshole asshole asshole*

He didn't see the light and he didn't see the car. The light was red and the car came from the other street and he crunched the rear fender, almost missed it even in his inattention. The car's horn went and the car itself skidded and slid, like a bumper car at a carnival.

My God, he thought, awakening from his misery. I'm *caught*.

"Driver's license and vehicle registration, please." The red lights of the police car flashed in his rear-view mirror, like laughing reminders of his future gloom. He mechanically handed both over to the officer, having already pulled them out of his glove compartment as he and the other driver awaited the policeman's arrival.

"You're active duty military?"

"Yes, sir." They were all "sir," everyone in any position of authority anywhere, even this pock-faced policeman who was no more than two years older than Swenson himself. But that was all a part of it, too.

"Where are you stationed?"

"At the Naval Academy, sir." Swenson rested his head on the steering wheel, knowing what would come next.

"Well, you can't drive this car. As a matter of fact, it looks like your whole frame is cracked. These damn fiberglass body structures. Are you on leave, or do you need to get back?"

"I need to get back, sir." He saw no sense in delaying it. "To be honest, I'm out of bounds."

"AWOL, huh?" The cop seemed to think it was pretty funny. Or maybe he was simply remembering. Swenson was uncomfortable with his smile, whatever had motivated it. "They don't mess around up at that place. I've heard the stories. Well, we have to inform your commanding officer about the accident, anyway. We'll let him know you're down here. Do you have a way to get back?"

Swenson sighed. "Not really. I guess you could drop me off at the bus station."

The policeman handed Swenson his license and registration. Swenson decided that his funny smile was actually commiseration. "You're really in the shit, aren't you? I'll tell you that. Let me get this accident report down, and I'll take you out to the Maryland border, and we'll talk the State troopers into driving you back."

"I appreciate it." Swenson's voice was worn down to a beaten moan. Suddenly, he was exhausted.

"No sweat. I was in the service myself. Army. But I know what's waiting for you back there. The Academies, wow. I had a platoon leader who went to West Point. He was a pretty good guy. You know, you hear the stories about how the Academy officers are all so straight and all, but he was really a good head. Anyway, you just sit tight right here and I'll drive you over. Oh. Do you have any preference for a towing company?" The officer had gone from an almost childish camaraderie to an overly officious manner within a second. "If not, I'll call the next one on our police department standby list."

"No, sir. I don't have any preference."

Sally Sue was a memory. His pretty Corvette was a broken plastic toy. The driver of the other car was walking around holding his neck, feigning whiplash. He had been caught over the Wall, an offense that would cost him at least a month of restriction, and probably seventy-five demerits. What the hell does it matter where they take my car, mused Swenson, watching idly as the police officer made a radio call back inside his squad car. I'll be an old man by the time I get to use it again, anyway.

# Chapter Two: 0400

"Aaaahhh! Ow! Oh!" The alarm had cut into the sweet fog of Dean's slumber and he had reached for it quickly as he jolted out of sleep, forgetting he was sleeping nude on his springs. In his haste he had caught his scrotum on a sharp metal edge, and pulled it as he reached for the alarm clock. Now he danced around the room in the pitch dark of a predawn Monday morning, holding his crotch, imagining all sorts of travesties befalling his precious family jewels.

Peckarsky rolled slowly from his slumber. "What the hell's the matter, John?"

"Aaaahhh! I caught my balls on a spring! Oh, my God, I hope I haven't torn the sack. Oh—" Dean stopped dancing, a jolt of fresh hope jarring his consciousness. "On second thought, I hope I have. Quick! Turn on the light!" Hospital, mused Dean excitedly. Holiday. Oh, please God, just a moderately severe tear. I'd even give one nut ... Just one, mind you. But I'd give one for a month in the hospital.

Peckarsky turned on the small light over the sink, rubbing his eyes from the fluorescent glare. Dean hobbled over, still holding his crotch, and then examined his scrotum under the white light. He shrugged. "Well, there's a small cut."

Peckarsky shook his head. "Where?"

"Right there. Can't you see it?"

"No I can't. Oh, that? Come on, John. That wouldn't even make a hemophiliac beg for a Band-Aid."

Dean examined the small scratch for another long moment, as if hoping it would grow with time. "Yeah, I guess you're

240

right." He sighed resignedly. "We'd better get moving. I've held us up long enough as it is."

"Do you have the list?"

"It's on my blotter."

Dean wearily pulled on his sweatgear. Monday had started, and would not stop until well after taps, eighteen hours later. He and Peckarsky had window-closing duty for the week. By the time they had tiptoed into all the upperclass rooms in the company and quietly closed each set of windows according to the meticulous instructions passed down among the plebes and kept on the list, Fogarty would be arriving to escort Dean on another early-morning jog.

And I have to tell him this morning, thought Dean, coming fully awake in his realization. I *have* to, before it blows up and he finds out through Thad.

But he had another hour before he could afford the luxury of thinking about that. He sighed, picking up the list and handing Peckarsky one page while he kept the other. "This is something like what a slave would do before the Civil War."

Peckarsky shrugged, shaking his head hard to clear the sleep from it. "Eat shit, John. That's the military."

"Yeah, you're right. And next year, some poor idiot will close our windows in the middle of the night. And the son of a bitch had better be quiet, or I'll kick his ass."

"Oh, listen to that, will you?" Peckarsky was reading through the list one final time. "Next thing I know you'll be going down and signing up for the goddamn boxing team."

"Don't hold your breath." Dean folded the list over once, an absent gesture as he walked toward the door. Suddenly he stopped, a small taunting smile finding its way onto his lips. "Why don't you come running with us this morning, Ski? Huh? You're a jock. Let's see *you* do the seawall in the dark."

"Oh, ho. Now he's going to play the hero to me. I don't see *you* volunteering to go keep Fogarty company."

"Yeah, but I'm doing it."

"Good. Remind me to piss Fogarty off today, so I can do it, too." Peckarsky was whispering as they crept to the end of the hallway. He touched Dean's small shoulder as they walked, speaking with the patient tones of a big brother. "But I'm proud of you, John. No kidding."

They reached the end of the hallway. Peckarsky and Dean faced in opposite directions. preparing to go into separate rooms.

Dean checked his list for room 6120, his first assignment. The collection of notes passed down by classmates through the winter was like a slam book, little hints and exclamations from others who had already done their week of window-closing. Horter light sleeper. Watch for stereo cord. Go on *right* side of desk. Leave right-hand window open two inches.

Dean crept into the room, standing for a half-minute inside the door to get his bearings in the dark. Horter snored peacefully from the right-hand bed. Venturelli, his roommate, rolled once on the left-hand bed, in the middle of a dream. His movements made Dean's heart beat more rapidly, with a mix of hesitation and morbid, undeniable curiosity. He was struck with the notion that he was penetrating their most private moments, watching them slumber.

Only relatives, roommates, and lovers deserve to see another person roll like that, he mused. These upperclassmen had the power to control his time and his physical and mental exertions and thus in many ways his life. But they looked vulnerable and childlike while asleep, as if all the fierce gestures and posturings were just that, facades conjured up along with the anger of the reveille bells.

He slowly pulled the left window shut and locked it, all without making a sound, then eased the right one down to its required two inches. There, he congratulated himself. Only twenty more rooms to go. He crept back toward the door.

"Dean."

"Yes, sir." He came to a brace. Impossible, he thought. Unbelievable. Horter was lying wide awake, motionless, his eyes fixed on Dean.

"Noon meal, Dean."

"Sir, the menu for noon meal is—"

"Just the main course."

"Sir, the main course for noon meal is Chicken Tetrazzini, sir." What a hell of a thing to ask at four in the morning, wondered Dean. But who am I?

"Thanks, Dean." Horter's eyes slowly closed.

"You're welcome, sir." Dean began to move quickly toward the door. Horter was awake anyway, and he had twenty more rooms—"

"And Dean..."

"Yes, sir?"

"Go around to Mister Swenson for waking me up."

Dean sighed, opening Horter's door. "Aye, aye, sir."

Outside, he carefully checked the list for the next room. Shelton leaves his books on the deck. Go around left side. Both windows tight. Dreiden *very* light sleeper. Get in and out quick.

Dean began to smile as he fantasized a glorious swan song to plebe year and the Naval Academy and the whole entire eat-shit military he had hated from his first moment. I'll knock Dreiden's door open with my foot, he planned, and scream at the top of my lungs, "I can't stand it any longer!" Then I'll walk right through Shelton's goddamn pile of books, kicking them all across the room, and slam their fucking windows shut, bam, bam! They'll be screaming at me, but I'll walk right out, kick a few books as I stomp out the room and slam the door. Then I'll go back to my own room and pack my clothes and leave.

*Plebe summer there had been a man whose name he no longer even remembered who had come back from his third trip running to the seawall and back because he couldn't march right, his M-1 rifle banging on top of his head, and a squad leader had yelled at him in the musty oven Annapolis summer heat about getting his rifle up where it belonged, and the squad leader had dropped him for pushups. The man whose name Dean no longer remembered had thrown his rifle to the deck and the squad leader had asked him, are you pissed? and the man had screamed back at the squad leader about how fucking pissed he really was and the man had tried to hit the squad leader. And Dean and a whole company of plebes had stood at attention in the middle of a company left turn, rifles at right shoulder arms, sweat dripping into their eyes, so afraid that none of them dared to even break attention as a horde of squad leaders beat the man whose name Dean no longer remembered, fifteen feet away and they did not dare to even look, the grunts and thuds settling into all their fears and paralyzing even their eyeballs. By the time drill was finished and they were racing through their rooms into new uniforms and another formation the man whose name no one could remember was gone and so was all his gear. No one heard from him again.*

Dean sighed, easing Dreiden's door open with such a delicacy that it might have appeared he was entering a king's domain. The men's snores wafted toward him as he crept into their cave, making sure he went around the left side of the desk.

One more room to go. Dean checked the list for 6101, where Swenson and McClinton slept. He felt he knew them both, all their angers and their joys, but he was surprised to read the handwritten scrawl that noted Swenson was a light sleeper and McClinton was a log. Swenson was usually so easygoing and unflappable that Dean had not expected him to be a restless sleeper. He felt he had learned a secret about his squad leader that he had no right to know.

But it didn't matter. Swenson wasn't in his rack, anyway. Dean almost sauntered to the windows and closed them quickly, then retreated. In the hallway, he checked the clock: five-fifteen. He had fifteen minutes of free time before Fogarty would drag him around another ice-choked loop of the Academy grounds again, time enough to shine his shoes, which were finally regaining their mirrorlike gloss after hours of repair.

"Dean!" An urgent whisper filled the empty hallway like a small explosion. Dean automatically came to a brace and turned slowly toward the voice. Swenson walked casually toward him, dressed in civilian clothes, looking gaunt and troubled.

"Yes, sir. It's me, sir. Good morning, sir."

"Don't remind me." Swenson grimaced. "Are you running with Mister Fogarty this morning?"

"Yes, sir."

"Well, tell him I need to talk with him. Oh, hell. Go to your room. I'll get him myself. You're sure he's up?"

"Sir, he told me to be waiting for him, sir."

"All right. He'll be up." Swenson walked back toward the Fourth Wing, then noticed Dean still standing alone, in his brace. "Carry *on*, Dean."

"Yes, sir. Aye, aye, sir."


"Ah, Fogarty." He jogged alone toward Swenson in the darkened hallway, his power sharp and directed, each stride like a blade. The clicks of his boots made echoes off the quiet walls. He was wrapped and bundled for the winter air, only his face showing from behind parka and wool stocking cap and leather gloves and sweatgear. "You crazy son of a bitch."

"Well, I'm glad to see you're back."

"I'm not sure I'm glad to be back. I'm in deep shit, Wild Bill."

Fogarty slowed to a walk, reaching Swenson. "You got caught."

"I wish that was all. I really do." Swenson's face was lined with exhaustion, wrinkles in his eyes and forehead that looked like granny beads. "I got in a wreck. That'll cost me. It was my fault. My car's a mess. The guy I hit is going to sue me. I'm getting Class A'ed for being over the Wall. I just got finished seeing the O.D. He was pissed because I woke him up." Swenson peered cautiously at Fogarty, his blue eyes wounded. "And Sally Sue was in there with another man." His eyes swam in tears. "God, can you believe it? She bangs me on Saturday night, leaves me on Sunday afternoon, and is in there with another man on Sunday night. The bastard was old enough to be my father, too."

"Well, maybe—"

"Hey, man. Let's stop playing games, alright? I should have a long time ago. They were both nude. The damn guy had gray hair all over his chest. I saw his *chest!* He was old enough to be my father." Swenson stood silently, staring at the floor. "I feel like God just took a dump, right on my head." Finally he shrugged. "Ah, what the hell can I do about it now? I'm screwed."

"Want to go running with us?"

"Are you crazy?" Swenson laughed softly, watching his former roommate. "Yeah, actually I guess you are. Mister gung-ho."

"I don't feel too crazy." Fogarty rubbed his jaw gently. "In fact, if I wasn't so busy setting an example for our man Dean, I might have bagged it this morning. My face hurts and I'm tired."

"Then go back to bed, man." Swenson reached for his own door. "Hell, I'm going to. The world can come crashing down on me in an hour, but I'm going to catch me some 'z's' till then."

"No, I can't go back to bed." Fogarty grinned, waving at his former roommate as he walked toward Dean's door. "Who the hell would make a leader out of the Gutless Wonder if we all slept in?"

They ran together under the crisp black sky, side by side, dressed the same, like double vision or maybe brothers. Crusts of ice broke under their boots as they jogged up the road past old houses toward the Superintendent's mansion, then turned the corner in front of it and headed for the chapel. Fogarty chided Dean as they ran.

"Well, let's see Dean, where were we, huh? Jesus Christ, you got a whole day away from me. Did you think about it all over the weekend?"

Dean gasped for air, the harsh winter frost attacking his lungs as he breathed. "Yes, sir, I—"

"Hey, dummy. That was really a boot thing to do, coming up to me and my woman like that yesterday. You don't do that unless you have something important to say. Quit making those sounds, Dean, you remind me of a foghorn."

"Aye, aye, sir." Dean's breathing was becoming more difficult and his throat was catching every time he sucked air in. "But, sir, I did—"

"Turn here, Dean. Run up to Stribling Walk. Yeah, you just stood there like a fucking maladroit, staring at my girl. What's the matter, Dean, you never saw a girl before?"

"Yes sir, but I had something else...I..."

"You sound just like a foghorn!" Fogarty breathed easily as he ran, his nose already dripping from the steam his breath was giving off. "Okay, hold it up. Stop right here."

They stood in the dark on Stribling Walk, surrounded by everything that made it an Academy instead of a mere college. Bancroft Hall was a bulky gray bunch of shadows on one end of the walkway. Mahan Hall was on the other, flanked by Maury and Sampson halls, the face of its ancient clock luminous in the dark: 0545. To one side, the Chapel dominated them. On the other, down a hill, the skeletal beginnings of what would soon be modern classrooms lay in the frost and mud. They were all named for heroes, for naval warriors. Fogarty and Dean lived in a museum, a monument to war.

Fogarty stood in the center of it, his arms up in the air like an orchestra conductor calling for a crescendo, waving at buildings and cannon and monuments. He called to Dean, his voice choked with emotional intensity. "So, what does it all mean to you, Dean? Huh? Doesn't this all make you...feel, every time you walk to class?"

Dean stood hesitantly, frozen by the raw power that exuded from Fogarty. He was almost afraid to move or even answer. "Uh, yes sir."

"So what does it make you feel?"

"Uh, well..." Dean looked all around him, as if for the first time. *Tired,* he thought, watching the face of Mahan Hall's clock. And *cold.* He clutched his arms to his own breast. No, that's not good enough. "Proud, sir." Fogarty stared at him with that expectant raw intensity, wanting more. He shrugged. "Just proud."

"Well, I suppose that's a start." Fogarty prodded him toward Mahan Hall and they began running again. Dean immediately began to rasp, his lungs bitten by the cold air. "Stop wheezing, dummy."

"Aye, aye, sir."

"Do you know what it makes me feel, Dean?" They turned along the road that fronted on Mahan and picked up Fogarty's usual route, passing the Naval Museum and the Tripolitan Monument. "Eternity." Fogarty glanced quickly at Dean's uncomprehending face. "That's right, eternity. I see all these things and I feel like I'm one small part of something so big and great that it'll never die, Dean. Never. This is our country. This is everything that ever made it grow. Stop making those sounds."

"Aye, aye, sir." Dean tried to breathe through his nose but could not pull the air in fast enough. He began to wonder if Fogarty belonged to a strange, secret religion that worshipped cannonballs and concrete. Shinto, he thought absently, trying to keep up. Samurai.

"I went to a funeral the other day, Dean. It was Saturday, I guess." Fogarty nudged Dean, pointing him toward the Hospital Point footbridge. "It was my best friend. It was sad. His wife was crying. But you know, I thought, watching him go under like that, I thought, he isn't really gone. He's alive as long as this place is alive. Do you get what I'm saying, Dean?"

If I say I do, mused Dean, fighting to keep up with Fogarty as they ran, he'll make me explain it. "Not exactly sir."

"This place made him what he was, and he made this place what it is. This place killed him, in a way, but he died for this place. He's as much a part of it as the goddamned Herndon Monument. And as long as there's a Naval Academy, Ron Loudenslager lives. Yes, sir, Dean. He touched my life, pushed me into myself and messed me around until I found out who I was, just like I'm doing to you." Fogarty glanced toward the struggling plebe again. "Only I wasn't such a goddamn maladroit. But that's eternity."

They crossed the narrow footbridge and ran the edge of Hospital Point. It seemed easier the second time. The ice crunched underneath Dean's boondockers and he slid on several little flat ponds, even falling once, but he no longer needed to be prodded or harassed by Fogarty. Fogarty jogged easily behind him, pointing out the slicker ice patches, grabbing him when he slipped, almost mothering him along. Finally they reached the road below the Hospital, and as they jogged through the looming spires and flat tombs of the cemetery, Fogarty again moved alongside Dean.

"So, tonight I'm going to finally get to sign up for the Marine Corps. Dean, I'll tell you. This is one of the happiest days of my life."

"Yes, sir." He is *crazy*, thought Dean, surrounded by the resting places of dead alumni. They're dying in droves in Vietnam, his best friend just came home in a box, and this is the happiest day of his life because he can be a part of that.

They followed Fogarty's usual route, passing Worden Field and the laundry and running the edge of Dewey Basin. Fogarty chatted idly as if they were strolling. Dean wheezed and gasped for air, his face completely numb from the cold and his legs gradually losing all feeling from the cold and from Fogarty's exhausting pace. Cold fear began to settle in Dean's lungs with the icy air. On the other side of Santee Basin, across a narrow width of Farragut Field, the seawall waited, icy and moss-covered, great surging shards of ice and flotsam just beyond its rocks.

I'm too scared, thought Dean fretfully, no longer listening to Fogarty's chatter. I'm too *scared*.

" ...I said, isn't that right, Dean?"

"Sir? I'm sorry sir. I didn't hear you." Steam rose from his mouth like smoke from a locomotive, puff puff puff, every time he gasped for air.

"You never say you're sorry, dipshit. How many times do we have to tell you that? You say, 'Excuse me.'"

"Aye, aye, sir." He gasped for air. "Excuse me, sir."

"I said, you're going to show the whole goddamned Brigade what a Fogarty-trained plebe can do, Dean. You're going to sprint the seawall with me, every step of the way. Right, Dean?"

*He can't order me to, I'll tell him that—* "Right, sir."

They jogged past Luce Hall, the Navigation and Seamanship building, another stone museum that had been there forever. Santee Basin was a junk-filled ice pond on their left. Bancroft Hall began to appear far to their right, the Seventh Wing's plebes coming awake now, their windows dotting the building like sporadic stars as they prepared for reveille.

"Here's what we're going to do." Fogarty was maddening as he ran, frustratingly fresh, in control. They had reached the edge of Farragut Field, the very place where the plebe whose name

Dean could not remember had committed his brief act of defiance those long months before. The foremast of the U.S.S. *Maine* grew in front of them like a pointing finger, marking the beginning of the seawall. "When we hit the seawall, I'm going to start sprinting." Fogarty smirked confidently. "I'm not even going to look behind me, Dean. I want you to follow me. You keep up with me, do you understand?"

Dean's eyes had already gone wide and hollow with dread. "Yes, sir."

"Just hit the rocks I hit. Stay away from the rocks I stay away from. Just concentrate, Dean, and you'll do okay. If you lose your concentration, you'll splatter your fat little head. Are you ready?"

"No, sir!" Fogarty turned quickly toward him, his face a threat. Dean shuddered as he jogged. "Yes, sir. Aye, aye, sir."

"Good." Fogarty picked up the pace, his own eyes going bright and round with challenge. "When I finish the wall you'd better be right behind me. Either that, or I'd better be able to come back along the rocks and find you dead. One or the other, Dean. Show me some guts."

"Aye, aye, sir." *I just hope you don't see my guts splattered on those* rocks, thought Dean, fighting once again to keep up with Fogarty as the first classman broke into long, graceful strides.

They hit the seawall at a sprint, Fogarty's head slightly bent, his shoulders tight with intensity. He was beautiful to watch, beautiful, and Dean lost himself for one small second before he concentrated on Fogarty's boots. The boots moved with a quick, balletlike grace along the rocks, going faster and faster, a wild hopscotch in the dark. Dean fought to match their movements, the skin of his face stretched tight in an anxious grimace, his own feet feeling like a bumbling toddler's as they tried to imitate Fogarty's movements. *I can't,* he thought wildly, losing control of his movements as the jagged rocks flew past him. *I can't keep up I can't do it I* can't—

*I've got to, this is my* chance, *but watch his boots.*

They bounced and leapt almost happily with the challenge, Fogarty's movements like the gleeful jumping of a deer in an open meadow, celebrating freedom. Dean pushed himself harder *but I can't—*

His boot slid on a black rock as though he had stepped in oil and then he was sailing forward and he could not keep it back, *"Sir!"*

The animal in front of him shuddered for a quick instant, caught in midstride by his scream, then toppled on the rocks, as if that leaping buck had been shouldershot in the middle of a jump. It happened quickly, a half-second and Fogarty was an unmoving clump on the dark rocks before him.

"Sir!" Dean stood up, unharmed, and walked carefully on the rocks to Fogarty, who now was rolling back and forth, his teeth clenched, holding his right arm.

"Aaaaahhhh! Aaaaahhh!" Fogarty rolled over onto one side and vomited off the edge of the rock, into a crevice that surged with the icy flux and flow of the Chesapeake Bay. He retched again, a dry heave, then sat still as he peered stoically at Dean, who was now standing in front of him.

"I'm sorry, sir! I'm sorry! I slipped and it just came out!"

"I told you not to say you were sorry, you goddamn maggot." Fogarty spat his words through clenched teeth. Behind them, to the east, the first piece of morning sky forced its way in a wide blue streak above the far shore of the river. "So what happened to you?"

"I just slipped, sir. I was trying but your boots move so fast. I was trying but I lost it and it just came out."

Fogarty's head was back against another rock, his face queasy and his eyes closed. He cradled the arm. "But you were trying?"

"Sir?"

"I said, you were trying? Really trying? You didn't bail out on me?"

"Sir, no sir." It was one small embryo of pride, even in his failure. He would not let Fogarty debunk it. "I didn't hair out, sir. I gave it everything I had, I swear to God."

"So how do you feel about it, Dean?"

"About what, sir?"

"Running the seawall. Growing some guts. Can you do it?"

"Sir, yes sir." Dean watched Fogarty's slack, nauseated face. He won't try it again. He broke his arm. He had to. He wouldn't throw up just because he bruised it. Not Fogarty. He's crazy but he won't run the goddamn thing again.

"Well, let's go." Fogarty struggled to his feet, using only his left arm, still cradling the right arm as if it were already in a sling. He tried to shake the hurt arm once and then grimaced, a small whine leaking uncontrollably from his throat, and pressed the arm back against his body.

"Sir, if you fall again, you'll destroy that arm, maybe for the rest of your life. In all due respect, sir. I saw you throw up. You should go to sick bay."

"Are you my mother?" Fogarty experimented with a jog. "Dean, if you promise you won't yell at me, I promise I won't fall." He grinned, slapping Dean hard on the back, a demand that he begin jogging also. "You gotta be tough, Dean. Today's the day I sign up for the Corps. You don't think I'd hair out on the seawall on a day like today, do you? And Dean," Fogarty pushed him again, "neither are you."

Fogarty began tentatively, then picked up speed. By the time they again reached the seawall they were both sprinting, Fogarty's left arm often high in the air as he compensated for the loss of balance his tucked right arm caused. It wasn't as fast as before, and Dean felt a small reprieve, staying immediately behind Fogarty, forgetting his fear as he concentrated on the dancing boots. It was a shuffle, a fox-trot march, a ritualistic tribal dance.

If someone had been watching from the field he would have seen two dark identical sillhouettes, bulky with wool, white ice behind them, the blue streaks of a new day creeping up from the shore beyond. Up and down the shadows moved, left and right along the rocks, a long boot ballet. And something else.

Finally they finished, Fogarty slowing their pace into a comfortable jog. He turned and saw Dean just behind him and broke into a huge, embracing grin that made Dean glow with pride, that lifted all the weariness from his numb legs and made his body feel light and even powerful.

"Well, how about that." Fogarty waited for Dean to catch up with him, and they ran side by side. He still clutched his right arm to his body, keeping it immobile. "Dean, you hot-shit son of a bitch, you made the seawall in the dark, like a true Fogarty-trained plebe. So, how do you feel about yourself, maggot?"

"I feel great, sir. I really do. Sir, I request permission to ask a question, sir. How is your arm, sir?"

"It's broke, Dean. How the fuck do you think it is?" Fogarty slapped Dean on the back with his good arm, bellowing into the empty black morning air. "Dean, you're a goddamn hero, boy! Hey, wait till they hear about this in the company area."

Click click click. In the hushed afterwash of reveille's infuriating screams, Lenahan's leather heels marched off a measured warning, an announcement. See them stumble from their hovels, dressed in rags, he mused playfully to himself as he toured the company area, saluting each midshipman who froze at attention in his bathrobe, eyes blurred with sleep. Do I today salute a future Nimitz? What tales will he tell of me a generation hence, remembering that mad captain who stalked these passageways at dawn?

"Hey, where the hell's Fogarty?" The double doors at the beginning of the company area were empty, and several midshipmen were mulling near the bathroom, sounding cheated of a ritual. They saw Lenahan and came to quick attentions, nodding to him as he approached.

"Good morning, gentlemen."

And then they heard the sounds, coming up the stairway. They all turned together and waited, curiosity bonding their stares.

"I can run all night—"

"I can run all night."

"And I can run all day—"

"I can run all day."

"I can run all night—"

"I can run all night.

"'Cause that's the Marine Corps way."

"'Cause that's the Marine Corps way."

"GOOD MORNING, ASSHOLES! IS EVERYBODY AWAKE?"

"You're late, Fogarty." One of the midshipmen dared to speak, pre-empting Lenahan.

"Well, that's because—" Fogarty appeared at the top of the stairway, all wet and muddy and dripping snot and steam down his front, revelling in his condition, grinning with good spirits. He saw Lenahan and came to attention also. "Oh, good morning, sir."

"Good morning, Mister Fogarty." Lenahan saluted him. Dean appeared behind Fogarty, wet and steaming as well, his red face burning with pride. "Ah, Mister Dean."

"Yes, sir. Good morning, sir."

Lenahan examined them, his face amused, standing at a loose parade-rest in his greens, clutching his gloves behind his back. "They were wondering why you were late for reveille, Mister Fogarty. I take it they wanted to start off the day telling somebody to get fucked, and you let them down." The six midshipmen who had gathered near the bathroom chuckled sheepishly.

"Uh, yes, sir. I was about to explain, sir." Fogarty clutched his right arm to his body in an unnatural attention. "You see, Mister Dean ran the seawall this morning, sir. The entire seawall, in a dead sprint in the dark."

"Well, Mister Dean." Lenahan looked closely into Dean's soft moon of a face and detected some new ingredient that had lit the eyes, even dared to conjure up the corners of the lips into a confident smile. "You have broken through the barrier, so to speak. What do you have to say for yourself?"

Dean peered straight ahead, in his tightest, most rigid brace. "Sir, I'm now a Fogarty-trained plebe, sir." The small crowd of midshipmen that had gathered made small jeers and chuckles to each other. Dean actually smiled back, then continued. "Sir, I would like to make a statement about Mister Fogarty, sir. Sir, I caused Mister Fogarty to fall on the seawall on our first attempt this morning. I think he broke his arm, sir. So he threw up and then ran the seawall again, with his arm like that, sir. I don't know if I would have made it if he hadn't done that, sir. It made me embarrassed to be afraid when he wasn't afraid. I guess that's leadership, sir. Anyway, I caused him to fall and I feel terrible about his arm, sir."

"You weren't surprised, were you, Dean?" It was one of the midshipmen who had gathered at the edges of the crowd. "You know what you get when you cross a marine with a gorilla? A retarded gorilla." Lenahan turned quickly around and the midshipman startled. "Oh, wow. Sorry, sir. I was talking about Mister Fogarty, sir."

"That's alright." Fogarty shot back his retort, his face lit with the challenge. "You know what you get when you cross a marine with your mother? The clap."

"That wasn't even funny." The crowd laughed, though.

"So? Marines are too dumb to make up good jokes."

Lenahan nodded toward Fogarty's arm. "Is it hurt badly?"

"Sir, after what you've been through from the war, you can't expect me to complain about a damn arm, can you, sir?"

"Is it broken?"

"I think so, sir."

Lenahan snorted. "Then for Christ sake, go get it looked at."

"Aye, aye, sir." Fogarty watched Lenahan walk away, back down the hallway toward another part of the company area. The others dispersed, busy with preparing for morning meal formation and come-arounds. He whacked Dean on the chest. "Dean, you asshole." It was an almost friendly insult. "I'd better not hear you tell anybody else that you did this to me. I did it to myself."

"But sir, I called to you. It was my fault, sir."

"But sir, but sir." Fogarty mimicked Dean. "That's what I hate about you, you sorry little troll." Fogarty seemed actually amused. "Stop thinking like a goddamned civilian." Fogarty stood in front of Dean and for the first time the plebe noticed the weary pain that had tightened his antagonist's face. "Now, I'll tell you what. You made such a goddamn hero out of yourself I'm going to give you the morning off. No come-around. Go take a shower and read the paper, Dean. I'll see you before noon meal."

Dean suddenly remembered, and his face went blank, paralyzed with dread. "But, sir, I need to talk—"

"But sir but sir but sir." Fogarty mimicked him again, walking away. "I need to go see a doc, Dean. Talk to me before noon meal."

# Chapter Three: 0845

Lieutenant Pruitt stood in front of the Battalion conference room, in the middle of the hallway, his hands on his hips and his chin jutting so far forward that he seemed to lean over under the weight of it. He pointed menacingly at a passing midshipman, calling him over to him.

"You, there. Mister!"

The midshipman looked up from his bored gaze at the floor, and quickly saluted Pruitt. "Good morning, sir."

"Come over here." The midshipman quickly obeyed, standing at a lanky attention, a full head taller than the baby-faced lieutenant. Pruitt stared up at him. "Do you know anything about the torpedo in the conference room?"

The midshipman squinted, glancing curiously down at Pruitt. "The torpedo in the conference room, sir? No, sir."

Pruitt was Perry Mason, pacing in the hallway. "Are you positive, Mister—what is your name?"

"Langford, sir."

"Langford." Pruitt wrote the name down underneath a host of others in his notebook. "What company?"

"Twenty-nine, sir."

"Langford. Twenty-nine. All right, Mister Langford. You don't know anything about the torpedo in the conference room, then? I don't need to remind you, Mister Langford, that midshipmen are under oath at all times."

"Yes, sir. I understand, sir. But I don't know anything about a—" Langford squinched up his face again "—torpedo in the conference room?"

"Alright. You may go, Mister Langford. Good morning."

"Aye, aye, sir. Good morning, sir." Langford saluted again, and continued on his way, shaking his head and even turning around at one point to squint back curiously at Pruitt.

Lenahan walked toward Pruitt, having come down the stairway during the interrogation, on his way to the conference room. He shook his head slowly, scrutinizing Pratt's favorite company officer. "What the hell are you doing?"

Pruitt looked up suddenly, his boyish face intense under an overlarge cap. "There's a torpedo in the conference room."

Lenahan squinched his own face, then stared at the ceiling for a moment as he tried to restrain his amusement. "Well, Pruitt, being a submariner and all, you should get a kick out of that."

"Commander Pratt is going to shit. I mean, he is just going to *shit*." Pruitt seemed uneasy, as if he himself might be named the culprit.

Lenahan could not restrain a chuckle. "Oh, you mean a *real* torpedo?"

"Of course I do." Pruitt seemed irritated, and continued to scan the hallways for other midshipmen to interrogate.

"Yeah, I'd say the good Commander *is* going to shit." Lenahan gave off a belly laugh. "Well, I'll be damned. Where is it?"

"Where is it? It's in the conference room! It's a big one, one of those old Japanese torpedoes they keep in the Yard over by Dahlgren Hall. It's laying right across the conference table, with the tail sticking out of the window. It's cold as hell in that room. How the hell are we going to have our conference with Commander Pratt this morning? Commander Pratt is going to flip!"

"It sounds like you already have, Pruitt. Take it easy, will you? It's only a goddamn torpedo. Now, what the hell are you doing out here in the hallway?"

"I've been *trying* to find out who put the torpedo in the conference room! What the devil does it look like I'm doing?" Pruitt shook his notepad at Lenahan. "I'm asking the mids who walk by whether they know anything about it."

"Oh, wow. Are you for real? I guess you are." Lenahan shook his head, despairing of Pruitt. "Did anybody call Public Works to get a couple guys over here and take the torpedo back to Dahlgren Hall?"

Pruitt stared exasperatedly at Lenahan, as if the suggestion were irrelevant to solving the crime. "No. Why don't you do that, Ted? You don't seem to have the stomach for this part of it."

"It ain't stomach that causes someone to stand out here and play this game, Pruitt." Lenahan patted him on the shoulder, his face so close that Pruitt registered a moment of fear on his own. "It's *asshole*."

Lenahan walked into the conference room and there it lay, lengthwise across the conference table itself, round and rusty and painted a bright green normally reserved for park benches. It filled the room like a cold phallus, completely covering the conference table. Lenahan laughed aloud again, holding his stomach. Joe Wentzel walked into the room and immediately began laughing also, the little aviator prodding Lenahan and then pouring them both a cup of coffee.

"Whoever did this ought to get a medal." Wentzel gestured toward the torpedo. "It's pretty funny, really."

Lenahan sipped his coffee. "Yeah, for about ten more minutes it's going to be funny. Then when that door opens—" he pointed toward Pratt's office door "—it will be *disaster*, major crisis." Lenahan crouched over, doing a searching mimic of Pratt. "Find the culprits! Geld them and lock them into their rooms!"

"Oh, Christ." Foote walked heavily through the door and stared at the torpedo, his eyes rolling, his meticulous morning destroyed. "It'll take us a half-hour to calm the Commander down."

"But really," Karalewski the clown was right behind Foote. He leapt onto a chair and then carefully sat on top of the torpedo, feigning relaxation. "I kind of like it, myself. It will bring a... park atmosphere to our meeting."

"Come on, Karalewski, this is serious." Wentzel guffawed. "The next thing you know, they'll be putting that airplane in Tecumseh Court again."

"They did that, too." Pruitt was back in the room, pacing around one end of the conference table, staring at the torpedo with exasperation. Karalewski waved at him and he shook his head, irritated. "This is bad. They hung a sign on the airplane that said 'Pratt sucks.' I tell you, he's going to *shit*."

Lenahan checked his watch. "Well, we've got two minutes. The question is, do we sit here at the table waiting for the good Commander, as he has instructed us to do each morning, or do we stand by at parade-rest outside his door, to disassociate ourselves from the torpedo?"

Pruitt knew all the protocol surrounding crisis management of Pratt's many moods. He sat down at the conference table, shivering from a gust of wind that coughed through the open window, and placed his notebook on the small portion of table in front of him that was not already blotted out by the large torpedo. "We sit and wait."

Lenahan and the others looked to each other, then shrugged. Karalewski stepped carefully down from his perch. Lenahan gave him a hand as he hit the floor, then shrugged. "Pratt's little brother says sit and wait, I guess the only thing to do is by God sit and wait."

They sat expectantly at the table, notebooks in front of them, unable to see over the top of the torpedo at the others sitting across from them. This is great, thought Lenahan, staring at the ugly green metal. Just goddamn great. And I forgot to call Public Works. He checked his watch. They still had a minute before Commander Pratt would stumble through the door from his office. Lenahan began to rise, thinking to call Public Works, and Pratt burst through the hallway door, his watery eyes round and almost frightened, a bundle of papers and notepads clutched under one arm. Poor guy, thought Lenahan, I really ought to try to leave him alone, just for one meeting. He ain't playing with a full deck.

"Somebody's in my office! Someone pushed back when I tried to open the door! Someone is in that room!" Pratt stared at his Company Officers sitting calmly around the torpedo, as if it were not even present, and squinched his face in disbelief.

"What are you doing?" They looked quickly at each other, as if collectively coming out of shock, and came to attention. "What is this?" Pratt stared dumbly at the torpedo, his bundle of papers in disarray underneath one arm, his cap still on his head, cocked at its customary tilt, wire frame glasses pinching the sides of his fleshy, shaved head.

Pruitt answered dutifully. "It's a torpedo, sir." Lenahan nudged Wentzel, swallowing back a guffaw as he and the others stood at parodies of attention.

"I know it's a torpedo, Lieutenant Pruitt. I don't have to be a submariner to know it's a torpedo. What's going on?" Pratt's free hand reached up and adjusted his cap, mashing it tighter onto the side of his head as he remembered. "There's someone in my office!" He dropped his papers onto the conference table and walked cautiously to the conference-room entrance to his office. Quietly he fit the key. The company officers remained in their places at the conference table, watching him with mild wonderment. Pratt softly turned the doorknob, then gave a wheeze and pushed the door hard, as if to surprise whoever had taken over his office.

The door gave six inches. Pratt screamed into the room. "You'd better give up, we've got you, you're on report!" Then he raised his face, staring at a wall of newspaper that went from floor to ceiling. "What is this?"

"It looks like newspapers, sir." Pruitt's blond child's head stared in amazement.

"It *is* newspapers. A whole room full of newspapers! My office is stuffed with newspapers!" Pratt looked inside the door for a long time, as if trying to decide whether to remove the papers or close the door. "How did this happen?"

"It looks like they wadded them up and—"

"I *know* how it happened, Lieutenant Pruitt." Pratt slammed the door and looked at his officers as if they themselves were responsible. "This is a breach of discipline." His eyes rested on Lenahan for a moment. "There will be an investigation. The men who did this will be punished. It is the ultimate form of disrespect." His words were agitated, sounding like they had been ground out of a warped record played on an old Victrola, all mixed in pitch and speed. A dribble of spit gathered in one corner of his mouth. Pratt was in a complete rage.

Finally he walked to the end of the conference table and stood, staring down the long nose of the torpedo. "Resume your seats, gentlemen. We will have our staff meeting. Then we will get to the bottom of this. In fact, I'm the Officer of the Day beginning at noon, and I do intend to solve this...problem." He sat down with an immediacy that was itself a command, and they all followed him. Lenahan bit the inside of his mouth to keep from laughing. The bottom of this, he thought, staring at the Commander. Pratt, you *are* the bottom of this.

Lenahan argued with himself as Pratt busily shuffled through his papers, trying to warn himself that, no matter how frivolous it all seemed, it was deeply important; it was his whole career. Do those things well that the boss checks, Lenahan mused as he awaited Pratt's message for the day, or you'll read about it on your fitness report. He doodled a big zero on his notepad. Ah, the hell with it. I just can't get excited about that kind of bullshit. I mean, seriously. He reached up and absently plinked the cold metal of the torpedo that still lay the length of the conference table.

"Why did you do that, Captain Lenahan?" Pratt had stopped shuffling his papers and was staring at Lenahan as if Lenahan had tweaked him on the nose.

"Sir?"

"Why did you just do that to the torpedo?"

Lenahan stared back, meeting Pratt's gaze, feeling suddenly defiant. "You mean this?" He plinked the torpedo again, a dangerous retort. "Hell, I don't know, sir. I'm a marine, you forget. You know what you get when you cross a marine and a gorilla, sir? A retarded gorilla." Lenahan leaned back in his chair and started to laugh. Wentzel joined him. Across the table, Karalewski's eyes were just visible above the torpedo, warning him. He looked at the end of the table and Pratt was scowling, obviously insulted. Lenahan cut short his laugh and shrugged. "I'm sorry, sir. I've just never seen a torpedo up close." Pratt was unmoved. "It's pretty hard to ignore, you have to admit."

"You think this is funny, don't you, Captain? You actually think this is some kind of a....a...game!" Pratt clutched his papers tightly, wrinkling the edges with both his hands. "The military is not a game. If these men are allowed to breach discipline like this, they will continue to make a mockery of the system when they are officers. Did you burn villages in Vietnam, Captain?"

"Sir?"

"Villages. Like on the evening news. The 'zippo' marines. Did you burn them?"

Lenahan shrugged, wondering about the relevance. "Every now and then. But it wasn't any sort of 'scorched earth' type of thing, Commander. You walk into a village and ask the villagers where it's safe to walk, you know, where there aren't any booby traps. Everybody in the village knows where not to walk. They have to keep their kids and waterbulls out of the way of the booby traps. So, you ask them where not to walk and they just stare at you like they don't know what the hell you mean and they sit there and watch your men walk right over the top of a booby trap. Boom. And you see some happy goddamn trooper go up in a cloud of smoke. So you try to let the villagers know that you're, how can I say it? Upset."

"And you burn their village."

"Ah, just their thatch porches. They fix them back up in a day or so."

"So, you make it a game. The military is not games, Captain. I'll bet you played the same sort of games when you were a midshipman."

Lenahan sighed audibly, and reached inside his sock for his cigarettes. No, he thought, I didn't burn one goddamn village, the whole time I was a mid. He lit the cigarette. It was going to be another two-pack day, he could feel it coming. Dear Lord, he prayed, staring at the green paint of the torpedo in front of him, if you will strike this dumb-ass dead of a heart attack, I will go to mass each Sunday for the rest of my life. Faithfully. Without exception. In sickness or in health. Amen, and all that.

Pratt began his morning harangue, reading over his notes from the Commandant's earlier briefing with a righteous zeal, finding issues of passion and justice in such mundane trivialities as uniforms and basketball games. *Here I am,* mused Lenahan, *an old man in a dry month, being read to by a boy.* Who said that? Eliot, I guess.

"Service selection is tonight. It will be orderly, beginning just after evening meal. The P.A. system will announce midshipmen by class standing." Pratt looked up from his notepad, staring directly at Lenahan as if renewing an old argument. "No shaved heads for marines. Any midshipman in my battalion who shaves his head will be placed on report for Direct Disobedience of a Lawful Order. No exceptions. Are there any questions on this point?" All six officers stared numbly at the torpedo, shivering from a gust of cold air that had just blown through the window.

Pratt went into another self-important drone, something about parking regulations when the first classmen were allowed to bring their cars into the Yard after spring break. Lenahan's mind drifted away, out to California in a corn-filled garden with his son, back into Vietnam past stinking waterbull pens, thatch porches burning in a village behind him, up to Bethesda as he sat in a chair in Neil Bard's room with Nurse Goodbody on his lap.

"Are you with us, Captain?"

"Sir?" They were all looking at him. Pratt was holding a piece of paper toward him. Lenahan looked at it, his eyebrows raising: another Form Two from the Commandant's meeting. "Yes, sir. I'm with you, sir."

"I said, how did reveille go this morning, Captain Lenahan?"

"Reveille, sir? It went fine, sir."

"Did you see anything wrong?"

"Wrong, sir? No, sir. The midshipmen were up and about. Morale was fine. The plebes were being run. They're kind of used to having me around by now." He nodded toward Pratt's hand. "Do you want me to do something with that, sir?"

"It's another one of your men, Captain." Pratt let the Form Two drop onto Lenahan's side of the torpedo. It slid down onto the table in front of him. "Everything's fine, but one of your men was caught in Washington last night, or should I say this morning. It seems he had a car wreck, or we might never have known."

Lenahan read the Form Two and whistled. "Swenson. He's a good man. Squeaky clean. He must have a pretty serious personal problem, sir. He wouldn't do this on a lark. He's not one of my wild ones, by any stretch of the imagination."

"Oh. I suppose we can expect a lot more out of your wild ones, then?"

Lenahan shook his head, a whimsical smile flitting across his face as he stared down at the Form Two, no longer caring to look at or even answer Pratt. He suddenly felt weary of the whole process, all the mindless debates that had done no good, all the mornings spent trying to inject his sort of reality into Pratt's fantasies. He plinked the torpedo again, an act of flagrant rebellion, then finally mustered the energy for a response.

"Yes, sir, Commander, on a good night my wild ones can make it all the way to Philadelphia and back."

# Chapter Four: 1150

"Hey, Wild Bill, wait for me!"

"Funny man." Fogarty stopped on the bricks of Stribling Walk and waited as Swenson approached him with his long-legged gait, a silly, almost embarrassed grin on his face. They began to walk toward the Hall together, a repetition of a thousand other times as they had grown into adulthood inside black uniforms, spending shoe leather in quick journeys along Stribling. "So how was math?"

"We proved one and one is two." Swenson said it with the reverence of the true academe. He noted Fogarty's sneer. "No, really, man. We *proved* it. It took forty minutes."

"Great. Every first-grader in the country thanks you."

In the distance a scream approached, high-pitched and piercing, and all thousand of the midshipmen on the walkway searched south, above the Chesapeake. Then here it came, like a small dark bullet, growing larger, taking on wings, an F-4 Phantom jet that shot straight up the Severn, just above the water, at five hundred miles an hour. They stopped on the walk with hundreds of others and screamed back, raising fists, electrified as the jet spun onto its back and then righted itself, a salute, like a high-school football player throwing the ball he had carried for a touchdown into the stands for his family.

Fogarty's face was raw with admiration. "Goddamn grads. He'll get in trouble from somebody for that. I'll bet McClinton is going ape-shit."

They started walking again. Stribling Walk buzzed with the aftermath of the grad's own special homecoming. Swenson grew pensive, staring at the Herndon monument. "Remember the day we climbed that, Bill? I don't think I've ever been so psyched. Standing there in the Field House while we waited for the class of 'sixty-five to throw their caps up into the air, and as soon as the first cap went up, running with that mob toward Herndon, trying to undress and carrying raingear. Do you remember, Bill? Carrying our goddamned raingear because the O.D. thought it might rain. I remember I threw away my raingear while I ran. Then standing there in all that mud and grease, feeling free. That was it, I felt free. Screaming and slapping the backs of all our classmates, we'd finally made it, there weren't any more plebes. Oh, damn, that was a good feeling. And when that cap finally went on top of the monument we went so crazy that the guy who put it up fell all the way from the top and broke his collarbone." Swenson tapped Fogarty's cast. "He looked like you."

Fogarty was solemn, too, fighting to keep a small grin on his face. "Yeah. And then that asshole Wilson spooned me when I got back into the company area. As if I was still a plebe and he was still God. 'Call me Bob,' he said. As if I couldn't anyway."

Swenson was in some sort of trance. "And then in one day we were in California, on board ship. Christ, it was freedom, freedom. Remember Seattle, Bill? I don't think I've ever been so drunk. 'The navy's in town,' that's what they said. We didn't buy a drink for four days and we were smashed the whole time. They liked us. And I fell in love in Hawaii. Remember?"

"You have a way of falling in love."

"Yeah, but there's nothing in the world as pretty as a half-Japanese girl, even if she was only sixteen. Remember? Trying to surf there on Waikiki and I hit her with my board." Swenson chuckled softly, obviously addled beyond his remembrances. "She taught me how to surf. I've never seen anything as pretty as that place when we came into Pearl Harbor. All the colors of the water, like a painting by somebody who had too much imagination. And then you punched out that sailor. Remember, Bill? He tried to cut into the chow line, screaming 'Regular navy, coming through!' like we were nothing but pieces of shit after having taken shit for a whole year, and you just stuck your arm out and he stopped and started to swing at you." Swenson eyed Fogarty. "You didn't have to hit him a second time, though."

"It felt too good to stop."

"Then when we got back here after youngster leave, finally upperclassmen, wearing that beautiful goddamned gold stripe on our khakis. It was like a reunion, seeing all our classmates again after a summer of bouncing around with the real navy, getting drunk and getting laid and falling in love. Remember, Bill?"

"What's wrong, Swede?" Fogarty put an arm on his old roommate's shoulder.

"They're going to throw me out, Bill." Swenson stared at the red bricks of the walkway, shaking his head with miserable certainty. "I can just feel it, man. They're going to toss me. Here

I've hated this place for four years, but I don't want to get thrown out. This place has cut me too deep. It's too much a part of me. They can't bounce me now, this is my *life*."

The A-4 was still in the middle of Tecumseh Court, although the Officer of the Day had sent a mate out to tear down the PRATT SUCKS sign. Swenson nudged Fogarty as they passed it.

"I'm sorry about last night. I wish I could live last night over again. I'm glad you put it there."

Fogarty grinned. "I hear Pratt absolutely shit when he tried to get into his office this morning."

The Court was filled with black-uniformed midshipmen scurrying back from class. On college campuses, people walked to and from class, and sometimes they simply walked around for the fun of it. At the Academy, time was a whip, beating on every man. Midshipmen did not actually walk anywhere; they strode or jogged or even ran.

Fogarty and Swenson entered the Hall through the Fourth Wing's Second Class doors, an entranceway reserved for third- and fourth-year midshipmen. Fogarty patted Swenson on the back again as they headed in different directions.

"They won't throw you out now, Swede. They've got too much money invested in you. Hell, man, all you tried to do was see a girl."

John Dean jogged slowly down the passageway, carrying several sets of uniforms over one shoulder, and banged abruptly on Fogarty's door before entering the room. He then took three giant strides inside the doorway and pressed his back against Fogarty's wall.

"Dean, my man! You're early for come-around, you fighting fool!"

"Yes, sir. I knew you might be having trouble at the Press Shop with your arm, so I thought I would bring you your uniforms, sir, in case you needed a clean set for noon meal formation, sir. It was no problem, sir. I had to go get my own stuff anyway, sir."

"You greasy smack." Fogarty was sitting back in his chair, his feet on his desk, reading a book. He glanced up at Dean's rigid frame, smiling with approval. "Put them in the closet. Hey, Dean, did you ever read poems?"

Dean returned from the closet and resumed his position against Fogarty's wall. "A little bit, sir. Not very much, though."

"Well, you ought to, Dean. Like Captain Lenahan says, it's good for you. A lightning rod, something like that. I just started and I like it. Really. I like the shit out of it." Fogarty studied the book in front of him. "Now, listen to this. It's by 'Anonymous.' This guy Anonymous is pretty good. They ought to write him up for the goddamn Nobel Prize, huh, Dean?"

"Sir, I request permission to make a statement, sir. Anonymous means—"

"Hey, he got the joke." Fogarty raised a hand, shutting Dean up. "Okay, turkey, listen up, I'm going to read you this and I want you to tell me what it reminds you of. Think hard, Dean."

"Do not stand at my grave and weep:
I am not there. I do not sleep.
I am a thousand winds that blow.
I am the diamond glints on snow.
I am the sunlight on ripened grain.
I am the gentle autumn rain.
When you awaken in the morning's hush,
I am the swift uplifting rush of quiet birds in circled
   flight,
I am the soft stars that shine at night.
Do not stand at my grave and cry;
I am not there; I did not die."

Fogarty looked up from the book and stared at Dean with a melancholy mix of pride and defiance. "So what does it remind you of, Dean?"

Dean's eyes remained on a far wall. His round face melted from intensity into a version of hesitant sadness. "It reminds me of what you said this morning about eternity, sir. About how your friend won't ever be dead if this place still exists, because it killed him but he died for it. I think that's what you said, sir."

"That's it. By God, Dean, you're a fucking genius!" Fogarty grinned sardonically. "No offense."

Dean dared a small grin of his own. "Sir, I request permission to ask a question, sir. Sir, how is your arm?"

"Broken, Dean!" Fogarty rose from his chair and bonked his cast on Dean's soft stomach. "What do you think, I'm wearing this cast to build up my shoulder muscles?"

"Sir, are you under any medication, sir?"

"What are you, my doctor?" Fogarty began brushing lint off of his uniform with a whisk broom.

"No, sir, but my father is a doctor, sir, and I was merely curious."

"They gave me some." Fogarty walked over to his cabinet and pulled out a small cylinder filled with pills. "Darvon." He pulled out another cylinder. "Valium. They said to take one of each every four hours and stay in bed. Can you believe that, Dean? Let me tell you about doctors, Dean: they're candy-asses. Take a bunch of pills and stay in bed just because you break your arm. It doesn't even hurt anymore." Fogarty allowed himself a small, conspiratorial smile. "Not much, anyway. But for Christ's sake, it isn't going to hurt any less if I'm laying down."

"Sir, it's standard procedure for a bad break, sir."

"Well, that's what I hate about standard procedures, you negat. Brush off my back, will you?" Fogarty handed Dean the whisk broom and the frail plebe carefully brushed off all the lint from the back of Fogarty's drill shirt. Fogarty quizzed him as he worked.

"So, what was in the newspaper today?"

"Sir, the Marines are still trying to retake Hue City, sir. Bad weather, heavy casualties, and a lack of special weapons for house-to-house fighting have slowed them down, sir. In the air, navy jets from the carrier Kitty Hawk bombed a radio center ten miles south of Hanoi through heavy flak, sir. And air force jets flew raids against one North Vietnamese field that had three Soviet bombers on it, sir. The Communists have lost more than thirty thousand men killed since the Tet offensive started two weeks ago. And the most recent Harris poll shows that support in this country for the war has risen sharply, from sixty-one percent in December to seventy-four percent today."

Fogarty grunted. "Does that surprise you, Dean?"

"The rise in support, sir? I have to admit it did, sir."

"I thought it would. It didn't surprise me at all. We finally get all these bastards out where we can fight them and we kick their asses. And then the crybabies like that Senator McCarthy and Bobby Kennedy start bitching and moaning. Americans don't listen to crybabies, Dean. If President Johnson's got a hair on his ass, he'll call for a counteroffensive, and there won't be a damn war left for me to fight by the time I graduate. Americans know that, even if those asshole crybabies don't. So who do you listen to, Dean?"

Oh, my God, thought Dean. Professor Thad, that's who. Dean ceased brushing Fogarty's shoulders and came to a brace against his wall again. Speaking of crybabies. "Mister Fogarty, sir. There's something I've got to tell you, sir. I've been trying to do it since Sunday. That's why I came up to you after chapel. I was going to this morning, but then we fell and you hurt your arm and I just—"

"So *tell* me, Dean! Don't give me all of this bullshit about why you haven't, just *tell me!*" Fogarty was laughing.

He said it as fast as he could. "Sir, my chemistry professor is turning you in for hazing, sir."

Fogarty stood motionless in front of Dean, his nose squinched and his mouth working in small circles. Finally he spoke. "*Hazing?* What the hell is *hazing?* Hazing is something you do in a fraternity. I haven't been hazing you, Dean, I've been indoctrinating the shit out of you."

"That's what I meant, sir. Violation of the plebe indoctrination regulations, sir. The professor calls it hazing, sir." Dean felt Fogarty's accusing stare. "Sir, I didn't do it, sir. I hope you'll believe me. I didn't do anything. When I failed the test last week he asked me some questions. I couldn't lie, sir. It would be an honor offense. He asked me and I told him. I even asked him to leave me alone, sir. I swear to God. He doesn't understand this place. But he's got a lawyer helping him, and—"

"A *lawyer?*"

"Yes, sir, he's got this lawyer friend who keeps talking about the Constitution. I don't know what's going on." Dean verged on tears. "He's filing a complaint today. He told me fourth period. Honest to God, sir, I tried to get him to keep his nose out of this. I wanted to make it on my own, sir. I didn't need anything like this."

"A *lawyer?*" Fogarty sat on the edge of his desk, nursing his broken arm. "What the hell does he need a lawyer for?"

"I guess he's afraid the Academy will cover it up, sir, and he wants—"

"Who the hell is this guy?"

"Professor Thad, sir. He's new here. He graduated from grad school last year." Dean caught himself. It was no time to praise Thad's credentials. He took a deep breath, staring at the far wall. "Sir, if it will do any good, sir, I will deny everything I said to him. I will—"

"We don't do those things. Criminals deny things. Are you an honorable man, Dean?"

"I try to be, sir."

"Then take shit head on. Don't give me any of this 'deny' bullshit. How the hell are you going to tell your men not to lie, cheat, or steal when you're willing to go out and lie?"

"It was just a thought, sir."

"Holy shit." Fogarty's face was numb as he sat slumped on the corner of his desk, his blue eyes filled with bafflement that went so deep it came out on the other side as wonderment. "Hazing. A *lawyer*." Finally he focused in on Dean again. "Well, what a bunch of happy horseshit *that* is. Right, Dean?"

"Right, sir." Dean swallowed hard.

"So we'll see you tonight at come-around. Sweatgear."

# Chapter Five: 1500

The phone rang and Lenahan picked it up, reaching over a pile of paperwork, room inspections, and Form Twos. "Good afternoon, Captain Lenahan speaking, sir."

"*Ted.*" It was warm as a feather bed, as relaxing as the stroke of a cello. Lenahan felt himself pass through warmth and exhilaration all the way to incestuous guilt and back again.

"Hi, Angie." He automatically pulled out a cigarette and lit it, shaking his head at his own excitement. "So, how've you been?"

"I'm worried about you. Are you all right?"

"You're worried about *me*? Well, don't worry about me. I'm all right, all right?" He dragged on his cigarette and blew several smoke rings across the room. "Sorry. I'm just getting tired of being asked that. It's nice of you to worry. So tell me, Angie, what the hell are you worried about?"

"It's hard to pin down." A child called to her in the background. "Just a minute." Lenahan dragged on his cigarette, staring at the ceiling. "All right. I'm back. What was I saying?"

"It's hard to pin down."

"Oh, yeah. Well, it is. You just seem to be in a *knot*, Ted! Really. I can't believe you choked that guy in the hospital on Sunday. And that nurse…"

"Are you jealous, Angie?" Lenahan's craggy face was wrinkled with a grin.

"Jealous? No, not really. If that's what you want, that is." Her voice took on a small purr. "Steve's traveling with the Admiral this weekend. He'll be gone three days. Thursday, Friday, Saturday. Three days."

"Thursday, Friday, and Saturday." Lenahan felt himself becoming aroused, in spite of his own attempts to stifle it.

"That's right." The child called again. "Hold on a minute." She held her hand over the receiver and called to the child. "All right."

"You're something, Angie, you really are. But what happens then?"

"What do you mean?"

"Thursday, Friday, Saturday. And then what?"

"Steve's going to Vietnam this summer."

Is this how it happens, mused Lenahan, his own mind whirling with a vision that was like a newsreel of himself two years before. Is this supposed to be my payback, to take from a brother, an eye for an eye until the whole goddamn world is blind? So what is love, and what are memories? Is this the whole stinking world?

"That's brutal, Angie. I mean, it's absolute *murder.* I'm sorry." He spoke through clenched teeth, as if the words were being pulled out of him with his entrails, leaving him all spent and gutted.

"I need you, Ted. I don't want to be alone. I can't stand the thought of being alone for a whole year."

"Then tell Steve that. I could never do it to him, *never.* Every time I see him now I feel like throwing up. I can't go through the rest of my life that way. I'm sorry, Angie. I really am. You're terrific, but it just isn't worth it. I can't do it again. Ever."

"So you're really taken by the nurse."

"I really like her. That doesn't have a whole lot to do with what we're talking about, but yeah. I really like her."

"She's a whore." The purr was gone and the claws were out.

"Angie, really. And what are we?" Lenahan stubbed out his cigarette.

"I'm sorry I said that, Ted. I really am." Her voice was calm again, no purr but filled with the cello's warm strokes. "You'll stay in touch? I'm really afraid. I'm not a very strong WesPac widow."

Her warm words conjured up his whole military past, June weeks swimming in the bay and watching all the girls in their pretty bathing suits, sweet Angie with his best friend, their hands clasped together in the most innocent of embraces, the one that said forever with a purity that no one, especially Ted Lenahan, had the right to defile.

"Of course I will, Angie. You're my best friend's wife."

She gave off a surprised, throaty chuckle, as if that fact had eluded her for the past several months. "I guess I am. And you won't stay away from me after this?"

"I like you, Angie. No, probably a little more than that. You're a huge part of my life, wrapped up in a pretty pink ribbon."

"That was beautiful."

"No, it was sad."

The child was screaming at her. "I've got to go. Can I still call you?"

"Any time you want."

"I will, you know."

"I hope you do. I'm kind of low on friends, myself. They keeping getting shot on me."

The child called to her again. "That's what I mean about worrying over you. When you say things like that."

"So, don't get shot."

"*Ted!*"

"'Bye, Angie."

"Good by-y-y-y-ye." She dragged it out, as if chiding him.

Lenahan sat back in his chair for thirty seconds, staring dumbly at his closed office door. Then he picked up the telephone again and quickly dialed four numbers. He grinned when the other party answered. "Wentzel, you cocksucker, how can you stand to be sitting around in your office when your buddies are over there getting shot at around Hanoi? Huh? It's Lenahan, who the hell did you think it was, Ho Chi Minh? Well, you don't have a hair on your narrow ass if you don't just walk yourself right over to the 'O' Club with me and have a beer. Huh? Tell Pratt to kiss my butt. We've got to be back here after evening meal for service selection anyway. Come on. I'll pick you up in ten minutes." Lenahan checked his watch, grinning again. "And I promise I won't tell your little lady."

He piddled around his desk for five more minutes, avoiding paperwork by straightening out his desk, finding little notes to throw away, generally killing time. The phone rang again.

"Good afternoon, Captain Lenahan speaking, sir."

"Hello, Captain Lenahan, this is Professor Thad, of the Chemistry Department, how are you today, sir?"

He would have known it was a professor if the voice had merely called in the weather. It had that irritating relaxation, that modulation that came from not being rushed, from never having been physically challenged. And it would be a younger professor, too. The older ones were different. Most of them had seen the other end of it, in the operating navy as officers or seamen. That made a difference, at least most of the time. This guy Thad, mused Lenahan, trying to remember. Oh, yeah. The other day. Dean.

"Don't tell me Dean flunked another goddamn test."

Thad seemed startled by Lenahan's abruptness. "Why, no, we haven't had any more exams since I talked with you before. Actually, I'm flattered you remembered my name, Captain. I had thought I would be required to go into a rather long preamble, and this is embarrassing enough without—"

"So, don't." Lenahan checked his watch, cutting Thad off. This son of a bitch is giving me a preamble about why he doesn't need to give me a preamble. "What can I do for you, Professor? By the way, I called Dean in and counseled him. I asked him if there was anything he needed to tell me and he said there wasn't."

"That's a pretty carefully worded question, Captain. Is that how your system works?" Thad did not conceal his irritation.

"I'm not a lawyer, Professor, I'm a Company Officer."

"That was a very lawyerly question. Did you ask him if any violations of the plebe indoctrination system had been perpetrated by upperclassmen on him? Did you specifically ask him that?" Thad's voice was trembling over the phone, with rage or fear or something.

"You're *wrong*." Lenahan gripped the receiver, staring at a picture on his wall as he and Thad communicated their hostility through the empty hiss of the telephone line. The picture showed two marine infantrymen working a machine gun from a fighting hole in Vietnam. One was black, the other was white. They both wore little buttons, a joke in their unit, probably, that said "WE TRY HARDER." Lenahan shook his head. Thad was still waiting for a response, or perhaps was struck dumb by the ferocity of Lenahan's rebuke. "Lawyers ask questions like that, Professor. I'm not a lawyer. I'm not interested in developing a goddamn *case*.

Dean's a big boy. I gave him the opportunity to let me know if somebody was bearing down on him too hard. He didn't seem to think so. My job is to make him a man, to teach him to get hit and keep going. He's going to be an *officer*, professor. He doesn't need somebody to sit him on their knee and burp him."

"I can see we disagree."

"Disagree? What the hell do you even know about it?" Another long, hissing silence. "Tell me, Professor, have you ever even been in Bancroft Hall?"

"I know about the regulations. I have a copy of them right in front of me. And I know about the Constitution of the United States."

"The *Constitution*?" Lenahan restrained the scream that had begun to force its way out of his throat. "A noble document, one I have sworn to uphold and defend. Which section talks about plebe year?"

"Why, due process!" Thad spoke as if Lenahan were a Neanderthal. "The denial of life, liberty, and the pursuit of happiness without due process of law!"

"Are you for real?"

"A man doesn't give up his constitutional rights just because he comes to the Naval Academy, Captain. He only gives up those which are spelled out in regulations. When the regulations are violated, the man's constitutional rights are breached."

Lenahan gestured to the machine gunners in the picture on his wall, as if they might commiserate. "I think this asshole is serious!" He grasped the telephone receiver tightly again, grimacing at his desk. "What the hell do you think we're up to over here, Professor, huh? *Huh?* Do you think we just sit around and glory in seeing people getting beat on, is that it? Well, you listen to me. We're not turning out goddamned *schoolteachers*. Every man who graduates from this place has got to be able to deal with pressure, and I don't mean the kind of pressure you get when you take a *test*, either. You know something? Every now and then I have a dream. I dream that I'm reading the newspaper, and there's a story about some dufus Academy grad doing something stupid and getting people killed. Maybe he blows it in combat. Or maybe he just freezes up when the pressure hits him inside the cockpit of a plane with a mechanical failure, or something as simple as keeping a ship on course in rough seas with an oiler right next to it, during underway replenishment. That isn't simple, by the way, it's just regular. So anyway, here in my dream, Professor, the guy screws it up and gets a bunch of people killed, and I read about it in the paper and I say, 'Jesus Christ, Lenahan, that was one of *your people!*' Do you get what I mean, Professor? Here I am, in my dream, that is, discovering that I didn't get some sorry-ass loser out of the Academy before he *killed* people. It doesn't have a goddamn thing to do with being smart, either. It's got a lot to do with being ... something. Taking heat, I guess. But that's my job, Professor. Part of it, anyway. I get paid by Uncle Sam to teach the good ones and get rid of the bad ones. And people like Dean, well, we just have to push them until we find which way they tilt. But that's my job. You teach them chemistry. That's your job. I'm not telling you how to do it, and I don't know anything about it. But stay out of my job. All right?"

"Part of my job," Thad droned on, ignoring Lenahan, obviously attempting to be done with a formality, "part of *my* job as a professor is to report violations of the plebe indoctrination system. That's exactly what I'm doing, Captain. I have sent a letter to the Commandant of Midshipmen and the Superintendent of the Academy, reporting the violations perpetrated on Mister Dean by Midshipman First Class Fogarty, also of your company. This is a courtesy call, Captain, to let you know that the letter has been mailed."

"*Fogarty?* Why, you cocksucker—" Thad hung up the phone. Lenahan swore into it anyway. "I'll catch your act in hell, you goddamned mouse!"

# Chapter Six: 1800

John Dean chopped down the passageway toward Fogarty's room, dripping wet in his sweatsuit, having just finished two hours of extra duty. His face was flushed beet red. He took a deep breath as he reached Fogarty's door, pausing for one secret moment before he burst through it.

"Midshipman Dean, fourth class, reporting as ordered, sir."

"Dean, you goddamn animal." Fogarty said it without his usual exuberance. He was at his desk, reading another book. He looked up and examined Dean's soaked sweatsuit. "You *are* a drippy piece of mung. Go put on a dry set of sweatgear."

"Sir, I request permission to make a statement, sir."

"You don't have a dry set of sweatgear."

"That is correct, sir. The two pairs I wore this morning are still soaked, sir. This pair was my last dry pair, sir."

"Dean."

"Yes, sir?"

"I didn't ask you if you had a dry set of sweatgear, I told you to go put on a dry set of sweatgear. And in two minutes, you will be back inside this room with a dry set of sweatgear on, do you understand me?"

Dean swallowed, his eyes hollow with the amazing knowledge that he was going to obey this order even if he had to kill for a dry set of sweatgear. "Yes, sir."

"Now, Dean, I am going to blink, and when I open my eyes, you will be gone. And in two minutes I'm going to open my door, and you are going to be standing in the passageway with a dry set of sweatgear on. Got it?" Fogarty wasn't even watching him anymore. He was reading the book again.

"Sir, yes sir."

"Good." Fogarty looked up from the book, smiling faintly. "Blink."

Dean sprinted furiously for Fogarty's door and raced down the hallway, squaring each corner as he made his way back toward his room. An upperclassman called to him and he froze in the passageway, screaming at the top of his lungs, his face contorted in its energy and purpose.

"*SIR I REQUEST PERMISSION TO MAKE A STATE-MENT SIR I AM ON A COME-AROUND TO MISTER FOGARTY SIR AND I HAVE TWO MINUTES TO BE BACK INSIDE HIS ROOM WITH A CLEAN SET OF SWEATGEAR I REQUEST PERMISSION TO SHOVE OFF SIR!*"

"All right, all right!" The unseen upperclassman chuckled. "Get out of here!"

"Sir aye aye sir!" Dean resumed his sprint and finally reached his room. Peckarsky was sitting at his desk, shining a pair of shoes. Dean began throwing off his wet sweatsuit. He screamed at Peckarsky. "Give me your sweatgear! Hurry up!"

"Are you crazy?" His athletic roommate watched him furiously undressing and rose from the desk, eyeing his own sweatsuit with protection. "Hey, I don't want you sweating in my stuff, John. And besides, they'd fit you like—"

Dean's voice was a fierce growl, stunning Peckarsky. "I didn't ask how they would fit I said *give* them to me, asshole! Hurry up!"

Dean ran to Peckarsky's locker and grabbed a clean sweatsuit, not even looking at Peckarsky.

"Hey, man—"

"Fuck you!" Dean turned toward Peckarsky as he hurriedly pulled the sweatsuit over his gym shorts and shirt. "Give me a hand, will you?"

Peckarsky helped Dean pull the trousers through his tennis shoes. "Fogarty, huh?"

"Well, no shit." Dean tied the drawstring. "Thanks." He bolted out of the room, leaving his roommate shaking his head with a mix of bemusement and admiration.

Fogarty had just begun to open the door when Dean raced down the passageway toward it. Dean sprinted harder, wheezing, trying to beat the door. He came to a puffing, red-faced parade rest just as Fogarty stepped out into the hallway, and snapped into a brace as Fogarty stood in front of him.

"Midshipman Dean, fourth class, sir."

"You look like Charlie Chaplin." Fogarty broke into a wide grin. "I didn't want you to catch cold, Dean, standing around in that wet sweatgear."

Dean still fought to catch his breath. "Sir, I appreciate that, sir."

"Greasy, greasy. Plebes don't appreciate, Dean. You know that. Now close your eyes and open up your mouth." Dean obeyed, and felt the tart sweetness of a piece of candy melting on his tongue. "My girl sent me a Care package today."

It tasted good. Dean sucked on it. "Thank you, sir."

"What is this thank you shit, huh? Swallow it whole. Ahhhh!" Fogarty raised a finger, catching Dean in the nick of time. "Just kidding, Dean. Come on in."

"Aye, aye, sir." Dean dashed into the room and put his back against Fogarty's wall. "Midshipman Dean, fourth class, sir."

"Ah, Dean Dean Dean." Fogarty sat back down at his desk and studied the soft features of his charge. "Are you learning anything?"

"Sir, yes sir, I decidedly am, sir."

"What?"

There was a knock at the door, authoritative, an Academy ring cracking on the wood three times and then Lenahan burst into the room, filling the doorway in his green uniform, cap and all, his heels clicking on the floor. Fogarty jumped up from his chair, standing at attention.

"Attention on deck, Midshipman Fogarty, first class, sir."

"Gentlemen." Lenahan nodded to Fogarty and scrutinized Dean closely, wrinkling his face at the overlarge sweatsuit, wondering at the jawbreaker candy in Dean's mouth. "What the hell is in your mouth?"

Dean sucked the juice free. "Candy, sir."

"*Candy?*" Lenahan turned back to Fogarty. "What is this, *The Little Rascals*? You got this guy dressing up in Daddy's clothes and sucking on a lollipop? I'll tell you, Mister Fogarty, plebe year isn't what it used to be."

"No, sir." Fogarty grinned sheepishly. "To be honest, sir, I'm not usually this easy on Mister Dean."

"So I've heard." Lenahan sat on Fogarty's desk, taking his cap off and shaking his head as he looked at Fogarty and then Dean. "In fact, if we are to believe Professor Thad, Mister Fogarty, you are something of a menace to society. Have you been told about the charges he has placed against you?"

"Mister Dean told me, sir. That's the only thing I've heard."

"So, tell me, Mister Dean. How did all this come about, anyway?" Lenahan looked at Dean with an expression that bordered on disgust.

"Sir, I..." Dean blinked and swallowed hard, his eyes all the way round, staring at the far wall. "Sir, I failed the Chemistry exam, sir. And Professor Thad wanted to know why. And then he started calling me, sir. He just started calling me. And then today after class he sat me down with a copy of the Commandant of Midshipmen Instructions on Plebe Indoctrination, sir. And he went through them, line by line. 'Has this happened to you,' he would say. 'Has that happened to you,' he would say. And I had to answer him, sir, or it would be an honor offense. Wouldn't it, sir?"

"Yeah, it would, Dean." Fogarty interjected. "Sir, it isn't Mister Dean's doing, sir. It just happened, that's all. I don't think it would be right for him to take the heat, sir."

"Well, Mister Fogarty, let's get a few things straight. *He* isn't taking the heat. You are. And you're on your way out of this place, if a few people have their way."

"On my way *out*, sir?" Fogarty stared quizzically at Lenahan. The prospect had never occurred to him. "Of the Academy?"

"That goddamn professor has written a book on you, Fogarty, a goddamn *book!*" Lenahan waved a packet of materials in front of Fogarty's stunned face, then opened the manila envelope and began flipping through pages. "Listen to this: 'Commandant Midshipman Instruction 1531.2B dictates that, in executing their responsibilities for Plebe Indoctrination, upperclassmen will be held *strictly accountable* for observance of the spirit and the letter of this instruction. *Cite:* Commandant Midshipman Instruction 1531.2B of 17 August 1965, section 4(b)'" Lenahan looked up at Fogarty, his eyebrows raised. "You like that, huh? Oh, there's more." He flipped the page. "'Fourth classmen will be treated with justice, dignity and respect. *Cite:* Section 4(d). This does not allow for such treatment as wiping snot on a fourth classman's belt buckle, grinding out the polish on his shoes (also violative of section 4(c) and 4(f), both of which will be dealt with below), or requiring him to sleep nude, on his springs (also violative of section 4e(3), relating to denying a plebe the opportunity to sleep during authorized hours. Section 4 e(3) has been repeatedly violated by Mister Fogarty as he has been requiring Mister Dean to arise well before reveille in order to perform exercises that are not authorized by the Physical Fitness Manual, and are thus violative of section 4(f). In all, I charge that Mister Fogarty has violated more than a dozen counts of the Plebe Indoctrination Instruction, merely over the past five days. As will be seen in the enclosure, such violations go against virtually every article of the Instruction. Mister Fogarty has failed to treat Mister Dean with justice, dignity and respect. Section 4d. He has encroached on time which is specifically intended for study. Section 4e(1). He has denied Mister Dean the opportunity to eat a full and complete meal. Section 4e(2). He has denied him the opportunity to sleep during authorized hours. Section 4e(3). He has caused Mister Dean to perform acts of a menial nature. Section 4e(4). He has caused Mister Dean to perform physical exercises not authorized by the Physical Fitness Manual. Section 4f. He has, most importantly, touched Mister Dean under circumstances other than to administer first aid.'" Lenahan held up several other pages. "There's an addendum with what he and his lawyers call 'specifications.'"

Fogarty had gone absolutely numb, standing in front of

Lenahan with his head slightly tilted, the sling from his arm cutting into his wide neck. His mashed nose was squinched, his eyes confused. "Wow."

"Yeah. You're what they call a 'test case,' Mister Fogarty. Either you're the exception with this stuff or you're the rule. If you're the exception, you get thrown out. If you're the rule, the Academy gets investigated, like it has been every year for the past four years, and the plebe system gets watered down, or done away with."

"I don't understand, sir. I'm not the exception or the rule. It was Dean that was the exception."

"No, no, you've got them all wrong. Dean is the *victim*. So how does it feel to be a victim, Mister Dean?"

Dean verged on tears again. "I don't feel like a victim, sir. I just feel like something's gone wrong, sir." He looked exhausted. Dark rings circled below his eyes, onto his cheekbones. He looked like a flushed, sick child in Peckarsky's sweatsuit. "I felt like I was finally making it, sir. I ran the seawall." Dean invoked the seawall as one might mention having climbed Mount Everest, or having swum the English Channel.

"They're not interested in building character, Dean, they're interested in facts. The facts are, the regulations have been violated—" Lenahan caught himself, hating this new notion of having to think like a lawyer "—allegedly, that is."

"Oh, hell, Captain, I violated them. I may as well get that out up front."

"No, you don't. You don't get anything out up front anymore. They're after your ass, Mister Fogarty."

"It would be dishonest not to start right there, sir—"

"The hell you say?" Lenahan's face wrinkled into a sad smile. "We're dealing with people from the *outside*, now, Mister Fogarty. They don't play by the same rules."

"Well, I can't handle that, sir." Fogarty watched Lenahan, feeling almost betrayed by the subtle urging for him to deny the obvious. "I broke the regulations, sir, but I made Dean. Where's the harm?"

"They're not interested in harm, Mister Fogarty, they're interested in facts." Lenahan stood up and placed his cap back on his head. "Don't do or say anything unless you check with me first. I just want you to know I'll be with you all the way on this one." He started for the door. "But I also want you to know that I don't really think we've got much of a chance."

# Chapter Seven: 1845

"Brigade, a-tenn, *hut*." Banks, the Brigade Commander, sounded almost timorous as he stood at the Anchor and called the Brigade to evening meal. Commander Pratt stood stiffly at the Staff table and watched Banks' every move, as if waiting to pounce on him with a Form Two. Pratt had ripped through Bancroft Hall twice already during his brief time as Officer of the Day, placing hundreds of men on report, causing midshipmen to literally flee down the passageways as they saw him approach.

"Attention to announcements. Service selection will begin immediately after evening meal in Smoke Hall. Class numbers will be announced over the P.A. system. Once first classmen have made their service selections, they will immediately clear Smoke Hall for the next entering group. Brigade, seats."

Screams echoed through the mess hall like buckshot blasts as first classmen contemplated the evening ahead. Service selection night was the first step out of the door and into the operating forces. Within a few hours, every midshipman in the class of 1968 would know his first duty assignment after graduation.

The whole Brigade was charged, and of course the plebes became the conduit for the emotion. One table over, two first classmen who had endured four years of the East Coast after growing up in California had ordered up a California Happy Hour, the four plebes on the table now dipping into laundry bags they had carried to the mess hall before formation and donning "baggy" swimsuits, sunglasses, Mexican sandals, and suntan lotion, and serenading the firsties with surfing songs. It was stupid, thought Fogarty, watching them, but it was fun, too. He called over to one of the firsties, a friend he had watched grow into adulthood locked inside the Hall.

"Hey, Skippy, what are you going after?"

His friend had put on a pair of aviator sunglasses and was conducting the plebes as if they were a symphony. "Anything that floats, man, as long as it's out of San Diego!"

Fogarty laughed. "That's what I call career planning."

"To hell with that. I'm going back to God's country!" His friend nudged the other firstie at the table. "What are you doing, Bill? You made your mind up yet?" They both laughed as Fogarty sputtered, not realizing it was a joke.

"I guess you haven't heard." Swenson leaned back from his chair, talking to Skippy. "Fogarty and I both just might be on the way to CivLant."

"CivLant?" It was a codeword for the civilian world. "I heard about your stunt, Swenson, but what the hell did *you* do, Bill?"

"He built some character in a negat." McClinton watched Dean's woeful face. "Some professor is out to get his ass."

"You're kidding." Fogarty's friend watched him as he tested a glass of tea. "Are they serious, Bill?" Fogarty nodded, still not looking up from the tea. "Well, what in the hell does a professor know about running plebes?"

Fogarty finally spoke. "Maybe he can take my place in Vietnam, too."

It wasn't funny, but everybody laughed. McClinton watched the antics in the mess hall, trying to change the subject. "Pratt's gone crazy, man. The whole Brigade is laughing at him. Hey, Bill, why aren't you up there giving Banks a hand at the staff table?"

"He might ask me about the torpedo and the newspaper. He's been asking every mid from our battalion. I swear to God he's fried two hundred people since noon. I was in the Main Office a minute ago and they're going crazy. The plebe Mates look like pony express horses. They're exhausted from chasing after mids for him. I don't need any of that right now."

"Still going to get your head shaved tonight?"

Fogarty grinned hopelessly. "I don't guess there's any way out of that, is there? I mean, what's Pratt to fifty years of tradition?"

"He'll fry you."

"He won't really fry anybody for that. It's just a threat."

"He'll fry anybody for anything, you know that."

"But it's a tradition."

"So is frying people."

A plebe trotted past the table, carrying a blueberry pie, his eyes fearful and wild, fixed on the Anchor. McClinton caught the movement. "Uh-oh, there goes some real trouble."

The others looked up. Swenson seemed astonished. "Look at his face! He's going after Pratt!"

They all stood, as did dozens of others who had caught the huge plebe's movement. Closer and closer the plebe jogged, balancing the pie in one hand, searching for an approach to the staff table. He stopped for a small moment behind the kiosk at the Anchor, on the other side of the staff table, gathering himself. Then suddenly he charged the table, his face contorted in fear and ferocity.

He approached Pratt from the rear. The midshipmen on the staff table picked up the plebe's advance just in time to push their own chairs back in startled disbelief, leaving Pratt with one finger in the air, in the middle of a sentence as his other hand scooped up a forkful of food.

*"Wild man wild man wild man wild man!"* The plebe dumped the whole pie on Pratt's head, then fiercely massaged it into his crewcut with both hands as he screamed. Then he wiped his hands on Pratt's cheeks and began sprinting down the long corridor of the mess hall, toward the Fifth Wing doors.

Pratt bounded out of his chair, spitting pie, both hands raised above his head in fists. "Catch that man! Mate, I want that man!" Pratt pointed after the fleeing plebe, and another plebe, his Mate from main office watch, sprinted after the attacker, waving a notepad. Pratt screamed along the corridor, his high-pitched tenor like chalk scraping across a blackboard. *"Stop that man! Stop him! Stop him!"*

Food flew at Pratt's Mate like a volcano erupting, un-premeditated, undirected, individual gestures of contempt for Pratt. The Mate was forced to stop for a moment in the midst of a barrage of meat and pie, scraping it out of his eyes, new food now whacking into him like baseballs. Another plebe raced out from a company table and flattened the Mate with a cross-body block as he began to run again, then himself raced out of the mess hall, following Pratt's assailant. The Mate crouched on the floor in the middle of a pile of food.

"You! You, you're on report!" Pratt had the microphone at the Anchor now, and was pointing at the second fleeing plebe. No sooner had his bellowing stopped than a fount of food sailed toward him from every portion of the mess hall.

It became a full-scale food fight, the kind normally reserved for the morning before Christmas leave began. Pieces of bread sailed the length of the mess hall like confetti, many of them bouncing off the Anchor, some of them hitting Pratt himself. He stood at the Anchor, dodging squares of bread as the mess hall became screaming madness, his head blue and pasty from the pie that had begun the debacle.

"Every company commander is on report! I want to see

every company commander at the Main Office right after this meal!" Pratt rang the bell at the Anchor again and again, trying to announce the end of the meal. "Fourth class, march out! Fourth class, march out!"

# Chapter Eight: 1930

"You know what I'll always remember about this place, Bill? The smells." Swenson lay back on his bed, his hands folded on his stomach, his service dress jacket folded neatly inside-out next to him. "I got here from Minnesota and I'd never smelled the sea before, and there it was, the beginning of it anyway, just off those rocks. And everything we did plebe summer, marching on Farragut Field or out on the YP boats, or even on Sunday when we got Yard liberty, the smells from the river and the bay were there, all musty and filled with fish and weeds. It was a good smell."

Fogarty sat in Swenson's chair, his feet up on the desk. McClinton lay on his own bed, reading *Playboy* magazine. The P.A. system cut into their conversation from outside the room. "First classmen with class standings of fifty to seventy-five report to Smoke Hall for service selection. That is, first classmen with class standings of fifty to seventy-five report to Smoke Hall for service selection."

"Yeah." Fogarty smiled wistfully. "And the smell of new whiteworks and new sheets and new everything, and the smell of the dust from all of the construction. And the smell of mildew from your sweatgear because it never got dry."

"No, I think I'll remember the sounds." McClinton eyed a Playmate with approval, then looked over to them, smiling. "Really, man. Where else in the world does a loudspeaker cut into every part of the day, telling you what to wear and when to do things? And Mahan Hall's clock, banging out the bells every half hour like all four thousand of us are on a gigantic goddamn ship. And that pile driver. Here we suffer through four years of a pile driver, bam bam bam, and never get to use the new classrooms they're building over there."

"And chow calls." Fogarty nodded, still smiling. "You're right. Do you realize it's normal to us to hear somebody scream at the end of every hallway, every meal formation? And plebes screaming every time you walk into their room? And the bells in the messhall telling you when you can leave the table? And goddamned *reveille*?"

"It's all weird, man. It's all weird." McClinton returned to his magazine. "And in four months I'm going to be down there flying that jet."

"No, it's not weird. It's just the way it is." Fogarty eyed Swenson. "So what are you going to sign up for, Swede?"

"CivLant." They laughed uneasily, without humor. "No, I think I'll try for something out of Pearl Harbor. A destroyer, I guess. I liked Hawaii."

Smoke Hall was like a candy store on service selection night. Computer printouts were taped all over its cavernous walls, outlining the needs of the naval service. Each midshipman was allowed one pick, according to his class standing. If he stood high, as did the scholarly Swenson, the choices were almost limitless, from immediate master's degree programs in certain fields to submarines or ships of the line or sophisticated staff jobs around the world. If he was near the bottom, as was McClinton, he took the leavings, which often ended up being such positions as an engineering officer on a pre-World War II destroyer out of Norfolk. But from the instant a first classman strode out of Smoke Hall after choosing his graduation assignment, he was changed. After service selection night, the class of 1968 would no longer be a collection of midshipmen struggling to endure the Academy regimen; they would each be betrothed to their separate military futures.

"You didn't lose that fight, you know." McClinton hid behind his magazine. "I know you don't want to talk about it, but I just wanted to say it."

"Ask Chervanek."

"He knows, man. He knows." McClinton peered over the top of the magazine. "It's going to take you a while to get over that, isn't it?"

"Look, man." Fogarty shook his head. "Loudenslager's fucking dead, my arm is broke, and some professor is trying to throw my ass out of here. I don't have time to worry about it." He caught Swenson's knowing smile. "All right, it will always piss me off. Always, till the day I die. Okay?"

"I knew it would." McClinton returned to his *Playboy*. "It's not like you, otherwise. You don't work for something for four years and have it grabbed away from you like that and then not feel cheated."

"Remember Nunzio, Bill?" Swenson was remembering again. Fogarty was getting tired of it. It was like admitting defeat. "That asshole. And we stuck that dead fish under his radiator when he left for Christmas leave. It smelled so bad that the O.D. thought someone had died in the room."

"Let's do something besides remember. all right? I'm too young to be remembering. That's for the old grads who come back here for Homecoming and get all blasted down in the mess hall." The loudspeaker announced class standings of seventy-five to a hundred. Fogarty grinned, nodding to Swenson. "Go get it, big Swede. Surprise us all and sign up for the Marine Corps."

Swenson hurriedly dressed, then grabbed his cap, no longer trying to hide his excitement. He waved to them as he dashed out the door. "Don't hold your breath. As my granny used to say, one fool in the family is embarrassing enough."


"First classmen with class standings of three- hundred twenty-five to three-hundred fifty report to Smoke Hall for service selection. That is, first classmen with class standings of three-hundred twenty-five to three-hundred fifty report to Smoke Hall for service selection."

"That's me." Fogarty rose from Swenson's chair, checking his watch. "Christ, McClinton, at this rate they'll have to tell the window-closers to wake you when your number comes up." He grabbed his cap. "So long, folks. The next time I see you I'll be a marine. Sort of."

Swenson chuckled softly, having returned two hours before after signing up for a guided-missile destroyer out of Pearl Harbor. "They'll be glad to see you, Bill. The marines aren't doing very well. Too many firsties have been following this Tet offensive, seeing marines and soldiers splattered all over the cameras."

"That's what they get for letting us watch TV first class year." McClinton was on his fifth back-issue of *Playboy*. "Now you want to know why I didn't go to West Point like my old man?"

"Well, anyway," Fogarty stood at the doorway, "they're just getting far enough down the class standings to pick up the marines, that's all. Dumb mids always make the best marines, you know that."

"That sort of says something, doesn't it?" Swenson could not hold back one final taunt.

"Yeah. It says that a man who spends forty minutes proving one and one is two had better not be calling in artillery when the shit hits the fan."

"Touché."

He walked down hallways that had sucked his youth up like a dry sponge, basking in memories, little pockets varnished with so many layers of his own energy and pain that he knew a part of him would always stay in Bancroft Hall. He walked past the room where he and his two roommates had endured plebe year, brutality and homesickness clinging to the doorway with an aura that was almost visible. And here was Loudenslager's old room, now haunted by a ghost. He turned a corner and passed a room where he had stood in the autumn of his plebe year, behind a closed door, as four first classmen had beaten him with a cricket bat, telling him to admit it hurt, just admit it hurt, and they would stop. They had finally broken the cricket bat and he had left without telling them, running back into his own room and sticking his head inside his laundry bag for fifteen minutes as he cried, hoping his roommates would not catch his tears. They had broken him but they had never known. No one had ever known. That was plebe year: finding yourself, knowing your weaknesses, but keeping them from anyone else.

Fogarty walked into Smoke Hall as if marching at parade. Midshipmen and officers bustled about, giving the huge old room a frenetic, undirected energy that reminded him of an open-air marketplace. But he had not come to shop. The marines were set up in a small side room to the left as he entered the Hall, as if they had opened up a recruiting office. A Marine Corps flag hung over the room's doorway and a half-dozen officers stood at the entrance, like sirens luring him into their sanctum. They were fathers, they were brothers. After years of waiting at their fringes, he was finally going to join them.

He was only the sixteenth to sign the forms, out of more than three hundred who had selected their future billets. The Marine Corps would not make quota in 1968, for the first time in years. The Tet offensive was scaring men away, even at the Academy. Scanning the list of midshipmen who had signed up for the Corps, Fogarty noted the absence of several men who had

claimed for years that they would become marines upon graduation. He marked their names in his memory with cold disgust;
they had become invidious, like draft dodgers on the other end of
the spectrum. They were danger dodgers. Better here than there,
he decided, reading the list again.

But in a moment it was done, like a marriage ceremony,
years of anticipation and years of union linked together with five
minutes of formality. Captain Lenahan was waiting for him by the
doorway. He put an arm on Fogarty's shoulder and handed him a
Marine Corps tie clip.

"Take care of your men, Mister Fogarty." Not "Congratulations." Not "Obey orders." Not even "Welcome to the Corps." "Take
care of your men." It was a commandment, carried in Lenahan's
combat scars as if they were etched in stone.

Fogarty fingered the tie clasp. It seemed an almost trivial
gesture for such an overwhelming moment, as if he had just won a
trinket at a carnival instead of entering a life's work. But the
emblem gleamed at him and Lenahan patted his thick shoulder
again and he felt warm, thrilled, explosive. He wanted to hit
something for the Marine Corps. "I will, sir. I swear to God I will."

He strode down the same hallways as before, but they were old, or
maybe he was new. He felt vaguely like a snake shedding old skin,
anxious to get on with this business of leading men, to shed the
navy blue and wear the green. *I will be a marine like the Commandant
has always dreamed of, I will run all night and I will run all day and I will
face whatever bullet, charge whatever hill, I will take it to the enemy and
stuff it down his throat, kill him dead for Corps and Country and I will
plant the flag. I will go to Vietnam and I will find the son of a bitch who
killed Ron Loudenslager and I will kill him back, make him die a slow
death make him bleed to death.*

He never even made it back to Swenson's room. At the
edges of the company area his classmates gathered silently in the
hallway, grinning widely, elbowing each other but not yet speaking
to him. So many of the ones who had shared the pride and the
misery, who had suffered the pains and celebrated the joys since
that first hot summer afternoon when they all stood together
sweating and wheezing in the dank oppressive heat of Dahlgren
Hall and took the oath of a midshipman after having been run to
exhaustion in the steambath air by dead Loudenslager, so many

who in a few short months would labor off to duty all around the world, combat and isolation their reward for four years of sacrifice and regimen, now paced gleefully, preparing to shave him bald.

He stopped in the middle of the hallway, grinning sardonically, knocking on his cast with his knuckles. "You wouldn't attack a cripple, would you?"

"The hell we wouldn't." Dreiden stood in front of him, smiling easily, carrying a set of electric hair clippers. "You ain't getting off that easy. We been putting up with all this Marine Corps bul-l-l-lshit for four years." Lesse stood next to him, grinning like a clown. Boggs was there, and George, and even McClinton. He knew it was no use to fight. Besides, who cared, really? It was a tradition.

"Okay, Okay. But let's go into Swenson's room. anyway. You've got to plug the goddamn things in."


Sore jaw, broken arm, an onion for a scalp. It's been that kind of week, mused Fogarty, walking slowly down the passageway. He pounded hard on a closed door, then flung it open. Dean and Peckarsky looked up, startled, and came to immediate braces.

Fogarty leaned against the wall, grinning at Dean. He pointed at his scalp. "You know what this is, Dean?"

Dean stared at the ugly whiteness. Fogarty reminded him of a Martian. "It's a shaved head, sir."

"No, it's a military heart." Fogarty chuckled as he noted Dean's uncomprehending, furrowed face. "Yeah, I've pushed myself to exhaustion, Dean, stood out there on that drill field with the dust blowing up my nostrils and that goddamn drum beating inside my head until I felt it was my own heart beating, boom, boom, boom boom boom, a heart with a cadence, you know what I mean? A military heart. And that's what this is, Dean." Fogarty rubbed his head roughly. It itched when he touched it. "It's the only place in the world where you feel good when they make you look hideous. I like this, Dean. I earned it. Do you know what I mean?"

"Yes, sir." Fogarty continued to stare at him. It occurred to him that he might be required to explain it. "Well, sort of, sir."

"That's good enough. Anyway, have I got news for you, Dean! In honor of my Marine Corps"—Fogarty lowered his voice slightly, somewhat embarrassed— "and, in consideration of my present physical state"—he glanced at Peckarsky—"not to mention the letter your professor wrote about what an asshole I am, we are going to take tomorrow morning off. No run."

It sounded curious to Dean, as if Fogarty were attempting to exert a measure of control over that which had already been removed by Thad and Lenahan. Still, he felt relieved. "Aye, aye, sir. Thank you, sir."

"Don't thank me, Dean. I already told you about that. Anyway, you ran the goddamn seawall! You don't need me anymore for that. Start sleeping on your mattress again, too. You grew up this morning. You rate a rack."

Incredible, thought Dean. Thad does not exist to this guy. *And I did it on my own.* "Aye, aye, sir."

Fogarty tapped his scalp again, reaching for the door. "Look around the mess hall tomorrow morning, gents. You'll be able to pick out the elite."

"You, there! Mister! Halt, I said. Halt!"

Fogarty turned and looked behind him and saw the unmistakable waddle of Pratt blustering down the hallway, fifty yards away, moving toward him with a visible fury. He thought to turn and run as so many had done that afternoon and evening, but decided against it and instead froze in his tracks, sighing resignedly. With this cast and a bald head, he mused, the man could find me in a pitch-black room, much less the mess hall tomorrow morning. Running away was a Class A offense.

"Yes, sir. Good evening, sir."

"You have a shaved head." Mad Pratt closed in on him, his hat at its characteristic tilt and his head cocked in the other direction, as if to balance it.

You noticed, thought Fogarty, a nauseous ball rolling through his stomach despite his cavalier manner. "Yes, sir. Right down to the scalp, sir."

Pratt came nearer and squinted closely, then finally recognized him. "It's you, Fogarty! You're in my battalion. You shaved your head."

"No, sir. My classmates shaved my head, sir." Fogarty shrugged lamely with his good shoulder, looking hopefully at the battalion officer. "It's a tradition."

"You let them, Mister Fogarty. That's the point."

"Sir, I—"

"Are you aware of my instructions on shaved heads?" Pratt's face was a foot away from Fogarty's. Fogarty noticed a small glob of blueberry pie that still clung to the inside of one of Pratt's ears.

"Sir, yes I was, but I didn't shave my head, sir."

"I issued an order, Mister Fogarty. You disobeyed it."

"I really didn't have any say in the matter, sir." Fogarty felt completely sick, as if he would soon throw up. "It's hard to stop people from taking part in a tradition."

"You're on report, Mister Fogarty. Give my Mate your alpha number." Pratt eyed him closely as he mumbled his alpha number to the harried plebe. "Mister Fogarty."

"Yes, sir?"

"Do you know anything about the midshipman who hit me with a pie tonight?" Pratt's words drove into him like flat blades: here came the Honor Game. Pratt could ask him about anything in the world, any aspect of his life, and he would be honor bound to answer. A year before, one midshipman had caused a classmate to be expelled for an honor offense because the man had lied to his girlfriend. Honor was a microscope. It could also be a guillotine.

"No, sir."

"You're sure, Mister Fogarty?"

"Yes, sir."

"Do you know anything about how my office was stuffed with newspapers last night?"

There it came. It was the reason midshipmen had been running from Pratt all day, as if he were the harbinger of death. Fogarty held Pratt's gaze, feeling a helpless fury as deep as any hate he had ever known. "Yes, sir."

"You do?" Pratt's whole face widened with a mix of surprise and delight. "What do you know, Mister Fogarty? Were you involved in it?"

Behind them in the hallway other midshipmen in the company were peeking out of their rooms, curious and afraid of the volatile Commander. The plebe Mate stood just to Pratt's left side, his pen held attentively to his notepad, as if he were a reporter interviewing Fogarty.

Fogarty adjusted his sling. His arm suddenly hurt. "Yes, sir." He continued to hold Pratt's eyes. "I was, sort of, pretty heavily involved in it, sir."

"You were?" Pratt looked over at his Mate, as if to say

something, then looked back at Fogarty. "The torpedo?" Fogarty nodded. "The plane in Tecumseh Court?" Fogarty nodded again. Pratt began to bounce up and down on his toes, and spoke with the flat viciousness of an omnipotent warden about to ban an inmate to solitary. "Why did you do those things, Mister Fogarty?"

"No excuse, sir."

"I want a reason, Mister Fogarty!"

"There is no reason, sir." Every muscle in Fogarty's body was still. He stood at an unblinking attention, his face emotionless. The middle of his mind was back in plebe year, watching someone torment him from another room. Pratt could have cut his arm off and he would not have moved.

"You can't say that to me." Pratt pouted, his eyes boring in on Fogarty. "Who was involved with you?"

"Sir, you can't ask me that."

"What do you mean I can't ask you that?" Behind them, all the heads had disappeared. Wild Bill Fogarty was in Deep Shit, and it did no good to watch Pratt do his number. It was bad luck. "What do you think this is, Mister Fogarty, a game? The military is not games, Mister Fogarty. I asked you a question."

Fogarty's lips tightened, his only visible display of emotion. "Sir, I am my company's representative to the Brigade Honor Committee, sir, and I happen to know you can't ask me that. It's entrapment, sir. You can't ask me that."

Pratt considered him for a long moment, still bouncing on his toes. The hallway had become quiet as a tomb, as if Fogarty and Pratt and the attentive plebe Mate were the only men in Bancroft Hall. "Were the others who were involved in your company, Mister Fogarty? I can ask you that."

"Yes, sir. You can ask me that." Fogarty held his attention, then suddenly sighed. "Yes sir, they were in the company, sir."

"I knew it!" Pratt turned to the Mate. "I want every man in this company in the passageway, Mate. Immediately! Immediately!"


They stood along both walls in the hallway, staring at Commander Pratt with looks that varied from open hate to outright fear, dressed in long gray or blue bathrobes or the whiteworks uniforms that served as casual clothes, some in their dress blue uniforms after having returned from the library or from Smoke

Hall. Fogarty stood with Pratt and his Mate in the center of the passageway.

Pratt called to them, his voice surging and slowing, walking with a measured, exaggerated pace in front of them. "Every man who had nothing to do with the newspapers in my office, or with the airplane in Tecumseh Court, or with the torpedo in my conference room, can secure." The men looked at one another, and slowly many of them began to file away, leaving perhaps thirty midshipmen in the passageway. "The rest of you are on report. Conduct Unbecoming a Midshipman." He gestured to the mate. "Take their names."

# Chapter Nine: 2330

Eighty marines. Eight goddamn warm bodies. Well, mused Lenahan, walking out of Smoke Hall toward the Main Office, there goes somebody's career. Eighty is not a hundred.

Lenahan chuckled sardonically, climbing the stairway to the Rotunda, remembering some of the reasons midshipmen had given him for changing their minds about going into the Marine Corps. My daddy promised me he'd buy me a car, says one big goddamned football player who signed up for minesweeper duty. My mommy was crying on the phone, another one tells me. I can't afford to pay for all the new uniforms, one guy who's been talking about the Corps for three years decides.

And in every pair of eyes he could see a television screen reflected once, filled with the agony of a marine grunt being hauled all beefy and bleeding out of Hue City on a tank. I wonder what would have happened if Iwo Jima had been on TV, he thought absently, reaching the top of the stairs.

Report to Madman Pratt. Report to Madman Pratt. Lenahan started to sing it to himself as he strode across the Rotunda, making it a child's jingle. Report to Madman Pratt. Report to Madman Pratt. Report to Madman Pratt, cause he is where it's at. It made a pretty good song. He could feel doom waiting for him on the other side of the Officer of the Watch's door and he approached it with the same sort of gallows humor that he had felt when he knew he was walking into a likely ambush in Vietnam. What the hell, he laughed nervously to himself, knocking on Pratt's door. Like the troopies used to say, it beats working for a living.

"Come in."

He opened the door and took three giant steps inside, standing at a casual, practiced attention in front of Pratt's desk. "Captain Lenahan, reporting as ordered, sir."

Pratt dropped a stack of Form Twos on the edge of the desk. They were half an inch thick. Lenahan retained his attention, knowing they belonged to his company. He felt a mix of rage and amusement that left him merely standing in front of Pratt, smiling feebly. It had been so dramatic, Pratt's presentation of the conduct forms. This man really believes it's a crisis, Lenahan mused, examining Pratt's customary forced glare. I feel sorry for him. No, I really do. This is real to him, this funny Formica veneer of formality and Form Twos. And the part that should be real doesn't exist. He's not a stupid man. I don't know what the hell it is. I wonder if he gets laid at home? I should ask him that.

"For me, sir?"

"Don't be facetious, Captain. Quite frankly, I'm tired of it." Pratt motioned toward the pile of Form Twos. "It's the torpedo. The torpedo and the newspapers and the plane in Tecumseh Court. 'Pratt Sucks.' You liked the torpedo, didn't you, Captain? You even taunted me with it this morning. It was your company. I should have known it was your company. A military unit manifests the attitudes of its leaders. You have a terrible attitude, Captain. It pains me to say that, considering your combat record."

"Sir, really, this is kind of ridiculous getting—"

"I knew you would think that. Thirty men in your company have just been placed on report for improper conduct and you think it's ridiculous. 'Pratt Sucks' and it's ridiculous to put them on report. It was the ultimate form of disrespect. And do you know who was the instigator, Captain? Do you?"

*You* were, thought Lenahan, silently holding Pratt's gaze. "No, sir."

"Fogarty. We sent him to the Brigade Staff. We made him a four-striper. And what do we get in return? 'Pratt Sucks.' And his head was shaved." Pratt dropped another Form Two onto the desk. "How many warnings did I announce about shaving heads?"

"A lot, sir. But I told you then, a man who gets his head shaved can be trying like hell to obey your order."

"Then what do you have?" Pratt's face was querulous. He leaned back in his chair, regarding Lenahan as if he were a child. "How do you control? You go to the source of the problem. Fogarty is the source."

"Sir, really." Lenahan sighed, coming out of his attention and scratching the back of his head as he scowled at Pratt. The Commander came forward in his chair, watching Lenahan's movements closely, as if he were waiting for Lenahan to jump across the desk after him. "Mind if I light a cigarette, sir?" Lenahan drew his pack from his sock, not waiting for Pratt's assent. He lit a cigarette and drew heavily from it. "In all due respect, sir." He was tired of saying that to someone he did not respect. "Who the hell was hurt when Fogarty got his head shaved? It was a tradition. You can't deny troops tradition and still expect them to stay proud of their uniform."

"We're not talking about tradition, we're talking about obedience. I issued an order."

"It was a stupid order."

There, thought Lenahan. I've said it. The silence was tangible. Outside, the conversation of two plebes who had just been relieved of the watch and were heading back to their rooms rose and fell with tales of chasing midshipmen through the Hall at Pratt's behest. Lenahan dragged on his cigarette again. Pratt still watched him as if he would explode at any moment. Finally Lenahan continued. "But the important thing is, Fogarty didn't disobey it! Can't you see that? It's like... It's like..." He couldn't think of anything it was like. He stared at the floor, shaking his head, then suddenly flung his eyes into Pratt's. "It's like telling somebody not to get robbed, and then throwing them in jail when they get robbed. That's what it's like. No, it's worse, actually. I don't know what it's like."

He couldn't even tell if Pratt was listening. The fat-faced Commander simply stared at him, unspeaking. He tried again. He had to win this one, because the other one was worse. "Listen, sir. You couldn't march down to a goddamn people store, if there was such a thing, and pick out all the perfect parts for a combat commander and have them fit together any better than they already do with Fogarty. This guy is smart, he's tough, he's dedicated, and he cares about his people. He's got the *spirit* of a leader. He's taken all this place has to dish out and he's come back for more."

"Your idea, that is." Pratt finally spoke, hesitantly, almost pouting.

"Sir?"

"Of a leader. Your idea." Pratt leaned back in his chair, folding his arms on his chest. "He lacks respect, Captain Lenahan. Maybe he gets it from you, I don't know. 'Pratt Sucks.' Is that your idea of spirit? A torpedo. Newspapers. His head was shaved. He shows no respect for the system. He's like you."

Lenahan rubbed the back of his head again, looking sideways at Pratt. It wouldn't be any use to talk about the other thing with Pratt. In fact, it would be the worst possible thing to do. Pratt would flip, and Fogarty would be packed and gone within a week. Regulations, thought Lenahan, still peering at Pratt but now thinking of Thad's letter. Now we have regulations about how to lead. Don't use your head or your force or your spirit. Follow the instructions, as if you're building a model airplane or a goddamn computer. They don't trust people anymore. And if you put a word *regulation* on it, Pratt will stand by it like a preacher pointing to the Bible.

"Ah, the hell you say, sir. This guy's given us everything he has. It just isn't fair."

"Captain Lenahan," it had become almost a motto at the Naval Academy, "who the hell said life was fair?"


I can't believe I'm doing this.

It looked like a castle, all high and huge and dark, portentous and somehow haunted by its own memories. He could not get used to the idea of wandering on his own up the front sidewalk, uninvited, or of actually standing at the front door. Visitors to official functions were required to use the side entrance. He never would have done it at all if it had been daylight. But at midnight it seemed absurd enough, frightening enough, to be possible, if not appropriate. Some things are forgivable at midnight, while odious at noon.

He rang the doorbell and waited, beating his hands against his body to try and warm them. A hall light came on. He continued to wait, and the locks in front of him clicked and turned. It stunned him to see the Superintendent himself standing in front of him in a weathered West Point bathrobe, his thin gray hair disheveled and his eyes bagged with sleep. Lenahan had expected a steward, and had rehearsed a short speech about the need to drag the Admiral from his sleep.

"Captain Lenahan." It surprised him that Kraft actually remembered his name. The Admiral deliberately checked his watch. "Don't tell me. The enemy is at Gate Three and you've come to evacuate the old men and the civilians."

Lenahan found himself laughing, throwing up both hands into the icy night air and shaking his head with embarrassment. "No, sir. I'm really sorry about this, sir. I just don't have anywhere else to turn, and I have a problem that has to be addressed tonight. I know this is really presumptuous, but I need your advice, sir."

"Well, hell, I'm awake anyway. And I've never been one to turn down the chance to give somebody advice." The Admiral's wrinkled face split with a grin as he opened the door. "Come on in."

Lenahan followed him down a hallway, to a high-ceilinged sitting room filled with ornate, Colonial furniture. The Admiral sank heavily into one overstuffed chair, and gestured toward another one, crossing a pajamaed leg. "So how did service selection go?"

"The marines took a bath. Too much TV coverage of the war." Lenahan took his cigarettes from his sock. "Mind if I smoke, sir?"

"Do I mind? Hell, let me bum one, will you?" The Admiral leaned over and took one of Lenahan's cigarettes. "Thanks." Lenahan lit it, and then his own. The Admiral leaned back, too polite to prod Lenahan into speech until he was ready. Lenahan sat forward in his own chair, fearing he would become lost in the padding if he leaned back. The room was so formal that it chilled him. It seemed to him that they were sitting in one of those roped-off areas reserved for tourists at the homes of famous early Americans.

Admiral Kraft had a leader's developed sense of his subordinate. He picked up Lenahan's uncomfortable awe immediately. "You know, the first few times I sat in this room I was afraid even to light a cigarette. I thought I'd burn a hole in this goddamn precious fabric, or something. But then I decided that I was part of history. Just think, Captain, if we burn a hole in the rug tonight, some tour guide will make it a part of her speech in a few years!" He grinned again. "It's not exactly home sweet home, but you get used to it."

"Sir, I really need your help." Lenahan scrutinized the Admiral's lined face, feeling a kinship with his history and his style. Kraft's sort, men who had shunned staff jobs for years in favor of command at sea, were being mothballed right along with the ships they once commanded, which now sat stripped and powerless in murky brownwater berths at the Philadelphia Naval Yard. Kraft was not a technocrat who could run a nuclear submarine, and he was not a politician who could be comfortable with the sophistry of Pentagon politics. He was a sea dog and a combat leader. The navy had chewed on him for thirty years, and it would soon spit him out.

"All right." The Admiral checked his watch again, smiling at Lenahan as if he were actually enjoying the midnight mystery of it all. "I assume you need it tonight, Captain?"

"Yes, sir." Lenahan shrugged again, smiling weakly. "I'm really sorry to be doing this, sir. In fact, I feel downright ridiculous sitting in this chair staring at you in your pajamas." The Admiral laughed, and Lenahan chuckled softly. "How old is that B-robe, sir?"

"Thirty-two years." The Admiral said it proudly, his over-large mouth again breaking into an almost innocent grin that belied the wrinkles on his face. "I won it on the 1935 Army-Navy game." He looked down at the thinned, faded gray fabric of the robe. "It isn't any more worn out than I am."

"Ah, sir. You're got a lot of fight left in you." Lenahan said it almost hopefully. He stubbed out his cigarette. "Admiral, I've got a man in trouble on a plebe-indoctrination charge. We got a letter today from the plebe's chemistry professor. A lawyer helped the professor draft the letter. It's filled with legal language. All kinds of junk. It's one of these situations where, if you look at the letter of the regulations, the man was a bastard. But if you look at what actually happened, hell, Admiral, this plebe made out like a bandit. Fogarty taught him more about himself in four days than he'd learned in nineteen years."

He checked Kraft's face. It was emotionally void, a noncommittal blank. "So, anyway, I know what's going to happen when this letter gets to Commander Pratt tomorrow morning. He'll freak out. My man won't stand a chance."

"You say a lawyer helped him draft it? Do you know how a lawyer got involved?"

Lenahan sighed, feeling abandoned. The Admiral was asking the wrong questions. "I checked up on this professor. He's a young guy, real smart, kind of mushy—one of those brainchildren who like to come here to stay out of the military. I've got a buddy over in the Science Department who I called today and asked about him. My buddy says this guy hasn't stopped bitching about the plebe system since he set foot in the Yard. I don't know what the hell he's up to. He's just got a lawyer, that's all."

"What did Fogarty do?"

"A bunch of the old stuff, sir. That's all." Lenahan shrugged. "Nothing that hadn't been done to him or me or probably even you during plebe year." Lenahan studied the Admiral's face, searching for something to key on. "Are you a Catholic, sir?"

"No." No commital, only that same small smile.

"Well, I'm a Catholic. And you know, when I was growing up, the priest and my mother and everybody used to say, 'Lenahan, if you eat meat on Fridays, boy, you're gonna burn in hell. It's a mortal sin.' And then one day they changed their minds up in the hierarchy and now it's okay to eat meat on Friday. I don't know what they've done with all of those mortal sinners down in hell who never repented from a sin that I can't even commit anymore, but anyway, it's changed. Only, deep down inside, I'll always believe it's a mortal sin to eat meat on Fridays. Do you know what I mean, sir?"

Kraft seemed entertained, but hardly comprehending. Lenahan made two fists in front of his face, as if signaling his intense frustration. "I guess I'm not getting very far. But here we have Fogarty, on the verge of getting thrown out of the Naval Academy for giving a man a few days of a plebe year like the one he had. Can you sense the irony in that, sir? I know times are changing, that it isn't nineteen-sixty-four anymore. I know there were abuses. But here you have a guy who spends his own plebe year getting the hell stomped out of him because everyone is telling him, right from the Admiral on down, that this is what will make him a better officer. So he takes all the crap and he finally learns to believe in it. And then somebody who can't even do twenty pushups anyway decides that pain is immoral, and we have a few congressional investigations, and the system starts changing. Only it doesn't change inside this guy's head, because he knows what worked and what didn't when it happened to him. But of course nobody asks the people it happened to, because they're all supposed to be mindless or something after it happened to them. So anyway this guy remembers what works on different kinds of plebes and he selects the right treatment for this one screwy plebe—we call him Baby Blue in the company, Admiral—and goddamn, what do you know, it works on the son of a bitch! But that's using discretion, and nobody trusts discretion anymore. In the meantime we've worked up regulations about how to lead, how to discipline, what you can say, what you can ask. So my man has violated the regulations. Big deal. Go ask Baby Blue if it hurt him. For the first time in his life he feels proud of himself. He ran the goddamn seawall in the dark this morning. Christ, he wouldn't even go *outside* in the dark a week ago."

"What do you mean, he ran the seawall in the dark this morning?" The Admiral seemed suddenly interested.

"Well, Fogarty's been taking him out before reveille for a run. Fogarty does it by himself, has been for years. He's crazy, Admiral, you'd love him, sir." Lenahan was grinning brightly, feeling he had finally awakened the Admiral. "So, anyway, Fogarty takes Dean along the seawall, just like he does himself every morning, and this morning the yellow-bellied little turkey actually *ran* the damn thing! Admiral, I'll tell you, I thought Dean was going to absolutely bust when they got back, he was so goddamn proud."

"You were there when they got back?"

"Hell, yes, sir." Lenahan started to get comfortable in the chair. The Admiral's eyes were electric in their new intensity, finally full awake. "That's another story, actually, but I've been holding reveille on my company for the last five days or so. It's sort of a little payback from Commander Pratt because some of my people got caught sleeping in at reveille. So I've been around, and I can tell you, sir, I've seen what Fogarty's done for this man. It's been incredible. And now all they can see is the goddamn regulations—"

"You've seen it, Captain? You were there, in the Hall, while this was going on?" It wasn't interest. It was something else, not quite fear and not quite anger, and it settled over Lenahan like cold rain when he realized it, waking him and chilling him at the same time. "What did you do about it?"

"*Do* about it?" The chair seemed overstuffed again, and Lenahan sat on its very edge, like a plebe in the mess hall.

"Do you realize the implications if this gets out, Captain? You were there when these violations were going on. If you didn't do anything about them, you were a part of it. It's like aiding and abetting." The Admiral caught himself. "No, I don't want to make this criminal. It's like giving command sanctions. You're my representative in the company. It's like *me* approving of it."

"Don't you, sir? Approve of it?"

"It's not that simple anymore." The Admiral had uncrossed his legs and was sitting forward, folding his arms on his knees and staring into Lenahan's pinched, querulous face. "I can't counsel the abuse of regulations, Captain, and neither can you. Even if the end justifies the means."

"So who makes up these goddamn—"

"It doesn't matter anymore." The Admiral noted Lenahan's disappointment. It was as if someone had stuck a pin in him and let the air out. "Think about your priest just for a moment, Captain Lenahan. The fish on Friday thing is done. But we've got priests in this country, a lot of them, who are counseling people to use birth control devices. All right, that's realistic. But if the Catholic Church finds out, it can discipline the priest. It could even defrock him. He might argue to Rome that the Pope doesn't understand reality, but that's not going to get him his priesthood back, is it? When you stand on principle, you take your chances, that's all. If we sided with your man Fogarty, we could lose the whole plebe system."

Lenahan grimaced, unimpressed. "To who?"

"What do you mean, 'to who'?"

"I'm sorry, sir, to *whom*?" The Admiral did not join him as he chuckled at his own little joke. "I mean, when you lose a system, a way of life, you usually lose it to something or somebody. You don't just ... lose it, like a baseball glove you left out on the athletic field."

The Admiral studied him closely from only a few feet away, looking weary. "That just doesn't matter anymore, Captain. If we stood by you, we'd be saying that the system is out of control."

"What the hell is out of control when a man simply—"

"How many times do I have to say it, Captain? It doesn't matter!" The Admiral had stood and was nodding formally to him. "In fact, we've lost more than Fogarty. I'm afraid you've just become a casualty yourself."

A casualty, thought Lenahan, rising also from his chair and feeling suddenly light-headed. A casualty. Hey, I like that. My men always did say I took so much shrapnel I must have a magnet inside of me. He came to his famous loose attention that met all the requirements of attention but yet looked like he was leaning against someone's wall. "Great, sir. Do I get another Purple Heart?"

"No." The Admiral began walking him toward the door. "You get orders out of here, before somebody decides to investigate you."

# PART SIX:

---

# MONDAY, FEBRUARY 26, 1968

# Chapter One: 0930

"I swear to God, Neil, you look *terrific!*"

Lenahan sat back in the metal visitor's chair, his feet on Neil Bard's bed. Bard was sitting up, his bed having been cranked into that position. The bandages were off his head and he looked like a muppet with his woolly, undirected hair. He smiled merrily to Lenahan, his face filled with a childish, semicomprehending smile. Lenahan dragged on his cigarette. "But you need a haircut, boy! I told Maria that, and she says they're still afraid they might nick your scalp. Hell, I said. You worry about nicking a man's scalp after some monkey of a VC went and blew half of it off the back of his head? But you know nurses, Neil. And doctors, too. They don't think the way we do."

Bard smiled back. It was nice to see him smile again. Lenahan blew a ring of smoke in his classmate's direction and Bard responded by squinching up his face and grinning back to Lenahan. "So anyway, Neil, here I go again, back to the Nam. Fastest set of orders I ever got in my life. That just goes to show you, boy, when the bureaucracy gets a hair up its ass, it can be efficient as hell! Oh, yeah. It's a sad state of affairs when a few candy-ass lawyers and a couple of congressmen who wouldn't know a come-around from a walk in the woods can knock a whole institution on its ass. Is that too strong, Neil? I don't know. I'm pretty hacked off. When you keep Dean and throw away Fogarty, it gets a little scary. Not that we should throw away Dean. Ah, hell. I'm talking out of both sides. But you tell me who you would have wanted on the next boat or in your medevac helicopter after Luke the Gook gave you a new hole in your head, huh?"

Bard merely continued to smile. Lenahan hadn't expected any more from him, not yet anyway. It was great to see his friend able to communicate. Lenahan had been spending several hours, four or five times a week, trying to lure the wounded lieutenant back from the hollow insides of his own head. And it seemed to be working.

"So I won't be able to see you for a while, old buddy. I'm going out to California and help my boy plant some corn. That sounds dumb, I know, but what the hell are kids for, anyway, except to help you enjoy doing dumb things? And then I'm going to get on that big Bird and fly. Okinawa, Viet-fucking-Nam, oh yeah. Get me a grunt company again. But I'll write you letters, Neil, and you can get Goodbody to read them for you. They'll be cra-a-a-zy, but that's all right. Nobody ever promised you it would all make sense, did they? Besides, they'll keep you laughing. Huh? Come on, Neil!" Lenahan stood up and pounded on his chest, jumping up and down in front of Bard, who began laughing again.

"Hey, Lenahan, are you all right?" Goodbody filled the doorway behind them, leaning into the room, her moon eyes hesitant and sad. "You haven't flipped out, have you?" She paused, then added almost hopefully, "I think we can get you a psychiatric profile if you want one. It would keep you out of Vietnam."

He had stopped jumping. "So who wants to stay out of Vietnam? Besides, Maria, a man would have to be *crazy* to want one of those things. Ha ha. Hey, take care of my little buddy, will you? He's going to be talking any day now, I can feel it." He walked toward her, exploring her voluptuous curves with his eyes, and put a hand on one rounded shoulder. "I'm going to miss you, Goodbody. I'm not—"

"Don't call me Goodbody." She almost pouted.

"Hey, Neil, she's figured it all out!" He pulled her to him briefly.

"They've got no right to do this to you, Lenahan. I watched you lay on your back in that room across the hall for *months* and it just isn't fair. You should do something about it."

"I asked to go back. All they did was kick me out of Navy."

"You should just get out of the marines, Lenahan. You could get a good job doing a lot of things." She put her head against his chest. It lay on his ribbons and shooting badges.

"So who wants to get out? And then what, huh? No, it's what I always wanted to do, lead troops, and you can't do that in CivLant. Fifty grand a year, a company car, two martinis at lunch, and then what?" He grinned frivolously at her, trying to cheer her up. "I love the military, Maria, all the way down to my nerve-damaged toes. It's the chicken-shit I hate."

"*Lenahan!*" She pounded on his chest in her frustration

"More sir, harder sir, faster sir, I love it, sir." It was an echo from his own plebe year, an epoch ago.

"Oh, you're impossible." She hugged him. Bard smiled again.

"What I was saying was, I'm going to miss you. I'm not

303

exactly in the position to tell you to sit at home at night and crochet while I'm gone, but, uh"—he shrugged helplessly, his foolish grin intact—"I hope you'll be around when I get back, anyway. I'd really like to continue this discussion. See you in a year?"

"Oh, Lenahan, Lenahan." She was hugging him tightly, shaking her head, her tears melting into the green woolen fabric of his uniform. "Just come back, all right? Please, please, Lenahan. Just come back."

He laughed, an involuntary chuckle as he patted her shoulder. "I'm coming back, Goodbody. I'm just not worth a damn when it comes to dying."

# Chapter Two: 1100

So here it is, thought Wild Bill Fogarty, sitting on his desk and peering at the stripped mattress on his bed. The last picture in my Navy scrapbook. One seabag, two boxes of books, and a suitcase. And me, head shaved as close as the first day I got here, my punching arm shattered from trying to make a man out of a boy, and tears as big as horse turds dripping off my chin.

He didn't want to leave, that was all. He wanted to sit on top of his desk in his blueworks uniform and be a midshipman until it came out right again. It seemed like such a final act, shedding his blueworks for the last time. He didn't like civilian clothes. He didn't even like civilians. He would never really be a civilian, no matter what they did to him, not after all he had sacrificed to rise beyond it and earn the right to be something more. True, he had already applied to Marine Corps officer candidates school, and it appeared they might accept him. But in the meantime he had to wear those funny shirts and shoes that he had grown away from four years before, that he had mailed home in the same suitcase that had carried away his youth forever.

Goddamn Gant shirts, Bass Wejun shoes. What a disgrace. I mean, it's all right when you decide you want to wear them on liberty or something. But when you *have* to wear them it's different. It's like failure.

Outside his room the P.A. system cut into his doldrums.

"The uniform for morning class has been changed from working uniform blue alpha, wear reefers, to working uniform blue alpha, wear reefers, carry raingear. That is, the uniform for morning class has been changed, from working uniform blue alpha, wear reefers, to working uniform blue alpha, wear reefers, carry raingear."

Spring was coming with the rain. In a month the Dark Ages would be on the wane and then after that would come exams, and Dead Week leave, and finally June Week, the class of 1968's final days of parades and frolic, terminating on a Wednesday morning, a scarce three months away, with more than eight hundred caps thrown into the air out of joy and release and something else. So *close,* mused Fogarty, holding his own cap as if it were an emerald. So goddamn close.

He casually tossed it into his trash can. It was only his class cap, anyway. He had given Swede his best, "grease" cap, passing the perfectly manicured piece of uniform down like it was an heirloom. Swede wasn't very good on caps.

Swede would graduate. That was good. He would be restricted until June Week, but what was three months compared with a diploma and a commission, to being able to say he was a Grad? And leaving his cap with Swede was sort of like leaving a part of himself with the class. Maybe Swede would throw his cap up into the air on graduation day. There would be some sort of symbolism in that. Not being able to participate in that final act was almost worse than being denied the diploma. It was as if he were a Siamese twin connected to eight hundred others through an invisible emotional umbilical cord, being fed the same diet of duty and pain and pride, enduring all the long lonely hours, performing all the tasks, only to be scraped aside just before birth as unfit to be associated with the others. The rest of it he could deal with, but graduation day would be hard.

I didn't do anything wrong. I didn't even do half the things that had been done to me.

Linda was picking him up at noon. It was almost beyond his pride to think of climbing into his car next to her, dressed in civilian clothes, like a reject from the institution that had spawned her father and her brother. Her whole family had been understanding, enraged at his dismissal, but that didn't change facts. Facts are what people are interested in these days, he thought again, thinking of Lenahan's admonishment. Linda had hinted at getting married immediately, a gesture of her own loyalty, but he would not think of doing it before his class graduated (a superstition, perhaps), and he could not imagine himself having anything other than a military wedding. He would wait until after Marine Corps OCS, and be married in his uniform. Maybe Swenson and McClinton and and some of the others could come from wherever they were assigned and be ushers. Maybe they would even let him be married in the Academy chapel. Somehow, he doubted that. He wasn't sure why.

Oh, hell.

He'd given away all of his uniforms, whiteworks and blueworks and service dress blues and khakis. He didn't have any use for them. All that remained were the set of blueworks he wore, and his full dress blues. Full dress blues were personal. They fit each man like a sunburn. No one needed an extra set.

He rose from the desk and picked up his full dress coat from the bed, staring at the antique, short-waisted uniform that was a vestige of more than a century of Academy tradition. He had choked on its high collar through a hundred sleep-inducing sermons in the chapel, smothered in its woolen heat through scores of boring dress parades on Worden Field. He had watched it take on ornaments as he made his way through the Academy, the humiliating clean sleeves of plebe year taking on the notions of rank as he progressed. During his second year a long diagonal stripe had appeared on the left sleeve. Linda, he remembered. And Ron Loudenslager's cap up in the air. During his third year, two diagonal stripes. Running plebes, he thought, with a small shiver, and a summer on an aircraft carrier in the Mediterranean. And finally, his fourth year had seen both sleeves burgeon with concentric stripes, four of them on each sleeve, with a star above. A Brigade striper. Those little golden rings had been his reward for having poured his youth, every last hot ounce of it, into that uniform.

He dropped the uniform back onto the bed, shaking his head. It was too much. He didn't like feeling sorry for himself. But he felt immediately sad, looking at it rumpled on his mattress. It was uncharacteristically covered with lint, forlorn and empty, tangled in its own sleeves. It belonged to a midshipman who no longer existed, and he knew he was its ghost.

Finally he picked it up again, and slung the jacket over his shoulder, carrying it by the sleeves as he walked into the closet and worked his way into his reefer coat, babying his broken arm. Then he strode out of the room, purposefully, and out of Bancroft Hall.

Stribling Walk would never change. It was funny, the fluidity in his own mind as he marched toward Mahan. It was today in the raw cold of a Dark Ages morning but it was also every other time he had strode along it to class, all merged into memory and future, one long march. His mind could place itself back in his own plebe summer as the Walk filled with white-uniformed platoons, a thousand boy-men marching to evening lecture, all whistling the theme song from *The Bridge Over the River Kwai*, a haunting echo bouncing off of the ancient buildings, a secret melody of resistance. Then Mahan Hall itself filling with a chorus of "We Gotta Get Out Of This Place" when evening lecture was finished. No one liked Navy, until they had to leave. Then he could blink and Stribling was filled with other plebes, he their oppressor, as they sang and whistled in the hot summer night, their own spirit and their own resistance, this time against him. But all the moments blended and were in his mind at once on Stribling. They all lived together in his present, and that, he thought, was really what eternity meant anyway.

He left Stribling and crossed a small parking lot, then entered Sampson Hall, the Science building. He climbed the worn dark stairway with a missionary stride. On the second level he walked slowly past several classrooms, peering through the doorways and searching faces in the classes. He had never met Thad. It seemed ironic, or maybe simply appropriate, that the man who had brought about all of this embarrassment and hurt was nothing but a name. Finally he saw Dean, halfway back in a classroom, taking meticulous notes with the sure air of a scholar. It had to be Thad in front of the class, fleshy-faced and somewhat plump, not too much older than Fogarty himself, lecturing on the interrelationships of hydrocarbons with a love that was almost palpable.

Fogarty walked casually into the classroom, noting the curious stares from the plebe students, and nodding perfunctorily to Dean as the frail plebe's whole frame stiffened with something that resembled fright. Thad picked him up from the corner of one eye, and then turned to face him, with a forced air of authority.

Fogarty stopped, halfway to Thad. He nodded again, taking his full dress blues off of his shoulder and holding them by the collar with his one good hand, in front of him. "You're Professor Thad?"

"I am." Thad did not move from behind his podium.

"I'm Fogarty."

Thad went visibly taut. He searched behind Fogarty for the doorway, then glanced quickly at his class "What do you want?"

"Nothing." He took a step forward, and Thad took a step back. The classroom was so quiet that they could hear the casual tones of the professor across the hall. "I just wanted to show you something." He held up the uniform. "These are my full dress blues. I can't wear them anymore." He held the uniform up higher, nodding toward the ornamented sleeves. "I was really proud of this." Thad had taken another step backward, and was flush against the blackboard. "You scalped me, man. Do you know what I mean? You scalped me."

"I think you'd best leave, Mister Fogarty. You're disrupting my class."

"So who should wear these, Professor?" Fogarty nodded toward the stripes on the sleeves. "And who should get those, huh?" Thad seemed on the verge of calling for help. But Fogarty didn't want a scene. If he made a scene, the Marines would hear about it and he wouldn't be accepted at OCS.

"Take it easy, Professor, I'm leaving. But here." He hung his full dress blues on Thad's podium. It was like leaving his best friend behind in the sterile classroom. "You decide."